Forever Crushed

The Forever Series

1

Amber Paige

Copyright © 2023 by Amber Paige

All rights reserved.

No part of this book may be reproduced in any form or by any electronic or mechanical means, including information storage and retrieval systems, without written permission from the author, except for the use of brief quotations in a book review.

Cover Design: Amanda Santos (@ehmandinha)

Edited by: Jeanine Harrell (@indie.edits.with.jeanine)

Proofread by: Kirsten Kanyaya (@book.dragon.author.services)

❧ Created with Vellum

For anyone who dared to dream that their long-term crush would notice them and maybe even fall in love.

Dreams are worth holding on to.

Trigger Warnings

Gaslighting, love bombing, toxic parents, mental abuse, cheating (not between the main characters), depression, anxiety, and sexual content.

Gwen's Playlist

Crush—Mandy Moore
It's Gonna Be Me—*NSYNC
Black Magic—Little Mix
I Can See You (Taylor's Version)—Taylor Swift
Candy—Mandy Moore
Style—Taylor Swift
Into You—Ariana Grande
Fictional—Khloe Rose
Say My Name—Destiny's Child
Wannabe—Spice Girls
SNAP—Rosa Linn
Juliet—LMNT
Next Time—JESSICA
Is It Just Me? — Emily Burns
Baby I—Ariana Grande
Enchanted (Taylor's Version)—Taylor Swift

Ash's Playlist

Be Alright—Dean Lewis
Jet Black Heart—5 Seconds of Summer
Cheers—New Rules
The Search—NF
It Is What It Is—Jamie Miller
Older—Sasha Roselyn Sloan
Ghosted—Jeremy Shada
Love & War In Your Twenties—Jordy Searcy
Disconnected—5 Seconds of Summer
I Am Yours—Andy Grammer
Let You Down—NF
24 Hours—New Rules
Before You Go—Lewis Capaldi
Slow Hands—Niall Horan
You Found Me—Kelly Clarkson
Mine (Taylor's Version)—Taylor Swift

Spotify Playlist Link

The playlists include a mix of throwbacks and current day songs. While the book takes place in 2015, I included current day music because it fits their personalities and tastes. I write my stories based on vibes, and this playlist is a perfect mix of where I was when I wrote this book. So, have fun and enjoy!

Chapter One

Gwen

Remember that show from the late '90s to early 2000s, the one with the talking babies who went on imaginary adventures? Well, it's the first thing I wake up to every morning. I play the show on an endless loop. I can't fall or stay asleep without it. Something about the easygoing predictability of it comforts me.

My bare legs are cool against the cotton sheets as I stretch under my blanket. Fall is right around the corner, but living in the Northeast means it's still hot and sticky outside. I blast my AC to avoid sweating in the middle of the night. Pulling on my blanket, I scroll through my phone mindlessly. It's a habit I should break, but it helps wake me up. I snicker when I land on Chrissy and her twin brother, Zack. Her signature goofy duck face always manages to ruin a decent photo.

Sitting up, I glance out the window across the room. My

studio apartment is two blocks away from the University of Castle Brook. I tried dorm life, but it didn't last past my first fall semester. My roommate was a nightmare. She took advantage of her first semester away from home. By that, I mean she fucked different guys.

Every damn night.

I ended up sleeping in the hall or the library half the time. My parents helped me get this apartment, but I got a decent enough job at a local cat café so I can chip in half of my monthly rent, because who can afford even a studio apartment on their own? I worked all summer, picking up extra shifts and putting some money aside in case of an emergency.

Checking the time, I groan. 8:09. My first class starts in fifty-one minutes. Today marks the first day of junior year.

My hair flops over on the top of my head as I sit up. I have to stop falling asleep with my hair in a sloppy bun.

Just as I hop out of bed, my phone buzzes.

> Good morning, bitch. Hope your ass is up because I'm on my way!

I roll my eyes. She's always been a morning person, even in high school.

> I'm up. I just need to shower. See you soon :)

I drop the phone on my bed and stand. My knees crackle and buckle. I swear, for being twenty-one, I'm aging like a fifty-year-old man. Walking to the bathroom, I stumble over my shoes that I kicked off after my shift last night.

"Crap!" I catch myself.

Some people see clumsiness as a personality trait. To me, it's a damn curse. Perhaps that explains why my body is aging the way it is . . .

Chapter One

Oh well. I shrug my shoulders and walk across the cool tile floor. Even though it's hot outside, I set the water temperature to blazing because who doesn't love to burn themselves in the morning? After shimmying out of my cotton boy shorts, I pull my white T-shirt over my head. I ignore the mirror, knowing exactly how I look—like a hot mess minus the hot part.

Once I hop out of the shower and dry off, I run a brush through my shoulder-length dark blonde hair and leave the bathroom to grab some clothes. Opting for a pair of black biker shorts and a navy-blue mid-length T-shirt, I throw them on. I stopped caring about what I wore to classes after freshman year. I don't draw attention, anyway.

Gathering my books for today's classes, I hear Chrissy singing "It's Gonna Be Me" by *NSYNC down the hallway. I unlock the door, and she struts in mid-dance. I can't help but grin at her as she sings horribly, handing me my usual iced chai latte. When the chorus starts, I join her, and we're jumping up and down, singing like tone-deaf walruses, not caring if I get a noise complaint later.

When the song ends, she pulls out her earbuds and smiles widely. Chrissy has always been beautiful. Her naturally, tightly curled blonde hair, rosy cheeks, and blue-speckled eyes are dangerous, and she knows it. When she meets my gaze, she frowns and purses her lips together. "My dear Gwen, is that what you're wearing?"

I roll my eyes and pick up my two books for the day before placing them in my bag. "Absolutely. Now let's go," I say while taking a sip of my latte.

She drops her shoulders and pouts. "You're never going to get a boyfriend looking like that." Chrissy groans as I step into the hallway.

"Who said I *wanted* one?" I throw back, bumping into her as I turn to lock the door.

Yes, a boyfriend would be nice. The last time a man touched me was, well, high school, 2012 to be more precise. While I'm not a virgin, I don't think I've ever experienced a legit orgasm, only the ones I gave myself, which is embarrassing and a deep, dark secret.

"I know you, Gwen. Deep down, you crave the touch of a man." Chrissy runs her hands over her body seductively as we step outside, and I choke on my tea.

"Jesus, Chrissy, it's only 8:35 in the morning."

She skips ahead of me, clearly having had a couple shots of espresso. "Only 8:35!? I've been up since 6:11. Now hurry. We've got places to be!"

Once I catch up, she grabs my free hand and pulls me down the sidewalk.

The atmosphere changes when we reach campus. Castle Brook is well known for its rolling landscape and castle-like structures. The trees are still green, and they whistle in the breeze. Students line the courtyard, wasting time before classes start. When we walk under the archway, the path changes to cobblestone, something the campus directors refuse to replace. The aesthetic is appealing, but the functionality? My ankles scream and brace themselves, knowing damn well I'm bound to break a bone or two before I graduate.

"Gwen," Chrissy whispers with a hint of teasing laughter. I finish my latte and glance over to where she's pointing. "What if Ash Waylen was your boyfriend?"

I squint in confusion, and my stomach jolts when I see him. Ash, Chrissy, Zack, and I all attended the same high school. Ash was the crush I thought I could escape when I moved away for college. Boy, was I wrong. How did I not realize we attended the same university?

Ash is the type of crush that leaves a lasting impression on

Chapter One

you. At one point or another, a different guy may enter your life, but that damn crush always creeps its way back in. I watch him intently, daring to wish he would glance my way just once. I could never capture his attention in high school, and I don't blame him. I'm unremarkable, not to say I don't think I'm pretty. My hair has a natural wave, and my eyes are deep sapphire blue. But standing next to someone like Chrissy? I'm damn near invisible.

"Dare me to catcall him?" Chrissy teases, and I flush instantaneously.

"Don't you dare," I hiss, but she shouts right over me.

"Looking good, Waylen!" She whistles at him like some perv off the street.

I look his way again just as he smirks. *Oh my god, that smile.* I can see his dimples from here; I nearly melt along the cobblestone when he waves back at her. His hair is wavy, but he slicked it back to add some height above his brow. The color is a beautiful chestnut brown with hints of gold when the sun hits him. His face is flawless and clear, longing to be stroked and caressed. My heart pitter-patters just as his milk-chocolate eyes scan over me. I silently beg for him to notice me, even if it's just for a moment. But when he drops his gaze and glances over me, all hope is lost.

"There she is!" Just when I thought the embarrassment was over, Zack tackles me in a bear hug, squeezing the life out of my lungs. "Oh, how I missed you!" He messes with my hair and continues to squeeze me.

"You saw me yesterday," I choke out. Doubling over, I catch my breath when he places me back on the ground.

"You know I can't last not seeing you for a day." His wide smile etches one on my face as well.

"And what about me?" Chrissy clears her throat and taps her foot against the path.

Zack waves his hand, dismissing her. "You cause too much trouble. I can live without you for a bit."

Chrissy punches his arm, and he winces. Zack is about five inches taller than Chrissy and me. While his sister's hair is blonde, his is so black it shimmers blue. His eyes are the same shade as Chrissy's, and he has light freckles trailing over his nose. He's a lady killer, and while he doesn't know it, everyone else does.

Zack and Chrissy are twins. I grew up next door to them. I met Zack first in first grade, but Chrissy wasn't too far behind. We're all the same age, and before I go any further, Zack is like an older brother to me. He's very protective and has made my dating life, or rather, my attempt at a dating life, impossible. Chrissy, on the other hand, is so outgoing it's painful. Zack's head combusts at least once a month from dealing with Chrissy and her antics. I at least made his life easier.

Dating for me is . . . interesting, to say the least. I found it hard to get a guy's attention because they were always googly-eyeing Chrissy. If I caught someone's eye, it never went past a third date.

"Gwen, don't you have a class in like five minutes?" Chrissy pretends to check her watch-less wrist, and I panic.

"Shit gotta go! See you guys later!" Relieved that I slipped on my sneakers this morning, I bolt toward the science building, which is on the other side of campus.

My first class today is Biology 103, and my second class is Biochem 102. My major is very science heavy because I'm striving to graduate with a Bachelor of Science degree in Biochemical Engineering. My long-term goal is to become a Biochemist and drive research developments. I'm a science nerd through and through.

I make it to class just in time. My lungs burn as I gasp for air, and I almost twisted my ankle weaving through the

Chapter One

crowded hallways. I compose myself as I step into the classroom, finding a seat in the middle of the room just as the professor strolls in.

Biology is one of my favorite subjects, although I can't pinpoint why. I love learning about life and all its mysteries.

An hour goes by before we're dismissed. The first day of classes is always overwhelming—syllabus day is horrible. I swear we need a grounding session before and after going over that packet from hell.

When class ends, I shake myself out of the trance I was in. Chrissy meets me outside and loops her arm through mine.

"You seem *really* excited about this biochem class," I tease.

She rolls her eyes and grins wider. "I'm always excited."

We round the corner and stand outside, waiting for class to start. We scroll through our phones and share funny clips with one another, laughing obnoxiously. The introvert in me is screaming, but Chrissy's extroverted nature silences it.

Ten minutes pass before Chrissy and I wander into the classroom. We take our seats in the first row on the left-hand side. If I don't sit close to the front, my mind wanders. I love science, but I get distracted easily. The room fills just as Professor Stilts walks in, the same professor I had last year. With him teaching, I know Chrissy and I will pass for sure.

"What's he doing here?" Chrissy whispers so only I can hear her.

My eyebrows raise when I look over my shoulder, seeing Ash wander in. My gut flips, and my right leg jostles. I look around the room and panic when I realize there's only one seat left.

And it's right next to me.

"Chrissy, change seats with me." I gather my things as the panic takes over my voice.

He must be walking over because she clicks her tongue and smiles that mischievous smile of hers.

"Oh no, girly, now's your time to shine."

My face flushes when I feel his presence. I place my notebook back down and force my attention toward the board. My eyes flick to the right, feeling his gaze on me.

"Hi, Gwen."

I meet his caramel eyes and smile as calmly as I can. Meanwhile, my body is screaming, *"How the fuck does he know my name!?"*

"Hi, Ash."

Dimples appear on his cheeks near the corners of his full lips when he smiles. I twirl the pen in my hand, trying to settle my nerves. Looking down at my notebook, I start to doodle like a second grader. Out of the corner of my eye, I watch Ash pull out a pair of black wire-rimmed glasses, and when he sets them on his face, my body bursts into a flurry of hot chills. I sink into my chair and glance over at Chrissy.

When she meets my gaze, she grins, and I mouth, *"I hate you."*

Professor Stilts hands out the syllabus when she mutters, "You're welcome."

There goes my GPA, and there goes my damn chance of passing this class.

Chapter Two

Ash

Gwen Roman and Chrissy Willows are two peas in a pod. I saw them a lot in high school, always laughing and practically conjoined at the hip. Grinning around them was inevitable. Those two are comedic geniuses. The best part is they don't even realize it.

As soon as I sat next to Gwen, Chrissy beamed and Gwen averted her gorgeous blue eyes. Her cheeks flushed the same color they would back then. I wish I could say I noticed her prior to today. It's possible I needed glasses sooner than I thought because this girl is a bombshell. Who knew curves like that could exist on a woman? I certainly didn't.

My eyes linger on her longer than I'd like. I promised myself no flings or relationships this year. I'm still getting over my last girlfriend. Alex Finnley really did a number on me. I met her last year and fell hard. Alex has the looks of a goddess but the bite of a demonic entity, which I realized too late. We would spend our days together, and she would sleep over at my brother's house, where I live. Then we would wake up together and go to class. She consumed my life, and she took it just as easily.

When the professor walks in, I slide my glasses on, and Gwen's eyes glance my way, only to retreat just as fast. Something about her makes my chest feel strange. I'm going to have to focus hard on not looking at her. Next class, I'll be sure to grab a different seat. This girl may just kill my GPA and who knows what else . . .

I make it a whole ten minutes before my eyes gloss her over again. She's twirling her pen and drawing silly doodles in her notebook as Mr. Stilts goes over the syllabus. Her phone keeps lighting up in her shorts pocket, but she ignores it. My eyes climb over every inch of her thighs in those formfitting shorts. My heart kicks into overdrive. High school Ash was an idiot to have never noticed her.

I didn't know we attended the same university. Not until I saw her today when Chrissy called out to me, which I didn't take offense to. It's just who Chrissy is.

When Gwen's cheeks painted themselves hot pink, the world stopped. I knew I was doomed if I saw her again, and of course, we share the same biochem class. So, I get the pleasure of seeing her every Monday, Tuesday, and Friday, plus lab on Thursday.

My mind shields me from feeling anything further. I'm far from over Alex. She shattered my heart and stomped all over it. What's even worse, she won't leave me alone. I wake up to her text messages and phone calls every morning, and she's not getting the hint. She betrayed me in the worst way possible, and that's not something anyone can recover from in just a few months.

The class dismisses, and I shake myself from my thoughts.

Chapter Two

After I've gathered my things, the words escape my lips before I give them a second thought. "See you guys later."

I make eye contact with Gwen; her eyes trap mine, and a grin slips across my lips. Her mouth drops open, and I hold back a chuckle.

My next class is dull. I despise the first few days of new semesters; all we do is go over the syllabus, and time always drags on. My phone buzzes as the English professor rambles on about books we're expected to read. My phone vibrates against my thigh again, and when I pull it out, I groan.

Hey, cutie, how are you?

What doesn't this girl get? Is she so selfish that she can't give me the one thing I want?

Fine, are you free later?

For you? Absolutely!

I think it's about time to have a one-on-one with her. Paint the picture plain and clear.

Leave me alone and let me heal. That's the least she can do for me, after everything she put me through this past summer.

Chapter Three

Gwen

The hour goes by in the blink of an eye. I couldn't concentrate the entire time. I tried to focus, but my eyes kept wandering to my right, taking in every moment I could just admiring Ash. He probably won't sit next to me next class. I need to soak it in while I can. He smells like fresh pine and apples. His muscles bulge through his simple black tee, and he shakes his leg up and down as he takes notes.

It also doesn't help that my phone keeps buzzing. I already know it's Chrissy sending me heart emojis and heart-pumping memes. She's always such a cheerleader, even when the outcome is dire. Professor Stilts dismisses the class, and everyone packs up. I slide my notebook into my bag and pull my phone out of my pocket.

> OMG, since when did he start wearing glasses!?

Chapter Three

I can smell him from here! You must be dying!

He keeps looking at you!

The last message makes my eyes widen. I glance over at Chrissy, and she's nodding with a wide, toothy grin.

"See you guys later." Ash smiles directly at me before walking away.

I can't keep my jaw from dropping to the floor. My phone buzzes again.

WTF!?

"I'm right here. You can just talk to me," I mutter.

She jumps up and down as I sling my bag over my shoulder.

"He knew your name. Oh my god." She fans her face with the syllabus. "Gwen, Gwen, Gwen, you have to tell me." She leans forward, almost toppling the desk over. "How do you feel?"

"Confused."

She pumps her arms in the air while hooting like she's at a sporting event.

I scoff, trying my best to ignore my heated cheeks as we walk out of the room. I don't know why she's getting so worked up. The last I checked, Ash had a pretty serious girlfriend. Not that I stalk him on social media or anything . . . which only makes me question my intelligence.

Did I really not recognize the familiar looming castles in the background of his profile picture? Maybe I need to re-evaluate my major . . .

Remember, Gwen, Ash only sat next to you because there

were literally no other seats available. Don't get yourself worked up.*

Zack approaches us, and Chrissy combusts from all her excitement.

"Zack! Oh my god! Guess what!" Chrissy shouts.

He looks at me, clearly concerned about her mental state.

"You need to calm your sister down and tell her to lay off the espresso," I say, and she punches me in the arm. I don't think she intended to leave a mark, but she definitely did.

"Guess who sat next to Gwen in biochem." She dances, and people glance our way. "Ash Waylen!" She doesn't wait for his response.

When she makes her announcement, he looks my way, beyond baffled.

"There were no other seats available." I pass it off like it was nothing.

Zack arches an eyebrow, letting that brotherly protective glare peek through. "He goes here?"

Maybe I'm not as dense as I thought I was.

I hold my hands up and walk away before Zack can question me further. "I have to go get ready for my shift. See you guys tomorrow." I skip away before Chrissy or Zack can stop me.

On my walk home, I can't help but smile. Ash Waylen knew my name.

My name!

I never would've thought that what just happened could have happened. Part of my brain is chastising me for getting so worked up. But my heart has been yearning for a moment like this for years. I know it was a chance encounter, but perhaps it means chances are in my favor. Yes, he has a girlfriend, but even his small glances are enough to satisfy me.

I drop my bag on my apartment floor and get dressed in my

Chapter Three

work uniform. It's nothing crazy. Since I work at a cat café, it's pretty casual. I slip on a pair of ripped jeans and a white, collared polo. I twist my hair up into a clip and walk out the door within five minutes of returning home.

On the way to work, I jam my earbuds in and put on "Black Magic" by Little Mix.

The cat café I work at is about ten blocks from my apartment. I carry mace with me even though it's a decent neighborhood. Tea and Kittens is one of a few cat cafés in the Northeast, so we can get pretty busy. I've always loved cats, but my parents never let me have one because they're deathly allergic.

I had a decent childhood. With no other siblings, it was always just me. Unless Chrissy or Zack invited themselves over. You would think that because of this, I was the center of my parents' attention, but not all one-child households work that way. Both of my parents crammed their lives full of work and their own pursuits. They took vacations together and went to the movies and dinners without me. It was something I grew up thinking was normal. Until I mentioned it one time when I was at Chrissy's house. Since then, the Willows family invited me to everything.

And I mean *everything*.

It took time for me to realize that my parents were assholes, and since I grew up, it hasn't gotten better. I don't talk to them much, but at the end of the day, they love and care for me. My father, Richard, is an accountant at a local bank back in Pennsylvania. My mother, Bree, works for a travel agency. Growing up in a small town back in Pennsylvania was . . . well, it sucked. There was a reason I wanted to go to college out of state. I moved to Massachusetts without a second thought, and when I found out Chrissy and Zack were joining me, I was elated.

Rounding the last corner, I step in front of the glass

Forever Crushed

window. One of the new kittens is lounging on a cat tree, lazily batting at a fluffy mouse that dangles from the post.

I smile and open the door. "Pickles, what are you doing, lazy boy?"

His pink nose wiggles as I lean in to give him a kiss. I pat his head while admiring his white, brown and black stripes. The tip of his tail is also white, and it reminds me of a paintbrush. I give him one last scratch before turning around to face the café.

The main room is modern, with hardwood floors, dark navy-blue walls, and plants hanging from the ceiling. Cat trees and towers galore line the left wall, and to the right are booths and tables. Many people come here just to play with the cats and chill, which I've also been guilty of.

Pulling myself away from Pickles, I clock in. Popping my head into the back kitchen, I wave at Ryan, my manager, who is only a couple of years older than me.

"How's it going, Ryan?"

He glances my way and sighs. "Would be better if these damn cats would stop shedding," Ryan whines before blowing his nose into a tissue. "Living the dream, Gwen. Living the dream."

I snort as he tosses the tissue in a trash can. Ryan has the craziest red hair I've ever seen. Not only is it deep crimson, but it's also wild and curly. I probably would have a crush on Ryan . . . if he didn't have a boyfriend.

As if on cue, Blake strolls in and lifts me from behind, twirling me around the room. When he drops me on the ground, I have to steady myself from the giggling and dizziness. Blake is a football player, and he has the most flawless olive skin I've ever seen. His black hair is neatly trimmed, and his glasses are always falling off the bridge of his nose.

"Are you working today?"

Chapter Three

Blake shakes his head at my question. "No, just wanted to see that guy." His eyes land on Ryan.

In two strides, he reaches him and plants a big kiss on his lips.

I look away with a smile. It must be nice having someone to love like that. I wonder if I'll ever get to experience that level of devotion.

I get to work cleaning the litter boxes and playing with a few of the older cats. Sitting on the ground, I grab a laser pointer as a group of younger college students enter the café. I overhear them as they place their drink order with Ryan. Turning around, I keep my back toward them and focus on Brooksly.

Brooksly is an older cat, the longest resident we have here. I'm not sure why. He's the sweetest boy on the planet. When I scratch underneath his chin, strands of black fur float through the air.

Raising my hand to itch my nose, I freeze when a shadow casts over me.

"Nice pussy," the stranger blurts out, and his friends chuckle behind me.

Rolling my eyes, I do what I do best when it comes to customers like this.

I ignore them.

"Cat got your tongue?" The guy kneels to my side, but I don't meet his piercing stare. "Come on, talk to me." Reaching forward, he takes my chin and forces me to meet his gaze. "See? That's better."

Fury seeps through me. Heated goosebumps erupt along my skin in response to his touch. Brooksly growls when someone else takes a step forward, causing them to halt.

"Want to get out of here?" He lowers his tone, trying to sound seductive.

If I had food in my stomach, it would have crawled up my throat and landed on his face. I know if I pull away, he'll get angry. But if I don't, *I'll* get even more angry. Mom always told me to be nice to strangers, but this wasn't in the handbook.

"Hey! What are you doing?" Ryan shouts from behind the counter.

His footsteps follow soon after, causing the guy to release his grip. I scramble backward as a rush of relief floods over me when Ryan steps in front of me.

"What do you think you're doing?" Ryan interrogates.

"Nothing."

"Oh yeah? It doesn't look like *nothing* to me. Why don't you get the fuck out of here before I call the football team for backup? My boyfriend would love shoving his foot down your throat," Ryan threatens, and the color drains from the stranger's face.

Keeping my attention on Ryan, I don't move until the café is empty again. Gasping for air, I run my fingers through Brooksly's fur as he sits on my lap.

Ryan drops to his knees and sighs. "Are you okay?"

All I can do is nod.

"Gwen, you can't let anyone treat you that way. If it's not a disgruntled customer, it's some perv trying to get your number. You have to stick up for yourself. What would have happened if I weren't here?"

I don't want to think about that possibility. While he's right, people pleasing is etched in my bones. It doesn't matter how I feel in the end.

It never does.

"I'll try to do better," I promise, even though I know I won't be able to keep it.

With a sympathetic smirk, Ryan stands as the café door's

Chapter Three

bell chimes again. "Take all the time you need. I can handle the customers."

A new couple walks in and approaches Ryan to order some drinks. When they sit, I notice the woman's attention lands on Brooksly.

I release a tense puff of air and clear my mind. My job here isn't to sit on the floor and feel sorry for myself. My job is to find these cats a home.

Leaning down, I whisper to Brooksly, "Now's your time to shine."

Getting up, I walk toward the couple. Kittens play at their feet, but their eyes sparkle when they see Brooksly trailing by my side.

"Hi there. How are you guys today?"

Brooksly wastes no time. He rubs on the woman's ankle, and she melts in her chair.

"I think you just made her day," the man says while smiling at the woman.

Brooksly weaves in between them, chirping and purring his heart out.

"Our cat passed away a few months ago. I haven't had the courage to walk in here since."

I smile sympathetically; her pain is real. While I've never lost a cat, I can only imagine what their absence must feel like.

"Well, lucky for you, Brooksly is fantastic at putting a smile on anyone's face." Right on cue, he jumps on her lap and cuddles close. I get to witness the exact moment she falls in love.

"Is he available to adopt?" A weight is lifted off my shoulders when the man asks the question.

"He is." I smile again, and tears threaten to coat my eyes.

I fell in love with Brooksly the moment I saw him. But I

knew I wasn't right for him. He deserves constant love and affection, but with classes and work, it's impossible for me.

"Where's the application?" the woman chimes in, excitement filling her voice.

I excuse myself to print it out. While I'm in the back, I focus on regulating my breathing and heartbeat. It's not long before fury settles in my bones and my stomach churns with the memory of what happened earlier. That asshat invaded *my* space. Touched me without *my* permission. I wish I had the guts to scream at him and his friends. Scare them off myself and not have to rely on another man to do it for me.

The moment is over, and I'm safe. I need to get my shit together because what if Ryan or Blake aren't here next time, and that happens again?

I need to do better for my sake.

Fuck what Mom taught me all those years ago. Strangers like those guys don't deserve my kindness. I just need to remember that and woman up.

The paper is hot off the printer, so I grab it and head back to the couple waiting with Brooksly. As I emerge from the back, my eyes meet Ash's again. This makes two times in one day. But when I see who's trailing behind him, the warmth in my chest vanishes, and I drop my gaze.

Chapter Four

Ash

I brought Alex to the cat café because I thought it was a hole-in-the-wall coffee shop. Also, Alex hates cats, and I wanted to piss her off. I wasn't expecting to see Gwen again. Just my luck. I didn't know she worked here, and seeing her face fall when she saw Alex and me, stung a bit. I wish I could explain why. I've only spoken to Gwen once, and that was today. And we barely talked, so why is my heart racing just at the sight of her?

I force my eyes forward, walking to a booth in the back of the room. I need to make sure I do the one thing I set out to do tonight.

I need to stand up for myself.

As soon as I slide into the booth, my legs shake vigorously. Alex tries to sit next to me, but I point to the seat across the table.

"Don't be such a baby, Ash." She settles in her seat and

flashes me her flawless smile. I don't fall for it. "You look good." Her voice softens as she reaches for my hands. "Did you want to order anything?"

I take them off the table, avoiding her touch. "No, thank you."

We sit in awkward silence. The only distraction is from a cat tower on the other side of the room, with a kitten on it, batting at a bell from a cat toy.

With a sharp intake of air, I get straight to the point. "Listen, Alex. I need you to leave me alone." I've never had to do this before. All of my previous girlfriends ended things with me. I don't find joy in this, but Alex deserves *everything* I'm about to say to her. "You're borderline harassing me, and I'm sick of it. What you did—" Anger starts to spew from my mouth. "Fuck you, you selfish asshole, and leave me alone." I don't expect her to back down, and when she doesn't, I ready myself for the fight I desperately need.

"What I did!? What about what you did? Flirting with my best friend!?" She leans forward, meeting my rage with her own fury. Her straight black hair dangles in front of her empty black eyes.

"How many times do I have to tell you? How can I flirt with your best friend if I never even knew you had one?" I know how cheating affects relationships and home life. I witnessed my mother and father go through it more than once. There's a reason I opted to go to college out of state and move in with my brother. I couldn't take the toxic environment anymore.

"It was a mistake! You're making it out to be worse than it really is." Her voice rises, and I remember that we're in public.

"This will be the last time I'll tell you. *Leave me alone.*" I drop my voice, hissing my final words.

Chapter Four

She stands abruptly and storms out of the café. I run my hands through my hair and let all my emotions surface.

Fuck her, and fuck me for trusting her.

Chapter Five

Gwen

Alex Finnley is extremely gorgeous. Her eyes are dark brown, nearing black, and her black hair is free of frizz, always straight and neat. I freeze when they walk past me to sit at a booth in the back. I focus on the couple at hand. Offering them the application, I tell them to hand it to me when they're done, and if all goes well, they can take Brooksly home tomorrow.

I can't help but watch Ash and Alex afterward. Absent-mindedly, I pick up Pickles and let him chew on my fingers. I pull my phone out of my pocket and text Chrissy one-handed.

>Guess who's here.

Don't even joke with me right now.

Is it Mr. Biochem!?

She texts me back rapid fire. I can always count on Chrissy

Chapter Five

to respond within seconds. I'm the same way as well. It's the millennial in us.

> Mr. Biochem? Never mind, I don't want to know. Ash is here with Alex.

> Alex!? They broke up over the summer.

I squint in confusion. Pickles paws my nose, and I place him down with a hint of laughter. He falls over and wrestles with my shoelaces.

> You must be wrong because I'm watching them. Right now.

> Social media is never wrong, Gwen!

I glance over my shoulder as Alex points angrily at Ash. My eyes bug out, and I quickly turn around again.

> Okay, maybe you're right. They're fighting.

> In the cat café?

> In the cat café. The cats are going to be scarred for life.

She sends a slew of laughing emojis before I place my phone in my back pocket. I turn around just as Alex rushes past me, brushing my arm. She doesn't apologize. She just storms through the door with fiery rage evident in her expression.

I look toward the back booth just as Blake stands by my side. "Isn't that Mr. Biochem?"

You've got to be kidding me. The look I give him makes him raise his hands in surrender.

"Chrissy's a wildfire, okay? Now go, save the day." He teases me with a heroic pose before walking out the door.

I stand still for a moment, unsure of what to do. Sucking in one last breath, I find the courage to go and talk to Ash.

Fuck it.

I start to walk, but Pickles clings to my laces for dear life. Looking down at him, I wonder if this is Zack in cat form, always preventing me from talking to guys. With a sigh, I pick him up and cradle him in my arms while walking over to Ash. I hold Pickles close to my chest when I face him. His eyes are sunken, his face now pale and tired. A stabbing sensation pokes at my heart.

When his eyes meet mine, he offers me a small smile. "Hey, Gwen."

My knees nearly buckle at the sound of his voice. I hold Pickles out, not knowing what else to do. "I wanted to introduce you to Pickles."

He meows right on cue, and I smile awkwardly. Ash snickers and reaches for Pickles. When I place him in his hands, our fingers brush.

And just like that, my damn hand is on fire.

Ash smiles at Pickles. My heart melts as Ash strokes him and Pickles falls under his spell. The bastard actually cuddles up to him.

"He must like you. All he does is bite me."

Ash meets my eyes and laughs. "Well, if you taste as good as you smell, I don't blame him."

Remember when I said my knees nearly buckled? Well, they're jelly now. I giggle as my cheeks burn, still standing in front of the booth like a fool.

"Want to sit?"

I sit the moment he asks, which only makes him chuckle

Chapter Five

again. I watch Pickles, and my lips curl. *What an asshole.* He snuggles along Ash's shoulder.

"How was your summer?" I break the silence. It looks like he needs a bit of a distraction.

"It wasn't bad. I went home to visit my parents, went to the beach, nothing crazy. How about you? I didn't see you around."

My brows rise from both confusion and shock. I don't remember running into him during my trips back home. When did he see me? How did I miss seeing him?

"I worked a lot and didn't want to go back home."

He nods mainly to himself. As he moves his gaze to the table, his eyes gloss over.

"Do you want to talk about it?" I ask. He looks at me again, and I continue. "It's okay if you don't want to. Sometimes it's nice to vent to a stranger."

"But you're not a stranger, Gwen."

I shrug. "I'm close enough."

He grins and pets Pickles before sighing. "I caught Alex cheating on me back in June. It's been . . . rough."

I tilt my head to the side. Without thinking, I reach over and hold his hand that rests on the table. I rub tiny circles on his soft skin with my thumb.

"I'm sorry. No one should have to go through that."

He looks down at our hands, and my internal temperature rises. He grins just as Pickles nibbles on his ear.

"Ow, fucker." He holds Pickles in both hands and returns him to me.

"Now, that's the Pickles I know." We both laugh as Pickles chews on a loose strand of hair that escapes my hair clip.

"Well, I better get going. See you tomorrow?"

My gut explodes with butterflies, and I nod. "See you tomorrow."

I think I'm gonna die.

Chapter Six

Gwen

The next morning arrives, and the thought of going to class makes me want to hurl. My stomach flips upside down, tossing and turning repeatedly. I'm rubbing my belly like a pregnant lady when Chrissy walks into my apartment.

"Is there something you forgot to tell me?" she asks with a furrowed brow.

With a sigh, I run my fingers through my shoulder-length hair. I didn't tell her about my shift last night. I was afraid that if I let the words out, the moment would disappear, and who am I kidding? Nothing *really* happened. I just held his hand . . .

"I feel like I'm going to be sick." I grab a ginger ale, silently praying it will settle my bubbling anxiety.

"Anxious about seeing Mr. Biochem?" She shimmies and grins, teasing me. I can't hold back the smirk that threatens my lips. "Oh my god, what aren't you telling me?"

I slide my phone into the back pocket of my jean shorts and pull my hood over my head, not caring that it's ninety degrees

Chapter Six

outside. I walk away from Chrissy and step through the doorway.

"Gwen!" She chases me out the door, and I lock it. "If you don't tell me right now, I swear to god I'll blow up your phone all day and embarrass the living shit out of you."

I roll my eyes, still wearing the same grin. "You won't believe me if I told you."

Her eyes bug out, and she smiles widely. We start the trek to campus, and I share all the details.

"No wonder your stomach's a damn mess!" She holds my hands and jumps up and down, the complete opposite of my current feelings.

Sure, the prospect that Ash might be into me is a dream come true. But for all I know, he let me hold his hand and comfort him simply because I was there, someone to confide in during his time of need. I've fantasized about a moment like that for years. That doesn't mean anything will come of it. There's no need to get my hopes up.

We walk toward the science building; my schedule is the same as yesterday. Tomorrow, I have English 103 and Calculus 102. I link arms with Chrissy as we skip down the cobblestone path. She pauses, and I trip over my feet.

Her face lights up as her cheeks blush. "I'm gonna tell Zack."

The realization hits me, and I try to smack her phone out of her hands. "Like hell you are." The last thing I need is him ruining any chance I may have—if there's even a chance at all. "What Zack doesn't know won't hurt him."

I pull on her arm again, leading us inside. She and I bicker back and forth all the way up to the third floor.

"I have to tell him. He's my twin brother!" she whines.

My eyes roll so far back they almost get stuck. "Did you tell him about Miles?" Her face drains of all color.

"Summer fling Miles?" I add.

She covers my mouth with her hand, and I can't stop laughing.

"Fine, deal! Just shut up!"

Zack rounds the corner, and he tilts his head in our direction. I raise my hand, and Chrissy does the same, not removing her other hand from my mouth. Zack walks away, not daring to ask what's going on between us. She removes her hand and wipes it on her skirt. I snicker to myself as I walk away.

"Get your ass to biology," Chrissy lectures me with a teasing tone.

The class goes by agonizingly slow, yet the minutes seem to blur. Biology is a comfort for me, but my stomach still twists and aches, wondering what biochem might hold for me. It's silly. I'm being ridiculous. There's no way he would sit next to me again. If anything, he would show up earlier so he could avoid sitting next to me.

Class is done, and I can't remember what we went over today. I'll have to check the syllabus and make sure I didn't miss anything. *Maybe those things are useful after all.* This is so unlike me; I need to focus and stop thinking about Ash.

Ah, crap.

My eyes follow him as he walks toward the biochem classroom. Chrissy steps in front of me and immediately follows my line of sight.

"This is going to be so good!" she squeals as my stomach tumbles.

The first time I saw Ash was in tenth grade. We shared the same social studies class. The moment he strolled through the door, I fell for him. Ash was the cool guy, not a jock, just a normal dude everyone liked. He's witty, smart, and down to earth. It wasn't just his looks that drew me in. It was his personality.

Chapter Six

The looks were a bonus.

And now? It's all crashing back. I haven't seen Ash in person since my senior year of high school. I'm still unsure how I never realized we attended the same university. This has been the most interaction I've shared with him—ever. Just the simple "Hi, Gwen." in class was enough. Then he and Alex showed up in the café, and I somehow got the nerve to approach him. Where did that even come from?

Chrissy pulls my hood off as we stroll into biochem. "You look like you're about to rob a bank with that hood on."

I forgot I still had it draped over my head.

I feel his eyes on me before I see them, ignoring Chrissy's blatant snickering. She leads the way to the seats we sat in yesterday, and Ash is in the same spot as well. I press my lips together, letting out a long exhale. After plopping down on my chair, I pull out my notebook, still feeling his gaze on me. From the corner of my eye, I can see his eyes trail up my legs, pausing on the midriff from my cropped hoodie, and then land on the shy smile I'm trying my darndest to hold back.

My phone buzzes, so I pull it from my back pocket.

He's checking you out right now!

I glance over at Chrissy, placing my phone on my desk, screen down. Her mouth drops open. She hates it when I don't respond to her texts, and now I'm doing it to push her buttons. My phone goes off as Professor Stilts walks in. I smile to myself when it goes off again and again and again.

"Gwen?"

I turn slowly, meeting Ash's intense stare. Those glasses . . . just when I thought he couldn't get any hotter.

"Aren't you going to get that?"

My phone vibrates again, and I feel Chrissy's burning glare.

I smile, knowing exactly what I'm doing. "No, it's just a spam call."

My phone vibrates violently against the table. I pick it up in a panic.

"Bitch, pick up your damn phone!" Chrissy yells in a hushed tone.

I shoot daggers at her. Ash snorts, so I decide to have a little fun.

I slide the answer button on the screen. "Hello, this is Gwen."

Ash beams, holding back a chuckle as I use my polite phone voice.

"Yes, this is Chrissy. I just wanted to tell you that you're a—"

I end the call before she can finish her sentence.

"Ladies, settle down." Professor Stilts scolds us.

I sink in my chair as Chrissy leans toward me.

"You're not my best friend anymore," she mumbles.

I stick my tongue out at her as she uses her best angry voice.

"You guys are ridiculous," Ash remarks, and my eyes bounce to the right. His cheeks are blushing red, and the smile on his lips melts my insides.

Focus, Gwen.

I force my attention onto Professor Stilts. I took Biochem 101 with him last year. He's about six feet tall, very lean, and not bad to look at. He has auburn hair, and he wears these black wide-rimmed glasses. A lot of people take his courses because he's ranked one of the hottest professors at Castle Brook. I'm pretty sure that's why Chrissy and I ended up in the same class. Unlike her, I take his classes because he's good at what he does and I admire his teaching techniques. No matter

Chapter Six

what subject he lectures, I catch on and never find myself confused.

He's currently introducing new methods to balance equations. I stare at the board and jot down as many tips as I can, making sure to pay attention and not let my eyes drift to the man on my right.

A piece of scrap paper lands in the middle of my notebook. I stare at it in confusion before dropping my pen to unfold the crumbled-up note.

Hi ;)

I glance at Ash, who smiles at me while leaning back in his seat. I mouth "Hi" and let my own goofy smile slip free.

I seriously can't believe any of this is happening. I can't fathom that someone like him would talk, let alone pass notes, to someone like me. Another note lands on my notebook. I try to act cool and nonchalantly open it.

You're pretty cute . . .

I drop the note, trying to hide my flushed face. The urge to pull my hood over my head overwhelms me. My cheeks burn hotter than the sun, and it only gets worse when he chuckles and tosses another tiny paper note.

I'm bored . . .

I tear off a piece of paper and write a quick message.

Nice glasses.

I chuck it at his chest before going back to note-taking.

I try to focus, but I fail horribly. For the rest of the class, my mind wanders. I feel Ash's eyes on me, and I melt under his gaze. My body lightens and tingles. I dare to wonder how his hands would feel on my thighs, along my bare back...

I release a tense huff.

We're assigned a set of problems for homework, and as everyone packs up, I feel slightly disappointed when Ash doesn't throw another note my way.

"Till next time, ladies." Ash's gaze lingers on me for what feels like an eternity. He places his glasses in his shirt pocket before turning around to leave the room.

"Hey, Gwen." I look over at Chrissy as she wipes the corner of her mouth. "You've got a little drool right there."

"Shut up." I smile to myself while shoving my notebook into my bag.

When we walk out of the room, I notice Ash standing across the way, talking to his friends. Chrissy pulls on my arm and leads us farther down the hall.

"Want to have a little fun?" She wiggles her eyebrows.

"Oh no." I already know what she wants to do, and it's not good.

"Time for a little recon."

Oh, fuck me.

Chapter Seven

Ash

Last night was rough, but Gwen was there, and in the blink of an eye, I smiled and found comfort in her presence. I was expecting to have an awful night, but it turned out to be the opposite.

I can't explain how much brighter the world became when she appeared, holding that scrawny kitten. I was never a pet person, but after yesterday? I might be. I felt like I could tell her anything. That no matter what came out of my mouth, she wouldn't judge me.

I've never spoken the words out loud; she was the first person I shared it with, besides my brother, that is. The moment I said "I caught Alex cheating on me," a weight lifted off my shoulders. Then she took hold of my hand, and I fell still. She formed little circles along the back of my palm, setting my hand ablaze. I wanted to stay, but I didn't. I needed her to pull me into her arms and ease my pain. I let my mind regain control, and I left.

Today is different. The urge to talk to her is renewed, and I need to follow through.

I can't help but tease Gwen. The last time I wrote a note was in high school. I found myself writing it before I even realized what I was doing.

Our notes fly back and forth, bringing a stupid grin to my face. And when she compliments my glasses, my cheeks burn, and I can't toss another message her way. My brain is screaming at me to stop. I'm breaking the promise I made to myself after I broke up with Alex.

I need time to heal.

I can't seem to control my mouth when I'm around Gwen. Just as class ends, I speak before thinking, letting my naturally flirty personality take control. I love seeing her blush whenever I give her any form of attention. It rouses something deep within me. She makes me feel like more than just some "random cool guy." I'm used to everyone wanting to be my friend. I'm the definition of an extrovert. What I'm not used to is being looked at like I have something within me I didn't even know was there. Maybe that's why Gwen intrigues me so much.

Back in the hallway, I meet up with some guys from my computer tech class. I don't need to take biochem for my major in computer analytics, but I wanted to. No one ever believes me when I share my love for chemistry.

I feel her presence when she steps outside. I take deep breaths and force myself not to give in and admire her. My muscles ache, begging me to turn around. Luckily, before I give in, I feel her fade away.

"Ash, you all right, buddy?"

I'm pulled back to reality and force a smile before nodding. "Yeah, just forgot to eat this morning. I'll meet you guys in the computer lab in a bit."

Chapter Seven

These guys don't know me well enough to know when I'm faking my ass off. I made friends here at Castle Brook but only had one best friend. The same guy who went behind my back and slept with my girlfriend. So, I guess he wasn't much of a friend after all.

I would be lying if I said I didn't miss him. Brandon was the only one who knew what I went through back home. He knew when to call me out on my shit and how to get me back on track if I slipped up. I don't have anyone who does that for me anymore. I'm trying to learn to do it myself, but that's not going well so far.

Stepping outside, I walk toward the cafeteria. One reason I chose to go to college in Massachusetts was to get away from my parents. The other reason was because I fell in love with the campus. It was like being teleported back in time, going from modern, perfectly paved sidewalks to delicately placed cobblestone paths. The yards are covered with trees and various flowers. Finding shade is easy when you're in the courtyard. I stroll down the path with my head held high until I see her.

Fucking Alex.

Here I am, wallowing in self-pity, and there she is, laughing her pretty little head off, flirting with some random guy with neatly slicked-back blond hair. If I could just get a glimpse of his face, I would warn him away from her. No one deserves to go through what she put me through. My eyes linger on them the entire time, but I don't catch the guy's face. Not wanting to look at her anymore, I open the door to the cafeteria.

I wasn't lying when I said I didn't eat breakfast. I normally don't, if I'm being honest, but today my stomach grumbles and begs for nourishment. I walk up to a vending machine to buy a bag of chips and a bottle of water. I'll get something for lunch after my next class.

A few students line the tables, but since it's not twelve yet, it's pretty deserted. Walking over to a table, I stop when the sensation in my muscles returns. Looking up, I find her instantly.

Gwen and Chrissy are sitting at a table in the back, hunched behind a laptop, gazing at the screen. A playfully dangerous smile creeps onto my lips. My feet move in their direction, ignoring all warning signs from my brain.

Chapter Eight

Gwen

Recon, according to Chrissy, means flat-out stalking and not just via social media. It's around ten when we settle in the cafeteria. The room is massive, able to accommodate around eight hundred students. The floors are white tile that almost glisten, and booths and tables fill the room.

Chrissy pulls out her laptop and types away. She could drop her current major and start her own private detective business. She pulls up Ash's social media page and slides the computer closer to me.

"Remind me again why you want to be a psychiatrist," I whisper.

She pulls up his photos that were only visible to his friends a few days ago. "Are you friends with him on here?"

She snorts in response. "Don't ask questions you don't want the answers to," she says while scrolling through his photos. My heart pounds against my eardrums. "Remind me again why I never dated him in high school?" Chrissy clucks her tongue before smiling like a smart-ass.

She knew I liked him, so she followed the girl code. To be honest, Ash isn't her type, anyway. He's too brainy.

I admire all his photos. In most of his pictures, he's caught off guard, laughing, or smiling. A few are of this past summer, shirtless on the beach. Then there's him and Alex, and a pit forms in my stomach. I crave having someone look at me the way he looked at her. It must be such an otherworldly feeling.

"I can't believe she cheated on him," I sputter without thinking.

"She what!?" Oh, I should have known better. Chrissy draws a few unwanted glances our way. She always does.

"I thought you knew," I hiss at her.

She shakes her head vigorously before taking control of the computer again to pull up Alex's page. Remind me never to get on Chrissy's bad side.

"Both of their relationship statuses are listed as single." She doesn't pull her eyes off the screen as she talks. "And who is this?" She pulls up a picture of Alex and someone who looks oddly familiar.

"Why does he look familiar?" I ask.

"Brandon Johnson, he went to our high school."

Then it hits me, and when she notices the light bulb over my head, she nods.

"Ash's best friend?" I mutter under my breath.

"Oh yeah, she two-timed him with his best friend."

I can't close my mouth. No wonder Ash is a wreck.

"Hey guys, what are you up to?"

I nearly jump out of my skin; Ash's voice was the last thing I expected to hear again today. I slam the laptop closed, and Chrissy and I play innocent.

"Nothing," we say at the same time.

Chapter Eight

He smiles while quirking a brow and takes a sip of water. "That's not suspicious at all." He sits down while popping a chip into his mouth.

"We're naturally suspicious. We can't help it." I nod at Chrissy's words.

"It's a bit of a curse," I say.

He watches us intently before eating another chip. "How's Pickles?" Ash asks.

Chrissy's confusion is obvious, but all I can focus on is Ash and those damn dimples.

"Who the fuck is Pickles?" Chrissy blurts out.

Ash holds my eyes hostage, and I've never felt more at ease and captivated. I let myself get lost in his wild chocolate eyes.

"The kitten at the café. You've met Pickles before," I say without looking at her.

Ash licks his fingers, and I gulp.

"Oh, the one that chews on you?"

Ash nods at Chrissy's question, and I see Zack out of the corner of my eye. He's jogging over to us. I hold my finger up just as he crashes into me.

"Dammit, Zack!" I almost fall out of my chair, but Chrissy catches me.

He rubs his knuckles over the top of my head.

"Zack Willows?" Ash's voice peaks as he recognizes Zack.

"Oh, shit, Ash Waylen!"

I'm released from the chokehold and fall against Chrissy. Zack and Ash hug and pat each other's backs fiercely. They start to chat and catch up. I side-eye Chrissy as she starts to tap on her phone.

> What did you do to that man?

> Nothing that I know of.

> Besides holding his hand to comfort him? ;)
>
> You got him wrapped around that pretty little finger of yours.

> I don't know how!

> Whatever you're doing, girl, keep doing it!
> You'll be in his bed by the end of the month!

My cheeks flush at the thought. Me and Ash in the same bed? I mean, who hasn't dreamed of such a thing? If Chrissy said something like that yesterday, I would have laughed her off. But with the attention he's showing me and his sexy gaze, I wonder if it's becoming a real possibility. My heart pounds, wondering just how he would look on top of me.

I need more ginger ale.

"Gwen?" I shake myself from my thoughts as Zack speaks. "Are you okay?" He sweeps his eyes over my expression.

I choke out a laugh. "I'm great." I force a smile, still trying to get the thought out of my head.

Ash grins almost wickedly when he notices my flushed cheeks.

"Okay . . ." Zack's words are laced with concern and wonder. "I'm going to show Ash where some of the other guys from high school hang out. See you guys later."

"Wait, don't I get a hug?" Chrissy stands with her arms extended.

Zack snorts and shakes his head. "Stay away from me, devil woman."

I can't help the giggle that rattles my chest. Chrissy has put Zack through hell and back. He's crazy protective and has even gotten into a few fights in defense of his sister. That's the kind of relationship they have, and I love it.

"Don't be a jackass!" Chrissy launches herself at him.

He struggles under her, and my cheeks ache from smiling so much. I don't even notice when Ash moves to stand in front of me, not until the smell of his natural scent mixed with pine and apples fills my nostrils. My breath catches and stops dead in my lungs.

"Are you working later today?" His lips form a natural smile.

I grow dizzy. "Not today, tomorrow though."

He nods while boring his eyes straight into mine. "See you then." His tone melts my insides.

"Okay," I manage to mutter out.

Zack clears his throat, noticing just how close Ash and I are standing. "Gwen, don't you have homework to do?"

I roll my eyes before staring at him dead on. "Don't you have hemorrhoid cream to apply?" I sneer.

Chrissy snorts and shoves Zack's shoulder. "Get out of here, prick."

She's still laughing when they walk away. I swear Ash glances over his shoulder before they leave the room, but perhaps it was just my mind playing tricks on me.

Chapter Nine

Ash

Zack Willows is the definition of a goofball, just like his sister. He and I were decent friends back in high school, not super close, but the kind of friends where, even if years pass, the relationship resumes the moment you see each other again. I appreciate his candor and sense of humor; I could really use a friend like him right now.

So when he asked me if I wanted to hang out and see some other guys from our graduating class, I was all in. I let Zack lead the way, but before we leave, I glance over my shoulder, needing to look at her one more time.

"Are you okay, dude?" Zack asks curiously.

I whip back around and prop the door open. "Yeah, just thought I forgot something. All good."

Zack's jaw clenches, and his shoulders tense. Whenever I would see all three of them together, I used to watch how Zack and Gwen would interact. Their relationship is interesting.

Chapter Nine

One moment, they're fighting. The next, they're teasing each other relentlessly.

Zack blabbers on as a twinge of jealousy makes my skin itch. Are they more than friends? Every time he sees her, he rushes to Gwen and crushes her in his arms. He doesn't do that with Chrissy, so why Gwen? I shove my hands in my pockets as soon as I feel them ball into fists. Why am I getting so worked up? I don't know Gwen like that, and even if I wanted to, I can't. I promised myself no girls this semester.

We enter the pavilion, the most exquisitely historical site on campus. The building is grand and magical. If we were in Europe, this would be the kind of castle the Tudors would have lived in.

"So, how've you been?" Zack turns to face me, walking backward down the hall.

I wonder how many people know about the breakup and how many know the truth behind it.

I shrug my shoulders in response. "Can't complain."

Zack matches my nod with an enthusiastic grin. He leads me into one of the rec rooms down the hall, and my mood changes instantly.

"Holy shit, Rome?" I chime.

Rome matches my shocked expression before standing and pulling me into a firm hug. "Ash fucking Waylen!? Good to see you, man!"

Rome stands about five inches taller than me. His skin is tan, and his forearms are toned from playing football. We used to be in the same coding club back in the day. He also used to raid my parents' refrigerator every time he would come over.

"No fucking way."

I turn around and get the same greeting from Miles Summers. This man took me under his wing during my first year of high school. He was one year ahead of me, yet that didn't stop him from wanting to be my friend. He's the coolest, most down-to-earth guy I know. His dark skin is as flawless as ever, and he examines my features with his amber eyes.

"How's it going, dude?" He grabs me by my shoulder and gives me a firm shake.

"I'm okay," I respond with a faint smile.

He tilts his head to the side, and I think I finally may have found someone who's able to catch me in a lie.

"Heard about you and Alex. Was it a tough breakup?"

Does he not know? Is he playing dumb?

"Leave him alone, man. He'll talk about it when he's ready," Rome adds while plopping on a couch. "Zack, how's Chrissy doing?"

Zack groans while sitting next to Rome. "Don't get me started."

The three of us can't help but snicker at Zack's pain. Chrissy loves love and anything physical. Zack sure has his hands full with that one.

"Did you guys see Gwen Roman? She got hot, man."

I fall into a chair next to Miles as Rome blabbers. I shift my gaze to the floor, trying to will the stifling emotions over Alex away.

"Shut the fuck up, Rome," Zack hisses, earning him another round of chuckles.

I pretend to focus on my bag, willing myself not to say anything. But if I find Miles or Rome near Gwen? I don't know what'll happen.

"What's up with you two, anyway?" My ears perk at the question Miles dares to ask.

I lean forward, resting my elbows on my thighs. Now, this is something I need to know.

"What do you mean?" Zack takes a long drink from his water bottle.

Chapter Nine

"Are you fucking or what?"

And there goes the water. Thankfully, no one was sitting across from him.

"She's like my sister, asshole!" Zack punches Miles's arm.

A smile pulls on the edge of my cheeks, and the smallest wave of relief washes over me.

The thought of her and Zack together upsets my stomach. It boils and unsettles my body. *What the fuck is wrong with me? Why am I feeling this way about some girl I only truly noticed yesterday?*

I rub my hands over my eyes, catching Miles glaring at me. "Ash, what the fuck did Alex do to you, man?"

I feel like it's written all over my face. The confusion over my feelings for Gwen, the hurt and shattering distrust Alex filled my heart with. Oh, and don't forget the backstabbing pain Brandon inflicted upon me as well.

I'm screwed up.

"Promise not to call me a pussy?" I need to talk about this, and these guys are my friends. I feel safe in this group, and I know that no matter what I say, they'll have my back. They did before, and they will again.

"Spill it, man." I sigh at Rome's words.

Miles nods his head, and Zack offers me a sincere smile.

In order to heal, I need to start from the beginning. Something I dread having to do, but if I want to move on, I need to take one step at a time.

"Hope you guys have a free period because this is going to take more than a minute."

I tell them all about Alex. How I met her, and how the instant I fell under her gaze, she consumed me. I would spend days with her, never wanting to leave her side. We had a perfect relationship in my mind; it lasted nine months, but it was all fake. I took her home over the past summer to meet my parents when summer vacation started. Something felt off the moment I introduced her to them, but I shook it off as nerves.

That same night, we went to Brandon's. He was throwing a crazy party since his parents weren't home, typical college student. She acted strange the entire time. She barely held my hand or looked me in the eye. So, I did what any confused young adult would do. I drank my feelings away. I lost her in the mix of vodka and music. It wasn't until I was trying to find my way to a bathroom that I accidentally stumbled into a guest bedroom.

I sobered up the moment I saw them together. There she was, the woman I thought I was in love with. And there he was, the only best friend I ever had.

In bed together.

I wish I could get the image out of my head, but it's burned into the deepest corners of my mind. I remember admiring her skirt that night. It was short and teased her ass whenever she took a step forward. I resented it when I found it hiked above her waist. She rode Brandon like he was a Greek god. Throwing her head back, smiling, drunk off his dick. His hands gripped her hips, moving her back and forth like she wasn't doing it well enough on her own.

The anger didn't rise quickly enough, something I'm ashamed to admit. I think the shock and vodka got in the way, but when I realized who I was watching, I blacked out. Hot rage blinded me. I have vague images of Alex jumping off Brandon's dick, pulling her skirt back down. Brandon's pale face when he noticed who'd walked in on them. I'd never thrown a punch in my life until that night, and I threw one right at my best friend. His nose cracked under my fist, the sound was more than pleasing. I needed him to hurt. I needed revenge for the knife they both plunged deep into my back.

Alex screamed, begging me to stop hitting her new fuck toy.

Chapter Nine

I didn't listen. The fact that she was begging fed my desire to keep hurting him, and I didn't give him the chance to fight back. Call me whatever you want, but I found joy in kicking him while he was down. It wasn't until two random bigger guys pulled me away that I relented. They weren't stupid either. I remember one of them saying that Brandon deserved it. Because who fucks someone else's girlfriend while their boyfriend is downstairs? What kind of best friend would do that?

I left her shit on the porch and offered to buy her a plane ticket home, but she refused. I don't know where she spent the rest of the summer. But I have a strong feeling I already know the answer.

Their faces are blank, and I can't get a read off them.

Everyone is quiet until Miles speaks up. "She fucked Brandon?"

I clasp my hands together and nod.

"And you walked in on them?"

I nod again, digging my fingernails into the back of my left hand.

"Dude, I don't even know what to say."

I look toward Rome, understanding just how he feels. "You don't have to say anything. It just feels good to get it out."

My eyes shift back to Zack. He walked in on me talking to Chrissy and Gwen, and now he knows I'm single. Am I getting this death stare because he thinks I'm going after one of them? Well, I've got news for him. When I want something, I tend to get it.

And right now, I feel a pull toward Gwen Roman. No matter how hard I try to deny it.

Chapter Ten

Gwen

Wednesday arrives, and another set of classes begins—English and calculus. Thankfully, they're only twice a week.

I stroll outside and check the time. It's around one in the afternoon. I have about two hours before my shift at the café. And then I remember Ash's words. *See you then.*

I wonder if he'll actually show up. The thought makes me nervous yet ecstatic. How I became the center of Ash's attention after all these years is beyond me.

Sure, we all looked awkward in high school. I know I did. But I don't think I changed that much. I'm still the same height, and my hairstyle hasn't changed. If anything, it's just longer now. The only other thing I can think of is the fact that my body leaned out, and I gained new curves. I'm not skinny like Chrissy, but she often tells me how envious she is of my hourglass figure. My chest filled out as well, but I wasn't wearing

Chapter Ten

anything to show it off when I first caught his attention. I have to be missing some key evidence here.

I walk over to a bench canopied by some trees and pull out my biochem notebook. Might as well get the questions assigned from the last class out of the way. I zone in on the textbook and hammer the questions out, following what notes I managed to take yesterday.

Ten questions in total don't sound bad. What makes this difficult is that each question takes about ten minutes to think over and complete.

I check the time again and leap off the bench. It's 2:30. I gather all my belongings and scurry. With thirty minutes to change and walk to work, I bolt by passing glares, managing not to hit anybody or sprain an ankle.

I burst through my apartment door, drop my bag, and change into a clean uniform. My stomach growls as I pull on a pair of jeans. I'll have to grab something at work. Before running out the door again, I push my earbuds in. Despite fumbling with my keys, I manage to lock up in record time. Jogging down the stairs, I check the time once more. I have fifteen minutes to get to work, and while I know Ryan won't care if I'm late, it still bothers me.

I stop right before the café and compose myself. I made it with five minutes to spare, only having to sacrifice my lungs and burning thighs. Catching my breath, I stroll in through the door.

And, of course, we're busy today . . .

I clock in and get to work right away. When I check in with Ryan, he asks me to get behind the register while he gets Brooksly ready to be picked up.

"They were approved?" I ask as my heart pounds.

Ryan nods proudly. "Now he gets to go home forever, all thanks to you."

Tears threaten my eyes, and I look over at his normal spot on the cat tree. "Let me know before he leaves?"

Ryan squeezes my shoulder and smiles. "You got it. Now, let's get to work. Looks like we got a crowd coming in."

The door opens as I step behind the counter. Being a small shop means that most of the time, it's Ryan, Blake, or myself working. Tonight, it's me and Ryan. So, I get to manage the orders, my least favorite part of my job. I tie an apron around my waist just as the group approaches the counter.

"Welcome to Tea and Kittens," I greet before looking up.

"Gwen!" Zack tries to run behind the counter before I stop him.

"You stay right there!"

He's like a damn golden retriever. Zack brought Ash and a few other guys from high school with him.

Ash walks up and rests his elbows on the counter. "Hey, you."

My body sings when I hear his voice.

Zack interrupts, though, ruining the moment within milliseconds. "We'll take five coffees, my lady."

I glare at Zack as he stands in front of the register.

"Twenty bucks." I hold my hand out.

"Twenty bucks!? That seems a bit much." He reaches for his wallet before slapping a twenty in my hand.

"It includes tip." I smirk.

"Ryan, I'm being swindled over here!" he calls to the back as I place eight dollars in the tip jar.

"You probably deserve it!" Ryan shouts from the back.

Ash and I both chuckle. My eyes land on him, discovering he's already watching me.

"Where's Pickles?"

I gather the mugs and point to the window. "His normal spot."

Chapter Ten

He looks back at the window and crosses the floor while Zack watches.

"Who's Pickles?" Zack asks, sounding intrigued.

"Guess you'll find out. Oh, and he *loves* snuggles," Ash says as I try to smother my giggle.

I hope Pickles makes Zack scream. I would pay good money to hear that.

I turn my back and prepare the drinks for Zack and his friends, stealing a glance at their booth as Ash returns with Pickles cuddled on his shoulder, just like the other day.

"Hey, Zack. Want to meet Pickles?"

Oh boy, here it comes. I lower myself behind the counter and peer over just in time for Ash to hand Zack that puff of crazy fur. Zack pulls him in and screams as Pickles chomps on his finger.

"Gwen! Your damn cat bit me!"

I burst out in laughter, losing my balance and falling on the floor. Pickles trots to where I'm settled.

"What a good boy." I pat his head as Zack bitches up a storm.

I wipe the tears from my eyes and carry the drinks to the booth. Zack is sucking on his finger, and I hear it before it even happens. Just before I place the drinks down, Pickles scampers from behind the counter and launches himself at Zack's ankles. Zack hollers again, and the laughter that builds in my throat boils over. Ash beams as the others crack up.

"Did you train him to do this?!" Zack shrieks, and I can't control it anymore.

"I wish I could say that I did." I bend down to pick up Pickles. As much as I want him to eat Zack's ankles, I can't have his pained screams scaring away other customers. "We have to leave Zack alone now, okay?" Pickles places his paw on my mouth. "Let me know if you guys need anything else."

Forever Crushed

"Thanks, Gwen." Ash's smile is addictive and dreamy.

His cheeks are blushing from either the laughter or from something else entirely.

I nod and walk over to a cat tree, where I drop Pickles off with some of his other friends before getting back to my next task.

An hour goes by before the couple from yesterday returns. Ryan set up a bundle of goodies for them to take home.

I rush over to Brooksly and hold him one last time.

"I'm going to miss you, buddy." I kiss his cheeks, and he rubs his nose against mine.

I walk over to the woman, and she grins the moment she sees Brooksly.

"If you need anything, be sure to call us." Ryan opens the cage, but I hand Brooksly right to the woman.

"We will, don't worry."

I fight back tears as the woman cradles Brooksly in her arms.

"Thank you." She beams, and I nod with a sniffle.

"I'm glad he found such a loving forever home." Tears escape my eyes the second I open my mouth.

I excuse myself, not having the strength to see this all the way through. I walk past the guys, trying my best to hide my tear-stained face. Strolling over to Ryan's desk near the back, I grab a tissue to blow my nose and wipe my eyes dry just as the door swings open.

Chapter Eleven

Ash

I tried not to admire Gwen as she worked. I didn't want her to feel like I was watching her every move like some pervert, waiting for her to bend over so I could stare at her ass. Instead, I found myself watching her for a different reason, and I couldn't resist following her with my eyes. She makes it clear she loves her job by the way she smiles and plays with the cats, giving each and every one of them individual attention. I don't think she likes the drink-making aspect, but the cats and kittens? She's all over that.

I really took notice of it when a couple came in to pick up an older cat. The way she kissed the top of his head and teared up saying goodbye made my own eyes gloss over. She didn't notice I was watching her when she passed our booth to go to the back, and with Zack preoccupied with Pickles taking bites out of literally every part of him, I take my chance.

Opening the door, I step into the back room. It's dark, but a faint light comes from a lamp on a desk.

I take small steps toward her, not wanting to scare her off. "Are you okay?"

She peeks over the tissue at the sound of my voice, and I have to fight the urge to run over to her and wipe her tears away.

"I'm fine." She tries to laugh it off, throwing the tissue away.

I step closer, needing to be near her.

"I'm just being silly," she says while wiping away the rest of her tears.

Standing in front of her, my gaze lingers over her swollen eyes and puffy cheeks. I raise my hand and thumb away the tear that rolls down her face. Her skin is soft like silk. It makes the tips of my fingers tingle.

"He's been here since I started. He would greet me at the door and lie on my lap during playtime. I know he's going to a good home, but I'm going to miss him."

Gwen's tone holds so much passion and love. I can't help but wonder what it feels like. What would it be like to have someone care for me as deeply as she cares for Brooksly? What would it be like to be loved by someone? *Truly* loved?

Gwen is passionate about what she does, and she cares about everyone around her. Who knew someone this sweet and caring could ever exist?

"It's not silly. If you ask me, it's kind of cute." I take another step forward, making her back up against the desk. Slowly, I reach toward her, tucking a loose strand of hair behind her ear, causing my heart to swell inside my rib cage. "How come I never noticed you before?" I'm at a loss for words. How could I have grown up in the same neighborhood as her? How did I go to school with her for years and never notice? "Maybe I needed glasses sooner than I thought."

Chapter Eleven

My comment makes her giggle, and the room brightens in that moment.

"Better late than never, I guess." Her eyes flick to mine.

I could happily drown in those ocean eyes of hers. I can't stop myself from scanning every inch of her expression. When my gaze lands on her lips, all the oxygen in my lungs vanishes. Being this close to Gwen, smelling her eucalyptus and vanilla scent, and touching her even in the slightest way is enough to make me dizzy.

"I see you now, Gwen Roman. I see you clearer than I ever have."

I lean in on instinct, and our noses feather over one another. Her attention is on me, holding me captive. My heart thunders against my chest, making me wonder if she can hear it. Our breathing falls in sync, both shallow and full of longing. Placing my hand on her waist, I close my eyes, and as our lips brush along one another—

"Gwen, get your damn cat!" Zack screams from the other room.

I release a sigh before opening my eyes.

"I better go save him," she whispers against my lips.

I nod before taking a step back, placing my hands in the pockets of my jeans. I barely touched the girl, and I'm already turned on.

"Gwen?" I call out as she walks away.

Spinning back around, she faces me with red cheeks. "Yeah?"

"Never mind." The faintest smirk forms on my lips again.

When she leaves, I trail my finger along my mouth. My lips ache with longing. I was so close. Just the idea of kissing her has me riled up. I need to figure out what's up with this girl and why she's eliciting such responses from my body.

No. I shake my head free of those thoughts. I made a promise to myself, and this one I cannot break. It doesn't matter how my feelings for Gwen seem to be growing. I need to focus on myself and my studies. No exceptions.

Chapter Twelve

Gwen

It's not all in my head. Ash sees me, actually *sees* me. His flirting isn't all fantasy. I dare to wonder what might have happened if Zack wasn't such a baby.

When I get home, I send Chrissy a picture of Pickles nibbling on Zack's ear. When she doesn't respond, I check the time. It's only nine, but that woman loves her beauty rest.

I strip out of my jeans and take off my bra. After pulling on an oversized T-shirt, I curl into bed. Tomorrow is the first lab for biochem, and the thought of seeing Ash sparks a fire between my thighs. I trail my fingers over my lips, imagining how his would feel against mine. I groan into my pillow as my thoughts run wild.

I've only had a handful of experiences with boys. Back in high school, I let Jessy Matthewson fondle my breasts as we made out. When he reached into my underwear, I had to fake it. He didn't know what he was doing, and I was too embarrassed to correct him. I wonder how Ash's fingers would feel. I

Forever Crushed

know he has more experience in that department than I do, and the thought ignites my body with electricity. My nipples harden under my shirt, making me whimper in frustration.

Shoving all that from my mind, I roll onto my side and put on my comfort cartoon, then reach over to my bedside table and turn off the light. I need to get some rest.

I have a feeling tomorrow is going to be one hell of a day.

Boy, did I call that one.

Chrissy pounds on my door as I fumble with my toothbrush in one hand and my shoe in the other. I slept through my first, second, and third alarms. After managing to get the door open, I slip my sneaker onto my foot and run back to the bathroom to spit out the toothpaste.

"Maybe if you didn't set an alarm so late in the morning, you wouldn't be rushing around," she calls after me as I put on my other sneaker.

I toss a random movie tee on and grab my bag.

"Ready." I fight to catch my breath, and Chrissy taps her foot impatiently.

She looks around my room. When she finds what she's looking for, she goes to grab it.

"Sit." She pushes down on my shoulders, forcing me back onto my bed. "You're not going to impress Mr. Biochem with your hair looking like this."

Chapter Twelve

I wince as she pulls my hair into a high ponytail. "I get the feeling he doesn't care about my hair."

She jumps off my bed. "What do you mean?"

I swing my keys around my finger and walk out the door. "If you answered my text last night, maybe you would know." I smirk as I lock the door behind us.

"What are you not telling me?!" she shouts as I jog down the stairs.

When we step outside, I begin to replay it all for her, and my grin grows as I watch her face light up.

"Gwen! You're about to get your freak on!" She backs up against me and twerks.

I push her away while laughing.

We go back and forth as we near the laboratory. With each step, her voice goes in one ear and out the other. My body comes alive and my heart throbs, knowing I get to see him again.

We enter the lab and head over to a spot in the corner. After sitting on a stool, I place my notebook on the clean, waterproof bench. Chrissy plops down next to me, boxing me in. She twirls her pen in between her fingers, and I scroll through my phone, willing my heart to calm down. Chrissy hums away and enters her own little world.

Looking at Chrissy, no one would know how much she's been through. Her home life was perfect, but she had a rough time when we were younger, especially in middle school. She used to get picked on because she was kind and pretty. All the girls hated her for it.

I've never been in a fight before, but I would defend Chrissy to the death. Looking at the two of us, one may think, "What do they have in common?" The answer is simple. We understand a person's worth is more than what's on the outside. I was there for Chrissy as she was there for me. We get every little nuance about one another. If she's sick, I know the only thing she wants is chicken nuggets and bakery rolls. If I'm upset, Chrissy knows to get a bag full of gummy candy and to put on a true crime doc. Best friends are special in that kind of way, and I'm truly grateful I have Chrissy. Without her, I wouldn't be the person I am today.

"Ladies." Ash's voice pulls me from my thoughts.

My leg shakes as my stomach lurches.

"Hey, Ash." Chrissy blows a bubble with her gum.

I glance his way as he raises his eyebrows.

"Chrissy, why don't you sit next to David? I overheard he thinks you're hot."

She begins to doodle in her notebook, not getting the hint. "No, thanks." Chrissy's smart, but she has her airhead moments.

"I'll give you five bucks."

"Deal." She jumps up and snatches the bill from his hand. Gathering her things, she winks at me before leaving.

One thing any college student is desperate for is money.

"Good to know I'm only worth five bucks!" I call after her, not caring who hears me.

She smirks at me before sitting next to David, whatever his last name is.

"Coffee's on me, bitches!" She waves the five around.

Ash chuckles as he gets comfortable on the stool next to me. "You two are hilarious."

Professor Stilts walks in and goes over the curriculum. I drop my gaze to my notebook, ignoring the fact that Ash put on his sexy librarian glasses. My feet bounce on the stool's foot bar but freeze once Ash nudges his knee against mine. How did he get so close without me noticing?

His leg sends vibrations through me. I glance over, discovering that he's staring straight ahead. Does he not realize our legs are touching?

My eyes trail down, and I gulp when I notice how good he looks in jeans. His thighs are toned, his muscles firm under the fabric. I move my eyes upward, noticing his arms are built.

Ash drops his pen and bends to his right. His hair brushes against my arm. I look toward Chrissy, more than bug-eyed. Her mouth falls open, and her smile is wide, exposing her slightly crooked white teeth.

When Ash picks up his pen and straightens his posture, he nudges against my arm. I almost have to excuse myself to go faint in the bathroom. Professor Stilts goes over the experiments we're to perform in the coming weeks, but I tune him out. I watch as Ash drops his pen against his notebook. He reaches into his pocket for something but doesn't pull anything out. Instead, in one smooth motion, he plants his hand on my upper thigh, and I tense under his glorious touch. He trails his thumbs along the fabric covering my leg, gripping ever so slightly. I glance in his direction, but his attention is still on Professor Stilts.

What the fuck is going on?

Ash drops his hand to my knee, then slides it up again. I forget how to breathe; I have to focus on just blinking. He brings his hand up to my waistband, and I suck in as much air as I can. I feel his finger feather against my bare skin, barely there but I feel it down to my toes. Before anything else happens, he removes his hand and picks up his pen. I look down at my notebook, trying to make it seem like I'm not completely out of breath.

The rest of the hour whizzes by. At the end of class, I feel his eyes on me once again before he slides his phone over to me. Without an exchange of words, I tap my number on the screen.

When I'm done, he picks it up and pushes his glasses farther up his nose.

"See you later." He winks at me.

Fucking winks at me!

He strolls past Chrissy as she charges at me. "What the fuck was that!?" I shush her, and she lowers her tone. "You got all squirmy!"

I scoff and shake my head. "I did not get all *squirmy*." I pick up my bag and stand.

"You were squirmy." Chrissy and I look at the guy who sat across from me.

"Shut up."

"You don't even know her!" Chrissy chimes in, and the guy rolls his eyes before leaving.

I pack up my things and leave the room feeling hot, heavy, and confused. I can't wrap my head around these last few days.

I give Chrissy the play-by-play as we walk outside. She lights up but ponders over my question.

"Why do you think he's suddenly interested in me?"

She scoffs as we walk down the path. "Because you're hot."

I blow air out between my lips. I'm not willing to accept that answer.

"I think it's time for recon part two."

This time, I agree with her.

Chrissy and I end up wandering around campus, easily getting in our ten thousand steps for the day. This would have been easier if we knew his schedule. My feet ache, and Chrissy slumps her shoulders forward.

"Where the hell is this guy?" she groans in frustration before pulling out her phone. "I'm texting Zack."

I trip over my feet. "Why didn't you do that earlier?" I whine, fighting the desire to fall to my knees.

"Why didn't you?"

Chapter Twelve

I stick my tongue out at her, knowing she has a valid point. She sends the text and holds the phone to her side, swaying in the humid breeze. I can't wait for fall to arrive in the next few weeks. As I wipe the sweat from my brow, my phone buzzes against my hip. I pull it out and almost drop it when a number I don't recognize pops up.

"Chrissy..."

She looks over at me as I show her my phone screen, and she snatches it with wide eyes.

"Boy, he doesn't waste any time." She hands my phone back just as hers chimes with a message.

I stare at the text, and I feel like I should hide under my blanket and never leave.

>Maybe Ash: Hey, beautiful, guess who.

I fidget with my phone, flipping it over in my hand, not knowing what to do. Do I respond or make him wait? What would I even say? *Hey, Mr. Biochem, thanks for massaging my thigh today!* I cringe at the thought. I'm discovering I'm not good at talking to boys.

"He's with Zack in the pavilion. Let's go!" she exclaims with a burst of energy.

I call after her as she books it to the pavilion. It takes all my mental capacity to make sure I don't roll an ankle on the way there.

The pavilion is one of the main castle-like structures on campus. It reminds me of a princess tower. The building is constructed from light gray brick, and there's a double-stone staircase that leads into the pavilion itself. Each corner has rounded towers. Every time I see them, I imagine a princess dangling her hair out the window, waiting for her prince to whisk her away.

Chrissy vaults up the steps two at a time, leaving me in the dust. When I finish climbing the stairs, I trail behind her as we "sneakily" enter through the grand entryway. Chrissy takes the left side as I take the right, peering around every corner and down every hallway. We near the staircase, and just as I peek into the rec room, I backtrack.

"Chrissy." I wave her over and point to the room before me.

She peers into the room and gives me a thumbs-up. Ash is hanging out with Zack and some guys from the café yesterday. They're all gathered in some lounge chairs.

"Text your brother," I whisper.

"And say what?" Chrissy whispers back, and I shrug.

"I want to see how he reacts to your text messages."

She lights up and taps away on her phone screen. I hear a ding from the other room and peer over enough to see Zack.

"Oh, fuck me." Chrissy and I force back our laughter as Zack growls in frustration.

"What did you send him?" I meet her gaze, and her eyes glisten.

"That I have a hot date and want to know if he has any spare condoms."

Zack bitches and moans. The other guys chime in, asking him what's wrong.

"It's just my damn sister. I wish she would keep her legs closed." Our mouths fall open when the words spill from Zack's mouth.

"That son of a bitch!"

I cover her mouth with my hand as I hold back the urge to crack up. I let her calm down before I remove my hand from her glossy lips.

She peeks into the room, and without looking at me, she says, "Text Ash back."

My heart plummets to the floor.

Chapter Twelve

"What do I say?" I hover my thumbs over the keypad, truly at a loss for words.

"Um, ask him if he finished the biochem homework for tomorrow."

I nod and type out the message. I take a minute to work up the courage to press the send button. Once I do, I watch Chrissy's expression.

"He's pulling out his phone." She smiles and grabs my hand. "He totally just blushed."

My phone buzzes, and I look at the message.

> Not yet. Want to work on it together?

A scream builds up in my chest when I show it to Chrissy.

"Move over, vibrator, because you're getting some dick tonight!"

My eyes bug out, and Chrissy realizes she just blew our cover.

"Chrissy?" Zack's voice echoes from the room.

Chrissy sidesteps under the archway and beams at the guys.

"What's up, bro?" She flashes him the peace sign, trying her best to act innocent.

My phone vibrates, and when I look at it, my cheeks blush bright red.

> You're right next to Chrissy, aren't you?

I step into view and flash a smile.

"What's up, guys?" I pull a Chrissy and flash them another peace sign. "Didn't expect to see y'all here."

Oh, just end it now. End this never-ending embarrassment. Ash's eyes land on me, and a knowing smirk paints his face.

"What are you two doing here?" Zack crosses his arms over his chest.

Chrissy and I shrug in sync. "Nothing," we respond simultaneously, and my hand flies across my forehead.

"We were just talking." Chrissy clicks her tongue, thinking she just came up with the greatest excuse in the world.

"About?"

I stare at Zack between my fingers and decide to stop letting Chrissy come up with all the excuses. "How Pickles kicked your ass yesterday."

The other guys snicker, and my heart thumps when I hear Ash's light yet husky chuckle.

"Okay, we gotta go now. Lots of important things to do today." I pull on Chrissy's hand as she waves goodbye.

"Bye, Zacky-poo!"

The room erupts again, and I swear one of these days, Zack just might actually explode.

Once we step outside, the urge to throw up makes me stop to breathe. My stomach tosses and turns. I'm not sure how I'm supposed to live like this.

My phone buzzes in my hand.

"I'm going to throw up. Just tell me what it says." I offer Chrissy my phone, and she accepts it.

> Meet me in the library in ten minutes?

I groan as Chrissy reads the message out loud.

"You don't have to go." She hands my phone back with a soft smile.

She knows my struggle with anxiety, and right now, it's way past "through the roof."

"No, I'm going. I need to woman up."

Chapter Twelve

She claps her hands and jumps up and down. "That's my girl!"

We part ways as I head to the library, my mind swimming and drowning at the same time. My thigh tingles from where Ash touched me earlier today, and I can still feel his thumb and grip on my skin.

I decide to follow through. Younger Gwen would have a heart attack if she knew this is our life right now.

Chapter Thirteen

Gwen

The library is one of my favorite places on campus. Rows and aisles of endless books tower up to the third floor. I've managed to comb through about fifteen percent of the library during my years here at Castle Brook. There are tons of little nooks, crannies, and hiding places you can tuck yourself into when you need to study or rest. I often find a secluded corner when I have to cram for a test or during finals week. Whenever I study at home, I always get distracted. Normally when I come to the library, I'm alone.

But not today.

I pace outside the main entrance, wishing I had time to change my shirt. This one is drenched in nervous sweat. Holding my notebook close to my chest, I focus on my breathing. In through the nose, hold for five seconds, and then out through my mouth. I do this about ten times and get myself under control.

"Hey, sneaky girl."

Chapter Thirteen

And there goes all my hard work. I turn around to face a cool, grinning Ash.

"We weren't sneaking around," I blurt out, picking at the frayed paper sticking out from my notebook.

"No, but you were spying." I go to defend myself again, but he interrupts me. "You know I'm right."

My cheeks flush when he flashes those melt-worthy dimples. "I don't know what you're talking about."

He steps closer, and my heart sinks into my gut. He leans in close to my ear, brushing his cheek along mine.

"If you wanted to see me again, all you had to do was ask." His voice drops a decibel, sending shivers up my spine.

I close my eyes, letting his tone run wild in my mind. I could listen to this man talk all day. I fight the whimper that dances on my lips when he pulls away.

Ash wraps his hand around mine and leads us into the library. He chuckles when I hesitate. I'm starting to wonder if he gets a kick out of my blushing cheeks and awkwardness.

I let him pull me to an area in the back of the library, trying hard not to focus on how his hand feels against mine. The sheer strength he possesses is impressive. His hand alone has more muscles than I could ever imagine. He holds onto me for dear life, like I would dare drop it and run away. He makes me feel like I'm on a cliff that crumbles beneath my feet. But he also makes me feel safe. His touch is comforting. I get the strangest feeling that he would protect me if he had to.

When he releases my hand, I have to stop the pout that threatens my lips.

Ash tosses his bag on the table and settles into a chair. I get comfortable across from him and glance around the room. A few students hover over textbooks sitting at other tables, and some browse through the bookshelves. Overall, this spot is pretty empty and peaceful.

When I open my notebook, I quickly slam it shut. I forgot I started the problems yesterday, about half of them, to be honest. Ash notices my sudden movement, so I smile nonchalantly.

"I saw that." He pulls out his glasses and slides them onto his face.

"Saw what?" I try my best to play dumb, but he doesn't fall for it.

He reaches for my notebook, brushing his fingers along mine before taking it. He flips through it before landing on the exact spot where I left off.

"Nice work." He hands me my notebook and slides his over to me.

I pick it up gingerly and flip through it. When I land on the completed work, my mouth drops.

"You lied to me."

He snickers as I feign disappointment. I grab my chest and sniffle. "We've only known each other for a few days, and you're already lying to me. Just break my heart, why don't you?" I flip open my textbook, sensing his amused grin.

"I would never do that to you."

Twirling my pen in my hand, I meet his gaze. "Lie to me or break my heart?" I feel a different side of me come out, almost flirty but not quite.

He leans over the table, his sculpted forearms making me gulp. "I think you know the answer to that question."

My subconscious screams in glee, but my brain steps in. Worry seeps into my being, and my bubble returns. What if Ash breaks my heart and never looks back? Why would I ever be his or anyone's priority or first choice? I'm no one special.

Forcing my eyes down on the textbook, I pick up where I left off the other day.

"If you completed the work, why did you ask me to join you?" I don't lift my eyes from the page as I question him.

Chapter Thirteen

"I enjoy looking at you."

I can't help but scoff. Now I know he's messing with me.

"Why are you laughing?" he chuckles.

I look up and see his broad smile, showing off his perfectly straight teeth.

"You like looking at this?" I gesture to myself, knowing how much of a mess I look right now. Pretty sure my hair frizzed out the moment I stepped outside.

His eyes sweep over my body, instantly making me regret what I just said. He bites his lower lip, and I wonder what's going through his head.

"I take it back. I *really* like looking at you."

His sincerity convinces me he's telling the truth. No words dare escape my mouth. His gaze traps them all inside me. I hammer out the equations, knowing full well his eyes are on me.

"So, Gwen." I raise my eyebrows but don't let my eyes leave the page. "How come I know so little about you? Even though we grew up in the same town."

I giggle to myself. That's easy.

"Because I'm me, and you're you." I drop my pen and raise my hands in victory. Biochem can officially suck it.

"What does that mean?" he asks, confusion infusing his tone.

I smirk like a smart-ass.

"It means you're cool, and I'm not," I respond honestly.

"That's not true." His dimples appear on the edges of his lips.

"You said you'd never lie to me."

He pushes his glasses up his nose absentmindedly. "I never said that."

He winks at me, and I realize what he meant was, *I'll never break your heart.* The thought of him having my heart makes

73

me feel like I've jumped off a two-hundred-story building. But could I claim his heart as he did mine? Hell no, this is Ash Waylen. And besides, he just had his heart broken. The last thing he needs is my obsessive ass.

I open my mouth to say something but close it the moment I realize the words that threaten to fly off my tongue.

"You can ask me, Gwen."

Is it possible he knows what I was about to ask?

"I'll ask you only if you want to talk about it." Do I want to add fuel to the flames? Is it my place to even ask such a question?

I feel Ash's heart chip away as he studies my expression.

"Just ask me." His tone is quiet yet comfortable.

I debate with myself for a moment. How would I feel if someone were to ask me this question? My gut is telling me this is information I need to know before anything happens. I don't want to put myself in a precarious position.

"Are you okay?" I focus on him, not his relationship with Alex.

The pain in my chest mirrors the pain in his expression, and I'd give anything to ease it.

I don't think he was expecting me to ask that question. He takes his glasses off and rubs his eyes. When he looks at me again, his eyes glisten from holding back tears.

"I'm getting there."

I move without thinking, standing from my seat to sit in the chair next to him.

Chapter Fourteen

Ash

"Sorry." A self-conscious laugh escapes, and tears build in my eyes. "I'm not used to people asking me that question."

Her sweet grin comforts me. In one swift movement, she wraps her arms around my neck, and I collapse against her shoulder. She traces circles along my shoulder blade, and my dam breaks. I dampen her shirt within seconds. She doesn't jerk away like I expect her to. Instead, her hand trails into my hair, massaging my scalp.

No one asks me that question. Not Miles, Rome, or Zack when I told them. I thought she was going to ask me what happened.

So when she didn't, it all came rushing out. I should've felt ashamed when the tears tugged at my eyes. I thought the moment I dropped the cool guy act, she would run away and never look back. Never in a thousand years did I expect her to keep showing up.

In high school, she was this nerdy little thing. I only knew she existed because of Zack and Chrissy. Now? She's in her prime. She oozes femininity and emotional intelligence. There's something else, though, but I can't figure it out.

I can't get over how smooth her skin feels against mine, how her eyes could drown me if I admire them for too long. I crave her when she's not around. Not just because she's fucking gorgeous, but because she's funny and kind. She cares for everyone and anything. I'm not used to people like her. I find myself doing things around her without thinking first, something I never do. It worries yet excites me at the same time. That's the effect Gwen has on me.

The last thing I want to do is scare her away. I don't know what I'll do if that happens. As much as I want to stay curled in her arms, I pull away. When I do, she meets my eyes again, placing her hands on my cheeks and wiping the remaining tears away.

"Don't worry. You're still cool in my book."

Just like that, she gets a smile from me. She trails her thumb along my cheekbone, down to my jawline.

"You know—" Her gaze meets mine, causing me to stutter for a moment. "No one has asked me that since the breakup."

She offers me a warm, sympathetic smile. She can't help but care. It's who she is. It's in her DNA.

"Well, I'm going to ask you every day, and you're going to hate me for it."

My breath freezes in my chest. The idea of her checking in on me every day fills my heart, slowly mending the shattered pieces.

"No, I don't think I will."

And I mean it. I could never tire of Gwen. Not her voice, not her laugh, not how her cheeks flush red from a simple

Chapter Fourteen

glance. I can't bear the idea of telling her the specifics of what happened between Alex and me. Not yet, at least. I want to enjoy Gwen and forget about my past.

Maybe she's different. And maybe, just maybe, she can show me what real love feels like.

Chapter Fifteen

Gwen

I can't sleep. The events from today replay in my head repeatedly. I toss and turn before looking at the clock. It's only eleven at night. Sleep might not find me tonight, which is saying a lot because sleep and I are best friends. With my trusty comfort show playing in the background, thoughts cloud the forefront of my mind, shoving any prospect of sleep out the front door.

I first noticed Ash when I was fifteen, and every day since, he's plagued my mind at one point or another. I'd move on if I didn't see him for a while, but then the moment he would reappear, I fell right back into my crush. In every book I read, I would picture him as the main love interest. He's the star in all my dreams and fantasies. And today, I played with his hair and stroked his back. He held my hand and gripped my thigh. His touch has left an everlasting impression on my body.

I'm trying not to dive in head first. It may not seem like it, but I am. The tether he has on my heart is roping me in faster

Chapter Fifteen

than I can control. I don't have the right experience with love to know how to guard my heart, and I just hope he meant what he said earlier today, that he won't break it.

My phone buzzes against my cooling sheets, and I roll over onto my other side. As soon as I see his name, I yank the charger from my phone and plop onto my back.

> Are you up?

> Unfortunately . . .

He responds instantly. The thought of having his undivided attention makes me giddy.

> Not unfortunate for me <3

> What are you doing up? :)

> Alex won't stop blowing up my phone. I blocked her, but she keeps getting different phone numbers via apps.

> So you texted me instead?

> Well, yeah.

I snort, knowing how his voice would sound at this moment. How dare I think he would do anything other than text me, silly me.

> What does she want?

A bunch of screenshots take over my screen. I scroll through them, reading everything Alex is sending to Ash. She's sorry she went behind his back, how terrible she feels, how she misses how he used to kiss and fuck her. I could live without that image in my head. What I see next makes me gasp. *I was stupid to think Brandon could live up to you.* Damn, Chrissy and I are good. We had that mystery figured out days ago.

> I just silenced her notifications. I would think the talk we had in the café was enough, but I guess not.
>
> Besides, there's someone else I'd rather be talking to right now.

His texts fill my screen, and I smile like a goof at his flirtatious messages. I would text Chrissy right now if she weren't asleep.

> Flattery will get you everywhere <3

> Lol you're so adorable. Do you live on campus?

> I tried but didn't make it past freshman year. I have a studio apartment a few blocks away. How about you?

> I live with my brother off campus. He owns a house and is never home.

> Are you and your brother close?

I honestly didn't know he had a brother. Apparently, the recon wasn't as successful as we thought.

> He's a bit of an asshole, but he's my brother. What can I say?

Chapter Fifteen

> I just have my parents, and honestly, they suck lol.

I hear that . . .

My head tilts in curiosity. I wouldn't have thought his parents would suck as much as mine. But who knows? Everyone has their secrets and crappy families.

Tired yet?

> No . . .

Good :)

We spend a good remainder of the night texting back and forth. I learn he's majoring in computer analytics but loves science, so he takes extra science classes for fun. I tell him my major and how I work at the cat café part-time, even though he already knows about Tea and Kittens.

If I send you something, promise not to call me a creep?

> Well, now I'm scared, but I promise.

The picture that follows surprises me. Ash took a picture of Pickles and me, and I'm not getting eaten alive. I'm cradling him in my arms by the front counter.

> This is more sweet than creepy but maybe just a little creepy.

Don't tell me that!

I laugh loudly and almost drop my phone on my face.

> Don't make me laugh so hard. I almost injured myself!

He follows my message up with a series of laughing emojis.

> I'd still think you're pretty, don't worry ;)

Oh my god, my heart. Every inch of my body flutters and tickles from his nonstop compliments. My eyes land on the time in the corner of my phone.

> We have to be in class in four hours . . .

> Meet me in bed later for a nap?

> In your dreams.

> Well, you're not wrong there . . .

> I can't handle you right now lol. See you in a few hours.

> Can't wait :D

I don't know how, but I fall asleep, and of course, Ash crawls into my mind and takes over my dreams.

Just like my reality.

Chapter Fifteen

I whine when my alarm goes off, begging my phone for five more minutes, but I know if I wait any longer, Chrissy will storm in here and drag my ass out of bed. I turn my cartoon off and grab a pair of jean shorts and an oversized white T-shirt. Hopping in the shower, I hope Chrissy brings me a latte; I'm going to need all the caffeine I can get today.

I'm dressed and brushing my hair when Chrissy knocks at the door. I open it and sigh in relief when she offers me my usual chai.

"You're a lifesaver," I moan when the plastic lid hits my tongue.

"What's wrong with you!?" Her face lights up. "You finally got some dick, didn't you? And not just any dick, Ash Waylen's dick." She raises and lowers her eyebrows suggestively.

"What? No." I shake my head. "But . . ." I trail off to create some suspense.

"What!?" I toss her my phone, and she taps in my passcode. "Gwen Roman, were you up all night texting back and forth? You naughty girl," Chrissy chimes, and I snort in response.

"That's not all." She beams in response, and as we leave, I tell her all the juicy details from the library.

We reach campus just as I finish.

"My little girl is growing up." She wipes away fake tears when we cross under the archway. "Don't look now." I keep my gaze on Chrissy, trusting her. "Alex is right there." She points to the left. "And she's watching you like a hawk."

"Me!?" I ask, flabbergasted, and she nods.

I stare forward, refusing to meet Alex's deadly glare. Does she know Ash and I have been talking? Maybe she saw us in the library? Chrissy peers over her shoulder and mutters. "Oh, boy."

Chills run through my body. This can't be good.

"She's walking toward us," Chrissy whispers.

Keeping my head down, I try to hide behind Chrissy. The last thing I want is a confrontation. I'm not one to stir the pot, and Alex is ready to bubble over.

"Gwen!"

Oh, thank god. I'm normally never relieved when I hear Zack's voice, but today, I'll let him tackle me.

"Zack!"

We run at each other, and I leap into his arms, meeting his embrace just as enthusiastically.

"Now, this is what I call a hug!"

My legs swing in the air frantically, almost hitting Chrissy. I land on the ground just as Alex walks past us. She or her friends must have seen Ash and me talking. That's the only reason I can come up with to explain her seething rage.

Zack notices and does a double-take. "What the hell was that?"

I shrug, playing dumb. "What do you mean?" I smile just as my phone buzzes.

Chrissy nudges my arm. "Alex is jealous that our Gwen here is stealing her man."

Both Zack's and my eyes widen.

"Welp, I gotta go!" I skip away from them, knowing full well the lecture Zack is preparing to give me.

Zack has always seen me as a little sister. He lumps Chrissy and me together, even though we're all the same age. I used to think it was cute how protective he would get whenever a boy would approach me. Now? At the ripe age of twenty-one, it's not cute anymore.

"We'll talk later!" he calls after me, but I ignore him.

Slowing my pace, I check my phone. My smile drops when the message isn't from Ash.

How's my baby girl doing today?

Chapter Fifteen

I press my lips together just as another message appears in our group chat.

> How's the first week of school going?

Oh, if only she knew . . .

> Both are great.

The line of questioning stops after that. My parents love to keep things straight and to the point. Which is fine with me. I'm not into talking to them much these days.

I head straight to biology, clutching my precious latte all the way there.

The caffeine didn't work. All it did was raise my heart rate and make me jittery. I nodded off in biology. I remember going over the functions and parts of the brain, and then class ended. I totally blacked out and woke up with my heart running a marathon. I can't let Ash keep me up all night like that again. I don't want my grades to slip because of a boy. Rubbing my eyes, I collide with Chrissy as I exit the room.

"Oh, girl. You need some sleep." She links her arm through mine as we head to my new favorite class. "Maybe if you slept instead of texting your new friend all night, you wouldn't be yawning."

Her words fade away when Ash comes into view, but my heart stabs me when I see who he's talking to.

Alex.

Chrissy feels my arm tense around hers, and she pulls me close as we pass them. We try to overhear what they're talking about, but all I can make out are harsh, hushed whispers.

"I don't think she's getting the hint," Chrissy leans in and whispers in my ear.

"No, she's not," I mumble.

Alex's expression is defensive, and her arm movements become frantic as she talks. She should feel guilty about what she did. She should apologize profusely, but she's not. She's not even concerned that Ash is in pain. It's all about her.

When Ash strolls into the room, his face is hollow. His normal glinting eyes are now shrouded in despair.

"I think he needs another Gwen hug," Chrissy mumbles.

He doesn't look our way as he sits in his chair and runs his fingers through his wavy locks. I get the hint, loud and clear. I place my phone on my notebook and make good on my promise.

> Are you okay?

I side-eye Ash, waiting for him to get the text. Nothing happens though. He stares down at his notebook and focuses on his notes. My heart tugs toward him, begging me to comfort him and ease his heartache. An idea pops into my head. My muscles twitch to move without a second thought.

Chapter Sixteen

Ash

Last night was the most fun I've had in a long time. I woke up this morning not caring that I was tired. I couldn't wait to get to biochem, sit next to Gwen, and tease her again. I needed to see her cheeks flush. I had to get her to smile just so I could return the favor. I think she has a thing for my dimples.

The moment I hopped in my car, my phone chimed. I picked it up, eager to talk to Gwen again, but no, fucking Alex didn't get the hint.

Hell, it wasn't even a hint. I flat-out told her she needed to leave me alone. She's so damn selfish that she can't even give me that. I've seen her around campus with other guys. I'm not stupid like she thinks I am. Even if I were stupid, I wouldn't allow myself to fall under her charm again. I'm tired of selfish women, my mother included. I had to witness her cheating on my father when I was younger. She didn't care who I saw strolling in and out of her bedroom. She thought I was too young to remember. Why do women like her think I'm so damn gullible?

Perhaps that's why I'm so intrigued by Gwen. She's far from selfish. She wouldn't hurt a fly if it landed on her ice cream. She would give that insect her damn frozen treat, and the thought of it kills me. No wonder Zack is so protective of her. No wonder he scoops her up in his arms every time he sees her and never wants to let go. I get it now because those same feelings are stitching their way across my heart.

I wish I knew how Alex nailed my schedule. On my way to biochem, I found her leaning against a wall, smirking at the sight of me.

"Hey, handsome."

My lips curl into a sneer at her comment.

"What do you want?" I try walking past her, but she digs her nails into my forearm.

"Why aren't you returning any of my texts?" she says while fluttering her long eyelashes.

"Because I told you to leave me alone, remember?"

She scoffs at me, waving her hand like she's dismissing a servant. "You didn't mean that."

My nostrils flare, and blood rushes to my cheeks. "I meant it, and the fact you're not listening proves I did the right thing when I broke up with you." I drop my tone, sensing Gwen before I see her. "I'm not doing this anymore."

I tug my arm away from her and walk away without another word.

I'm wrapped in my own selfish pity. Here I am, bitching about selfish women, and I'm pulling the same shit. As I stroll into biochem, I decide to stay quiet; I won't ruin Gwen's day. She doesn't deserve the depressive aura that radiates around me.

I feel her eyes on me, begging me to meet her gaze. As

much as I want her to comfort me, I can't. I don't want to taint her beautiful soul. My phone goes off, but I ignore it, even though I know it's Gwen. I refuse to pull her into my cloud of despair.

"Cover for me?"

Those words grab my attention.

Gwen stands in front of me, offering me her hand. "Let's go."

Just like that, she does it again. I place my hand in hers, and a small smile plays across my lips.

Chapter Seventeen

Gwen

I'm trying hard to ignore the tingling sensation on my palm. Ash's hand grips mine, fitting perfectly. I'm using all my strength to stand upright and not falter. I don't even know where we're going. I just know he needs an escape.

"Look, I'm not going to lie. I don't have a plan," I admit.

He chuckles as we step outside. "You kidnap me, and you don't have a plan?" His lips curl into a smirk.

"I didn't *kidnap* you," I whisper as a smile forms on my face. "I borrowed you."

My eyes lock on Zack. He's on the grass, sprawled out with a girl facing him. I can't let him see me with Ash, let alone holding Ash's hand. I pull on his arm, and we head down the path.

"We'll go to my place." I won't have to worry about Zack lecturing or embarrassing me there.

"I don't get wined and dined first?"

I ignore the obvious smooth talk and shield my face as we

Chapter Seventeen

pass Zack. Luckily, the girl is distracting him with her flawless looks and hand gestures as she talks.

"Don't worry. I'll feed you." I stand on my tippy-toes and ruffle Ash's hair.

Seeing Ash in my tiny apartment is surreal. I can't take my eyes off him. He examines every little knickknack, every book, even my extensive video game collection. I step out of my sneakers and collapse onto my bed, my body aching for a nap. My eyes flutter closed until the bed shifts. When I open them, Ash is hovering over me, so close that our noses brush against one another.

How do you breathe again?

Focus, Gwen. Ash needs a friend right now. Wipe the drool from your lips and provide him with the friendly care and attention he needs.

"You said you were going to feed me."

I said what? His eyes capture mine, and everything goes blank.

"Gwen?" He tilts his head.

"Yes?" I manage to say.

"Feed me."

Mindlessly, I pull my phone out of my pocket and hand it to him. "Takeout?" I offer.

His hand grazes mine as he takes my phone. Backing away,

he leans against my pillows, in the spot I sleep every night. I'll be breathing in his scent for as long as it lasts.

He peers up at me, and my heart jolts. Hot flashes flood my body, especially the spot between my thighs.

"You're adorable," he smirks before scrolling through my phone. "In the mood for anything in particular?"

I open my mouth and close it, catching myself before saying "You." Which would have been beyond devastating.

Sitting up, I cross my legs. "I'd kill for a good order of french fries."

My one and only bad habit besides skipping class, apparently.

"You're an easy woman to please." He looks up at me again, and I gulp. "I like that."

I scream and squeal internally.

"Got any good pictures on here?"

He's expecting a reaction out of me, but I'm a good girl. No nudes on there.

"Unless you like looking at cat pictures, I'm afraid not." He hands me back my phone, defeated. "Nice try though."

I order the food just as my stomach grumbles.

We wait in silence, but it's not agonizing or awkward. It's actually the opposite. We're both scrolling through our phones, sharing funny memes and videos with each other, something Chrissy and I do all the time. I'm lying on my belly at the foot of my bed, fighting my fatigue. When a series of knocking sounds from my door, I scramble to my feet and trip over my shoes.

"Geez, and I thought I was hungry." Ash chuckles as I open the door and accept the food.

I present the pizza and bag of what I'm hoping is deep-fried deliciousness.

Chapter Seventeen

"I know before you even say it." I drop the food on my bed. "I'm a good provider."

He snorts at my comment before grabbing a slice of pizza. I open the bag, and drool escapes the corner of my lips.

"What did you do? Order all the fries they had?" I ask Ash before shoving two in my mouth. "I think I love you," I moan without thinking.

I need to get better at the whole *think before you speak* thing.

"Sit down, silly girl."

I do a little dance before sitting on the bed. Potatoes make me happy. I'm a simple girl.

I get comfy as Ash's phone rings. I see who it is and notice just how quickly his face falls.

"She's still trying to get a hold of you?" I eat the fries two at a time, observing him.

With a sigh, Ash nods while looking down at the phone.

Reaching forward, I take his phone. "Trust me?"

With another nod, I confiscate his phone, tossing it near the bag he left by the front door. "It's just you and me now. Deal?"

His eyes shimmer, and he smirks. "Deal."

I scoot up toward the pillows and lean against them, right next to Ash. I offer him my bag of fries.

"Should I feel honored?" He places his hand over his heart.

"I don't even share my fries with Chrissy, so yes. You should feel very honored."

He lights up again and flashes me that wonderfully charming smile.

I check the time when we finish eating. I have a shift tonight at the café, but not for another four hours. Lying down, I place my hand over my stomach. I could really use that nap right about now.

Ash places the pizza box and bag of fries on the kitchen

counter, lying back down next to me, our hands grazing together.

"You never answered my question from earlier," I say with a yawn before rolling onto my side so I can look at him.

He turns his head, and my body warms.

"I'm better now," he says with a soft grin. I beam, proud that I cheered up Ash Waylen. "Do you have a shift later?" I nod before releasing another yawn. "Maybe you should get some rest. I can head out."

I take hold of his hand to stop him from leaving. "Please stay."

He watches me for a moment before getting comfortable again. Lying on his side, he faces me. We stare into each other's eyes, and my chest flutters. I shift closer to him and lean my forehead against his chest. He rests his hand along my waist, touching my bare skin.

"Is this okay?" he asks. His mumble is hot against the top of my head.

This close to him, I hear his heart quicken and his breathing deepen.

I nod, relishing in this moment. When I close my eyes, I sway from fatigue. A few moments pass before I hear his breathing slow. I fall asleep feeling safe and on edge at the same time. Here I am, with Ash in my bed, and what do we do?

We take a nap.

Chapter Eighteen

Gwen

I wake up to my phone vibrating against the bed. I pick it up, sleepy eyed, and look at the text from Chrissy.

Tell me everything! Where are you!?

What the hell is she talking about?

Placing my phone behind me, I turn around and remember as my vision clears. We inched closer after we fell asleep, my nose near his. Ash's arm rests over my waist, a strange yet comfortable weight.

"Are you awake?" I whisper.

His eyes flutter open, dark and glossy.

"I am." His voice is still groggy from sleep, somehow even more attractive than his normal tone.

With a shaky breath, I place my leg over his hip. Ash pulls me closer, and I gasp when I register how hard his length is.

My entire body flares in heated goose bumps when he

brushes a few strands of hair away from my face. Making the first move, I move closer and press my forehead against his. My body is begging me to give in, but my mind is screaming that it's too soon.

Ash takes my face in his hands. When I move forward, our lips brush, and I shudder.

This is it; it's happening.

I forget about breathing; I don't need oxygen. I need Ash, plain and simple. He leans in even closer, and just as I close my eyes, an earth-shattering bang resonates from the front door.

"I know you're in there, Gwen! Let me in!"

I peer into Ash's eyes and grunt.

"She'll go away," I whisper before moving to close the agonizing gap between us.

Another series of banging rattles my eardrums.

"I think we both know Chrissy isn't just going to go away." Ash smirks.

His eyes travel from my lips to my eyes. I drown in his hooded gaze and groan as I roll over to stand. Feeling extremely light-headed, I walk toward the door but stop when Ash speaks up.

"Gwen."

I turn around, still feeling breathless.

"I'm sorry." He strolls closer and takes hold of my hand. "I-I don't think I'm ready." He stumbles over his words, his tone full of regret and pain. "I'm still a mess over you-know-who, and while I want to see where this goes, I can't. Not yet, at least."

My heart cracks with his words, and I nod solemnly. He's right. Clearly, he hasn't recovered from Alex. It would be foolish to start something new. It could get messy.

"Friends?" I ask while squeezing his hand.

He gives me a lopsided grin. "For now."

Chrissy knocks harder, making me jump out of my skin.

Chapter Eighteen

"You better get that before she breaks your door down."

As much as I don't want to, I drop his hand. I turn my back toward him and open the door.

"You son of a bitch, you can't leave a girl hanging like that!" Chrissy storms in and halts when Ash comes into her view. He's picking up his bag when she notices him. "Oh, shit."

"Nice to see you too," he says with an airy laugh.

Chrissy's mouth drops to the floor, and she looks at me with a mischievous smirk.

"You just got plowed, didn't you?"

"I did not just get plowed!" I say frantically, just as Ash chuckles and squeezes past us.

"You so did!"

"I did not!"

We go back and forth as Ash walks to my apartment door.

"See you guys later."

My eyes follow him as he descends the stairs and leaves the building, taking my heart with him. It must show on my face because Chrissy stops bickering and closes my door.

"Maybe you didn't just get plowed."

I lift my palms to cover my eyes. There's no reason for me to cry, so why are tears forming in my eyes?

"I just got 'for now' friend zoned."

She shakes her head in utter confusion. "What the hell does that mean?"

I move to my dresser and unbutton my shorts. "It means that he's not over Alex, and while he wants to kiss me, he won't." I pull on my jeans and get ready for work.

"I still don't get it," Chrissy whispers in deep thought.

I sigh while putting on my work shirt.

"At least he's not using you as a rebound," she offers, trying to comfort me.

She's right. He could have gone a lot further than kissing

just now, and I would have let him. Not caring or even realizing that all I could be to him is a rebound.

"I wouldn't lose hope." She grabs me by my shoulders and flashes her famous Chrissy smile. "You'll always have biochem."

I roll my eyes and finish getting ready for my shift.

Chapter Nineteen

Ash

I'm a fucking idiot. Did I just do that? Did I really friend zone Gwen Roman? God dammit, I'm a fool. I let fear blind me. Once again, fucking Alex manages to ruin my life.

Gwen was within my grasp. My body begged for her. I felt it when I woke up. Fuck, I felt it the moment I saw her today. Not sure how I fell asleep in her bed with her pressed against me. I was surrounded by her scent, the desire to have her right then and there overwhelming. What made it worse was that she wanted it too.

Thoughts crash through my mind. I know I'm not recovered; my trust is shattered. My friendship with Gwen is a positive thing, but do I want to drag her through my darkness? Is it selfish of me to hope that her compassion might fix my heart after another tore it to shreds? I want to give Gwen my all. I don't want her to experience the broken side of me. She deserves more than that.

I walk back to the campus parking lot, head in the clouds.

Well, more like my head is still back in Gwen's apartment. So I only notice them because my eyes are focused ahead. I don't believe it at first. I even rub my eyes and look again, but there they are, hand in hand.

Zack and someone who looks extremely familiar.

They walk past me, completely immersed in conversation. I didn't know Zack was seeing anyone. But that's not what's bothering me. That girl, where do I know her from?

"Zack," I call after him, but he's oblivious. "Zack!" I raise my voice, managing to break the trance the girl has over him.

Zack spins around and greets me with a wide grin.

"Ash! What's up, man?"

My eyes scan over the girl as she clings to his arm.

He looks around, and confusion sweeps over his face. "Do you live around here?"

I open my mouth just as Chrissy skips our way.

Shit.

Her eyes gleam when she sees the three of us. She notices Zack's defenseless back first. With a running start, she leaps and clings onto his back like a monkey, rubbing her fist in his hair to top it off.

"What's up, brother!" Chrissy cheers.

The girl drops Zack's hand and watches me. Zack fumbles with Chrissy, making sure she's safely back on the sidewalk. She waves at me like she didn't just see me in Gwen's apartment.

"Ash, good to see you again." She not so casually winks.

"Again?" Zack's eyebrow arches, and I swear his jaw clicks.

"Oh, yeah. He was just at Gwen's place." The moment the words leave her mouth, her eyes widen, and her cheeks grow pale. She mouths the word *shit* directly my way.

"Ash, why were you at Gwen's apartment?" A vein in his

Chapter Nineteen

forehead pulses, and I suddenly feel like I've come face to face with an overly protective father.

"We were studying."

Chrissy gives me a thumbs-up, and I'm starting to worry about this woman's mental capacity. Does she think only I can see her right now?

"What the fuck was that, Chrissy?"

Her eyes widen again, nearly popping out of her eye sockets. She turns on her heels and registers the other girl's presence.

"Who's this?" Her normally playful, carefree tone drops. She now takes control of the parental role.

"Don't change the subject, Chrissy. Ash, what were you doing back at Gwen's?"

My eyes scan the girl. Her long brunette hair reaches her waist. She has freckles along the bridge of her nose and hazel eyes.

"I had a rough morning, so we skipped biochem. She brought me back to her place for takeout, and then we fell asleep." I tell him the truth because something tells me Zack would figure it out one way or another. And I don't want to be on the receiving end of his anger.

I can't tell if he likes this answer any more than my first one. He still wears the same blank, stiff expression.

"Great, now answer my question. Zacky, who is this?" Chrissy asks while placing her hands on her hips.

"I'm Roselyn," she tells us with a broad smile.

I tilt my head when she drags her fingernails along Zack's arm, softening his demeanor.

"And what are you doing with my brother?" Chrissy asks, not caring about the sass that rolls off her tongue.

"We're going on a date," Zack answers with a soft smirk.

"Why do you look so familiar?" Chrissy asks like she's playing twenty questions.

"We went to the same high school," Roselyn says.

And that's when it hits me. Roselyn Wilson was a cheerleader back in school. I used to see her when I would attend Rome's football games. She would stroll the halls in her uniform, always with her head held high. I don't remember liking her then, which explains how I'm feeling now.

"We'll talk about this later. Chrissy, please get back to your dorm." Zack's posture relaxes when he talks to his sister.

"Yes, sir!" She stands at attention and gives him a firm salute.

Just before Roselyn turns around with Zack, her smile drops.

Chrissy and I watch the new couple walk away, hand in hand, down the rest of the block.

"Chrissy."

She turns to face me with worry wrinkled along her brow.

"I don't have a good feeling about that." Apprehension fills her tone, and I completely agree with her.

Chapter Twenty

Gwen

The entire ten blocks to work, my mind races and the skin that got to feel Ash tingles. Never in my life would I have imagined that I would ever catch his attention. I mean, hell, I never even worked up the nerve to talk to him in high school. Fifteen-year-old me would have a heart attack if she found out we were close to kissing him. And somehow, I turned him on. The way he felt pressed up against my thigh lit a fire in my soul. Burning white flames erupted in places I never felt before.

Everything between us happened naturally. I didn't feel rushed or pressured. I wanted him, my body begged for him, and just as everything lined up, he backed away. I get it. I really do. It doesn't make it hurt any less though. I hope Alex knows just how much she fucked with his head, and if she doesn't leave him alone, I fear I may never get a real chance.

I walk into the café, and the aroma of fresh coffee wafts through the air. Blake is standing behind the counter, serving drinks left and right. I hop over Pickles as he tries to launch himself at me.

"Not today, sucker!" I say before waving at Blake.

"There she is! Mind helping me out here?"

I tie an apron around my waist and start taking orders. Since classes have started, business has slowly picked up. For a Friday night, it's decently busy. Familiar faces fill the booths and tables, some studying as others simply hang out, playing with the cats. I look down at my feet as Pickles chews on my shoelaces.

"Go make some new friends." I bend down to pet him but regret it the moment he nibbles on my hand. "Okay, fine. Be that way."

Blake chuckles beside me as Ryan strolls through the back door. Ryan leans over the counter, grinning slyly.

"So, Gwen. How's Mr. Biochem?"

Blake gasps like he forgot all about him. I open my mouth to speak but am interrupted by the bell hanging above the door. I glance toward the entrance, and my smile turns into a deep-set frown. Zack strolls in, holding the hand of someone I hoped I would never see again.

Her hazel eyes fall on me, and a wave of harsh chills creeps up my spine. I glance at Zack's grin and tilt my head.

"Gwen!"

I get the same greeting I always do. I step from behind the counter and let him pull me into a bear hug.

I wrap my arms around his neck and whisper in his ear when he sets me down. "What are you doing?"

"You remember Roselyn, right? She was in the same year as us in school."

No shit, Sherlock.

Not only did we go to the same high school, we shared a lot of the same classes. And that girl was a bitch. She used her title

Chapter Twenty

as the head cheerleader to get whatever she wanted. She thought she was better than everyone else, and she acted accordingly. I remember dodging her every chance I could get. She was cruel, especially to the quiet kids. She used to call me names and tease me enough to rile my emotions. Roselyn Wilson was a glorified mean girl, and she doesn't even remember me.

"Are you okay?" he asks.

Roselyn joins Zack's side, and I ball my hands into tight fists.

"Hi there," she greets with a faux innocent tone.

Years can change a person. I would be a fool to deny that. But I learned to trust my gut, and right now, it's screaming *"She's not a good person."*

"Hi," I bite out.

Zack's eyebrows crease together in response to my tension. "Are you okay, Gwen?" he asks cautiously.

I nod and fake a smile. "Just a rough day."

"Okay. Well, I'm here if you want to talk," Zack says before telling me their drink order. When I finish making them, he takes them over to Roselyn and sits beside her.

Keeping my eyes on them, I observe as they slide into a booth near the back. Something isn't right here . . . I can feel it.

Turning around, I meet Ryan and Blake's bewildered stares. I subtly shake my head, and they both nod at the same time, getting the hint to ask questions later. They pretend to go back to work, knowing I'll end up telling them everything.

I go back and forth between watching the door and monitoring Zack. On the one hand, I'm willing Ash to stroll through and take back everything he said to me earlier. On the other hand, if he walks in here, he'll see me watching Zack and Roselyn like a hawk.

I feel her eyes on me when I'm not looking. It's not

constant, but when I do feel it, it's not a kind stare. Which only solidifies my instincts.

"You're holding out on us, girly." Blake shakes me from my thoughts.

"You got her when she was thinking, Blake!" Ryan slaps Blake's arm.

I face them both and cross my arms over my chest. "There's nothing to tell."

They glance at one another like they know more than they're letting on.

"That's not what Chrissy tells me." Blake snickers.

My hand flies to my forehead. I'm not upset with her; I never told her it was a secret. If I did, I would trust her to keep it.

"I got 'for now' friend zoned," I whisper, and they both arch their eyebrows.

"For now?" Blake fixes his glasses as Ryan itches his head.

"He's still hurt by his ex."

"Ah, that makes sense," Blake offers.

"Give him time. He'll come around." Ryan places his hand on my shoulder and squeezes it.

"Oh, boy. Someone better go grab the stick." Blake sighs while covering his eyes with his hand.

Scrunching my forehead, I glance over my shoulder. Roselyn is pressed against Zack, and they're all hands and lips.

You've got to be shitting me . . .

Chapter Twenty-One

Gwen

Classes have been in session for a week, and I'm already behind on homework and reading. It's Saturday, and I'm hiding in my usual corner in the library, trying to catch up on my classwork. I didn't tell Chrissy about last night. I need to talk to Zack on my own, and it needs to happen today.

After a few hours, I step outside. The sun is bearing down, and I wipe sweat from my brow, releasing a pent-up sigh. I guess it's best to get this over with. I pull out my phone and text Zack.

> Free to talk?

> I'm meeting up with Roselyn in a few minutes. Can it wait?

> It's important.

> Meet me outside the pavilion.

I don't waste a second. I'm not letting him leave without talking to me first. I need to make sure he knows what he's getting himself into. Even he needs protection every once in a while.

My legs cramp and burn, but I make it to the pavilion in record time. I don't get my usual greeting when I see him. He knows I mean business.

"Everything okay?" His blue eyes twinkle with concern. The sunlight makes his freckles pop along the bridge of his nose, reminding me of his boyish charm.

"I don't want you to think I'm overstepping, but I need to know. What's going on between you and Roselyn?"

He doesn't get mad. I don't think he could ever get mad at me.

"I could ask you the same thing, but regarding Ash."

I run my hands through my hair and sigh. "Zack . . ." I groan in frustration. "This is serious. I'm trying to protect you."

His eyebrows arch. "From Roselyn?"

"Do you not remember how she was in high school?"

He lets out a puff of air and runs his fingers through his slicked-back ebony hair. "People can change, Gwen."

"I know that, but something doesn't feel right. I mean, don't you remember all the times she used to tease me? How upset you would get?"

"I remember, but again, people can change," he rebuts. "I used to make fun of people all the time. Look at me now."

He has a point, but still . . .

"I don't have a good feeling."

He releases a tense sigh in response. "Roselyn and I have been talking for a few weeks now. She's nice. I think you would like her if you gave her a chance."

I cut Zack's bullshit off. I can't listen to this anymore. "You know how ridiculous that sounds, right?" I don't fight my

Chapter Twenty-One

clipped tone. "How many times did you catch me crying because of her?"

I witness the moment when realization dawns on him, but he doesn't get the chance to respond. Roselyn whirls in and flings her body against Zack, wrapping her arms around his neck and her legs around his waist. She kisses his cheek, and he gets sucked back in, sending a pit the size of Texas all the way to my stomach.

"Ready to go?" she asks cheerfully.

He swings her around and grabs her waist, not noticing the pain and worry written all over my face.

"Hey, Zack!" one of his friends calls, and he jogs over, telling us he'll be right back, leaving Roselyn and me alone.

Tension surrounds us, suffocating and thick.

"I don't buy this new act of yours, and I don't know what you're up to, Roselyn, but if you hurt him"—I point to Zack; he shimmers under the sun's caress, too innocent for this world—"you'll regret it."

"Are you threatening me?" She clicks her tongue and furrows her brow.

I didn't mean to make it sound like a threat. But if she hurts Zack, she'll have more than me to answer to.

"He's not a toy you can play with. He's not someone you can fuck and dump."

She steps closer to me. Out of the corner of my eye, I see Zack walking back over to us.

"Is that what I'm doing?"

I smile coolly, not letting her get under my skin. "Roselyn Wilson, that's all you used to do."

A wicked grin spreads across my lips, and the overwhelming urge to protect Zack etches into my core.

"Ready to go?" Zack reaches for Roselyn's hand, and when

she meets it, she smirks like the devil herself. "See you later?" He notices my stance and squints his eyes in worry.

"Have fun." I force a smile and turn on my heels, walking away before I let Roselyn get the better of me.

I'm so unbelievably glad it's Saturday. I really need to sleep and not wake up to an alarm tomorrow morning. On my walk back home, I pull out my phone and text Chrissy. She needs to know what's going on between Zack and Roselyn. She'll put her sleuthing skills to work, and we'll have all the answers we need in no time.

"Hey, you."

Chapter Twenty-Two

Ash

I'm not good at keeping promises to myself. Waking up this morning, I needed to see Gwen again. Even after I friend zoned her, which was one of the dumbest things I've ever done. The thought of not seeing her until Monday makes my heart ache in ways I've never experienced. Luckily, it's Saturday, and I'm going to take full advantage of it.

I jump out of bed with my gut twisting and turning with nerves. I'm never nervous. I used to be able to keep my cool and go with the flow. Until I locked eyes with Gwen. She seems to awaken more than one unfamiliar emotion within me. I let it motivate me because the fact that Gwen can make me anxious only makes me want her more. I'm tired of letting other people control my narrative. It started with my parents, then moved to Alex. I need to take the reins. Even if nothing catches from the sparks between Gwen and me, I'll still be able to say I tried, that no one stopped me from giving it my all.

I don't know what'll happen. For all I know, she'll break my heart and stomp it to smithereens. The Gwen I know, though, would never do that. I've seen her kind-natured heart and how she cares about everyone who crosses her path. She's shown me patience and compassion time and time again. If anyone is worth taking a risk on, it's Gwen.

I take a quick shower, lathering every inch of my body in soap. I get the feeling she likes the way I smell. I caught her a few times just smelling me. Any normal person might think it's weird. I find it strangely cute. If I could, I would smell her all day too.

I even make sure to think my outfit through. Who the hell am I? When did I start caring about what I wore? Toweling steam away from the mirror, I ruffle my hair in the process. After slathering on deodorant, I pull on a plain white tee and step into my jeans.

I take a deep breath and let it out. You would think this was my first date. *Is this a date?* Or is it just two "friends" hanging out? I don't care. I get to see Gwen, and that's enough for me.

Once ready, I jog down the stairs and slip on my sneakers by the front door. I'm not surprised to see a note on the table when I stroll into the kitchen. I don't even have to read it to know what it says. It would go something like this:

Hey Bro,

I won't be home tonight. Hopefully, I'll see you tomorrow. Just do me one favor, no girls.

Max is a good guy, an asshole lawyer, but a decent human being. He took me in without a second thought.

The day after he graduated from high school, he moved out of Mom and Dad's. I could tell he didn't want to leave me

Chapter Twenty-Two

behind; he knew the kind of environment he was leaving me in. He couldn't take me though. I just started middle school, and he was starting college.

We're six years apart, and while he got all the smarts, I'm more chill and take things as they come. He's the kind of person who needs to have a plan for every little thing.

I hop up to sit on the kitchen counter, taking a bite out of an apple. Mindlessly, I scroll through my phone, watching silly clips and stupid recorded moments that only I probably find funny. I take another chunk of the crisp fall fruit just as she messages me.

> Hey :) How are you today?

And my day just became a thousand times better.

She meant what she said the other day, and she kept her promise. I'm not used to people checking in on me. I'm expected to keep my composure no matter the situation. Gwen sees the pain I'm holding, and she coaxes it out of me, slowly draining all the negative energy from my core. Apparently, I held onto more gloomy despair than I originally thought. Every time she asks me if I'm okay, I feel the emotions obstruct my throat, and I want to tell her everything—my family trauma, how I feel like I can't trust anyone because every time I do, something shatters it.

My mom and dad, Alex, and Brandon. They all took my trust and smothered it under a pillow, leaving me in pieces in the aftermath. Because in the end? They didn't care. They were fine leaving the mess for the next person. Not caring about the real-life human they left in shambles.

> I'm good, how are you?

> I'll be okay. Leaving the library now. I need a nap lol.

I grin at my phone screen, knowing she won't get to take that nap. Hopping down from the counter, I grab my car keys.

Now's my chance.

I'm hoping to catch her off guard. I want to surprise her. She deserves a bit of happiness, especially after what she did for me yesterday.

Twenty minutes later, I find a spot right in front of her apartment building and wait impatiently.

> Hey, pretty lady, whatcha up to?

Checking my surroundings, I don't see her, which either means she's already inside or still not home yet. Thankfully, she responds right away.

> Walking home now. I ran into Zack. Have I mentioned he's an asshole?

> You definitely have lol.

He seems to get under her skin. I'm going to have to tell her what happened yesterday. If Chrissy didn't get to her first, that is.

I leave my car and stand beside the sidewalk where she won't miss me. When I see her, everything slows. Her light brown hair blows in the wind, drifting that perfume mixture right to my nose. Her eyes are down, looking at the sidewalk. Is she afraid of tripping, or is her mind off somewhere else right now?

"Hey, you."

Chapter Twenty-Two

The look on her face is priceless. Her expression glows and she grins ear to ear. I match it effortlessly. This girl is something else, and I get the feeling I made the right move in showing up out of the blue.

Chapter Twenty-Three

Gwen

I stop right before the staircase to my apartment complex. Ash is standing beside the sidewalk with his hands shoved in his jeans pockets. His hair is still damp from a shower, and his white shirt clings to his chiseled chest. My cheeks burn, and my core erupts in a volcano of fluttering butterflies.

"Hey." My breath catches in my chest, almost unable to form the one-syllable word.

"Are you free? I was hoping we could hang out."

Forget the nap. I'll never sleep again if it means I get to hang out with Ash.

"What did you have in mind?"

A wicked grin spreads across his full lips. "That's a surprise." He extends his hand toward me.

My feet free themselves from the sidewalk, eager to be near him again. I let him take my hand and lead the way.

"Why do I feel like I'm the one being kidnapped this time?"

We both chuckle as he opens the car door for me.

Chapter Twenty-Three

"Don't worry. I'll feed you."

I snort while sliding into the passenger seat. My phone rings as Ash settles in the driver's seat. He plucks the phone out of my hand before I can answer it.

"Sorry, Chrissy. Gwen's not available right now. Talk to you soon."

Chrissy protests, which only makes him smile wider.

"Okay, love you. Bye!" He tosses the phone in the back seat before doing the same with his phone.

"You know she's going to kick your ass next time she sees you, right?"

Shrugging, he offers me a heart-melting smirk. "It'll be worth it." He reaches for my hand and squeezes it. "Just you and me, deal?"

He turns the key, starting the engine.

I buckle my seat belt and sit back, not letting my eyes wander away from his. "Deal."

I can't wipe this stupid grin off my face. I'm trying to. It just won't go away, no matter what I do or think. It might have to do with the fact that I'm sitting in Ash Waylen's car. Or maybe it's because he whisked me away and doesn't want anything to distract us from one another.

We reach a part of town I've never been to before. When we pull alongside an arcade, my face lights up from the neon lights.

"Are we going where I think we're going?" I ask, hope filling my tone.

Ash winks at me while unbuckling his seat belt. "Video games and food. Let's go have some fun." Ash's dimples pop onto his cheeks as he smiles.

I launch out of the car, jumping up and down like a kid at a water park. Ash reaches for my hand, and I grab his gladly, not caring about the "for now" friend zone aspect.

Forever Crushed

When Ash opens the door, classic video game noises greet us. The arcade is retro and super nostalgic. Old-school games line the walls, along with a bar farther back. The entire room is dimly lit with plastic glow-in-the-dark stars on the ceiling, and the rug is straight out of the nineties, complete with geometric patterns and neon colors. The aroma of popcorn and fried food invades my nostrils, and my eyes dance along the ceiling as Ash takes me to the bar.

He chuckles when he stops me from crashing into a barstool. We place our drink orders—I opt for a fruity cocktail while he gets a soda.

"Where do you wanna start?" he asks while chewing on his straw.

My eyes light up at all the possibilities.

"Two things you should know about me. One, I love fries, but you already know that. Two, I'm a sucker for a good zombie shooter," I exclaim.

Ash twirls the plastic straw around his tongue. Even though it's dark, I can see his broad smile.

"My kind of gal." He offers me his arm, so I intertwine mine around his.

I don't think he was expecting me to rock his world and kick his ass. Not only did I beat him in every game, but I did it with a drink in my hand. I don't think I've ever laughed as much as I have today. I laugh with Chrissy, but I always have fun around her. Ash makes me double over from giggling so hard. We tease one another, and he flirts relentlessly, making me flush every time. I trip over my feet as we finish our last game and stumble right into Ash.

"All right, time to get you some food."

I pump my arms up and down, giggling as I lean against his arm, feeling him up in the process. For someone who doesn't play sports, he's pretty built. I wonder if he works out in his free

Chapter Twenty-Three

time or if he has a strict meal plan. There's a reason I'm curvy and busty. That reason has one name—french fries.

I bob along to the music, my little introvert bubble completely popped. My eyes fall on Ash's back, trailing down to admire the way his ass looks in those jeans and climbing back up to devour his arms, his neck.

Dammit!

I place my drink down and shake my head. We're friends, just friends. I need to stop eating him alive with my eyes. He just makes it so fucking hard with the constant teasing and smooth compliments. Maybe I should put a bag over his head when we hang out . . .

Nah, that wouldn't do shit.

"Are you okay?"

I drop my hands and flash him a smile when he returns with food. "Don't steal my line," I say before popping a fry in my mouth.

"Are you having fun?" he asks with a lopsided grin.

I nod and go back to swaying to "Say My Name" by Destiny's Child, which blares above us.

"So much fun." My body ignites when he offers me a lopsided smirk. Maybe I should try that bag idea . . . I need to change the subject. I'm not sure how long I can last under his gaze. "Do you come here a lot?"

"No, I found this place just for you."

Oh my god, change the subject again.

"What's your favorite holiday?" My quick topic switch confuses him. He looks up again with his eyebrow arched. "Mine's Halloween. I've always wanted to go to a haunted house, but Chrissy and Zack aren't into it as much as I am." I nod my head and munch on more fries. "What about you? And don't be a basic bitch and say Christmas."

"What if it is Christmas?" he asks me as I point a fry at him.

Forever Crushed

"Then you're a basic bitch." I smirk teasingly. "Why do you like Christmas?" I ask him as he dips a fry in ketchup.

"Most of my favorite memories from my childhood are from Christmas. I guess I like the magic and beauty of it. How everyone is kinder to one another."

My insides melt, and now I feel guilty for calling him a basic bitch.

"Why do you like Halloween?"

"How am I supposed to top the answer you just gave me?"

His dark caramel eyes and dashing grin unleash a whirlwind of tingles and emotions in my veins.

"Are you afraid to answer because you might be the basic bitch?" he teases.

"One hundred percent." I purse my lips.

We finish our food and walk back to the car. After a couple of hours, I've sobered up and regained my wits. As I sit, I brush my hair away from my neck. Ash gets settled, and I feel his eyes on me again, the trail he's blazing with his starlit eyes. My chest heaves up and down before I dare to meet his longing gaze.

"Do you want your phone back?" he asks in a hushed tone.

"Just you and me. That was the deal, right?"

"Right." His smile almost glows brighter than the evening sky.

I gulp as his attention floats down to my lips. Without looking away, he fires up the engine. When he drags his eyes off me, I shiver.

The drive back home is silent. He had a random radio station playing, but it was low. I worry he can hear my heartbeat and staggered breathing. I run my hands over my legs nervously. *Was this a date? Or two friends just hanging out?* If this was a date, does that mean he might try to kiss me? Oh crap, just the thought makes my throat go dry.

He pulls off to the side, and I notice we're outside my apart-

Chapter Twenty-Three

ment. Night has fallen, but his features are dimly lit by the lights on the car's dashboard.

He reaches for my balled-up hand and interlocks our fingers together. "Gwen?"

I'm getting squirmy again. "Hmm?" I can't even talk; he must find me embarrassing.

Ash shifts in his seat to face me, so I unbuckle the seat belt to do the same.

"Can I tell you something?"

"You can tell me anything," I mumble.

He releases a deep sigh. "I told you Alex cheated on me, but you should know how."

"Are you sure?" I ask, and he nods softly.

Ash tells me how he walked in on Alex and Brandon during a party. I maintain a straight face, but deep down, I'm screaming. I wouldn't wish that image on my worst enemy. The fact that Ash not only went through it but that he saw it first-hand devastates me.

With another sigh, he meets my gaze, his lips twitching into a small, awkward smile. I squeeze his hand, trying to offer reassurance.

"You didn't deserve that, Ash. You know that, right?" I whisper. He drops his gaze and nods. "You're more than your past. While your experiences help define you, they don't make up who you are. You get a say in that matter, and if you ask me, you're a pretty good guy."

I reach over the center console and rest my palm against his cheek. The moment I touch him, my body sizzles, like when smoldering lava meets cooling water.

"I have one more question for you. What do you think this was tonight?"

His tone rams right into my heart. I fall still when he picks his head up and captures my gaze with his beautiful irises. He plucks the question right out of my brain.

Do I play it safe? Or do I tell him what I'm hoping it was?

He unbuckles his seat belt and leans toward me.

"I don't know." My voice fails me, my answer coming out in a whisper. He captures it, along with every other sensation in my body.

Ash caresses my cheek with his right hand, pulling me in.

"What are you doing?" I mumble.

He leans in and brushes his nose across mine, his gaze falling to my lips. "I want you to know just how much I want to do this." His voice is deep, drowning in desire. "I just want to make sure you get *all* of me, not a shattered, distraught version."

"I'm right here. I'm not going anywhere, I promise." I brush his hair away from his forehead and run my thumb over his cheekbone.

"I wish we were friends back in high school. Maybe if we were, I wouldn't be so fucked up."

I scoff. "You're not fucked up; you got fucked *over*. Besides, I was too cool for you back then." I get him to laugh.

When he opens his eyes, they glisten against the dim lights from the dashboard. "Wait for me?"

My heart flutters in response, and a soft smile spreads across my lips. I waited for Ash for seven years. He doesn't know that of course.

"Pinkie promise." I wrap my pinkie around his.

I can feel just how much he wants to close the gap. But he won't, not until he knows he can give me one hundred percent.

"See you later?" His whisper coats my lips.

I nod against his forehead, and it takes all my strength to tear myself away from him. As soon as I break contact, I crave him, needing to touch him again.

Chapter Twenty-Three

"You know where to find me," I whisper as I let go of his hand and step out of the car.

I start up the stairs, stopping when I hear him again.

"Gwen?"

I turn back around, and he tosses me my phone. Luckily, I catch it.

"Maybe text Chrissy. I really don't need her kicking my ass the next time she sees me." I give him a thumbs-up. "Good night, beautiful."

A whimper of desire escapes my lips, and I pray he doesn't hear it.

"Good night, Mr. Biochem."

His brow wrinkles in confusion.

I turn around, needing to create some distance because if I don't, I fear we may both succumb to our needs, whether we're ready or not.

Chapter Twenty-Four

Gwen

Three weeks pass, and Chrissy and I are still keeping our eyes on Zack and Roselyn. Zack hasn't noticed our watchful gaze; he's too deep under Roselyn's spell. We just want to protect Zack. Chrissy and I will handle Roselyn if she breaks his heart. That's a definite.

Ash gave me the okay to tell Chrissy everything. He didn't want me to feel like I was keeping a secret from her, and I'm grateful he trusts me. We'll be sure to keep his story to ourselves. In the end, it's his journey, and it's his to share.

Ash and I are taking things slow. We talk and flirt with one another, more so to poke fun at each other. I feel his eyes on me in class, lingering over my body. Taking in every inch and curve, almost as if he's trying to memorize me. The days creep by. Every second without his touch is agonizing. I replay the day in the lab, feeling the strength and longing desire from his hand. I repeat the moment I woke up and felt him pulsate against me, how his fingers feathered over my waist. He's all I

Chapter Twenty-Four

see when I close my eyes, all I think about when my eyes are open, and it's slowly killing me.

The official start of fall is this weekend, and the air is already cooling down. I can't wait to cuddle up in a sweater and walk around my apartment wrapped in a blanket. The first month of the fall semester is done, which only means one thing: exams...

"Gwen!" Chrissy crashes into me like her brother normally does.

"Where were you? I was about to head to class without you," I ask as she reapplies her lip gloss while linking her arm through mine.

"I was talking to Professor Stilts. I wanted to confirm what was going to be on the test next Monday."

"You could have asked me."

Her cackle bounces down the walls along the hallway. "Because I trust that you're paying attention in biochem."

I frown playfully and wipe away an invisible tear. "You don't trust me."

She pulls me through the doorway and grins. "Hell no, and it's all his fault." She points right at Ash, pulling his attention our way.

"What's my fault?" He fixes his glasses before not so subtly checking me out, focusing on my chest.

"Nothing," I respond with a shy smile.

"It's your fault she's not paying attention in class."

My eyes bug out as I sit down. I lean over, gently shoving Chrissy's shoulder.

"I pay attention." I lower my voice to a harsh whisper.

"Yeah, right, you pay attention to the sexy librarian over there."

My face burns, and I know Ash heard her because he snorts.

"Don't think I won't tell Zack about you-know-who."

She blows a bubble and pops it at my words. "Don't you even!"

We go back and forth, not realizing Professor Stilts has walked in.

"Watch me." I stick my tongue out, knowing full well she still has a thing for Miles Summers.

She plays the perfect student and snaps right into observation mode as Professor Stilts clears his throat. I glance toward Ash and smile when I catch him smirking at me. He pulls out his phone, gesturing that he's about to text me.

Looking good today . . .

Were you looking? I didn't notice ;)

I'm always checking you out ;)

You don't have to butter me up.

Is that what I'm doing?

Shut up, Waylen.

xD

I glimpse over at Ash, shifting in my seat, when I catch him smiling down at his phone.

Ready for the test this Monday?

Hell no, and it's all your fault.

How is it my fault? :O

Chapter Twenty-Four

I know exactly why he thinks I'm to blame, and I have no shame about it. It's the same reason I blame him for my lack of preparedness.

> Want to come to my place on Saturday and study? We can use the pool before my brother closes it for the season.

My heart stutters, and I feel myself go pale. Go to Ash's house? Me? I bite my lower lip and ponder over the offer. I shoot Chrissy a text.

> Ash just asked me to hang out at his place on Saturday to study.

> You're so going to get plowed! Finally!

I cover my eyes with my hand. I should have known better.

> You better go! I think getting some good dick will loosen you up.

> Are you texting Chrissy?

Oh, crap. I took too long.

> No . . .

> Liar. Down for this Saturday?

> Definitely, sounds like fun.

My body houses a thousand butterflies whose wings are made of feathers. Maybe nothing will happen. I mean, his brother should be there. And it's only been a few weeks since our "date." There's no way he's ready for anything more serious.

Right?

"You're doing what!?" Zack shouts a little too loudly when Chrissy and I meet him outside.

"You told him!?" I aim my shock at Chrissy.

"I was excited for you!" she shouts back.

We all go back and forth on the sidewalk like a disgruntled family.

"Excited!? This isn't exciting, Chrissy!" Zack shouts.

Chrissy clings to my arm with a pout. "Yes, it is! She's growing up right before our eyes." She wipes fake tears from her eyes as I sigh.

"You know I'm not a virgin, right?" I say, unamused.

"Yes, stop reminding me!" Zack covers his ears.

"Why do you care? I'm pretty sure you're boinking Roselyn," I chime in with disgust, and Chrissy nods as I fire back at Zack.

"Boinking? What are we, ten?" Zack asks me, sounding uncomfortable.

"Boinking is a legit term." Chrissy defends me like she always does.

"Would you prefer I say I'm pretty sure you're fucking Roselyn?"

He covers his ears again and leans backward.

"I can't believe we're talking about this right now." He walks away but comes right back. "You're not going."

I grin wickedly. He should know by now that he can't tell me what to do.

"I'm going this Saturday, and I'm going to enjoy *every* minute of it." I step toward him and stare right into his sapphire-blue eyes.

"Come on, Gwen! You're supposed to be the easy one. The one I don't have to worry about!"

I roll my eyes, letting out a tiny, frustrated laugh.

"Fuck, Gwen. I'm trying to protect you. You don't know how fucked up Ash is."

His words take me aback. "What do you mean?"

He stumbles over his tongue just as Roselyn steps out of the pavilion. "He's broken, Gwen. Alex ruined his mentality. Who knows what else could be wrong with him?"

"Oh, shit." Chrissy watches us go back and forth.

"Nothing is *wrong* with him! You're supposed to be his *friend*, and friends don't say that about one another. What has gotten into you?" I hammer at him.

"What's going on?" Roselyn latches onto Zack's arm, not gaining his full attention.

"Oh, I see. That makes complete sense," I sneer.

"You're not going Saturday," he states with full authority.

I smirk at him, knowing full well what I intend to do. Roselyn watches our interaction just as Chrissy does.

"Zack? We're going to be late for algebra." She pulls on his arm, but his eyes don't leave mine.

"Do you hear me, Gwen?" Zack asks.

I cross my arms over my chest before looking right at Roselyn, then back at him.

"Text me when you're done being a prick." I turn around and walk off campus.

Chrissy catches up and links her arm through mine.

"I think we need more recon missions," Chrissy whispers, and I nod my head solemnly.

It's pretty clear that Roselyn intends to drag Zack around like a motherless puppy. The last thing Chrissy and I want is for Zack's heart to break.

"I know. We'll figure something out," I murmur.

Zack's words flood my mind. What did he mean by what he said? Ash isn't broken. He was fucked over time and time again. It makes sense that he's different than he was all those years ago.

Hell, we all are.

Chapter Twenty-Five

Ash

"Ash!" Max shouts from the other room.

I open my bedroom door to yell down at him. "What's up!?"

No response. I grab the keys from my desk and head downstairs. Gwen is coming over today, and I have to leave within the next ten minutes to pick her up.

My feelings for her intensify each second. Every text message, every little glance and blush on her cheeks, all the teasing and blatant sexual tension. My heart called for her the first moment I saw her. I was stupid to try to ignore it.

Now, I'm ready to give her my all.

Three weeks isn't a lot of time. I get that. I've taken the time to self-reflect. I looked up videos on handling trust issues and trauma. I'm learning to recognize the signs and even talked myself out of a few anxiety attacks. I know I'm not one hundred percent, not sure I ever will be again. But with Gwen's support and reassurance, I'm feeling better than I thought I would. The thought of one more day without her being mine feels like a punch in the lower intestine.

Max is in the kitchen, sipping out of a coffee mug, glaring down at some sort of legal document. All my life, I was told Max and I look alike, and it's true. We share the same eye color, the same honey-brown hair. Mine just happens to be less tame than his. He needs to present a professional front, but I know just how chaotic he is deep down.

"You called?" I grip the edges of the kitchen island, keys in hand.

"Where are you going?" He doesn't look up; he keeps examining that sheet of paper like it's the most interesting thing in the world.

"Picking up a friend, is that okay?" Now I've got his attention.

"Is this a *girlfriend*?" His amber eyes pierce mine.

I didn't plan on asking him about having Gwen over today. Didn't really think he would find out, if I'm honest.

"She's a girl, and she's a friend. So, yes?"

He holds my gaze, arching his right eyebrow. It takes a few moments of silence before his eyes drop back down to the paper.

"Fine, just don't have sex in the pool or anywhere we eat."

My cheeks burn hot. I didn't plan on having sex with Gwen today. Of course, I would be lying if I said I didn't hope *something* might happen. We haven't even kissed. Let's not get too far ahead of ourselves . . .

"Don't worry. We're just going to study for a test on Monday."

A grin spreads across his lips. "Whatever you say."

I turn to make my leave but stop when he speaks up again.

"Are you sure you're ready for this? I saw how Alex left you. I saw the wreck you were."

Chapter Twenty-Five

Facing him again, images of Gwen crash through my mind. I trust her, truly. I'm ready *because* of her. If it were anyone else, I would take his question more seriously.

"She's helped me through a lot these past few weeks. I think you'll like her."

He nods and takes another long sip from his mug.

"As long as you're ready, that's all that matters." He drops his gaze again just as I turn around. "Have fun," he says as I close the front door.

The sooner I get her, the longer we can hang out. If it were completely up to me, she would be here already.

Chapter Twenty-Six

Gwen

I can't do this. I wasn't made for shit like this. My stomach is having a field day, and all the ginger ale in the world isn't helping. I haven't been able to focus since yesterday. I don't remember working my shift at the café last night. My mind is consumed with all the possibilities that could play out today. I'm probably overthinking it. I mean, Ash and I are friends. Friends who hang out and casually flirt.

Totally normal...

I collapse onto my bed and scream into my pillow. I can't even lie to myself. Nothing about this is normal. My feelings for Ash are escalating even though I know he's not ready. Today will be us hanging out as friends. Nothing more, nothing less.

Packing my bag, I make sure to remember the biochem textbook. I need to study today, no matter what happens. I put my swimsuit on under my jean shorts and a plain sky-blue tee. I can't believe this is happening. I'm going to Ash Waylen's house. I'm going to hang out with him, study and swim in his

Chapter Twenty-Six

pool. Girls would kill to be in the position I'm in. And here I am, having a damn panic attack.

A series of tapping sounds from my front door, making me freeze. Ash offered to pick me up since I don't have a car. I know how to drive, but since I'm so close to the university and work, I opted out of having my parents give me their old Toyota Camry. They're already paying half my rent. I don't want any more of their handouts. I pace, giving myself a pep talk.

"I've got this. I'm a strong, independent woman who's just going to hang out with her drop-dead gorgeous crush. Totally normal." I let out a breath of air and open the door.

"Were you just talking to yourself?" Ash asks with a hint of laughter.

To say I'm admiring him is putting it lightly. I'm *devouring* him. Ash leans against the doorframe, his head tilted to the side as he observes my flushed cheeks. His forearms are muscular, and his hair is messy and wet from showering. The doorknob clicks under my clenched fist. I nearly slam it shut from embarrassment.

"What? No."

His smirk turns my insides to molten lava, my knees unsteady.

"You're such a terrible liar." His smile widens, and my heart pounds against my ribcage. "Are you ready?" He raises his eyebrows, and I nod.

I grab my bag and lock the door behind me.

As we walk to his car, he turns around, walking backward. "Are you nervous, Ms. Biochem?" He winks at me, and with that, I'm all red and flustered.

"No." I trail out that simple word before continuing. "I'm so cool right now."

He opens the passenger door for me, and before I slip in, he touches my arm.

"Keep blushing like that, and we'll never make it to my house before the storm hits."

My forearm catches tingles under his grasp.

"Is it going to rain today?" I ask while glancing up toward the sky, noting a few scattered clouds.

I forgot to check the weather app this morning. My nerves got the best of me.

He leans against my forehead, his breath fresh and minty. "In more ways than one."

He drops my gaze and walks to the other side of the car.

What the hell is that supposed to mean?

Ash lives farther from campus than I originally expected. Throughout the car ride, my leg shakes restlessly. How does Ash make driving look so cool?

His eyes are on the road ahead, so I take the opportunity to eye fuck him. The weather's decently warm, but that didn't stop him from wearing a pair of black joggers that somehow embellish every muscle he has. He paired the joggers with a loose, sleeveless white tank that exposes his waistline through the armholes, allowing me to steal glimpses of his sculpted pecs and abs.

I grab the hair clip from my bag and twist my hair up to give myself something to do. We stop at a red light just as a song I recognize plays on the radio, "Style" by Taylor Swift.

"Is your stomach okay?" Ash catches me off guard. Why would he think it's not okay? "I saw all the ginger ale on the kitchen counter."

"Oh, yeah. I'm fine. Ginger ale helps my nerves." I feel myself getting shy and climbing back into my shell.

I ball my shirt in my fist and stare at my feet as my leg continues to jostle.

"Don't be nervous. It's just me."

He covers my thigh with his hand and squeezes it. His

touch somehow comforts me. I've been on edge since yesterday, craving some part of him. What I didn't know was that once I had his attention, all my uneasiness would fade away.

"You trust me, right?" He makes me smile just as the light changes to green.

"Right." I take it upon myself to increase the volume, dancing in my seat just as the chorus blares through the speakers.

Ash chuckles but doesn't let his eyes drift from the road. I feel myself loosen up, throwing my shell right out the window.

Twenty minutes go by before we pull into a lavish gated community. I have to hold my jaw because I'm afraid it might drop. Ash waves to the security guard as he opens the gates. I gawk at the opulent houses and neatly trimmed front yards. We round a bend and pull into a driveway. His brother's house is a fucking mansion, modern as hell, too. The house is two stories built out of brick that resembles volcanic ash but not as dark. The path leading to the front door is surrounded by trimmed summer green grass and neatly planted assorted flowers.

"You live here?" I ask in awe.

He turns the car off and twirls his keys around his index finger. "With my brother, the asshole lawyer, remember?"

I nod my head, still in utter disbelief.

"He's not home right now, so it's just you and me."

He beams that damn Ash smile, riling up my nerves.

Just him and me, great . . .

Chapter Twenty-Seven

Gwen

We head through the gate straight into the backyard, and I follow Ash to a set of lounge chairs. The pool takes up about half of the grounds, the clear water glimmering in the sunlight. The cement that surrounds it is lined with crystallized rocks.

I drop my bag alongside a lounge chair and sit just as my phone goes off.

> Are you still alive? Say pineapple if you need help!

> I'm fine, lol. I'll let you know if anything changes.

> Don't worry, I'll be sure Zack knows exactly where you are today ;)

I slide my phone into one of my bag's pockets and free my biochem textbook. Ash throws a towel at me, and of course, I don't catch it. It unravels across my face. When I peel it away, he strips his shirt off.

Oh, fuck.

He's everything I imagined and more. His back is facing me when he throws his shirt to the side. I sink farther into the chair, clutching the towel so tightly that the threads pull, the snapping sound causes me to loosen my grip. His thumbs tug on the waistband of his sweatpants. Cascading white flames burn down my body, landing right between my legs. He steps out of his sweatpants, revealing his blue swim trunks underneath, and showing off just what I expected. His legs are toned and blanketed with dark hair.

He turns to look at me, his eyes glistening in the blazing sun. "Coming?" His tone is undeniably sexy.

I avert my gaze, pretending to admire the garden along the fence.

"Aren't we going to study first?" I sit up while removing the towel from my face.

"We have all day to study. Let's have some fun first." His lips curl into a deviously handsome grin.

"Promise?" We really should study; I can't afford to fail the first test in this class.

Ash strolls over to kneel before me. "Pinkie promise," he says while offering me his pinkie.

I wrap my tiny finger around his, letting him pull me up against his chest.

He takes my book and sets it down on the chair. "Strip, sneaky girl."

Admiring me with hungry eyes, he backs away from me. I unbutton my jean shorts, gliding them down my legs, not breaking eye contact. I step out of my shorts, stopping right before I take my shirt off.

"Ash, wait!"

He steps backward off the edge, splashing right into the pool. When he comes up for air, I double over in pain from laughing so hard.

"Are you okay?" I choke out, unable to suck in any air between my cackling.

"Yeah, I did that on purpose," he says after he spits water out of his mouth.

"So smooth. Ten out of ten." I take my shirt off before he can say anything else.

I didn't wear something I knew I would be uncomfortable in. Chrissy offered me one of her strapless bikinis, but being two cup sizes bigger than her, my breasts would have spilled out of it. That's a look for some girls, but I don't have the confidence for that. So I went with a swimsuit I was familiar with, and I think it's cute. It's a lilac-purple one-piece with sheer fabric around the sides of my waist.

He runs his eyes over me from head to toe, leaving me blushing and red within seconds.

I give myself a running start and jump into the pool. The water is cold, and I'm starting to think going for a swim at the end of September might have been a terrible idea.

Ash meets me when I come up for air. I gasp as my chest tightens from the shock of the brisk water, my teeth chattering uncontrollably.

"It's freezing!" Goose bumps cover my body, but as soon as Ash smiles, they vanish.

Our legs brush when he closes in. He reaches for my hair clip and releases my bound hair. He tosses it toward the chairs before running his hands over my soaking, wavy hair.

"*Fuck*, you're gorgeous, Gwen."

Chapter Twenty-Seven

My breath gets stuck in my throat, forming a lump that may need to be checked on by a medical professional.

"You're not too bad yourself."

He stares into my soul, and I forget all about needing to breathe.

"Want to play a game?" He swims away to create some distance between us.

I miss the warmth he emits the moment he leaves my personal bubble.

"What did you have in mind?" I raise my eyebrow, sinking farther into the water.

"Truth or dare?" His voice drowns in flirtation and mischief.

Let's play this safe for a bit. Not sure I trust him with a dare.

"Okay, truth," I say while drifting closer to him, not fighting the natural current.

"Were you and Zack ever a thing?"

I can't stop the disgust from taking over my facial expression. "God, no."

He chuckles, and his shoulders loosen up, relaxing more with each passing second.

"Truth or dare?" I ask him, while silently begging, *please don't say dare, please don't say dare.*

"Truth," he responds coolly.

"Why did you keep sitting next to me in biochem after the first day?" Time to get some answers I've been dying for.

"Honestly?" He arches his eyebrow before moving ever so slightly toward me. My insides twist with anticipation. "I liked the way you smelled." I snort out a laugh. "You asked!" I burst out in more laughter, and it takes a moment to compose myself. "Your turn," he says with a chuckle.

We come face to face as a slight rumble echoes in the sky.

"Truth."

His lips form a lopsided grin, highlighting his dimples. "Did you have a thing for me in high school?"

Okay, who do I need to murder? Chrissy, Zack? Who spilled the beans?

"Who didn't?" I wiggle my nose as the words leave my mouth.

"Answer the question." His fingers brush over my hand, and his heavenly eyes glisten against the water's reflection.

"I did." It comes out as a whisper. His mouth opens, but I cut him off before he can say anything snarky. "Truth or dare?"

"Truth."

Heavy rain clouds loom above us, shadowing the sun entirely.

"Did you have a crush on *me* in high school?" I flutter my eyelashes to tease him.

"If I knew you better, I'm sure I would have." I scrunch my face in response. "I know you now though." His fingers intertwine with mine; our legs rub against one another again. "Truth or dare?"

"Dare." The answer comes out of my mouth before I even think about it. I don't care though. This is another *fuck it* moment.

"You don't want me to dare you." His voice drops a decibel.

He places his free hand on my waist, pulling me against his bare chest.

"Dare me." I lean in, my nose skimming his.

His hand skates down my waist, landing on the backside of my thigh.

"Kiss me." His voice is deep and husky.

I curl my hands into his hair, pressing my chest against his. Our lips graze each other.

Chapter Twenty-Seven

Right before I follow through, thunder cracks in the sky, and rain releases from swollen, dark gray clouds.

"Fucking rain." I smirk as Ash curses the storm.

Lightning strikes, and it seems to land in the yard right next to Ash's. My back shudders from the ear-shattering crackle of thunder. The rain pelts us, quickly blinding our vision and soaking us even further.

"Okay, let's get inside," Ash says while taking my hand in his.

We scramble for our belongings. Ash gets my bag, and I grab my overly expensive science textbook. *There goes my chance at selling this thing back.* We enter through a side door, dripping water all over what looks like a mud room. He grabs another towel and wraps it around me.

"Are you okay?"

I nod breathlessly as he tightens the towel around my shoulders.

"Follow me."

I follow him through the hallway, trying not to gawk at the pricey-looking furniture and paintings that line the walls. Ash's room is upstairs and to the right. When he opens his door, a rush of cold air assaults me.

"Jesus, Ash. It's like the Arctic in here."

He reaches for my book and smiles apologetically. "Sorry, I'm a hot sleeper." He fans the book out, shaking the water from the pages.

"Figuratively or literally?" This time, I get him to blush, and it makes me grin.

He opens his drawer and pulls out a black tee and matching basketball shorts. "I'll put your stuff in the dryer."

I take the offered clothes and wrap the towel tighter around my shoulders as he points to the bathroom directly behind me.

Stepping through the door, I shiver when my feet touch the

Forever Crushed

tile floor. My eyes catch his right before I close the door. His expression is soft and wondrous before he drops his gaze.

After closing the door, I drop the towel and peel off my rain and pool-water-soaked swimsuit. Of course, I didn't pack a fresh set of underwear. I'll be sure to stay far away from Ash. *Far, far away.*

I pull Ash's shirt over my head, instantly becoming intoxicated by the smell of laundry detergent and his pine and apple cologne. I tie the shorts' drawstring ungodly tight before looking at myself in the mirror. I'm in Ash's house, in his clothes, in his room. What did I get myself into? I try my breathing technique to get my anxiety under control.

"You got this. It's just two friends hanging out. Everything is totally cool." My eyes roll in the mirror's reflection.

As much as I want to, I *still* can't lie to myself.

I try to shake off my nerves as I open the bathroom door. Ash changed into a pair of lounge pants and a plain white V-neck shirt.

He looks in my direction, and I swear his voice gets stuck in his throat. He grabs a fur-lined fleece blanket from the foot of his bed and walks toward me.

He wraps it around my body as he takes the wet bathing suit from my hands. "I'll be right back."

I nod as he leaves. His room is about the entire size of my studio apartment. I trail my hand over his desk, noting how organized and tidy it is. Posters line the walls, but they're not what I expected from him. They range from band to old-school movie art, specifically classic Star Wars. I stroll over to the bookshelf, admiring his taste in fiction and classic novels. A TV rests directly across from his bed.

The thunderstorm rages outside the window on the opposite wall, showing no signs of letting up anytime soon. I walk to

Chapter Twenty-Seven

my bag and grab my phone from the pocket. A few messages from Chrissy and Zack, but I'll check them later.

When Ash returns, he shivers. "Holy crap, it is like the Arctic in here."

My nipples harden, and I become acutely aware that I'm not wearing a bra right now.

"Told you so." My teeth chatter.

Jogging past me, he jumps right into his bed, curling himself under the duvet cover.

He pats the spot next to him before flicking the TV on. "Want to watch a movie while your book dries?"

"Where's *your* book?" I ask, arching my right eyebrow.

"Downstairs, but I'm too cold to move."

I sigh when he flashes me an innocent smile.

My toes ache to be warm, so I accept his invitation. One step at a time, I make my way to the other side of his queen-sized mattress. He lifts the blanket, and I sigh as the warmth wafts over my body. I sit next to him, curling my knees into my chest, making sure to leave at least a foot of space between us.

He lies on his side, head propped up by his arm. "What do you want to watch?" He offers the remote, and I put on a true crime documentary.

"Is this okay?"

He raises his eyebrows before nodding.

"I'm going to keep this in mind, Gwen." He flashes me a smile just as thunder cracks in the sky again. The unexpected noise makes me jump, and he chuckles. "You can't watch true crime docs and then jump at thunder."

I stick my tongue out at him, wrapping his blanket tighter around myself. My body is at war with itself. My heart is racing from being this close to Ash, but my skin has goose bumps from the freezing temperature.

"Still cold?"

I try to conceal the moment I shiver, but it doesn't work. "Only a little."

His eyes float over my body before settling on my face.

"Come here." He holds his arms open, and I need to remind myself this isn't a dream. "Only if you want to," he adds.

I want to. I'm tired of letting nerves control my life. I'm safe with Ash. I have no doubt about it.

I remove the blanket from my arms, covering us both with it before scooting down. I move close enough that our feet touch. He wraps his arms around me, and I'm captivated by him. I caress his cheek with my left hand. He blushes rosy red from my touch.

"Ash?"

His breathing quickens, just as mine does. "Hmm?"

I swallow hard. My muscles tighten, knowing what I'm about to say. "Truth or dare?"

He shifts down so we're face to face. "Dare." His voice caresses my lips as he nuzzles against my nose.

I lock my leg between his, running my hand through his wavy curls. "Kiss me."

He wastes no time, parting my lips with his and kissing me with so much passion I forget about everything. Fuck nerves, fuck oxygen. I need him and only him, nothing else.

Our kiss deepens, and before I know it, I'm on my back. I tangle my hands in his hair and moan so quietly it becomes a secret only the two of us know.

I've been kissed before, but never like this. His lips are full and assertive. Ash kisses me like he's been fantasizing about me for years.

I let him take the lead, and damn, it's the best decision I've ever made. A rumble vibrates from his chest, escaping his mouth as a satisfied groan. I shift my legs so he fits perfectly

Chapter Twenty-Seven

between them. His hand lands on my waist and glides up under my shirt.

"Wait." I raise my hand to his chest, and he halts.

"We can stop."

I shake my head the moment the words escape his mouth.

"No, I um—" I click my tongue before deciding to just be outright with it. "I'm not wearing any kind of underwear right now."

His erection presses against my inner thigh.

"Fuck me. Just when I thought you couldn't get any hotter, you prove me wrong."

He pulls on my lower lip with his teeth before devouring me again. His hand explores my bare waist, trailing up. He reaches my right breast as his lips trail down my neck, and he licks where my pulse is throbbing. He sucks on it gently, eliciting a moan in response.

"Why do you feel so fucking good?" His voice is raspy and sensual.

I can feel his fingers itching to crawl to my hardened nipple.

"Don't stop, please, Ash."

All the teasing, flirting, the damn sexual tension has gotten to me.

If he's ready, then I am too. I was waiting for him at the end of the day, and I think we're both done playing the waiting game.

His thumb hovers over my nipple. I've never been touched like this, but the second Ash glides his thumb over it, my back arches, and everything becomes a blur.

He lifts my shirt, exposing my entire chest to the bitter air-conditioned air, and then pulls the shirt over my head. While his lips cover my nipple, he maintains eye contact. His tongue is warm as he lavishes his attention on my breast.

With each glide and flick of his tongue, my body grows hungry for more. I moan just as he switches to my other breast, following the same movement. I fight to catch my breath under his touch as his hair tickles my chin. The sudden urge to feel him inside me is overpowering.

I tug on his shirt and pull it over his head. I glide my fingers along his pecs, down toward his core. His skin is warm under my palms, and the mere sensation makes me dizzy. When I reach his waistband, he clashes his lips against mine. His thumb finds its way to my shorts, but he struggles to pull them down.

"What did you do? Glue the drawstrings together?" He chuckles, and I grin between his kisses.

I untie the knot I made to prevent the shorts from falling to my ankles, then I lean up and pull on his lounge pants, gliding them over his ass down to his knees. Ash props himself using his arms, trapping me between his muscles. He shifts before kicking his pants off, kissing my stomach in the process. I giggle at the touch of his lips against my bare skin as he kisses his way down to the waistband of my shorts.

He tugs them down but stops to look at me. "You're sure?"

"I am. Are you?"

He kisses my belly button and nods before gazing up at me. "Absolutely."

He tugs my shorts off and tosses them to the floor. Ash inches his lips and tongue from my waist to my chest, nibbling on my neck, then back to my lips.

"I was ready the moment I saw you a few weeks ago," he whispers.

I reach for his boxers, but he pushes me back down with a sexy grin.

"So eager," he growls as he shifts onto his knees.

When he tugs his boxers down using his thumbs, the breath I was sucking in is cut short.

Chapter Twenty-Seven

I felt his erection on my thigh the day I brought him to my apartment, but *this* doesn't compare. It's not even close.

His cock is impressive, and he's magnificent. His lower abdomen dives into a deep V. Admiring him, I take in his abs and muscular pecs. Seeing him this way makes my head spin.

As he presses his chest against mine, I become trapped between his strong arms. He kisses the other side of my neck and explores the lower part of my stomach with his knuckles. It's not long before he's feathering his finger above my swollen clit.

"Has anyone touched you here before?"

If I were wearing underwear, they would be soaked right now. Something only Ash has done. His touch is nothing compared to my previous experiences. I'm withering under his command.

"Yeah, but they weren't really good at it," I admit as my chest heaves in anticipation.

He circles his finger around my clit, and my hips arch with the movement. Balling the sheets in my right fist, I gasp in response to his touch.

"I'll make you forget all about them," he whispers darkly.

I moan as he finds the right rhythm, learning my body, discovering what makes me tremble and beg for more.

"Ash." His name escapes my lips. I murmur, "Keep going," in undeniable ecstasy as his finger works my clit.

I wrap my legs around him, needing more of him. Shifting down a tad, I wrap my hand around his cock. He groans as I stroke him, and I take a moment to determine the right amount of pressure to use.

"Gwen, *fuck*," he hums in pure bliss as I kiss his neck.

Thunder booms outside, shaking the entire house, and the rain hammers harder against the window pane across the room.

"Shit," I curse while jolting from the sudden interruption.

Ash snickers and presses his forehead against mine. "Don't worry. I'll protect you."

He secures his arms on either side of me, and I feel safe under his gaze and between his arms.

"Hang on, one second." He reaches for the bedside table and slides the drawer open.

The second I see the foil wrapper, I open my mouth. "We don't have to use that. I've been on birth control for years. Not because I sleep around. I have irregular periods." I'm babbling.

This is not the sexiest thing to say right now. But the overwhelming desire to feel him, all of him, is blinding.

The last time I had sex was my senior year in high school, and I barely consider it sex. I don't think he managed to put his dick inside me, but I can't recall. By all legal terms, I still might be a virgin.

"Are you sure? I haven't been with anyone since Alex, and we always used one. The last time we did anything was before the Brandon situation, but even then, that was last March. Once I found out she was sleeping around, I got tested. I'm clean. I promise. I've never done it without one before. I would never put you at risk, Gwen."

A smile spreads across my lips, and my heart soars out of my chest. I'm not used to this. No one puts me first. Here I am though. Witnessing history being made.

The thought of being the first woman he has unprotected sex with is exhilarating. Fuck all consequences that may appear down the road. I'm not concerned about pregnancy. STIs and STDs are a possibility, but I trust him. He's not lying, I can tell. His eyes are on me, not dancing around the room. His breathing is fast, but given the situation, I can't use that as an indicator.

"Me neither. I trust you."

He places himself back between my legs and presses his

Chapter Twenty-Seven

erection against my clit, guiding it where it needs to be.

"Fuck me. If this is a dream, don't wake me up," Ash mumbles.

I lift my body toward him, and he rubs the head of his cock against my entrance. He leans his forehead against mine as he slowly buries himself inside me.

I suck in a deep breath as Ash sinks into me, and I contract around him. The stretching is slightly uncomfortable but also intoxicating. I grip his back, digging my fingernails into his shoulder blades.

Ash pulls away slightly, slowly diving into me again, and before long, he's fully nestled against my hips. The sensation of being bare with him should be illegal. Pure magic boils in my veins.

"Fuck, Gwen." He's fighting to catch his breath, just as I am. "Are you okay? You're so tight."

I nod. The ability to form words is thrown right out the window. He watches me closely when he pulls out and presses back into me. My mouth parts and I whimper against his lips. My body accepts him, and slowly, he increases his speed, making me moan louder with each thrust.

Hitching my legs over his arms, I scream when he hits my G-spot. *"Fuck,"* I cry.

Ash creates a burning flame in my core. It slowly extends and fills every crevice and pore along my skin.

"Ash, don't stop."

I need him to keep going. I need him to be the one to give me my first orgasm.

Pressing his forehead against my shoulder, he shudders and moans with electrified need. I'm inching closer and closer to the edge. He fills me completely, and he's hitting every sensitive spot.

He dives into me, making my legs wrap around him tighter.

I pull him closer, needing him to fill this longing I have for him. I whimper against his shoulder as my body starts to quiver. My eyes haze, and the my core tightens. A blistering, hot sensation builds in my lower belly, slowly spreading to my spine.

"Are you going to come for me?" he asks with a husky tone.

My breath hitches in my throat as he groans.

"Mhm." The thought of speaking is out of the question.

"That's my girl."

A wave of pleasure explodes in my core as he whispers in my ear. I dig my fingernails into his back, moaning as my new favorite sensation overpowers me. My muscles tighten, readying themselves for release.

"That's it. Give me everything, baby."

My cry of pure desire fills the room. This is nothing like the orgasms I've given myself. This is more intense, more addicting, and more gratifying.

Ash's back tenses under my hands, and his moan fills my ears. "Can I come inside you?" his voice strains.

I can sense he's holding back the urge to finish right here and now.

The thought of having him fill me is nerve-racking yet exciting. The fact that I got him to this point is beyond mind-blowing.

"Yes." The single word is all I can manage.

Ash releases himself in a series of curses and groans. I'm so sensitive that I feel the exact moment he finishes. His length pulsates and throbs against my inner walls.

The climax fades from us both. Ash lands to my left, pulling me into his chest. He brushes my hair away from my face and kisses my forehead as he fights to catch his breath.

Leaning forward, I meet his lips tenderly. Tasting the sweat on his lips, I giggle, knowing I'm also covered in perspiration.

"Fuck, Gwen. I think you might have just ruined all other

women for me."

I lean against his arm and kiss his cheek, inching down to his neck.

"My plan worked then," I giggle.

His breathing doesn't let up, and his body becomes hot and needy again.

"I don't think I'll ever be able to get enough of you." He pins me on my back, kissing me long and hard.

"Can I tell you something?" I mumble against his lips.

"Anything." His tone is dark, nearing a snarl, when he takes my lips in his again. Kissing me with such devotion that I melt in his arms.

"You're the first guy to make me—" I gesture down between my legs.

Ash raises his eyebrows in disbelief. "Really?"

"Really," I whisper, slightly embarrassed by the confession.

"Fuck, Gwen. That's hot." Colliding his lips with mine, he kisses me greedily. "Good thing the storm isn't going anywhere anytime soon."

I snicker as his lips tickle my neck.

"You're all mine, deal?" He glides his tongue below my ear and onto neck, eliciting the same need within me.

"Deal." I willingly submit.

He chuckles against my skin, and my cheeks burn from all his attention and stroking. He sweeps his fingers over my stomach, tickling me, skims his nose over mine, and holds me captive with his eyes.

"Promise?" His tone changes, almost like he's begging me not to leave him.

He let himself fall for me, even if he wasn't one hundred percent ready to fall again. I glide my thumb over his jawline and smile.

"You and me. I promise."

Chapter Twenty-Eight

Ash

Things went further than I originally intended. All I wanted was to kiss her. Look at us now, a tangle of limbs and flushed skin. Her bare back is facing me, rising and falling as she breathes. A grin tugs on my face, my cheeks aching from smiling so much. This woman turned out to be more than I could've ever imagined, more than I thought I would ever be worthy of.

She makes me feel loved, cared for, *seen*. I've never fallen in love. I thought I did with Alex, but that wasn't real. This? The way I feel when I think of Gwen. How she spikes my heart rate with a simple text. How every time I see her, I crave holding her in my arms. Could this be love?

I know true love exists, but am I worthy to experience it? If I were to ask her that, I know what her answer would be. This woman thinks I'm worthy of the stars. Meanwhile, she deserves the whole damn galaxy. I cuddle closer to her, needing to feel her warmth against me. With one arm draped over her waist, I

Chapter Twenty-Eight

lean my forehead against her shoulder blade. I let myself become drunk on her scent and touch.

If this is what love feels like, I'd give anything to keep feeling this way.

She shifts, pressing herself against my chest. I pull the blanket over her exposed arm, making sure to keep her warm.

Rain pelts the window on the other side of the room, making Gwen twitch and flip onto her chest. Her hair is a mess of tangled waves. Absolutely my fault.

I trace my eyes over her, needing to memorize every little freckle and pore this woman has. It's dark, but I can still make out the outlines of her face. Her full, soft, pink lips are swollen from kissing me. The way her forehead crinkles as if her thoughts never stop running, even in her sleep. I love how her curls get wild during the day, and I fucking love the way she smells even without that perfume she sprays on her body.

There's so much I don't know about her, yet I feel like I've known her for years.

I curl my hands into her hair and kiss her shoulder sweetly, letting my eyes flutter closed even though I would be content just to watch her sleep the rest of the night.

A harsh clap of thunder startles me awake. I groan and notice a shift in the bed. Gwen stands, pulling my T-shirt back over her head.

"Where are you going?" My voice is still groggy from sleep.

I reposition on my stomach, admiring how she looks in nothing but my shirt.

"The bathroom." Her face lights up when her eyes meet mine.

A natural smile pulls on my lips. "Hurry."

I watch her until she reaches the bathroom. Fuck, she needs to get back here, fast.

Burning a hole through the door with my eyes, I will her to hurry. I can't express the need I feel right now. I'm throbbing against the sheets, needing to be inside her again. I roll out of bed and walk over to the door. Just as she steps out, I wrap my arms around her. She squeals when I pick her up, my hands cradling her perfect ass.

"You scared me," she giggles as I carry her back to bed.

Pressing my lips against hers, I slide my tongue over her lips. My skin tingles from her touch. Everything about her is soft and beautiful.

"You took too long," I rasp before taking her lips again, sending me right off the cliff I've been teetering on.

I toss her onto the bed and hover over her. She backs toward the headboard, her laughter light, and the moment I plant my knees back on the mattress, I sense her desire as well. Her nipples harden beneath her shirt, and her cheeks blush bright red.

Pulling her down by her ankle, I secure myself over her full chest and lean in to feather my lips against hers. She wraps her right leg around my waist, securing me against her warmth. Her eyes gloss over, mesmerized.

"Aren't you tired?" she asks as I kiss her cheek, then begin exploring lower down her neck.

"I was. Until I saw you walking to the bathroom in nothing

Chapter Twenty-Eight

but my shirt." I lick her neck, right on the spot that made her back arch earlier.

I groan hungrily as I grip her thigh, rubbing my cock around her swollen clit. She leans forward and bites my lower lip, freeing a moan from my chest.

"Ash?"

Fuck, I love when she says my name. I could play it on repeat for the rest of my life. I hover my mouth over hers, barely touching her lips.

She closes the gap between us, shifting my balance and making me dizzy. She gets me on my back, straddling right above my length. Her lips ravish mine as she presses her chest against me. I wrap my hands in her hair, making it a sexy mess. When Gwen slides herself over my cock, rubbing on me with the right amount of pressure, my eyes roll to the back of my head.

"That's really ni—" A moan escapes my mouth.

Never have I felt anything remotely close to this. Why does she feel so *damn* good?

She kisses my neck, gently sucking and drawing gentle circles with her tongue. I grab her hips, rocking her back and forth, needing her to move faster. Lining herself up, she slowly lowers herself onto my cock. I hum in unbelievable pleasure when she meets my shaft. Gwen's muscles contract around me, massaging every inch of my shaft.

I watch as she finds the right rhythm, and knowing she hasn't done this many times before makes me want her more. It hasn't taken her long to learn how to please me. Within a few seconds, I'm begging her—"Fuck, don't stop."

I don't let my eyes close. I need to watch her. The fabric of the T-shirt I gave her grazes over her perfect breasts. Her curves dip and fill in just the right spots.

I squeeze her hips, urging her to keep going. She throws her head back, moaning and whimpering.

"You like that, baby?" I ask, already knowing the answer.

I bite my cheek as her hips gyrate faster, needing more with each movement. "Ride my cock, that's it."

We become a haze of moans and staggered breathing, tangling our bodies around one another.

"Ash, I need you harder." She falls against my chest, sliding up and down on my length, and I lose control.

Wrapping my arms around her back, I lift my hips to give her exactly what she asked for.

"Is this what you want?" I growl, and she shivers as I whisper in her ear.

Devouring her lips, I hold her in place and ram myself in and out of her tight pussy, hard and fast. I'm close, but I need to be sure she gets everything she deserves. Being bare with Gwen has ruined me. But I'm pretty sure she destroyed me the first day I saw her. Between her kindness and dazzling smile, she had me wrapped around her finger. Now, I'm completely done for.

A few more thrusts, and she unwinds. Her muscles contract around my erection, and she unleashes her beautiful sounds into my mouth, making every bone within me vibrate with her blissful song. My legs spasm just as her back relaxes. Every cell explodes in my body and renews simultaneously. Before I can pull out, she fucks the cum out of me. My movements slow as I fill her until we're both completely satisfied.

"Why do you feel so good?" I ask with a chuckle.

Gwen kisses my forearm and locks her fingers with mine. "I could ask you the same question." Her tone teeters between shock and awe.

I stare into her eyes, making her flush. When I place a kiss on her forehead, she releases a contented sigh.

Chapter Twenty-Eight

Although the way she looks at me fills my heart, I can't stop a dark thought from creeping in: Am I worthy of being loved by someone like Gwen Roman? Am I worthy of love at all? I can't even remember the last time someone told me they loved me. Alex and I never exchanged those words.

I pull her against my chest and hold on to her for dear life.

"Are you okay?"

There's that question again, the one that gets me every time. I grip her tighter, refusing to let her go.

"Ash?" She peers up at me, noting my glistening eyes. "Talk to me."

Rolling onto my back, I mumble "It's stupid" while pressing my palms to my eyes.

She shifts in my arms and wipes my tear-stained cheeks.

"Tell me." The softness in her voice reminds me of a lullaby.

"I've never felt this way before, and it's terrifying. You know I've had girlfriends before. I don't know how many boyfriends you've had or if you feel the same way I do. I can honestly say this feeling"—I place her hand against my chest—"is new to me. It's warm and addicting, but it makes me nervous. What scares me the most is that while I haven't known you for long, it feels like I've known you for years. I can't let you go, Gwen. I don't know what'll happen if I do."

She leans in, placing a kiss on the tip of my nose.

"Can I tell you something?" Her voice is faint, like what she's about to tell me is a deep, dark secret. "I've kind of had a crush on you since tenth grade. No matter what I did, I could never get you out of my brain. It was like you fused right into the perfect crevice. Which sounds silly now that I'm saying it out loud. And while I haven't had many boyfriends, the same feeling sits in my chest."

"Tenth grade?" I ask.

She pulls the T-shirt over her mouth. Her confession and cute action quicken my heartbeat.

But I don't let her get away that easily. "Have you been stalking me, sneaky girl?"

Her cheeks burn rosy pink, and the tears I shed a moment ago vanish when I see her grin.

"I wish I knew you." I wrap my arms around her and pull her closer.

"No, trust me. You absolutely did not want to know me."

Reaching over, I tug her shirt down so I can see her wonderful smile. "I wish I knew you then, truly."

And I mean it. I wish I hadn't been so self-centered back then. I wish I paid closer attention.

"I'm glad you sat next to me in biochem and that I didn't scare you away."

Lifting her chin, I guide her to my lips. I kiss her longingly, needing to show her just how much she means to me.

"You could never scare me away. Now, Chrissy, on the other hand."

She giggles against me. I grin, and she immediately runs her thumb over my dimple.

And that's the moment it happens.

Chapter Twenty-Nine

Gwen

It's happening.

My feelings for Ash are becoming real, no longer a dream or fantasy. I've never been in love before, but this? It might be happening sooner than I expected. The Ash I created in my head is nothing like the Ash lying next to me. This Ash is wonderful and raw. My mind couldn't have pictured him like this because I didn't know men like this existed. Ash is complex, funny, charming, down-to-earth, and sexy. But most importantly, he's real. I painted him as the "cool guy," not daring to think he could be more than that. I've never been happier to be wrong in my entire life.

Here I am, lying in his bed, cuddling with him. His arms are wrapped around me, refusing to let go. I don't want to fall, but I feel it happening. I don't know if I need to guard myself or protect my heart, just in case. Then I remember what he said back in the library.

"Remember that promise you made me?" I whisper.

He brushes a strand of hair behind my ear, leaving my skin marked by his touch forever.

"That I would never break your heart."

Every bone and connected joint melts when he says the words I hoped he would remember.

"Did you mean it?" I ask.

He kisses me again, setting my lips ablaze. "Every word."

I nuzzle into him and let myself fall. Ash always had a tiny piece of my heart.

Now? He has the whole damn thing.

Chapter Thirty

Gwen

There's something about staying awake with Ash, listening to the rain, lying in each other's arms, and just talking. Hearing him laugh and light up in the dark makes my heart sing. The rain doesn't let up, and I don't dare check the time. I never want this night to end. We talk about everything, not caring how dull the subject is because no subject Ash talks about could ever be dull. I witness a different side of him, a side that's ridiculous and funny.

He asks me about my family, and I let it all out. I tell him about my parents and why Chrissy, Zack, and I are so close. I can't believe he actually thought Zack and I were a thing. The idea makes me gag every time.

"What about you? What are your parents like?"

When he rolls his eyes, I understand perfectly.

"A bunch of cheating bastards. If I didn't have my brother, I would be completely alone. Not saying he's not an asshole too, because he definitely is." He runs his fingers up and down my arm, creating goose bumps over my body.

"The generation before us really sucked at parenting, didn't they?" I ask.

He snorts and squeezes my arm. "You got that right."

At least Ash has his brother. If I didn't have Chrissy or Zack, I would be a completely different person than I am today.

I'm unsure when the rain stopped or when the sun began to rise. I was too distracted by Ash. My eyes are growing heavy, and I'm fighting with them to stay open, dreading the idea of going home. I never want to leave this bed. I never want to leave him.

"We stayed up all night, again," he says while I drape my arm over his waist. He trails his fingers along my spine, relaxing and turning me on at the same time. "Please, don't go," he whispers in my ear.

I nod and sink deeper into his bed. "I was hoping you would say that. Just promise me one thing."

He murmurs an inaudible response.

"We have to study at some point today." As a groan of displeasure escapes his lips, I can't help but snicker.

"I can't promise you that," he teases as he holds onto me, embracing me in his warmth. "Let's just sleep for now."

With a kiss on my shoulder, we drift off. And for the first time in my life, I don't need my comfort show playing right beside me.

Chapter Thirty

I toss and turn in bed, swearing that my phone is vibrating. I curse under my breath, still needing more sleep. I try to ignore it, but it doesn't stop. Rolling over, I almost fall out of bed, and Ash whimpers. I stumble across the floor and fall to my knees, reaching for my bag. I yank out my phone.

Zack's calling me . . . and against my better judgment, I answer it.

"Hello?" I pull my phone away from my ear as Zack goes off. "Lower your voice, please," I whine into the receiver.

This is the last thing I want to deal with right now.

"Where are you?" he hisses at me.

A grin slides over my face as Ash tosses in bed.

"I'm home," I lie through my teeth.

I knew he would call me; it was only a matter of time.

"Like hell you are. Where does he live? I'm coming to get you now."

I scoff, itching to get back into bed.

"Gwen," Ash calls and reaches for me. "Bed." He pats the spot next to him.

"Oh, you're in big trouble, missy!" Zack shouts.

I roll my eyes and pull the phone away from my ear.

"Fuck you, Zack. I'm fine. See you tomorrow." I hang up and put the phone on silent.

I'll deal with Zack later. Besides, he can fool around with

Forever Crushed

whomever he wants, why can't I? I decide to do one last thing before jumping right back into bed.

> Get your brother under control for me, please :)

> You got it! Hope you're having fun! ;)

If only she knew...

I place my phone on the desk before jumping back into bed. Ash hums in contentment as I nuzzle against him. I fit perfectly in his arms, like two puzzle pieces snapping together. I kiss his shoulder and settle against the pillow.

"Want me to deal with Zack for you?"

I smile at the thought of Ash being willing to stand up for me. He knew I was going to get an earful from Zack, yet he's ready to take my place in the hot seat.

"No, it's okay. I'll send Chrissy instead."

Without opening his eyes, a smile creeps across his lips, and I don't blame him. I curl around his body, and before I know it, I'm falling right back to sleep.

I stretch before opening my eyes, yawning and brushing against Ash's hairy legs. When my eyes flutter open, I find Ash watching me, taking in every detail of my face. I pull the blanket over my head.

Chapter Thirty

"Were you watching me sleep?"

He joins me under the covers, pulling my body closer to his. "Maybe."

I hide my face behind my hands and purse my lips, knowing exactly how I look right now—all sweaty and crusty. Just when I thought it couldn't get any worse, my stomach growls.

"Oh, yeah. I forgot to feed you."

I peer in between my fingers. He's smiling broadly, flashing those dimples and perfect white teeth.

"I'll go get us some food. My brother's probably home, though, so stay here, okay?"

I nod behind my finger wall. "Well, given that I don't have any clothes at the moment, I don't think I have a choice."

He pulls my hands from my face and kisses me hard.

"I like you with no clothes though." He gently bites my lower lip, making me needy all over again. "I'll be right back." He gets out of bed, grabbing his joggers from yesterday, I glide my eyes over his bare ass. "Don't move." He points at me while walking backward, hesitating before leaving the room.

I press my lips together and twiddle my thumbs. Against my better judgment, I get out of bed and check my phone. Of course, it's blown up. Missed calls from Zack, texts from Chrissy, and something from my parents. Wait, how the hell is it almost three in the afternoon? Shit, we didn't even start studying for biochem. Don't even remind me about my biology test tomorrow.

Ash strolls back in with bags of chips and bottles of water. He drops them on the ground the moment he sees me standing at his desk. His mouth twitches into a sloppy smirk, gawking at my body, making my limbs go numb.

"Ash, don't." I hold my hand out, blocking him from getting any closer. "Don't you come near me."

He grins wickedly. In one quick stride, he tries to grab me. I run away while giggling, jumping to the other side of his bed, playfully smiling and laughing as he attempts to grab me.

"We need to study, Ash."

He stands on his bed, inching closer to me. I back up and get ready to bolt again.

"Fuck that. There's something else we need to be doing right now."

My clit swells, and desire pools in my lower stomach under his hungry gaze.

"Don't make me have to run out of here in just your shirt."

He arches his eyebrows, and I realize I made the situation worse.

"That's something I'd pay to see."

As quick as lightning, he charges toward me. Before I can respond, he lifts me and tosses me back onto the bed. He pins my arms over my head and presses our lips together. He parts my lips with his tongue, and we dance around each other, gripping and whimpering softly.

"Ash!"

My eyes widen in response to the unfamiliar voice. A knock sounds from the door, and I freeze.

Ash places his finger over my lip and whispers, "Be quiet."

I nod and zip my lips. He strolls over to the door, opening it just enough to talk to his brother. When I overhear that someone is here for Ash, my heart twists. What if it's Alex or a completely different girl?

"Who is it?" Ash sounds bewildered.

"He said his name's Zack."

Fuck. I roll my eyes and silently shift off the bed.

"I'll be right down." He closes the door and smiles apologetically.

Chapter Thirty

"I'm going to kill him." I cross my arms over my chest, fuming with rage.

"No, you're not." *Oh, but I am.* "He must be worried about you. Want me to send him away?"

I sigh. "No, if I stay, we'll never get to study," I say while pouting. I don't want to leave, and I can tell Ash doesn't want me to either.

"I'll get your stuff from the dryer."

I gather my things and pack my bag. My book is water damaged and withered but still usable.

Ash returns and hands me my swimsuit and clothes from yesterday. My heart tugs and stings, urging me to stay. And I want to, but I would have to leave eventually. Life always resumes.

I pull my shorts over my body, and right before I change out of his shirt, he places his hand on my arm. "Keep it. It looks better on you."

I don't get to respond because as soon as the words leave his lips, he scoops me into his arms, crashing into me again.

I wrap my arms around his neck, pulling him closer, silently begging him to ask me to stay.

"I'll walk you down," he says against my mouth before placing me back on my feet.

My eyes well with tears, and I know it's stupid. I wipe them away the moment they cascade down my cheeks.

"Gwen?"

"I'm sorry, I'm fine." I force a laugh, hoping the tears will stop.

I'm not ready. I can't stand the thought of sleeping in my bed. One night with the guy, and I'm screwed.

"I'm going to miss you too." He wipes away my tears, offering me a gentle smile. "But we'll see each other tomorrow."

"Promise?"

He places a kiss on the tip of my nose. "Pinkie promise."

After a longing kiss, I step away. He helps me with my bag, and we head down the stairs.

When I see Zack through the glass in the front door, I grind my teeth. He's standing outside with his hands shoved in his pockets.

Ash opens the door for me, and we both fall under Zack's scrutiny.

"Gwen." Zack's stance and tone are notably tense.

"Zack." I meet his demeanor with my own fury.

"Gwen!" Chrissy steps out of the car, running toward the three of us.

Thank god she's here. Zack's eyes glance over to Ash, and I feel the moment it happens. Ash tenses, and without looking, I know they're both staring one another down.

"What is this, a cowboy standoff?" Chrissy asks.

I turn on my heel and face Ash with a smile. "Call you later, okay?"

I stand on my toes and pull him in for one more kiss. His tension melts away when I touch him. I feather my lips over his before pulling away.

Chrissy's jaw hangs open when I turn back around.

"You so got laid." She beams at me, and my cheeks flush hot.

I pull on her arm and walk to Zack's car.

"Come on, Zacky!" Chrissy calls after him.

I glance over my shoulder just as Zack tears himself away from their death stare.

I open the backseat door, and Zack speaks up. "Gwen, sit in the front."

I roll my eyes without facing him. "No thanks," I say before settling in the back.

Chapter Thirty

I offer Ash a sincere smile and wave, all while preparing for the lecture of a lifetime.

Zack glares at me through the rearview mirror, and the car fills with heated tension, except for Chrissy. She's bopping along to music, either oblivious to the thick air or trying to ease the hostility.

My unease and rage boil over. Let's just get this over with.

"Fuck you, Zack." I come out blazing, ready for a fight.

"Fuck me!?" he fires back.

Chrissy turns the music off and readies herself to defend me.

"You're the one who went over to some guy's place knowing what his intentions were!"

"Why is it okay for you to do that with some bitchy ass girl, but I can't with someone I've known for years!?"

He slams on the brakes when we reach a red light and turns in his seat to face me. "Just because you had a crush on him for years doesn't mean you know him."

I smirk devilishly as he seethes.

"Bet you didn't know that we've been hanging out for weeks now. You may think I'm a naive idiot, but I'm not."

The light turns green. Cars around us honk, but Zack doesn't budge. He holds on to my gaze, clenching his jaw.

"How did you meet Roselyn again? Was it legit, or did you just fuck her in a broom closet?" I hiss.

Chrissy snorts, trying her best to hold back awkward laughter.

"Fuck you, Gwen," Zack snaps.

A smile slithers across my lips again.

"No thanks, I've had my fill," I say while crossing my arms.

He whirls around and presses his foot to the gas.

"Holy shit, that's my girl!" Chrissy cheers from the front seat.

We finish the ride back to my place in silence. When he pulls over, I storm out of the car and slam the door.

Chrissy flies after me and follows me upstairs. "I need all the tea. Girl's night!"

Chapter Thirty-One

Gwen

I promised Chrissy I wouldn't let Zack ruin our girl's night, but I'm just so fucking pissed off. I get that he sees me as a little sister, but there are boundaries no one should cross, and he crossed about fifty of them in an hour.

Chrissy turned on a true crime doc we hadn't watched yet. She popped some popcorn and plopped down on the bed next to me.

I snack mindlessly, tossing one kernel in my mouth, then shoving a fistful in my face as my stomach rumbles.

"Geez, slow down."

I ignore her and focus on my biochem notes, needing to cram every little line into my brain.

"I'm sorry my brother's such a prick."

I pull away from my notebook, still shoving much-needed food into my mouth.

"It's not your fault, you know that, right?" I ask with a weak smile, ignoring my phone as it vibrates between us.

"I don't think he's used to worrying about you. *I'm* the troublemaker. You're the well-behaved one. Not to say that you still aren't, but you deserve to have some fun," Chrissy says before glancing down. "Speaking of fun." She grabs my phone and points it in front of her face. Who the hell is video calling me? "Hey, Ash!"

I scramble for my phone as she greets him.

"Chrissy!" I call after her.

She dodges my hands, greeting Ash with a wide, mischievous grin.

"Are you ready for this test tomorrow? Something tells me you aren't." She winks at the camera just as I save Ash from her antics.

"Dammit, Chrissy, when did you get so fast?" I double over to catch my breath.

Ash's husky chuckle reaches my ears and causes a silly grin to spread across my face.

I face the camera and try to play it cool. "Ash, what's up?"

Chrissy snorts behind me, earning her a stare I was saving for Zack.

"Seems like you're having fun." Ash is shirtless, lying against his pillows.

My breath catches in my throat. The need to be with him stings my chest like a thousand angry hornets. I open my mouth but stop when I remember I have an audience.

"Be right back, Chrissy." I walk to the bathroom, chuckling when I hear her protest.

"Wait, no! I'll be good!" she calls as I close the door and lean against it.

"Are you okay?" Ash asks.

That lopsided grin pulls on my heartstrings. I sink against the door and sit on the cold tile.

"I miss you," I admit. I'd give anything to be in his arms.

Chapter Thirty-One

"I miss you too."

I bang my head against the door and sigh.

"Did Zack give you an earful?"

I press my lips together and nod. "Yeah, but I gave him one back."

He grabs a pillow and flashes me his dimples. "That's my girl."

Fuck me. I'm all weak-kneed again.

"Is it tomorrow yet?" I ask with a pout.

"Did you study yet?" He arches an eyebrow.

He knows I definitely didn't get to study. How could I? All I can think about is him.

I squint and shake my head.

"Me either. Can't seem to focus for some reason." His words stoke a blazing fire in my chest.

"Wonder why." I suck in my lower lip just as he smirks seductively.

Chrissy bangs on the door, smothering the moment.

"Gwen, I miss you. What happened to bros before hoes?"

Ash arches his eyebrow again and lets out a breathless chuckle. "Did Chrissy just call me a hoe?"

I open my mouth, but she cuts me off.

"I did!" she shouts from behind the door, making us both snicker.

"Guess I better get going. See you tomorrow?" I hold his gaze, struggling to end the call.

"Tomorrow, can't wait." His voice is low and alluring, sending chills all over my legs and between my thighs.

"See you tomorrow, Ash!" Chrissy shouts.

I roll my eyes before hanging up. When I open the door, I'm greeted with a bowl of popcorn.

"Tell me *everything*. I can't wait any longer." She shoves the bowl into my arms and skips to my bed.

Something tells me I won't be able to study tonight either...

I was right. Chrissy and I stayed up until a little after midnight before I passed out on her. I wish I could say I slept well, but I didn't. I tossed and turned, missing the weight of Ash's arm over me, craving his body heat and natural scent. I spend one night with the guy, and I'm addicted. I don't think I'll ever be able to sleep peacefully without him again.

I flip open my biology book and hook my arm through Chrissy's as we get ready to leave for the morning.

"Be my eyes. I need to study for this biology test." I hand her my keys and let her lock up.

"Don't worry. You're safe in my hands." She trips out the door, struggling to regain her balance. With a wide grin, she composes herself. "Don't worry."

She gives me an A-OK gesture before locking the front door.

I just put my life in danger, didn't I?

Chapter Thirty-One

Somehow, we made it, and I didn't get hit by a car or twist an ankle. I focus on the anatomy of the human brain and force myself to memorize every little detail. I have to shake my head more than once, attempting to free my mind of Ash and our night together. I would be lying if I said I wasn't a little disappointed when I didn't wake up to a text from him. It's probably better that way though. I need all my energy and willpower to go toward these two tests today. I study as long as I can, not removing the book from my face until the professor hands the tests out.

Like always, I panicked for no reason. I'm glad my brain took it easy on me today and helped me out. Now, my nerves are a mess for an entirely different reason. I'm not concerned about this next test. At this point, if I fail, I'll make it up next time. That's what Ash has done to me, and I don't hate him for it. The thought of seeing him today excites me. I never knew I could miss someone so much. My heart ached the moment I entered Zack's car yesterday. I'm ready for some relief.

"Ready to see your man?" Chrissy shimmies her shoulders and sticks her tongue out the side of her mouth.

"I think I'm going to throw up," I groan while rubbing my stomach.

"Aww, my girl's in love."

Am I in love? That's way too soon, right? Shit, does Chrissy know something I don't?

"Gwen, relax." She notices my pale skin and shakes me by my shoulders. "I was joking."

Is she though? Does she sense something I don't notice within myself? Chrissy has been in love before. She has the experience I lack. I'm not afraid to acknowledge those feelings for Ash. What I'm afraid of is being the only one who feels them.

When we walk into biochem, Ash isn't there. We take our normal spots, and I go over balancing equations. My leg shakes, and my heart pounds against my eardrums.

Out of the corner of my eye, I see movement. My leg freezes, and I peer to my right, but it's not Ash. Some random guy plants himself in Ash's chair, and I wrinkle my forehead. I turn toward Chrissy, and her confused expression mirrors mine.

"Oh, shit," she mutters. Panic boils in me when her voice drops. "He's sitting in the back, don't look."

I do as she says. I sink farther in my chair and twirl my pen around. I watch her as she shoots daggers at the back of the room.

"You don't think . . . ?" I mumble under my breath as Professor Stilts walks in.

"Don't think like that. Deal with it later."

I nod and try to force the negative thoughts out of my mind. *Why is he sitting in the back? Was I just used and thrown away the next day?* No, I don't believe that. If that were true, then he's an extremely good liar. He wouldn't have called me last night if he was playing some twisted game with me.

Right?

My vision starts to blur when the test is placed on my desk. I pass the stack to the person behind me, not paying attention to anything other than my thoughts.

"Gwen." I hear Chrissy but can't turn my head. "Focus."

Chapter Thirty-One

I suck in a long breath and release it slowly. She's right. I need to pay attention. This is what matters right now. Nothing else should deter me. I'm cool. I can handle this. *Just clear your mind and focus.*

One question at a time. Just take one question at a time. My mind shifts, and I feel myself empty, turning into a husk. The words on the test before me are all I register, and when I turn it in, I walk out with my head held high. I don't bother checking to see if Ash is done or not. I'm going to go home and get ready for my shift at the café.

"Hey, you."

I stumble over my feet when I hear his voice. Slowly, I turn on my heels, finding Ash leaning against the wall. He beckons me toward him with his pointer finger, and without a second thought, my body listens.

When I approach him, he reaches to brush a loose strand of hair behind my ear before smirking at me. "How'd the test go?"

He normally takes his glasses off after class, but he's still wearing them, almost as if to tease me.

"Why didn't you sit next to me?" I mutter.

He caresses my cheek, and I lean into his touch.

"Because neither you nor I would have focused if I did. Were you worried, darling?" he asks in a sweet tone.

"Just a little," I mutter, and he offers me a kind, lopsided smile.

The tension in my shoulders vanishes. All worry and negative thoughts disappear.

"I had a dream about you last night." He twirls my hair around his finger, biting on his lower lip. "If you take me back to your place, I'd love to show you what it was about."

A wave of chills erupts over my spine, weakening my muscles. He leans in and places a light kiss on my lips.

"Okay, let's go," I whisper eagerly.

Knowing he wants me as much as I want him solidifies my feelings. I'm not crazy for thinking he likes me. It's not all in my head. He didn't use me like Zack thinks he did.

I wrap my hand around Ash's and pull him down the hallway. We need to get back to my place within the next five minutes.

If we don't, I'm going to take him to the nearest janitor's closet.

Chapter Thirty-Two

Gwen

Ash inches his hands down my back, pulling on my leggings. He kisses my neck as I struggle with my keys to unlock the door to my apartment building. I manage to get the door open, and we stumble across the foyer in heated giggles.

I run up the stairs, desperate to get Ash in my bed. The desire he unleashes in me is blinding, and only he can satisfy this new need he's awakened. Behind me, Ash takes the stairs two at a time. Right before he reaches me, I shove open my apartment door and am already walking backward toward the bed by the time he strolls over the threshold.

Ash's pupils are blown with lust. After closing the door behind him, he locks the deadbolt. One step at a time, he draws closer to me, and my legs bump against the bed as he closes in. He smiles seductively, trailing his knuckles along my jawline.

"You're so gorgeous." His voice is raspy, dripping with passionate desire.

Starving and needy, his mouth clashes against mine. He tangles his hands in my hair, pulling me against his lips to deepen the kiss. It's somehow both tender and rough, something I didn't think was even possible. Then again, Ash seems to make the impossible very possible.

His thumbs travel down my waist, tugging on my leggings again. "Let's get these off, hmm?"

He sucks on my lower lip before kneeling before me. I kick off my flip-flops as Ash tugs my leggings over my ass and down my legs. When I step out of them, Ash glides his lips up and down my thigh, igniting memories of the other night.

"Ready to see what my dream was about?"

I stare down at him, suddenly aware of what he's about to do.

"I have to go to work in an hour," I whisper.

His dark caramel eyes capture mine, trapping me.

"That's okay." He places his hand on my chest, gently pushing me on the bed. "I only need a couple of minutes."

Oh, fuck me.

Ash takes hold of my legs and rests them on his shoulders, giving him full access. I gulp as my lungs contract.

"Ash?" I mumble.

He groans against my thigh, hooking his thumbs under the edges of my underwear.

"I—uhh." Damn, this is embarrassing.

Sensing my tension, he meets my eyes, his face wrinkled in worry.

"What's wrong?" he asks in a soft tone. I sigh, and his face lights with awe. "Has no one ever done this for you before?"

I cover my face with my hands and shake my head.

His deep, gravelly chuckle vibrates against my thigh. "That's so fucking hot, Gwen." When I lean forward just enough to meet his gaze, he asks, "Do you want me to stop?"

Chapter Thirty-Two

He peppers open-mouthed kisses on my thigh, sucking and leaving tiny kiss-shaped battle scars. If this were anyone else, I would want to stop solely because of the unknown. But this is Ash, and as silly as it sounds in my head, I trust him.

"No," I whimper under his touch and fall back against the cotton sheets.

Ash pulls my panties down, leaving me exposed to the air-conditioned air. I'm quickly warmed by his breath closing in on my core. I inhale deeply as his hands lightly skate up my thighs.

"Gwen?" he moans, and I whimper in response, waiting for him to make his dream a reality. "Are you ready?"

I open my mouth to speak, but I don't get the chance. I choke out a cry of pleasure as he devours my clit with his tongue. Ash grips my thighs, pulling me closer to his mouth, and my back arches when he glides his tongue around me. First up and down, then in small electrifying circles against my swollen bud.

I ball the blanket in my fists and let out a brief shriek of bliss. And when I thought he couldn't give me more pleasure, he finds a way to do so. Puckering his lips, he gently sucks and kisses my clit. My face burns so hot that I wonder if the AC stopped working.

"You taste so good," he grunts, the vibration making my legs spasm. He chuckles against me and holds onto my legs that are propped over his shoulder. "Already? I just got started."

I release a whimper of desire. I need more of him.

His tongue swirls around my folds and glides down toward my entrance. Just as I'm about to beg him to keep going, he sets my world ablaze when he dives one finger deep inside me, pumping in and out.

"You're so fucking tight, sneaky girl."

My toes curl from the intense euphoria of his touch. My body withers under his control. White-hot fireworks build in my lower stomach and ignite along my thighs. My back arches off the bed, and Ash brings me closer to his mouth. Curling his finger, he finds my G-spot and vibrates against it in time with his tongue.

I choke out a moan. "Don't stop," I beg him.

He doesn't stop. He goes harder. My muscles tighten around his finger. Sooner than I want it to, the ecstasy explodes throughout my body, and I writhe against him. The words that slip from my mouth are incoherent. All at once, blood rushes to my head, leaving me dizzy and out of breath. With one final kiss, Ash pulls away.

I'm fighting for air as Ash crashes next to me on the bed. When he kisses me, I taste myself on his lips, and I breathe him in like he's all I need to survive. Rolling on my side, I play with his hair, glancing down and grinning when I notice his erection.

"Did you have fun?" His voice is still flooded with desire.

"I did. Now it's your turn."

His eyes widen when I glide my hand over his length. His breathing becomes choppy, just like mine was a few moments ago. My lips brush over his as I slip his sweats off, leaving him in just his black boxer briefs. He grows under my touch, closing his eyes and grunting as I tighten my grasp around him. Warmth meets my lips as I kiss his cheek one last time. Shifting, I free him from his boxers and start to stroke him.

"Is this okay?" I whisper against his ear.

He grunts and nods, unable to form words.

Not breaking any contact, I shift down and hover over him. I stroke his cock teasingly. He groans, and his hips start to lift.

"You're killing me, Gwen," he mumbles as I kiss below his navel, trailing my lips over the waistband of his boxers.

My mouth waters from the anticipation. I never wanted to do this as badly as I do right now. In one swift, needy motion, I

Chapter Thirty-Two

take him into my mouth. I bob my head in time with my hand, making sure not to leave an inch of him untouched.

"Fuck me."

I manage to place him under the same spell he had me under. He fists his left hand into my hair, wordlessly asking me to go faster. I look up to find him in a state of pure bliss. His eyes are on me, lips slightly parted, his back arches, and his muscles bulge.

I moan against him when his lips slide into a pleased grin.

"Just like that, don't stop."

His cock throbs as I whirl my tongue around it. I quicken my pace and increase the pressure around him.

"I could watch you do this all day. Fuck," he grunts while thrusting his hips again.

I could do this all day. I've only done this a few times, but I never enjoyed it. The way Ash tastes on my tongue is divine, salty with a mix of his pine body soap. I love how he looks at me from this angle, like I'm a goddess that knows every inch of his body.

"That's it, Gwen."

His grip on my hair tightens, and his glasses slide down the bridge of his nose ever so slightly.

I didn't think men were very vocal in bed. I must have hit the damn lottery. I'll never get enough of his noises and pleas of satisfaction.

"I'm gonna come, fuck." His grip loosens, but I don't back away.

I want to take everything he has. *No fuck that.* I *need* to take everything he has.

"Gwen," he warns, but I don't budge.

The pleased yet shocked whimper is all I need to prove that I fucked him senseless.

I've never let a guy finish in my mouth before, but the

desire to taste Ash silenced my nerves. I kiss the side of his cock while swallowing.

I crawl up toward him and lean against his arm, playing with his curly locks and smiling as he fights to breathe.

"I was not expecting that." His grin widens as he wraps his arms around me.

"Was that better than your dream?" I kiss him, something else I could never get tired of.

"*So* much better."

Our lips part, and we flash one another broad, love-drunken smirks.

My eyes glance at the clock on my bedside.

I press my forehead against his chest and groan. "I have to get ready for work."

I snuggle against him, wanting so desperately to call out and stay here in bed with him. He runs his fingertips along my spine, rousing need in me once again. *How the hell does he do that?*

"How about this," he starts. I peek up at him just as he cups my face in his hands. "I'll stay right here, and when you get back, we can cuddle all night and do whatever else we want to each other."

My face brightens at the prospect. "Really?"

He squishes my cheeks and pulls me in for another kiss.

"I don't want to spend another night without you." His grin turns gentle and meaningful.

He tugs on my heart, and I'm starting to realize I may not be alone in the whole *falling in love* thing.

"Did you miss me last night?" I ask while blushing.

He takes in a long, deep breath before sighing. "You have no idea."

Warm, fuzzy frisson explodes through my body. I take his words to my heart and plan on holding them there forever.

Chapter Thirty-Two

"Now, go get ready so you can get that perfect ass back here."

I snicker against his lips before sliding off him. He watches me get changed, and I have to exercise all my willpower not to strip down and jump back into bed.

Chapter Thirty-Three

Ash

Gwen's apartment is one hundred percent her. When she first brought me here, I didn't get to explore as much as I wanted to. I was in a bubble of self-pity, too busy crying over someone who didn't deserve my tears. I love being in Gwen's space, and I want to know more about her. I know she adores cats, fries, and could kick my ass in pretty much any video game. There's more to her, though, and I want to learn everything.

I wouldn't say I'm snooping. I'm just looking through her desk, her bookshelves, her video game collection.

Fuck, I am snooping.

I collapse onto her bed, surrounding myself with her scent. Shoving my face into her pillow, I hum happily.

Great, not only was I snooping, but now I'm acting like a pervert too.

I should have begged her to stay last Sunday. The moment they drove away, I felt like a meteorite plowed right through

Chapter Thirty-Three

me. Why did Zack do that? How did he get my address, anyway? What gave him the right to show up and take her like that? I wanted to fight him. I felt my fists ball, clenching so hard my fingernails dug into my palms. I wasn't treating Gwen like some glorified trash. Never in my life would I ever fuck and dump her. Did he think those were my intentions?

When I stormed back inside, Max was leaning against the back of the couch. His jaw was clenched, and his brows were furrowed in concern.

"Gonna tell me what just happened?" he asked as he crossed his arms. "I thought you said I was going to like her."

"That wasn't her fault. Zack came here looking for trouble." I rubbed my palms against my eyes to ease the strain.

"Was that guy her boyfriend?"

Both of them have told me they are nothing more than friends. Brother and sister, if you will. Do friends who are that close act like this? Do I need to be worried? No, I trust Gwen, end of story.

"No, he's just an overprotective asshole." I took hold of the railing, needing to be back in my room. At least there, I could still feel her presence.

"Just be careful, Ash."

I took the stairs two at a time, needing to breathe her in again.

But it wasn't the fucking same. My room was empty. My bed felt too big for one person.

I rolled on the side where she had slept, missing every inch of her.

I couldn't think straight or keep my focus. I knew she thought she was doing us both a favor by leaving, but I know now that neither of us was able to study regardless.

And now I'm in her bed, excited to see her when she's done her shift at the café.

My heart spikes when my phone goes off. I answer the video call without hesitation.

"Miss me already?" I ask while rolling on my side, positioning myself in a way to tease her.

Her cheeks color rosy pink, making my stomach flip.

"You have no idea," she whispers.

How does she manage to turn me on just by talking?

"Ow, Pickles!" The camera shakes as she fights that little ball of energy off, who I can only assume is chomping on her ankle.

I smirk and snort. How did I get so lucky? I can't help but admire her carefree smile. I need to make her mine.

"Ash?"

I shake myself from my thoughts.

Chapter Thirty-Three

Gwen composes herself, positioning Pickles front and center of the camera. "I think Pickles misses you."

He closes in on the lens, sniffing that little pink kitten nose all over her phone. Just when I open my mouth, he takes a chomp at the camera lens.

"Wish I could say the same," I say with a fake grin.

Gwen chuckles, placing Pickles back on the floor.

"Gwen, who are you talking to?" another voice asks.

The redhead I saw before comes into view, beaming when he sees who's filling her phone screen.

"Is that Mr. Biochem? Nice to meet you. I'm—"

Gwen cuts him off, blushing feverishly. I've heard that nickname before, and every time I hear it, I grin.

"That's my boss, Ryan." She pushes him away, making sure to keep him out of the frame.

"So, Mr. Biochem?" I waggle my eyebrows up and down, teasing her.

She opens her mouth, struggling to find words to explain the nickname.

I lean in closer, making sure she hears my whisper. "Dare you to call me that in bed."

Her mouth hangs agape, making me chuckle.

"Okay, I actually called you for a reason," she giggles, brushing a loose strand of hair behind her ear. "Chrissy's going to stop by. She said she needs to see me when I get home. Is that okay?"

"Only if you promise I get you all to myself when she leaves."

Her neck flushes as I charm her. "That's a guarantee." She winks at me before hanging up.

I think I may be rubbing off on her, and it's fucking adorable.

When Chrissy lets herself in, I'm sprawled on Gwen's bed,

holding one of her blankets against my chest. My eyes flick from my phone when she closes the door behind her. Chrissy beams, jumping up and down at the sight of me.

"What's up, Chrissy?" I ask as she leaps on the bed, landing on her knees beside me.

She bobs up and down before throwing her arms around me.

"Thank you." She shakes me around, drawing out the "you" in her gratitude.

"For what?" I ask with a snicker.

She pulls back, holding me by my shoulders. "Because of you, my Gwen is now a woman. You're a gift to this world, Ash Waylen."

I squint, slightly confused. I'm touched, don't get me wrong, but I wouldn't consider myself a *gift to the world.*

"What do you mean? I thought she wasn't a vir—"

She cuts me off before I finish. "Oh, she wasn't. But that girl deserved a good time. Which you gave her." She winks at me before letting me go. "You're a good guy, Ash. I don't let my best friend go off with just anyone. Keep that in mind." She taps the side of her head before backing away.

I can't help but feel good after a compliment like that. I thought people would look at me differently after the breakup with Alex. I'm not a bad guy, but I don't know what Alex was saying about me behind my back.

"Maybe you can tell your brother that?" I ask.

Chrissy looks up from her phone with a tired smile. "Don't mind him. He's just an ass."

I sit up, leaning against the pillows.

"Do you remember Roselyn? The real Roselyn." Genuine wonder fills her tone.

"What do you mean? She was always nice to me."

She sighs, sounding defeated and tired. "Of course, she

Chapter Thirty-Three

was. You were Ash Waylen. But to Gwen and I, she was a total rich bitch. Do you know how many times she made Gwen cry? She teased that shy girl relentlessly."

I scrunch my face in response and curl my hands around the blanket on the bed.

"Does Zack know this?" I ask through gritted teeth.

"Yes. He was the one who comforted Gwen when I wasn't there. I don't understand. And now, he won't talk to me. It's fucking weird. I know we seem like we're not close, but we are. I tell him everything, and he used to do the same. Now? He treats me like an outsider." The pain that radiates from her usual bubbly self is worrisome.

"Does Gwen know how Zack has been acting?"

She shakes her head solemnly in response. "That's why I'm here. She knows he's been seeing Roselyn, but she doesn't know how he's been acting. I need to tell her so we can fix it." She clicks her tongue. "I take that back. She witnessed it firsthand during the car ride back home the other day."

"Was it that bad?" The idea of Zack yelling at Gwen doesn't sit right with me.

"It was nothing she couldn't handle." Chrissy smirks. "I knew she was strong, but I got to witness it firsthand. Zack said, 'fuck you,' and you know what she said?"

I sit up straighter, needing to hear just how much of a badass my girl is.

"She said, 'No thanks, I've had my fill.'"

I double over in hysterics, imagining Zack's face upon hearing those words, and Gwen's tone when she said it. Chrissy falls over, nearly slipping off the bed.

We're still laughing our asses off when Gwen strolls through the front door. Her puzzled look only makes Chrissy and I hold our middles as we laugh louder.

"What did I miss?" Gwen asks curiously, and Chrissy actu-

Forever Crushed

ally falls off the bed from laughing so hard. "Chrissy!" Gwen rushes over to her.

Chrissy pulls herself from the floor, wiping tears from her eyes.

"No thanks, I've had my fill!" she cries before falling over again, and when Gwen's eyes meet mine, I give her a thumbs-up.

"I'm so confused..."

When Chrissy and I gather our wits, we let Gwen in on the joke. It was a clear "aha" moment for her, and when it dawned on her, I let out another round of laughter.

Gwen brightens around Chrissy. I knew Gwen had a funny side, but I didn't get to witness it in person yet, not like this. Their friendship reminds me of what Brandon and I had.

"That was the PG version. Want to know what I really wanted to say?" Gwen teases.

Chrissy's mouth hangs open in anticipation. Gwen meets my gaze, and I grow antsy over what she might say.

Our time together Saturday was, simply put, out of this world. I never felt that way with a woman before. She changed my perspective and completely redefined it.

A wicked, playful grin spreads across her lips, making me thankful I still hold the blanket over my chest.

"Never mind, I think I'll keep that secret to myself."

Chrissy pouts in response, but Gwen completely ignores it. Her eyes burn into mine, matching how I'm feeling at this moment.

Completely and utterly turned on.

I could never tire of Gwen. She's unlike anyone I've ever been with. They don't even compare to her. I worry I'm becoming addicted to how she feels and, more recently, how she tastes.

"I'm still here." Chrissy breaks the silence, forcing me to

Chapter Thirty-Three

drop my eyes from Gwen. "Bunch of horny teenagers in here. Ugh, so jealous." She hangs upside down off the bed, dangling her hair along the floor. "Got any friends you can hook me up with, Ash?"

"Actually, do you remember Miles Summers?" I ask.

Gwen makes a funny face, her eyes wide, and a smile pulls on her lips, but she tries to hide it.

Chrissy sits straight up and points at me. "Miles Summers?" she asks with a hint of excitement.

"Summer fling, Miles Summers?" Gwen pretends to cough, trying to camouflage her question.

Gwen earns herself a punch in the arm, but karma gets Chrissy back just as fast. As soon as the punch is thrown, Chrissy falls off the bed.

Again.

They fill the room with laughter, and this time, I feel out of the loop. I don't care though. Their laughter and beaming faces are contagious, and even though I don't know why they're giggling, I join in.

Happy to feel a part of something again.

Chapter Thirty-Four

Gwen

It's not like Chrissy to be upset. When she asked if she could hang out at my place until I got back from work, it was a no-brainer. Plus, I knew Ash wouldn't mind. Chrissy's my best friend, and she needed a safe place. I trusted Ash wouldn't make her uncomfortable.

I already knew Zack was being an absolutely uncensored asshole. I didn't know he was treating Chrissy like an outsider. I don't know why either. Was this something Roselyn contributed to? Or something different altogether? Either way, there's no excuse for his actions. He'll come clean whether he likes it or not.

I'm glad Chrissy told me what's been happening. Now we can figure this out and start fixing whatever is happening with our brother.

"Miles Summers, maybe that's who I need right now." Chrissy's face lights up. "It would piss Zack off."

"Dare me to call him?" Ash wiggles his eyebrows.

"Don't you dare." She points at him like a mother would a misbehaving child. He turns his comical gaze my way. "Gwen, don't let him control you!" She grabs me by my shoulders, shaking me violently.

"Chrissy, you already know my balance is fucked up!" She lets me go, and I fall back on the bed on my side.

Ash's grin grows, exposing his dimples.

I ignore Chrissy's warning; he pulls me in, and I let him.

"Do it, Ash."

He bites his tongue, flashing us his phone screen. Already talking to Miles.

Chrissy's face goes still, paler than a fresh sheet of snow. Chrissy has had a thing for Miles since high school, like I had for Ash. The only difference is that she and Miles dated last summer. Of course, she knew he attended the same university as us. She sought him out, and he fell right into her charm.

"Hi, Miles." She waves toward the camera shyly.

That's how I know she still has a thing for him.

"Good to see you, Chrissy." Miles chuckles as Ash points his phone right at her.

He watches them interact while I take him in, needing to memorize how he looks right now. Ash's hair is disheveled, like he was lying in my bed before I got back. He's holding one of my blankets close to his chest, and that smirk? It'll be the death of me.

That's the first thing I noticed all those years ago. No, not the dimples. It was the way his lips curled, full and shaded blush pink. How his eyes sparked, never leaving who he was talking to. He lit up a room without ever needing to walk into it. If he was there, you just knew.

How could I have gotten so lucky? How did I, Gwen Roman, capture this man's gaze? How the hell do I still have it? His eyes move back to me, as if he knows the questions that are running through my head. With one look, I feel completely and utterly done for. My heart sings, my stomach flutters, and my lungs forget how to convert oxygen to carbon dioxide.

"I think I need to go, Miles. They're looking at each other that way again."

I dart my eyes back to Chrissy and open my mouth to apologize, but Miles talks over me.

"Would you want to go grab something to eat? With me?" Oh, like he had to add that last bit in.

Chrissy jumps up, already running out the door. "Thanks for the hookup, Ash. See you guys later!" And just like that, she's gone.

Ash shows me his phone, indicating Miles already hung up.

"Why did they break up, anyway?" Ash asks.

Now isn't that a story . . .

"Love is a mysterious thing, especially for Chrissy. Don't tell her I said anything, but she gets scared easily."

Chrissy broke up with Miles because she felt herself falling too hard, and she didn't think he felt the same. She loves love, but when it's actually happening? She runs away from it.

I stand and kick my shoes off, sighing once my bare feet land on the cool hardwood floor. I walk over to my dresser and open my shirt drawer. Seeing Ash's tee again, I unfold it and show it to him.

"Want this back?"

He stretches along the bed, flexing his biceps.

"Aw, you still have it? It's almost like you have a thing for me or something." He throws a wink my way, alerting the butterflies within me. His breath hitches in his chest as he trails his eyes over my body. "Put it on for me."

His stare hoods with desire, his eyes devouring every inch of my body, not so subtly lingering over my curves. Slowly, I unbutton my jeans and step out of them.

Chapter Thirty-Four

"Haven't you had enough of me?" I place my hands on the hem of my shirt, waiting for a response before pulling it off.

"Fuck no."

He makes my skin itch, needing him on me. I don't care if it's under or on top. I just need to feel his strength and pressure. I take my shirt off agonizingly slow. His eyes light my skin on fire. After tossing my work shirt on the floor, I reach around my back to unhook my bra.

Before undoing the clasps, I turn around, snickering as Ash groans, "You tease."

I pull the shirt over my head. I didn't get to wash it yet, so I'm covered in his scent and flashbacks from last Saturday. When I release my hair from the collar, it flows down my back. I turn around to face him, meeting a different expression than the one I saw earlier.

"What's wrong?" I climb into bed, positioning myself over his lap.

He places his hands on my hips, leaning back against the pillows. His gaze softens, making me feel light and fuzzy.

"Tell me you're mine, Gwen." His words collide straight into my heart.

Ash wants me to be his. *Me? Did I hear that right?*

His thumbs massage my hips, loving and yearning. I rest my forehead against his.

"I was yours the first moment I saw you." I press my lips to his.

Our kiss is timid, like we haven't kissed until this point. He pulls my lower lip between his lips tenderly. Before I'm ready, he pulls away, leaving me breathless and flushed.

"I think I'm falling for you."

His confession is unreal. There is no way he's saying this right now.

"Tell me I'm crazy because I feel like I am." He chuckles, and his cheeks blush.

"If you're crazy, then I must be as well," I whisper. Ash glides his fingers along my lower back, right above the hem of my underwear. "Tell me this isn't a dream, Ash."

"If it is, never wake me up."

I slip my hands into his untamed curls, needing to be closer to him.

"You and me." He pleads between our locked lips. "Promise me."

I wrap my arms around his neck, brushing my nose against his. "I promise. I'm not going anywhere."

He gently lowers me onto my back, propping his elbows above my shoulders. His eyes bore into mine, full and dark like a faraway galaxy.

"How did you capture my heart so quickly?" He trails his knuckles over my cheeks and jawline.

"How did you keep mine for so long?"

Chapter Thirty-Five

Ash

I can't believe she said it back. I was worried my confession would scare her away. But I couldn't hold it in any longer. I had to make her my girlfriend. That was a plan set in stone. I couldn't go another moment knowing she wasn't officially mine. My feelings for her are growing, bubbling in my chest, begging for release.

And when I said it? Her eyes lit up, reminding me of wild ocean waves. She beckoned me on the first day of the fall semester, slowly embracing me with her warm and comforting light. I don't need air anymore. As long as she is with me, I'll survive.

Right now? I just want to be with her. I don't care what we're doing. I just love being in her presence. Whether we're talking, lying in each other's arms, laughing, or teasing one another.

I was in a dark place before Gwen. Alex ravaged me, and then tossed me out like Tuesday's trash. With Gwen, I feel seen and cherished. She carried the torch that freed me from my darkness.

I glide my thumbs over her cheekbones, brushing her wavy hair to the side. She cups my cheek, and I lean against it.

"Would you just want to cuddle and watch some true crime?" I ask, wanting to hold her and never let go.

"That sounds perfect," she says with a smile, embracing me with unspoken love. "To be honest, I'm kind of sore, anyway."

We both grin and chuckle. We've been pretty active the past few days. I could use the break too.

She turns the TV on and scrolls through titles until she finds one she's content with. She rolls over to face the TV, letting me move closer, draping my arm around her waist. She fits so perfectly against me, something I didn't think was possible. How could two human beings fit together so wonderfully?

"Want to order some food?" She perks up at my question, offering me her phone instantly. "That's my girl."

She chews on the side of her mouth, flipping over to face me.

"I love when you call me that." Her nose wiggles, and she ruffles my hair. "Now, get to it, Mr. Biochem. You know what I like."

Gwen Roman winks at me, earning herself a mountain of fries.

Chapter Thirty-Six

Gwen

My damn phone won't stop vibrating. Ash shifts beside me and pulls me closer to his chest. I'm not sure how, but he makes me feel safe and like I'm going to be pushed off a cliff at the same time.

The blue screen blinds me as I flip my phone over. I groan at seeing a bunch of missed texts from Zack. What the hell does this jackass want?

> Hey, are you up?
>
> I'm sorry about the other day.
>
> Are you free to talk tomorrow?

"Who's texting you?" Ash's voice soothes my irritation.

I text Zack back just to get him to shut up.

> Fine, just please stop texting me. I'm trying to sleep.

I place my phone far out of sight before flipping onto my back. Ash groans sleepily, leaning forward to kiss my cheek.

"Should I be worried?" He slides his hand down my sides, slipping underneath my underwear. His breath is raspy from both lack of sleep and desire. "What's my girl thinking about right now?"

His fingers hover above my clit. How did he discover my weak spots so quickly? Ash bites my earlobe, trailing his tongue down my neck. My chest tightens, and every little muscle in my body clenches impatiently.

"You." Nothing else crosses my mind.

He lifts himself on top of me, not moving his fingers. Which is driving me absolutely crazy.

"Gwen." Ash gives me a drunken, lopsided smile, moving his hand from my core to underneath my shirt. Lifting my tee, he kisses my stomach, moving to my breast. When he flicks his eyes up at me, he's in an unrestrained state of passion and need. "Tell me what you want." His hand engulfs my waist, leaving me flustered and dizzy. "I'll do anything."

I bend my leg and rest my knee against him. "You, I want you," I whimper.

The moment his mouth is on me, I sigh, already needing more.

He devours me with his mouth, flicking his tongue over my nipple. Chills roll over my spine, shooting between my thighs. Ash's thumb brushes over my other nipple, following the same rhythm as his tongue.

When he pulls his mouth from my body to position himself on his knees, I almost whimper. After slipping his pants off, he drops them to the floor. He stays there for a moment, just watching me, inching his eyes over my exposed body, leading up to my chest.

I pull my shirt over my shoulders, then sit up to remove his. I need to feel his skin against mine. The moment I do, my lips land on his pecs, and my hands explore every muscle I can reach. I pull on his boxer's waistband, urging him to pin me down and take me.

"Oh, wait one second." He rolls over and reaches for the table on the other side of the bed.

I groan, making sure he heard me. I don't think he understands the need he's stirred within me. If he doesn't get back here right now, I will chase him.

When he returns, he pushes his glasses up his nose.

"Fuck me," I moan.

He pulls on my ankles so we're face to face.

"Is that what you want?" He hooks his thumb on the hem of my underwear, pulling them down.

I bite my lower lip, nodding vigorously.

"You have to say it." His fingers find themselves on my swollen clit again.

"Please, Ash."

This time, he doesn't tease me. He glides his finger over me, rubbing in gentle circles.

"Fuck, Gwen, you really like it when I wear my glasses, don't you? You're so fucking wet."

A slight whimper escapes my lips in response, and it sends him right over the edge.

He frees himself from his boxers, and within a matter of seconds, I feel his length against me. He meets my gaze, and I gasp when he presses his cock inside me.

He growls when his lips touch mine, the rumble vibrating against my chest, echoing within me. After pulling out ever so slightly, he plunges back into me again. The movement makes me quiver, and my body tenses from the growing need. Our bare chests press together, his muscles firm against my softness, and he's smoldering hot. His lips don't stop moving over mine, tugging and playing, never getting enough.

"Tell me you're mine." His words float into my ear.

"I'm yours." My breathing matches his as he pumps inside me.

His cock rams into me on repeat. A pool of warmth spreads into my core, and my body sings.

"Say it again," he orders.

"I'm all yours."

He growls as I cry through the building haze. "That's my girl."

With one final thrust, my body is overwhelmed by blinding and searing tremors from the climax. Ash slams into me rougher, and he holds my hips steady. His eyes travel from my eyes to my breasts, and he groans darkly.

"I can feel you squeezing my cock," he hums.

Unable to form a single word, I nod.

"Come for me again." He thrusts into me, making me dizzy.

"Fuck," I cry as the blissful tension reappears.

Chills creep up my thighs, settling in my lower stomach. One muscle tightens at a time, squeezing the base of my spine. Ash nuzzles against my shoulder, gently sucking on my neck.

"Come for me again. Come all over my cock."

Reaching down, Ash works his thumb over my clit, rubbing fast circles while hastening his pace. Wrapping my legs around him tighter, my chest heaves from the building pleasure.

The pressure in my center explodes. I cry incoherently as Ash presses his lips against mine, taking every sound that leaves my mouth.

"That's it, give me everything," Ash grunts, his voice deepening before he releases a groan himself.

Chapter Thirty-Six

"Yes. Yes. Yes. *Fuck* yes!" I kiss him feverishly as he curses.

His hips slow as he fills me. And I feather my fingers down his back, kissing the crook of his neck as he falls back onto the bed.

He's reduced me to a puddle. I've never come twice in a row, especially in rapid succession like that. Ash has left me pleasantly sore and wrung out.

Reaching over, I fiddle with his glasses and softly chuckle. He remembered the comment I made about them. He's learned how to send me straight from being composed to utterly helpless.

"You'd make a very good librarian," I tease.

A smirk tugs on his lips, and he lets out a breathless chuckle. "I better take these off before I get you going again."

I take them off for him and place them on my bedside table. "Too late," I snicker.

He pulls me in, tickling my sides. I fight against his hands, begging him to stop since I couldn't breathe to begin with. I fall into his embrace, letting him cradle me and kiss my cheek.

"What am I going to do with you?" he asks, his tone deep with pure ecstasy.

I smile, knowing what I want to say but also knowing I don't have the nerve to say it.

"You have time to figure that out." I place his hand over my lips, kissing it gingerly. "Because I'm not going anywhere."

Chapter Thirty-Seven

Ash

"Except to the bathroom." She jumps from my arms and leaps out of bed.

The sight of her bare ass dashing across the room makes me smirk. I toss my shirt at her, and it lands directly on her head.

"Put that on. I don't think I can handle another round today."

She sticks her tongue out at me before closing the door. Sitting up, I reach for my boxers and sweatpants. Just as I'm pulling my pants back on, her phone goes off again. *Who the hell keeps texting her?* I vaguely remember asking her, but I don't think she told me.

I reach over and flip her phone over.

Fucking Zack Willows.

> I'll see you tomorrow. We have a lot to talk about.

I can't help but roll my eyes. Who does he think he is?

Chapter Thirty-Seven

Texting my girlfriend at one in the morning? What do they have to talk about, anyway? He's the one being an asshole, not her.

There was a time when I trusted Zack. He and I weren't close in high school, but I knew he was a decent guy. He looked out for his friends and stood up for the people he loved. He was loyal and kind. I don't know what happened between when I first saw him in the cafeteria and now because today's Zack is a complete prick.

I wonder if he's enjoying treating Gwen this way. Did he think he rescued her last Sunday? Like I was the guy she needed saving from? The last time I checked, she needed protection from him and his dicky persona. I wonder if it has anything to do with Roselyn. She's a bitch in her own right. Could she be affecting Zack's personality? How would someone even do that, anyway?

He messages her again, and I feel envy boil in my chest even though I don't want it to.

I miss you.

It's only been two fucking days! How can he *miss* her?

No. *Simmer down, Ash.* Zack's just a friend, a brother even. Nothing romantic ever sparked between him and Gwen. Every time I ask, they say the same thing. Besides, I trust Gwen.

I trusted Alex too . . .

The walls around my heart rebuild. I try to demolish them the moment they start, but I can't control it. The thought of losing Gwen is too much to bear. I can't even think of it. I put her phone back down just as she opens the door.

Seeing her eases my racing thoughts. I have nothing to worry about. Just look at her. This woman is a masterpiece, a modern-day queen.

Her expression softens when she sees me, her shoulders relaxing and her eyes sparkling. She warms my heart with one look.

"Are you okay?" She closes the space between us, wrapping her arms around my neck.

I love the way her nose crinkles when she smiles and how naturally pink her cheeks and lips are. How her hair curls at the ends and wraps around my fingers.

"I'm perfect." I press my lips against hers.

Gwen's touch is like magic. I crave her the moment we part, and when we kiss, the universe stops just for us. I don't need to worry about her. I need to learn to shut my brain up.

"You made me sleepy." Her lips smile against mine.

I let out an airy chuckle. "Let's get you to bed," I say as I pull on her hand and lead us back into our cozy world.

Lifting the blanket, I hold it open for her. She climbs in, snuggling right against my chest. I tangle my hands in her hair, breathing her in.

"Gwen?"

"Hmm?" Her voice is sweet and sleepy. Clearly tired from today and everything that happened.

It doesn't feel like today was the day of the biochem test. That seems like a distant memory. Of course, I remember all the events that occurred after.

"I'm happy you're mine," I confess.

She buries herself into me, snuggling against my bare chest. I play with her hair, soothing her to sleep. We both have classes tomorrow, but I don't care if I'm tired. I need to make sure she's comfortable and well rested before I succumb to my fatigue. I press my lips against her forehead.

"I trust you," I whisper against her skin just as she drifts off to sleep.

Chapter Thirty-Eight

Gwen

I don't want to deal with Zack and his new bullshit. I do, however, owe it to him. Zack and I have been through a lot. I can't count how many times he's cheered me up, given me a shoulder to cry on, and protected me from mean words or bullies. I don't approve of his recent actions or behavior, but everyone deserves to share their side of the story.

I just hope his side doesn't earn him a punch in the face.

I'm starting to really like this new and improved Gwen. At the beginning of September, I was shy, a pushover. October will finally be here tomorrow, and with it, a new and changed woman. I'm not sure who I owe this change to. Did Chrissy finally rub off on me? Giving me the best parts of her? Or was it Ash? Did he solely pop the bubble I surrounded myself in? It could even be Zack.

Maybe I can give myself some credit too.

I've been through some shit in life. My parents are a good place to start. Because of their lack of guidance, I learned to take care of myself at a very young age. They pushed me without even knowing it. I appreciate them for it, nothing else though.

High school was another challenge. I was looked over. I was the quiet girl that Chrissy dragged along, the one everyone thought was mute. I fell into books and daydreams; there, I had courage and conviction.

The first time I saw Ash, my life changed forever. I was in the social studies class, reading while waiting for the period to start. He strolled in, book bag slung over one shoulder. He was by himself, yet he still wore a lopsided grin. My stomach rolled and tilted the moment my eyes landed on him. I sank in my seat, not wanting him to notice me but also hoping he would.

He took over my thoughts and consumed my fantasies, leaving no room for anyone else to occupy my mind. I would walk the halls looking for him. Needing to see that smile one more time. Just when his image faded, he would reappear. Reigniting the crush repeatedly.

In junior year of high school, we shared the same biology class, and, boy, was that a struggle. That was the year Chrissy caught on to my secret crush. She saw me gazing at him in the lunchroom.

He was the center of everyone's attention. He was kind and didn't confine himself to one specific clique or group. Everyone wanted to share his space, just one glance or moment of acknowledgment. He had that effect on people. Especially me.

I didn't dare try to talk to him, though, Chrissy tried her best to hype me up. There was no point. All the girls in school liked him, and I was no one special. I was shy and looked down upon. Why would he waste any of his precious time on me?

That all changed senior year.

I don't think he remembers, but we shared another class together. English 103 revolved around old texts and stories,

Chapter Thirty-Eight

specifically from the medieval era. Chrissy and Zack were in the same class too, which was rare. As always, I placed myself by Chrissy. Ash sat on the other side of the room, never glancing my way.

Until Zack pulled a classic one on me.

That was the year the tackling and bear hugs started. I remember how Zack's face lit up the moment he saw me. He charged toward Chrissy and me. I had no idea the embarrassment he would bestow upon me that day. Quite literally, he yanked me from my seat, picked me up, and spun around in place saying, "There she is!"

When he dropped me back on my feet, my cheeks flushed, and I got light-headed. I felt eyes on me, which didn't sit right in me. As I sat back down, Zack plopped into the desk behind me. I twirled my pen around my fingers, smirking when Chrissy and Zack started to go back and forth.

"How come you never greet me like that?" I could hear the pout in her voice.

"Because you get on my damn nerves, woman."

I giggled at his comment. He could always make me laugh and feel better about myself. When the teacher walked in, I looked to the left, and when I found his eyes on me, it was over.

Look at me now. I wouldn't consider myself a badass, but the younger me just might. I've gotten better at standing up for myself and going after what I want.

True, I didn't go after Ash. He was the one who talked to me. What I did, though, was very unlike me. I didn't hide or cower from his gaze. I stepped in front of it, claiming my attraction and daring to hope we could be something more.

I walk around campus with my head slightly higher, still needing to watch the pathway though. I don't trust my ankles and the cobblestone one bit.

I see Zack before he notices me. A deep sigh releases from

my chest at the sight of him. I'm not in the mood for a lecture, and honestly? I'm not going to let him give me one. He seems lax, almost chill.

When she appears, I almost trip over my own two feet. I witness the moment his posture stiffens, worry creasing his forehead.

"Where were you?" I hear Zack ask cautiously.

"The library," Roselyn offers innocently as she wraps her arms around his neck.

"Don't lie to me, Roselyn. I saw you with that guy again."

And that's when the wind stops blowing.

"What guy?" she asks while kissing his cheek.

"The same guy I saw you clinging onto yesterday." His once shimmering blue eyes are lifeless, and a rage of fire ignites in my gut.

"I don't know what you're talking about," she responds coolly.

I'm gripping my book bag's straps so hard my knuckles turn white.

"I know what I saw," Zack says while untangling Roselyn from his body.

"Are you crazy?" Roselyn responds with a laugh, and that's when I take action.

"Hey, guys," I greet, faking excitement.

"Hey, Gwen." Zack's eyes land on me, and relief washes over his features.

"I don't have time for this. Text me when you're done being a psycho." Roselyn stomps away like a child throwing a tantrum.

"What was that about?" I ask, pretending like I didn't just overhear the blatant gaslighting.

"Nothing, just a disagreement." The look that settles over his face isn't normal.

Chapter Thirty-Eight

The rage I felt minutes ago cools, the need to comfort him taking its place.

"What did you want to talk about?" I ask, knowing he needs a distraction.

He shoves his hands in his pockets, staring at the ground. "I want to apologize. What I did last Sunday was unacceptable, and I shouldn't have talked to you the way I did." He tilts his head to meet my gaze.

His hair shines, and streaks of blue glint under the sun. I let out another deep release of air to relax. I was ready to go at it again.

"You were kind of a jerk."

He looks down at his feet again. He's being hard on himself. He feels bad. Never in his life has he ever spoken to me like that, nor have I ever talked to him that way. We were both jerks. He was more of a jerk, but still.

"I'm sorry I freaked out too. We both got pretty heated," I apologize.

A smile creeps across his face, and the entire conversation takes a turn. "I can't believe you told me to go fuck myself, like five times."

He chuckles, and I snort before smiling.

"I only said that after you called me *missy*."

We both laugh, and everything starts to feel normal. Silence settles over us, and I'm about to say goodbye when Zack speaks up again.

"We can talk about anything, right?"

I nod, too nervous to say anything.

"I'm worried about you."

Why does he keep saying that? What have I done to warrant his concern?

"I don't understand."

The look he gives me unravels the tightly wound ball of

nerves I've been holding inside. Zack chews the side of his mouth, and his eyes dart around our surroundings.

"Just tell me," I grumble.

"Is Ash acting okay? After the breakup with Alex, I mean."

"He's fine. What happened between us wasn't a rebound, if that's what you're worried about."

Zack nods, and his shoulders slump forward.

I get why he's worried. Zack always has my best interests at heart, and he doesn't want me to get hurt, but that's the risk I'm willing to take. I like Ash, and I feel myself falling for him. I'm not going to throw that all away just because Zack's—unnecessarily—worried. He can't protect me forever.

"I'm a big girl, Zack. For once, let me take care of myself."

His sigh is one I recognize. It's the same one he gives Chrissy time and time again.

"Fine, on one condition." He opens his arms, and that silly Zack grin returns. "We have to be friends again."

I jump into his arms and let him swing me around. I'm glad I have someone like him in my life. I know he cares about my well-being, and I never have to worry about him being dishonest with me.

True, he can be a major asshole when he wants to be. If this were anyone else, I wouldn't have forgiven them so easily. He's got some shaping up to do, and he'll need to beg for Chrissy's forgiveness. He'll do the right thing though. He always does.

When he places me back on the ground, I can't fight the words bubbling up in my throat any longer. "Is she treating you well?"

"Who? Roselyn?" Zack asks, and I nod.

With a disgruntled groan, he runs his fingers through his hair and looks toward the sky.

"Something doesn't feel right. Any time I try to confront

Chapter Thirty-Eight

her about my feelings, she calls me crazy and brushes it to the side."

"Zack—" I start but stop myself, trying to piece together the words I want to say as delicately as I can. "Trust your gut. And know that you have support from your friends, no matter what. All you have to do is ask."

"Thanks, Gwen. But I'll be okay." Zack smiles sweetly, but I can see behind it.

He's hiding something deeper than he's letting on. And it's breaking my heart.

Chapter Thirty-Nine

Ash

Undiluted jealousy boils in my veins. She's in his arms. Fucking Zack Willows. They've known each other their entire lives. I get that. What I care about are his arms around her and the smile that floats across his face whenever she's near. It doesn't seem like one a brother would give.

I hate that these thoughts are running through my head. I don't want them to. I didn't even expect to see them on campus today. Gwen and I made plans to hang out at her place again, but that was for later tonight. When I saw her walking toward the pavilion, I started for her right away. Until I saw she was walking toward Zack. I halted and hid in the shadows like a creep, needing to see what transpired between them.

Is this how fucked up I am? Still? Did my parents and Alex really leave this much of a lasting impression on me? I want to trust Gwen. I've told myself over and over that I could. Deep down, though, in the pit of my chest, I feel it brewing. I'm

Chapter Thirty-Nine

waiting for her to misstep. I don't want her to, but I'm waiting for something to happen.

Before Gwen, I was an emotional wreck, faking how I felt on the outside. I had an image to uphold. I'm Ash Waylen, all around nice, decent guy. On the inside, though, I'm Ash Waylen, a distrustful and heartbroken jackass.

I wasn't always this way. In high school, I was carefree. I strolled the halls knowing who I was. My confidence was evident in every room I walked in. I knew all eyes were on me. I knew every girl craved my attention. I didn't take advantage of it though. I only dated a handful of girls in my life and genuinely cared for each one.

None of them live up to Gwen Roman.

After Gwen, I'm a new person. I stand a little taller. My heart doesn't ache because of Alex every damn second. When I look at her, the entire world changes into something lighter and more lasting. So why are these feelings appearing? I don't want to be jealous. I don't like this feeling sitting in my chest. She can hug a friend. *Stop it, dammit.*

I don't breathe until they part. I don't notice I balled my hands into fists until they step away from one another. The light doesn't return until I see her face. I'll be with her later. Maybe then I'll feel a bit more secure.

Right now, I have other things to tend to. I've been slacking on my coding project, and I need to get some of it done before I get distracted again. Not that Gwen is a bad distraction. If it were up to me, I'd let her distract me all day long. She wouldn't want me to fall behind in my classes, though, just like I don't want her to either.

The first day of October is tomorrow, and the trees have started to change color, making Castle Brook University look even more magical. The wind is crisp, and the atmosphere smells cleaner. I remember Gwen telling me her favorite holiday is Halloween. I'm going to have to try to do something special for her. She deserves it, that's for sure.

The computer lab is on the farther side of campus, a bit far off from the main centers. That doesn't mean this building isn't busy—plenty of students are majoring in computers and technology. The building is modern. When they designed it, they tried to make it similar to the other historic-looking centers on campus—gray brick with a fancy entryway. Inside are vast, spacious rooms, different compared to the other buildings. The center is three stories tall, and the lab is on the top floor.

I opt for the stairs, taking two at a time.

It doesn't come as a surprise when I enter the lab and see Miles. He's a year ahead of me, but we're working on the same project. He doesn't notice when I approach or obnoxiously settle in the chair next to him. He's too busy tapping away on his phone, texting who I can only assume is Chrissy.

"Miles," I whisper.

No reaction.

"Miles," I whisper again.

Still nothing.

"Miles." I grab his shoulder and give him a firm shake.

"Fuck, dude." His hand flies to his chest, making him drop his phone. "When did you get here?"

I tap my login info on the keyboard without looking at the screen.

"How was your date last night?" I raise my eyebrows and smirk at him, earning myself a scoff before he picks up his phone and goes back to texting. "Not gonna tell me? All right, that's cool. I see how it is."

I turn to my screen and load the coding program. I tap away at the keyboard, seeing Miles smile at his phone screen in my peripheral.

"It was good, man. Thanks for the encouragement."

Chapter Thirty-Nine

I smile, giving him a tiny form of acknowledgment. I get into the zone, typing away furiously.

"You won't be thanking me once Zack finds out," I say bluntly.

Miles grunts beside me. "I don't think we need to worry about him. He's too wrapped up in Roselyn. And I mean that literally."

My lips curl. Ever since Chrissy told me how Roselyn used to treat them, the girl makes my gut churn. I don't get what Zack sees in her.

Gwen and Chrissy will watch his back. He's lucky he has them. I could have used friends like them this past summer.

"Hey, are you okay?"

I shake my head and meet his gaze. "Yeah. I just don't understand why he's dating her. Apparently, she used to bully a ton of kids."

"Really?" Miles asks before the wheels in his brain turn. "That actually makes sense. Typical *high school cheerleader mean girl* shit."

"Exactly."

"Maybe she's changed?" Miles tries to offer her the benefit of the doubt.

"I don't know. Gwen and Chrissy both have told me Zack is changing. He's like a firework waiting for his fuse to be lit. He was never like that."

Miles purses his lips and shrugs in defeat. "We'll keep an eye on him."

Not long after our conversation, Miles leaves. He told me he was going to check in with Zack at his dorm. I hope he's there. I have a feeling he needs a friend right now.

My back aches, and my shoulders burn from not sitting straight. When I look up from the computer screen, I notice the sun is setting. I pull on my arm, stretching it out. I got a lot done today. Now I just need to make sure everything works, but I have until the end of this week. Right now, I need to get my ass over to Gwen's.

I buzz Gwen's number at her apartment complex, and she lets me in immediately. The door opens when I finish climbing the stairs to her apartment. She pokes her head out, and my body reacts in a series of ferocious flutters. She has her wavy dirty-blonde hair rolled in a hair clip. Her sweatpants are way too big, and they hang just below her belly button. She paired them with a baggy white midriff crop top. This woman is the definition of a hot mess, and she's never been sexier.

When my foot lands on the second floor, I sweep her into my arms. She's all giggles and smiles as I press my lips to hers. The moment I do, my feelings from earlier vanish. I knew I was being ridiculous, but seeing Zack hold her sent me teetering on an edge I didn't want to be on. I feel safer now, being with her, with her lips on mine. Nothing else matters.

I cup her cheeks when I place her back on the floor. The moment I pull away, she loses her balance.

"Are you okay?" I ask with a hint of laughter.

She holds onto my arm to steady herself. A gentle smile lights up her face. It's only then that I let out a chuckle of relief.

"If you keep kissing me like that, I definitely won't be."

I feather my hand along her arm, leaving tiny goose bumps

Chapter Thirty-Nine

in its wake. Pressing my forehead against hers, I close my eyes and lean down to kiss her again. Just as I near her lips, I feel a finger on my mouth.

"Unfortunately, this will have to wait." She's breathless, and it only makes me crave her more.

I kiss her finger just as she pulls away.

She walks into her apartment and to the stove. Opening it, she checks on something in the oven. Only then do I notice the aroma filling her apartment. Garlic, basil, onions, and tomato sauce invade my senses.

"You didn't tell me you can cook."

Her messy bun flops to the side, and her face lights up. "You didn't ask, now did you?"

I throw my hands in the air and sit on the edge of her bed.

"You just keep getting better and better," I tease as she tosses a piece of bread in her mouth.

"How was your day?" she asks while bopping along to music in her head.

I shrug, too busy watching her to think straight. "Fine. Much better now."

She smirks and giggles at my response. "I saw Zack today."

I was hoping she would bring it up. I feel better knowing she planned on telling me from the beginning.

"He apologized." Her eyes widen and beam in amazement.

"That's good. Glad he owned up to his shit."

A timer goes off before she can say anything else. She bends over and pulls out a casserole dish from the oven, and I can't take my eyes off her.

"You like baked ziti and garlic bread?" She stands on her tippy-toes, grabbing two plates from a cabinet that's barely within reach.

"I'll eat anything you give me." Oh, that definitely came out way more sexual than I intended.

She turns on her heels, pointing a spatula at me. "Keep it in your pants, bucko."

I can't help but beam at her lame threat. "Bucko?"

Her eyes dart to the side like she didn't realize what came out of her mouth. "Yeah, that's exactly what I meant to say."

She hands me a plate, the smell making my mouth water and nose tingle. After settling next to me, she flicks the TV on.

I don't remember the last time I had a homemade meal. At my brother's, we always have takeout or frozen dinners. Nothing this fancy.

The pasta is hot, but I don't care. My stomach is growling in anticipation, and it tastes even better than it smells. How is that possible? I shovel more food in my mouth, not caring about third-degree burns. Turning to Gwen, I give her a thumbs-up.

She giggles and leans closer to me. "Glad you like it." She places a kiss on my cheek before digging in herself.

If this is what life and love are supposed to be like, what did I experience before? I dare imagine many more nights like this, and with the thought, I smile to myself. I'm never going home again. If I do, she'll come with me. The idea of going a day without her leaves a gaping hole in the center of my chest. I would miss how she feels snuggled against me, how she smells, how soft her skin feels in the morning.

And don't even get me started on that smile.

I see the way she looks at me. We both feel the same way about one another, utterly enthralled.

Chapter Forty

Gwen

Don't ask me how, but I didn't fail that biochem test. I was blissfully shocked when I got it back and saw the handwritten B+. Ash passed too. Of course he did. That man is so smart it should be a crime. I mean, who takes biochem for fun? I'll tell you who. Ash fucking Waylen.

Speaking of Ash, a day hasn't gone by without him. He stays at my place most of the time. On days when he has to return home to get clean clothes or check in with his brother, I'm right by his side. I haven't met his brother yet. He's always preoccupied with some important legal matter. It doesn't bother me; I only care about Ash and having him by my side. I love that he feels the same way. The thought of being away from him, of sleeping alone, is dreadful.

The look in his eyes tells me he's falling just as hard as I am. Chrissy notices it too, which makes me feel lighter than air. She gets giddy when she sees the little glances Ash gives me when I'm not paying attention. I wonder how many times a day I miss those secret gazes. I know how many I give him. I could look at him all day, admiring how his cheeks flush without warning. I could drown in his chocolate eyes. Don't even get me started on his glasses.

I've come to terms with gravity. It doesn't exist when we're together. I never thought I could feel so loved and cared for in my entire life. I dreamed I would, and in those dreams, it was Ash. Did I wish him into life? Did I somehow find a way to make dreams come true? *I could really market that and pay off my student loan debt...*

What's even better? Ash melded into my little friend group with ease. It was like he was a part of it all along. Chrissy and him joke and pick on one another. She started confiding in him for boy advice, which I greatly appreciate. Just because I have a boyfriend doesn't mean I'm any good with them.

Zack is, well, Zack. He and Ash tolerate one another. I wish I knew what was going through their heads. When I talk with Zack, I feel Ash's eyes on us, lingering and watching carefully. When I'm with Ash, Zack gives me the same treatment. Like if I make any wrong move, he's ready to fight to the death.

I've told Ash time and time again that Zack and I are just friends. He's like my brother. And I know Ash believes me, but that doesn't mean the suspicion in his eyes doesn't hurt any less. It's like he's waiting for something to happen between Zack and me. Observing us, hoping to catch us in the act. That'll never happen though. The thought makes me gag.

The only thing I can do is reassure him. Show him how crazy I am about him. Which comes effortlessly. I'll keep showing him all the love and compassion he deserves. Slowly, he'll get better. Trust will come to him again.

Halloween is two and a half weeks away, and I'm beyond excited. Decorations and spooky lights are displayed

Chapter Forty

throughout the campus, and the chill in the air reminds me of classic eighties horror movies.

I wrap my arms around my chest and secure my sweatshirt hood over my head. I could wait inside the computer science building, but then I wouldn't get to breathe in this wonderfully crisp air.

"Aren't you cold?" My ears perk at the sound of Ash's voice.

I spin around, trying to hide my chattering teeth. "No, I love this."

The sun reflects off the frame of his glasses, but his grin shines brighter. "Crazy girl," he says.

I stand on my tippy-toes and wrap my arms around him as he scoops me into his arms. Shoving my face in the crook of his neck, I sigh in contentment.

"I have a surprise for you." His whisper makes me shudder.

I pull back and brush our noses together. "Are you going to kiss me?" I ask excitedly.

"Well, yes, but that's not the surprise. Wait, is it that easy?"

I twist my lips, feigning deep thought. "I think it might be. Yes, it definitely is," I say before nodding like a love-drunk fool.

"You're killing me, Gwen," he whispers before closing the tiny gap between us.

I tangle my hands in his curls and suck in as much air as possible through my nose. Kissing Ash can't be compared to anything. The word I want to describe it with doesn't exist in the dictionary yet. His lips are full, soft, ungodly warm, and full of longing. When he pulls away, I can't help but lean back in for more.

"Don't you want to know what the surprise is?"

I love when he's breathless.

"What is it?"

He sets me on my feet and shoves his hands in his hoodie

pocket. "Remember how you told me you always wanted to go to a haunted house but no one would ever go with you?"

My eyes widen with excitement. While Chrissy and I have a lot in common, the one thing she can't stand is being scared, spooked, or anxious. The thought of someone jumping out to scare her is enough to give her nightmares. Zack never wanted to go with me because he always thought it was lame. I, on the other hand, want to be spooked. That's what Halloween is all about, and I'm a basic spooky bitch.

"Yeah." I grin widely, drawing out my response.

"What if I told you I got us tickets to go to one?"

A bright smile plasters itself on my face, and I jump up and down like a five-year-old going to a theme park.

"And—"

"There's more?" I whirl around, almost losing my balance.

Ash grabs my hands and pulls them against his lips. "It's going to be a double date." My eyebrows twitch in bewilderment. "With Chrissy and Miles."

My mouth drops, and I swear Ash's eyes twinkle. "She's going to kill you," I whisper with a smirk.

"She'll be fine. She's got Miles. Besides, I'd die happy knowing the one person I care about has a smile on her face." He tilts my chin back toward his lips with his thumb.

"Why do I feel like you only invited her because you want to hear her scream?"

A wicked grin plays on his lips and across his dimples. "There's that too."

"You're pure evil, Ash Waylen." I laugh breathlessly. "It's kinda hot."

"I'll be anything you want, sneaky girl."

Chapter Forty-One

Ash

"I'm going to murder you, Ash Waylen," Chrissy groans in the backseat.

My eyes flick over to Gwen just as her mouth forms the words *told you so*.

"It's going to be fine. You'll have Miles—" I shut my mouth the second her volume increases.

"You think Miles is going to enjoy a screaming, flailing, crying Chrissy? Gwen can't even handle that!"

Gwen nods beside me. "It's true. It can be rather disturbing."

"You're supposed to be on my side," I whisper to Gwen, and she shrugs and grins playfully.

"If anyone scares you, Chrissy, grab Ash and throw him their way, deal?" Gwen says with a mischievous smile on her face.

I glimpse Chrissy through the rearview mirror. The pout she wears on her glossy lips turns into a devilish smirk.

"Deal."

Gwen took no time throwing me under that bus, and neither did Chrissy.

Finding parking is a challenge. We lucked out with a spot near the back though. After a ten-minute walk, I flash the cashier our tickets, and we step through the gate.

Chrissy shouts, "I'm off limits, ya hear me?" She grabs me by my forearms and shields herself behind me.

Gwen chuckles beside me and intertwines her arm with mine.

The sooner we find Miles, the better. I enjoy Chrissy and her antics. I just hoped she wouldn't actually be a huge baby about the whole thing.

Horror Fest isn't what I originally expected. Somehow, it's more, and Gwen's eyes light up. String lights weave through the trees and hang above the tables, and various food stands are spread out around the grounds. A live band plays in the center of the festival, but the real fun branches off deep in the woods.

The air is chilly, and the smell of fried food and fall leaves waft in the breeze. Gwen doesn't dress like normal girls. She knows to dress properly for cold weather. She wasted no time stealing one of my rather large hoodies and pairing it with jeans and sneakers. Chrissy, on the other hand, is wearing a thin long-sleeve shirt and leggings and is already blue and shivering.

"Aren't you cold, Chrissy?" I ask, turning my head ever so slightly to check on her.

"Yes, but it's all a part of my master plan," she giggles maniacally before Miles appears in front of us and wastes no time jogging over. "Watch the master at work." Chrissy clicks her tongue teasingly and steps out from behind me.

"Hey, guys," Miles greets with a broad smile.

"Miles, where's your jacket?" Chrissy's playful tone is long gone.

Chapter Forty-One

Gwen snorts beside me and clings to my arm. This part definitely wasn't a part of Chrissy's *master* plan.

Miles shoves his hands in his jeans pocket and shrugs. "You know I like the cold. If I wore a jacket, I'd sweat right through it." His grin beams in the dark, not enough to charm Chrissy though.

She sighs in defeat and turns around. Lucky for her, I'm already pulling my hoodie over my head to offer it to her.

"Here you go, *master*," I tease her.

She scrunches her nose playfully. "Thank you, new best friend." Her gaze shoots over to Gwen, who isn't paying attention.

She's too busy taking in the sights. Who knows how long she's been distracted.

"What are we talking about?" Gwen snaps back to us and snorts when she sees Chrissy drowning in my hoodie. "Hey, we match now." Gwen glows and bites her tongue while squinting her eyes.

These two are literally drowning in fabric and my cologne, and they're having the time of their lives.

"Uh, my name's Ash, and I'm so cool. You can call me Mr. Cool. Thank you very much." Chrissy drops her voice and bounces back and forth.

"No, no, it's Mr. Librarian, and you can totally check me out anytime." Gwen matches Chrissy's tone and winks obnoxiously.

Miles covers his forehead with his hand and drags it down his face. "What did we get ourselves into, man?" he asks.

I chuckle as Gwen and Chrissy banter back and forth, pretending to be me. "I don't know. I ask myself that same question every day."

As Gwen and Chrissy enter their own world, my cheeks are sore within seconds. I'm not sure how I lived without them in my life, they make everything light and brighter. I feel like I've known them both for years. Their laughter is contagious, and I feel bad for anyone who wanders past us and overhears their little snippets and snide remarks.

"I'm Ash Waylen, and I have a big di—" I rush in to cut Chrissy off.

My arms wrap around their shoulders, and I push them forward.

"Okay, that's enough," I say, trying to hide my embarrassment.

Gwen doubles over and fills the air with her wonderful laughter.

"Don't act like we all didn't see you wear those gray sweatpants in high school!" Chrissy squirms underneath me but doesn't get too far because Miles scoops her in his arms and whisks her away.

"Let's go get you a drink," I say before placing a kiss on Gwen's head.

She snickers and clings my arm. "Don't worry, Mr. Smooth. I'll give you my hoodie if you get cold."

"That's very kind of you." I hold her close. "But I don't have to worry about being cold around you." Color rushes to her cheeks at my comment. "Now, how about we go get you a drink and some food?"

"You know me so well."

We follow behind Chrissy and Miles, and when the breeze blows past us, I don't shiver. Gwen's mere presence is all I need to stay warm.

Chapter Forty-Two

Gwen

If I knew horror fests were like this, I would have dragged Chrissy and Zack to one years ago. We haven't ventured to the haunted attractions yet, but I know once we do, it'll be a blast. Chrissy's already pumped and ready to face the spooks, thanks to a couple of shots and a few sips of Miles's hard cider. I offered to be the designated driver so Ash could drink, but he politely refused. I decided to stay sober and eat all the food I could get my hands on, and so far, it's been fantastic.

I'm shoving two fries in my mouth as we walk toward the haunted corn maze. Probably not the best way to start the night, but Chrissy wants to do this first, oddly enough. Blindly, I offer Ash a fry, and he snatches it from my fingers with his mouth. I can't get over the fact that Ash remembered my favorite holiday is Halloween, and he went out of his way to get us tickets to the one thing I've always wanted to do. This man keeps surprising me. I probably used all the luck that was supposed to last me a lifetime in securing him, but I don't care. It was worth it.

"Are you ready?" Ash whispers in my ear as I toss out the empty french fry carton.

Chrissy bops up and down in front of us, getting more pumped as we near the front of the line.

"Not as ready as her," I admit with a giggle.

He wraps his arms around me and pulls me close. "I don't think I need to say this, but if you get scared, I'll protect you."

"You'll protect me too, right, Ash?" Chrissy whirls around, leaving Miles visibly confused and baffled.

"What about me?"

Chrissy stands on her toes and grabs Miles by his shoulders. "Oh, sweetie, you didn't even wear a jacket for me. How am I supposed to trust you to protect me against the bad guys?"

Understanding, Miles nods. "Good point. Ash, you'll protect me too, right?"

Ash runs a hand through his hair and shakes his head. "Why did I think this was a good idea again?"

With a little hop, I place a kiss on his cool cheek, and color flushes his face.

He nods. "Oh yeah, silly me. How could I forget?" He beams down at me and plants his hands on my hips.

"Okay, you two, let's go." Chrissy snatches me out of Ash's arms and runs full speed into the corn maze.

"Chrissy, this is a bad idea!"

We take a sharp right, creating distance between the guys rapidly.

"We'll be fine, don't be such a baby." Screams echo around us, and Chrissy stops us dead in our tracks. "Okay, maybe this was a bad idea."

We're shrouded in darkness, and rustling sounds come from deep within the corn maze.

"You just had to go and play the tough guy, didn't you?" I mumble before linking our arms together. "Let's take it slow,

Chapter Forty-Two

and you better pray Ash and Miles find us before someone scares both our pants off," I whisper.

Whoever had the idea to place directional signs with trivia questions throughout the maze was brilliant. If only Chrissy and I were good at trivia . . .

"How many pounds are in two tons?" Chrissy counts on her fingers.

"Aren't you supposed to be good at math?" I ask her, losing my patience.

Chills creep up my spine, and I get the sudden sensation someone is watching us.

"Aren't *you* supposed to be good at trivia?" she snaps back as I peer over my shoulder.

"What gave you the impression I was good at trivia?" I lower my voice even though no one is behind us.

"I don't know. Shut up. I'm trying to count. Is it four or six thousand?"

"I can't remember!" I pull on her arm, deciding for us. "It's a fifty-fifty shot. Let's go with six and hope we get the next answer right."

I come to the conclusion that we're really fucking dumb rather quickly.

After a few twists and turns, Chrissy pulls out her phone and gasps. "It was four thousand pounds."

"You didn't think to check that out before we took three more wrong turns?"

She shines her phone's flashlight right in my face. "Why didn't *you* think of it, smart-ass?"

I'm starting to wonder if we reached a part of the maze the actors didn't think of covering because who in their right mind would ever get *this* lost? Two science majors, that's who.

I keep hoping Ash and Miles will show up behind us and lead us out of this damn maze, but every time I turn around, thinking someone is behind us, no one is there. They probably got out within ten minutes, all while laughing their asses off.

"Do you hear that?" Chrissy points her flashlight behind me and peers into the darkness.

"I've been hearing shit the entire time. No one's there." Just as I turn around, the thicket of corn rustles.

"I hate you for bringing me here," Chrissy mutters, digging her fingernails into my arm.

"Technically, Ash brought us. But even more technically, you pulled us away from the guys and brought us here," I hiss through gritted teeth.

She whimpers and shoves her face in my back. The noise subsides, and we're left in silence once again. I turn around and wrap my arms around her.

"We can do this. We're two brilliant, independent women, right?"

Chrissy stands straighter and sniffles in response. "Yeah, we don't need a man to save us."

The second those words leave her mouth, the rustling reappears but right next to us this time. Chrissy and I scream simultaneously and haul ass down the packed-dirt path. Chrissy's much faster than I am, so she takes the lead and weaves us through the maze blindly.

We come to a stop after running for a few minutes. My knees meet the earth the second we stop. Chrissy runs her fingers through her hair and doubles over.

"Fuck this shit, fuck Halloween, and fuck haunted corn mazes!" she shouts to the sky.

A slight smile pulls on the corner of my lips as her panic turns to frustration.

"And fuck your boyfriend for dangling Miles in front of me. Again!"

Chapter Forty-Two

I burst out in laughter and fall onto my back as she continues to holler.

"Quick, Gwen, who was Henry VIII's third wife?" She ignores my cackling and moves on to the next trivia question. "Was it Anne of Cleaves or Jane Seymour?"

"Jane Seymour," I blurt out in between giggles.

"Are you sure?"

I fight to catch my breath as she dares to question my knowledge of that bastard Henry VIII and his wives.

"Don't you remember when I was obsessed with the history of the Tudors?" I ask her while propping myself on my elbows.

"Oh yeah. That was a dark time."

I dig my feet into the ground and ready myself to stand when I hear footsteps crunching trampled corn along the path. Chrissy screams bloody murder, and a man wearing a black hockey mask launches on top of me.

His knees dig into the dirt underneath my armpits, and the scream that bubbles from my chest is raw. I try to kick him in the balls, but with the position he put me in, it's impossible. He takes my hands and pins them over my head. His face nears mine as I struggle for air.

"Boo." His dark caramel eyes meet mine.

Everything slows and returns back to normal speed.

"You son of a bitch."

Chapter Forty-Three

Ash

Finding the girls was simple. All Miles and I had to do was follow their screams. I didn't think they would be bad at trivia though. Who doesn't know how many pounds are in two tons? Apparently, they're the only two science majors on the planet who don't. Miles and I are finding their antics and lack of survival skills more than entertaining. How the hell did they find the one section of the maze where there are no actors? Damn, I wish I knew. Gwen almost caught us more than once because Miles and I couldn't stop snickering and stumbling over our feet. And I gotta say, for someone who wanted to get spooked, Gwen's keeping up with Chrissy's cries of terror.

"I can't believe you paid that kid five bucks for his mask," Miles whispers as I secure it over my face.

"It's all a part of my *master* plan."

Once I noticed Gwen and Chrissy were veering off track, I had to take matters into my own hands, and how could I resist? If the actors weren't going to get to them, someone had to.

Chapter Forty-Three

"And fuck your boyfriend for dangling Miles in front of me. Again!"

Miles kneels beside me, and I can't fight the grin that spreads across my lips as Gwen collapses to the ground in pure hysterics. That girl's laugh is something I'll never get tired of—it's light and carefree.

"Quick, Gwen, who was Henry VIII's third wife?"

"How much you wanna bet they get this one wrong?" Miles asks, midchuckle.

"I'm willing to bet Gwen knows this one. Five bucks?" Snooping around her apartment wasn't a total waste of time. My girl went through a major Henry VIII and Tudor family obsession at one point in her life.

"Deal." Miles shakes my hand just as Gwen speaks up.

"Jane Seymour." My girl is always right on cue.

I look at Miles through my mask, wishing he could see my satisfied grin.

"Dude, she's getting up. Now's your chance."

I don't think Gwen will hate me for this. The girl did say she wanted to get scared. She just didn't specify who was allowed to scare her. I lunge the second Gwen's feet dig into the ground. I don't bother being stealthy; I want them to know someone is coming for them.

Chrissy's scream rattles my eardrums, but I avoid her. My knees dig into the earth, trapping Gwen beneath me. Her cry vibrates my core, and wait, is she trying to knee me in the balls? Really? Perhaps I shouldn't have doubted her survival skills.

Before she hurts me or herself, I pin her hands over her head and hover over her eyes. She offers me a lopsided grin when she catches on, smart girl.

"Boo."

"You son of a bitch," she mumbles as the color returns to her face.

I release her hands and remove the mask from my face.

"Did I get you, sneaky girl?" Her lips part, and I swear even that simple move makes my dick twitch. "*Oof.*"

Gwen's fist makes contact with the underside of my ribs, and I topple over. Damn, that girl can pack a punch.

"Miles, you asshole!" Chrissy hollers, making Miles cackle even harder.

Gwen leans over me and grins like she didn't just sucker punch me in the gut.

"I thought you were supposed to protect me, not scare me." Gwen throws another punch, but I grab a hold of her wrist before she hammers down on me.

"I'm sorry." I pull her down against my chest and chuckle. "I couldn't help it, especially after the two of you managed to outsmart the actors."

"I thought it was odd that no one was tormenting us." She pulls back in thought.

I sit up and curl my hands in her waves. "I gotta say, I enjoyed watching your ass all night."

"Are you trying to tease me?" The corners of her lips crinkle.

"Absolutely."

Our noses brush, and my eyes flutter closed. Instead of being met with a kiss, I'm met with a punch in the arm.

"*Ow*, woman."

Her lips land on my forehead as I cradle my arm.

"Nice try, Waylen." She ghosts her mouth over my lips before pulling away.

Why the hell am I hard right now?

"You're on my shit list, Summers." Chrissy stomps.

Gwen frees herself from my embrace and pats off the dirt from her legs.

"It was Ash's idea. He dragged me along." Miles tries his

Chapter Forty-Three

damn best to hold back his laughter, but the poor guy can't seem to catch a break.

"Ash gave me his hoodie, so he gets one freebie."

Miles looks over at me for help, but all I can do is shrug. No one, not even Gwen, can stop Chrissy when she's in one of her moods.

"Anyway." Chrissy looks over at Gwen and grins. "What's next?"

"You're completely mental," Gwen giggles as we make our way out of the corn maze.

"Yeah, yeah, whatever. We're already here, might as well have some fun." Chrissy leaps on Miles's back, and he gladly accepts the task of carrying her.

"Let's go to the haunted house," Miles offers with a wide grin.

"Let's do it!" Chrissy chuckles as Miles runs down the path.

Gwen giggles beside me and wraps her arm through mine. "Having fun?"

Her blue eyes shimmer in the moonlight. "So much fun." She stands on her toes and kisses my cheek.

"Night's not over yet, sneaky girl," I whisper just as Chrissy screams bloody murder. "Guess the actors finally found us." I chuckle before wrapping my hand around Gwen's. "Ready to get scared?"

"With you by my side, I'm ready for anything."

Chapter Forty-Four

Gwen

We make it out of the corn maze in one piece. I'm still having a hard time registering the fact that Chrissy wants to go to the haunted house. I tried warning her that the actors are allowed to touch you there, but she doesn't care. I think she wants an excuse to throw Miles at someone, a bit of payback for the corn maze scare, even though it was Ash who charged at us.

The moon and stars are bright tonight, adding to the spooky ambiance. A cool breeze envelopes me, so I cross my arms over my chest. Ash wraps his arms around me as we stroll to the haunted house.

As the night creeps in, the crowd starts to thin. The festival is over around eleven, so we have about thirty minutes before everything closes.

"I'm so ready for this." Chrissy jumps up and down.

"You said you were ready for the corn maze too," I tease.

She twirls around and points her finger at me. "I didn't

Chapter Forty-Four

know there would be trivia," she snaps back with a crooked smirk.

"Whatever you say, *master*." I stick my tongue out at her, and she mimics me.

We round the bend, bickering back and forth, but Ash and Miles shush us.

"Did you just shush me!?" Chrissy aims her sass at Miles, but he shushes her again.

"Isn't that Zack and Roselyn?" Miles asks.

The four of us stop talking and try to listen to their conversation.

"That's Roselyn, all right. I recognize her voice," Miles whispers in acknowledgment.

Chrissy takes a few steps forward to get a better look.

"What do you mean he's just a friend? Do you embrace and kiss all your friends?" That's Zack, no doubt about it.

I glance at Ash, noticing the moment he gulps past a lump in his throat.

"Zacky, calm down. You're overreacting," Roselyn soothes, a complete one-eighty from her previous stance.

"I saw you, Roselyn. And when I called you out, you yelled at me."

"I didn't yell." Her faux comforting voice makes my lips purse.

"I can't listen to this shit anymore." Chrissy stomps forward, and I waste no time following her.

"It's just who I am, Zack," is the last siren call she can mutter before Zack turns his head and notices us.

"Zack!" I jump into his unexpecting arms in hopes of cheering him up.

"What are you guys doing here?" he asks as he places me on the ground.

Ash wraps his arms around me from behind as a fake grin spreads across my face.

"What's up, man?" Ash greets, wearing what I can assume is a matching fake smile.

"I thought you didn't like this kind of stuff." Chrissy doesn't hide her irritation. In fact, it's wrinkled deep in her brow.

"I don't—" Zack stops midsentence because Roselyn interferes.

"It was my idea." Roselyn's perfect smile does nothing to break the growing tension. "Hey, Ash." Her smirk grows, and I swear, Ash has to hold me back.

"What were you saying to my brother earlier? Something about gaslighting?" Chrissy stares Roselyn down, knowing damn well she has backup if she needs it.

"What's gaslighting?" Zack asks, sounding way way more innocent than he intends.

Does this guy not know what kind of emotional manipulation he's under? He really did live a privileged life . . .

"Oh, it's when someone makes you question your sanity even though they know they're in the wrong." Miles provides the dictionary definition.

"No one is *gaslighting* anyone." Roselyn clings onto Zack's arm, acting sweet and loving. "We were just talking, right, Zack?"

Zack meets my gaze. I plead with him to call her out. He's smart. There's no way he thinks this is normal.

"*Zack,*" I mouth, begging him to use caution, urging him to listen to us.

"So, who did you see her kiss?" Ash's tone drops, resentment peeking through. "This is too familiar, Zack. Trust yourself."

"Don't listen to him. Alex told me he's completely unstable

Chapter Forty-Four

and selfish." Roselyn tries to use a polite tone, but it doesn't work.

"I swear to fucking god. Zack, you're coming with us." Chrissy grabs Zack's hand and pulls him away. "We need to have a chat about manipulation, brother," Chrissy says as Roselyn takes a step forward, but I remove myself from Ash's embrace and block her path.

"Not gonna happen." I stand firm, not because I have Ash behind me, but because I'm willing to go down if it means Zack gets away from her toxic ass.

"Step aside." And there goes Roselyn's fake politeness.

Ash's chest presses against my back. He's ready to step in, ready to defend me against her bite, but I don't let him.

"I said *no*."

"Who the fuck do you think you are?"

"Gwen Roman, nice to meet you," I sneer with a step forward.

She steps to the side, but I match her. Ash's absence behind me is noted, and while I appreciate his support, I can do this all by myself.

"Ash, move your *girlfriend* before I make her move."

"You know, Roselyn, I wish I knew what your problem is. I would pay good money to sit in on your psychological evaluation. I bet the trauma is deep rooted, if it's trauma at all. For all we know, it's some sort of rare villain gene, and you just get a kick out of tormenting your boyfriends." She tries to move by me again, but I block her. "You're not going anywhere, not until Zack is out of reach from your siren call."

"Ash, move her. *Now*."

I don't have to look at him to know he's not budging. Ash has my back. He always will.

"Sorry, darling. I'm not the girl I used to be. You don't scare me anymore. Chrissy and I will be sure Zack comes to his senses. Now leave. I'm losing my patience," I bite back.

Roselyn comes toe to toe with me.

"Unwrap that fist, missy." Miles steps closer just as Ash does.

"Move," Roselyn snarls.

"No."

She shoves me, but I don't stumble.

"Roselyn, fuck off already." Ash's voice barely registers in my ears.

I've never thrown a punch before, but my grandfather taught me how to make a fist. Vietnam vets are a rare breed. Ball your fist tight and be sure your thumb is out. You don't want it to break from the impact. I don't know what I'm aiming for, nor do I care. I'm tired of people like her affecting the men in my life. I'm tired of women like her thinking they can degrade anyone they come across simply because they think they're better. I won't let her win anymore, and I won't let her suck me in.

In the blink of an eye, I whirl my arm back and let my fist fly, and it connects with her nose. Given that was my first punch, I would grade myself on a curve, but I hit her just enough that she trips over her feet. My knuckles crack from the pressure, but I shake it off. Roselyn stands upright and charges me. And I ready myself.

"Okay, that's enough." Miles steps in and catches her in his arms as she flails in an attempt to free herself.

Catching me off guard, Ash lifts me over his shoulder to put distance between the two of us. I chuckle when I see Miles carrying Roselyn away as she pounds on his back, screaming.

Once Roselyn's shouting fades away, Ash drops me back on my feet and holds me by my shoulders.

"What the hell, Gwen?" he asks as he grabs my shoulders.

Chapter Forty-Four

I meet his concerned gaze. "Someone had to do it." My bluntness makes him chuckle. "Why are you laughing?" I snort as his laughter deepens.

Chrissy jogs around the corner with heated cheeks. "Zack's safe. I hid him in the bathroom. Why are you two laughing?"

"Gwen sucker punched Roselyn." Ash wheezes out before doubling over. "Damn, I wish I knew you guys months ago."

"You threw your first punch?!" Chrissy wraps her arms around me. "I'm so fucking proud of you. Let me see your knuckles." She peels away to examine my knuckles with a grin. "Oh yeah, that's my girl."

"Thanks, Mom," I tease while trying to regain my composure.

Ash straightens and places a hand on Chrissy's and my shoulder. "I'm so glad I met you two." He pulls us into one big, loving embrace.

"We love you too, Waylen." Chrissy looks up at him, but Ash pulls her jacket hood over her head.

"Rude," she calls as Ash makes eye contact with me.

His mouth twitches, and I swear he's about to say something, but when Chrissy frees herself, he just winks at me. That's all I need to know I did the right thing.

In one night, I defended my friend and took a stand for the two guys in my life I undoubtedly care for. Roselyn isn't Alex, but she's the same kind of woman, and I'm sick of people like her hurting the men I care for. And what's even better?

I'm proud of myself.

Chapter Forty-Five

Gwen

Waking up in Ash's arms and witnessing his resting eyes and slight pout always makes me wet. It doesn't matter if it's five or six o'clock in the morning. Just one glance is enough to send me straight from tired to needing him inside me.

I didn't get to wake up in his arms today, and it's depressing. He said he had to do something before biochem today for my surprise later tonight. Another surprise, like the last one wasn't enough to last me a lifetime.

If I knew telling Ash my favorite holiday was Halloween meant he would go above and beyond, making the entire month of October absolutely wonderful, I would have prepared myself. I'm not used to being showered with attention like this, and while it's nice, I'm definitely out of my comfort zone.

Ash is going to get spoiled rotten the entire month of December, whether he likes it or not. I don't know how, but I

Chapter Forty-Five

have time to figure that out. I want to make sure he smiles just as much as I have these past few weeks.

I've said it before, and I'll say it again, Halloween on campus is always a blast. I woke up earlier than usual because there's something I have to find before Chrissy shows.

"Ugh, where are you?" I've been head deep in my closet for thirty minutes now.

I resorted to throwing clothes and jackets behind me, hoping the one thing I'm searching for will pop out.

Out of the corner of my eye, I spot an orange sleeve and immediately lunge for it. "Gotcha."

Stumbling out of the closet, I pull the crewneck sweater over my head and pat it down to release the wrinkles. I run my fingers through my hair just as a rapid series of tapping echoes from my door.

After I step into my furry moccasins, I let Chrissy in.

"Happy Hallowe—oh no." Chrissy's broad smile drops when she notices the sweater I opted to wear today. "I thought I threw that thing out years ago."

"You tried to throw this out?" I frown, unsure why she hates this sweater so much.

The crewneck sweater is orange, with two dancing skeletons on the front. The second I saw it, Chrissy cringed, but how could I not buy it? Remember, I'm a basic spooky bitch. These kinds of things are my weakness.

"You're lucky Ash is in love with you. If he wasn't, I'd worry he might run away."

I raise my eyebrows in confusion. "Ash isn't in love with me." I scoff and grab my bag.

Chrissy purses her lips like she knows something I don't. "Gwen, my sweet, sweet Gwen." She grabs my hands firmly. "Have you really not noticed? Not only did you capture his attention, which you wanted to do for years, but you took his heart, wrapped it in a blanket, and mended all the cracks that horrid woman left in it. I'd kill to have a man look at me the way he looks at you."

Is Ash in love with me? My stomach twists at the thought. I've known Ash for years, but we've only really *known* each other for a little over two months. I'm falling for Ash, but I just haven't hit those three words yet. Does that make me crazy?

I open my mouth to try to formulate some kind of response, but nothing I can think of explains how I'm feeling right now. I've never been in love before. How am I supposed to know when it happens to me?

"Did I scare you, Gwen? I'm sorry, I thought you knew." Chrissy lowers her tone and treads lightly.

"It's okay." I grin softly and squeeze her hands. "I think I'm just scared."

"Which is normal. Just because I think he loves you doesn't mean he does. For all we know, he's planning your murder right now."

I snort and roll my eyes.

"Love is a funny thing, Gwen. Take your time and simply listen to your heart." She taps my chest gently. "Now, let's get your spooky ass to class. Ash has something rather special planned tonight, and I cannot wait."

"You know what the surprise is?" I ask.

Chrissy beams with excitement. "You bet your ass I do. Now come on, we're gonna be late." She pulls on my hand, and as we walk to class, she bounces and chatters along the way.

I wish I could join her excitement, but I can't seem to get her words out of my head.

You're lucky Ash is in love with you.

Biology class drowns my thoughts. The anatomy of the heart distracts me for the entire class period. When class is over, I'm strangely relaxed, and the thought that Ash might be

Chapter Forty-Five

in love with me doesn't feel as debilitating as it did an hour ago. If anything, it makes me giddy and anxious.

I was worried my feelings for him would always be one-sided. Even if I caught his wonderfully beautiful gaze, how would I keep it? How *did* I keep it? I don't know, but I'm sure glad I did. Because I think I might be falling harder than I'd like to admit.

"I've said it before, and I'll say it again," Chrissy starts as we stroll into biochem. "I'm going to kill Roselyn." Her cheeks paint themselves blistering red.

"I'll bring the shovel and a bottle of wine."

"Good idea, we should get nice and drunk before—what the hell are you wearing, Waylen?"

My eyes fall on Ash, and not even a moment passes before my cheeks ache from the smile spreading on my lips.

"What, you don't like it?" Ash does a little spin in front of his desk.

He went out of his way to pick up a Halloween-themed hoodie, except his is black and has a man painted across the front with a pumpkin head, lounging suggestively. "I wanted to match my girl."

"I think you found the best hoodie ever." I stand in front of him and pull on the drawstrings.

"I think you're both fucking mental," Chrissy mutters as Ash brushes his nose against mine, giving me the special grin he saves just for me. The one that makes my insides turn to molten lava.

"Are you excited for tonight?"

I get lost in his dimples, and my knees weaken. "I am, but I have one question." I stand on my tippy-toes and brush my lips over his. "Does any part of tonight end with us in your bed?"

His cheeks blush pink, and an airy chuckle vibrates from his chest. "Oh, that'll definitely happen."

Our eyes flutter closed, and I take a step to close the gap.

"All right, you two, either take a seat or go find an empty room to do whatever it is you're doing." My eyes shoot open as Professor Stilts calls us out.

Ash chuckles and pushes his glasses up his nose as I rush for my seat.

"I take that back," Chrissy whispers while I pull my notebook out of my backpack. "You're both fucking mental and completely in love."

Chapter Forty-Six

Ash

My life can be divided into two different categories. Before Gwen, I thought Halloween was a silly tradition. Sure, I dressed up as a kid and trick-or-treated door-to-door. My childhood didn't last long though. Since my parents were always too busy fucking other people, it was always just Max and me. After a while, the fun, carefree Halloween nights ended. While everyone was out on mischief night, going to haunted houses and drinking throughout the evening, I was home. It didn't matter that I was popular. I had to stay home because I didn't trust my parents not to let the house catch on fire.

After Gwen, I've gotten to experience a whole new side of Halloween. She's showing me it's okay to have fun and be carefree. I keep planning these surprises for her because I thoroughly enjoy the look on her face when I tell her our plans, and that smile is enough to knock me right on my ass.

I want today to be as special as possible. It's her favorite day of the year, after all. I normally wouldn't wear something like this, but I knew she'd get a kick out of it. I strolled down the cobblestone path toward the science center with a new sense of confidence. I don't feel ashamed or worried that I might run into Alex.

I can't fathom that someone like Roselyn managed to dig their talons into someone like Zack. Thankfully, he has two badass girls watching over him. He has nothing to be worried about anymore now that he's free from her.

Gwen's reaction to my Halloween hoodie wasn't exactly what I was expecting. I thought she would laugh and give me her signature amused smirk. Instead, she took my breath away and pulled on my drawstrings. I don't hear Chrissy's mumblings or Professor Stilts at first. Only after Gwen pulls away and sits in her seat, wearing the hottest shade of red on her cheeks, do I notice. Gwen Roman has me wrapped around her pretty little finger, and damn, I wish I was there years ago.

Midlecture, my phone goes off in my pocket. I tear my eyes off a rather sexy and concentrated Gwen and squint down at my phone and see a text from Chrissy.

> Do you need anything for tonight?

> Nah, I got everything. Just make sure she dresses up.

> She'd dress up even if we just stayed home and watched movies all night.

> And don't tell me that turns you on!

> xD

> Are you sure it's okay if Zack comes?

Chapter Forty-Six

Zack and I haven't talked since the incident at Horror Fest. He and I were cool back in September before Roselyn dug her claws deep into his spine and started controlling his actions. This is Zack, though, and I want Gwen to have fun with all her friends, not just me.

> I'm sure. He needs a friend after the spectacle a few weeks ago.

> He does . . . thank you.

> Anytime. 8:00 okay?

> You got it, Mr. Biochem!

Gwen arches an eyebrow when I slide my phone back into my pocket. I wink at her playfully and mouth *"it's a surprise"* before focusing back on Professor Stilts and the mechanics of disease transmission.

Have I mentioned how much I hate leaving Gwen? Because I fucking hate it. Normally I would follow her home, and we would cuddle in her bed and watch TV. Today, I'm driving back to my brother's place alone. I needed a big enough space for tonight's plans, and I knew Max wouldn't be home, nor would he care if I had a few friends over.

The wind blows around me as I step out of my car and walk toward the front door. When I cross the threshold, a scent welcomes me that wrinkles my nose.

"Max?" I call while poking my head in the kitchen. "Why does it smell like burned chocolate chip cookies?"

"Because I'm burning chocolate chip cookies." Max pulls a sheet of black, crispy hockey pucks from the oven and sighs.

Not only is the sight of this man cooking rare, but the sight of him wearing a lacey pink apron is shocking and unsettling.

"Why?" I rest my elbows on the kitchen island and eye him suspiciously.

"I knew you were coming home today, and I wanted to do something nice." I hold his matching caramel gaze with mine. "Okay, fine. I have a proposition for you." And here we go. "Mom and Dad want to come over for Thanksgiving."

My eyes roll to the back of my head. Max feels the same way I do about our parents. He, on the other hand, has a more forgiving side. Which is weird, him being a lawyer and whatnot.

"And . . ."

"And what, Max?" I sigh.

"They want to meet Gwen."

I push my tongue against my cheek. "You haven't even met Gwen yet," I say.

Max picks up a cookie and cringes at the texture.

"I haven't officially met her yet, which is why I want to meet her first. I have a feeling Thanksgiving won't be the greatest time to get to meet the woman who changed my little brother's life." He throws the apron on the counter and walks over to me. "And don't pretend like I haven't noticed. You're never home anymore. When you are, you're locked in your room, giggling."

"I don't giggle—"

Chapter Forty-Six

"You do when you're with her."

I run my hands over my face.

"It's not a bad thing, Ash. After all you've been through, you deserve someone who makes you giggle." Max grins, flashing me a dimple on the center of his cheeks.

"She wants to meet you as well, so we can do dinner or something. I'll talk to her about Thanksgiving. Truthfully, I might not even show up that day, but I'll let you know."

I haven't seen my parents since last summer. They saw nothing wrong with what Alex did to me. That was the day my barrier went up. I created boundaries that I should have cemented years ago. The last thing I want is to see them, and the last thing I need is for Gwen to meet my fucked-up parents.

"Just think about it." Max squeezes my shoulder and gives me a firm shake. "And do me a favor. Please don't trash the place tonight."

"Don't worry. It'll only be a few friends. Besides, Gwen won't let anyone get out of hand."

"Sounds like my kinda girl."

That's all I care about. It doesn't matter if Mom and Dad don't approve of Gwen. I don't need their blessing. Max's opinion is the only one I care about, and I know he'll fall in love with Gwen the second she flashes him that smile.

I know because I already have.

Chapter Forty-Seven

Ash

F our words that tend to end in trouble, just a few friends, won't be the case tonight. A party was the first thing that came to mind. Until Chrissy told me Gwen doesn't do well in crowded rooms. So I opted for the next best thing: a few friends, food, drinks, and games. It's subtle, but I know Gwen will love it.

"Rome, will you please stop eating and finish hanging the lights?" I groan as Rome shoves a handful of chips in his mouth.

"I'm sorry, man, I haven't eaten all day." Chips fly out of his mouth midsentence.

"I saw you eat two chicken sandwiches at lunch," I say with an arched brow.

"He's an endless pit!' Miles shouts from the other side of the room.

"I'm a growing boy, and I need more food," Rome says, not caring that his mouth is full.

"You're twenty-one!" Miles cackles.

Chapter Forty-Seven

I'm starting to think asking Miles and Rome to help me set up was a bad idea. Luckily, Max helped me out a bit before he headed out for the evening. If it were up to these two to help me from start to finish, we wouldn't be eating tonight. At least they dressed up. Initially, when I told them to, they whined and cringed. Secretly, I know they wanted to. Miles made a makeshift toga out of a white sheet. Rome put on his football jersey, but he smeared fake blood and dirt all over his face. You can't say they didn't try.

Miles finishes weaving lights around the stairwell banisters as I place spider webs around the tables and picture frames. It's not perfect, but it's better than nothing. With a few lit candles and some decor I found in the basement, I think we did a pretty decent job. The lights will be dim anyway. Our work doesn't have to be perfect.

"Ash, I gotta say." Rome strolls in with a cupcake in his hand. "I don't think I've ever seen you go this far to impress a girl." Rome opens his mouth to devour the cupcake whole, but Miles snatches it before he gets the chance. "Dude, not cool." He pouts.

"I would have said the same thing, Rome. But you haven't seen Gwen since high school. Not only is she hot, she's cool as shit, and she makes our Ash here very happy." Miles drapes his arm around my shoulders and takes a bite of his stolen pastry.

"I appreciate that, man, but if you ever call her hot again, they'll never find your body," I threaten him with a smirk.

Miles whistles and removes his arm from my shoulders.

"Gwen watches true crime docs." I wink at Rome as the color drains from his face.

"So, uh. Is Zack coming tonight?" Rome asks as he pretends to get back to decorating.

"He is," I say nonchalantly.

"No Roselyn, right? Miles asks.

"No Roselyn."

"I still don't understand why he started dating her. She wasn't a bitch to us all those years ago, but she was to other kids," Rome says while tying back his blond hair with a scrunchie.

"If she's anything like Alex, she made the narrative fit her story and played the hero," I say.

Typical narcissistic move. They love playing the victim. I'm not sure why people like her get a kick out of hurting people. Could be a long streak of mistreatment from her childhood. Could be that she's a prickly bitch and loves getting under people's skin.

Alex wasn't always cruel. I met her at the beginning of last year. It was her attitude I was attracted to. That girl knows how to stick up for herself and her friends, something anyone can appreciate. I was standing in line for coffee at the local café on campus. She was a few steps ahead of me when an older guy approached her and marked her as his target. I sensed the level of uneasiness right away. Her posture stiffened, and those dark brown eyes flickered around the room. I stepped forward, ready to make up any excuse to talk to her just to save her from the creep.

"I said no, Viagra cock. Walk away before I mace your asshole so hard the prisoners won't be able to find it."

I stopped in my tracks when the guy hauled ass. I didn't plan on talking to her after that. I was going to step back in line and get on with my day.

"Were you going to try to save me?" she asked with a click of her tongue.

"Uh." My eyes danced around the room, and I took hold of my bag's straps. "I was going to, but you had it under control."

Her eyes crawled over my body. "What's your name?" She sucked on her lower lip and grinned.

Chapter Forty-Seven

"Ash."

"Come have coffee with me, savior."

Looking back, I should have noticed how her eyes devoured me like I was something to conquer and mark off her to-do list.

I was never into sleeping with as many girls as possible. I craved connection, and I thought she did too. That was mistake number one.

My phone dings, pulling me from my memories. When I glance at it to check the time, I notice a text from Chrissy.

> We're on our way!

Chapter Forty-Eight

Gwen

It's finally time! Chrissy and I are getting ready, dancing around my living room/bedroom to "Juliet" by LMNT. Being around Chrissy means it's easy to get hyped up for anything, and while I don't know what tonight will entail, I'm not nervous. I'll have my boyfriend and best friends with me.

Chrissy hyperfocuses on the mirror in the bathroom, making sure to fill every crease on her lips with ruby-red lipstick.

Chrissy decided to go very classic with her Halloween outfit. And by classic, I mean she put on a lacey red bodysuit and paired it with a matching skirt. She said she was going for a sexy demon, minus the horns. My opinion? I think she wants to give Zack a heart attack.

I decided to dress as a character I relate to. There's a book on my shelf, tattered and worn after my many rereadings. The main character wore a necklace. It resembled a promise that never came true. I relate to her. I admire how she grew into the

Chapter Forty-Eight

woman she always wanted to be. In the book, she wears this matching navy-blue tunic and trouser set, extremely romantic and medieval royal style. I found a necklace I thought resembled the one described in the book, curled my hair, pinned a dainty tiara on my head, and painted on a thin layer of rosy-pink lip gloss. I'm strapping on my boots just as Chrissy pulls out her phone.

"Zack's here. Ready, princess?" She smirks and adjusts my crown for me.

"Am I going to hate this?" I blow out the nerves that start to jump around in my stomach.

"Not one bit, I promise." She offers me her pinkie, and I accept it. "Now, let's go harass Zack. He needs all the sisterly love we can give him."

The air outside is exactly how Halloween weather should be—crisp and cool. I take a deep breath as Chrissy and I walk down the pavement to Zack's car. Hopping in the back seat, I beam at Zack through the rearview mirror.

"Happy Halloween!" I wrap my arms around him, choking his neck, but I'm happy to see him returning to normal.

It took time to get him back to his pre-Roselyn self. She really did a number on him, considering they only "dated" for a month or so. Roselyn had more than a few manipulation tactics up her sleeve, but I had no idea the extent of it.

When I first heard about it, I think I was in denial. Gaslighting, love bombing, classic narcissistic tendencies. Then Horror Fest happened, and it was time to intervene. I don't regret my actions that night because she got everything she deserved.

The first few days, Zack was in denial. He kept blaming himself, questioning whether or not what he saw was real. Roselyn made him doubt his sanity, which is the first red flag. The second came when Zack started crying, telling us everything he did wrong, everything he did to upset her. When, in fact, it should have been the opposite. Zack treats women like gold. There's no way I was going to believe him when he said *he* fucked up. Hell, if I needed pads or tampons, Zack would be the first to go to the store for me. He's like a damn golden retriever.

I want Ash to talk to him. He can share what he went through with Alex and maybe offer Zack some comfort. I wish we could have gotten them together sooner, but between classes and shifts at the café, my schedule is all over the place. Maybe tonight would be a good time for them to have a one-on-one.

A sense of relief washes over me when we pull into Ash's driveway. Ash, Miles, and Rome are standing outside, chatting and laughing.

I don't wait for Zack to turn off the car. Once he sets it in park, I fly out the back and rush toward Ash like I haven't seen him in days.

"Hey, you—*oof*," he grunts as I wrap my arms around him and rest my forehead against his.

"Hey." I can't help but beam like a damn fool. "I missed you."

Even though it's dark, his eyes sparkle in response, and his smile is broad and contagious.

"I think I missed you more," he whispers, and my nose wiggles. "Happy Halloween, sneaky girl."

Our lips meet, and we kiss like we haven't seen each other for weeks. When in reality, it's only been a few hours.

"Okay, you two, break it up," Zack groans.

"Oh, let them have their moment," Chrissy gushes.

"Damn, Chrissy, you look—ow!"

Ash drops me to my feet just in time for me to see Rome doubled over.

Chapter Forty-Eight

"Want to try that again?" Zack asks while shaking off his balled fist.

"You look absolutely terrifying." Rome blurts before raking his green eyes over me. "Damn, Gwen, you—"

Ash tenses, and by the way Rome's face falls, I bet he's giving him "that" look.

"Look like I shouldn't be talking to you."

"Nice to see you too, Rome." I grin at the blood he smeared on his face.

"Are you a sexy librarian?" Chrissy gasps in amusement.

I glance at Ash and he is, in fact, wearing his glasses and a black button-up cardigan. No one should make a cardigan look this good, ever. Of course, Ash would manage to pull it off and more.

"Gotta keep up with all these nicknames somehow," Ash teases.

I smirk and wish I brought a change of underwear. I fiddle with his glasses and rest my head against his shoulder.

"All right, let's get this party started." Rome whoops and hollers while leading us all inside.

Chapter Forty-Nine

Ash

It was all worth it. This girl's reactions to my surprises never cease to amaze me. Miles dimmed the lights before we all stepped outside to wait for them to. I turn around just in time to see her take in the orange and purple light bulbs.

"What do you think?"

"Ash, it's incredible." She's breathless, at a complete loss of words. Gwen takes a few steps forward and wraps her arms around my neck. Standing on her tippy-toes, she feathers her lips over mine. "Why do you keep going out of your way for me?"

"I get a kick out of your reactions, and I usually get a kiss or two as a reward."

Those beautiful sapphire eyes captivate me. She swipes her nose over mine, and the next thing I know, I'm struggling for air.

Kissing Gwen can only be described as magical. The second my lips touch hers, they tingle and burn for more. My

Chapter Forty-Nine

stomach tumbles, a feeling I've never known before her. I want to whisk her away, and show her how much I adore her. I want to occupy her space and time. I want her attention on me forever, no distractions or lingering stares. I just want her with me, and I hope she feels the same.

"Gwen, I—" I want to scream it. I want the whole room to know that this woman has my heart.

"What's wrong?" Concern washes over her.

I inhale sharply, but it's cut short.

"I'm begging you. Please don't make me watch you two make out all night. I don't think I can handle it." I fumble as Zack separates Gwen and me from our little world.

Gwen's mouth hangs ajar before a gentle smile tugs on her lips.

"Poor Zack, do you need a ginger ale? Or maybe a belly rub?" I'm left cold when Gwen's eyes roll onto Zack. "Or perhaps a backbone to support your righteous hypocrisy. How many times have I walked in on you making out with some girl?" Gwen interrogates.

Chrissy snorts somewhere in the background. That girl's always listening.

"All right, you two, let's just have fun tonight, okay?" I can't help but grin as I break the two of them up.

Chrissy and Gwen are like sisters—I've gotten the chance to see that up close. Zack and Gwen are definitely like brother and sister. His stance and demeanor only reflect the need to protect her. I see it now, and I appreciate it.

"Zack, let's go grab a drink." I offer while patting his back.

Gwen winks at me, and I get the feeling she did it to get under his skin.

"What did I do in my past life to deserve two out-of-hand women?" he groans as she walks away and plants herself on the couch.

"Come on, man, they're not that bad," I say.

"Ash, these cupcakes are great," Chrissy blurts out as we walk into the kitchen. "Miles, want to try one?"

Miles scampers in like a puppy. "I'm a sucker for cupcakes. Feed me?" He kneels before Chrissy, and I swear Zack has a heart attack.

"Not that bad, huh?" Zack huffs.

Okay, maybe I get it now . . .

Chapter Fifty

Gwen

I don't know how Ash managed to make his house look like it came straight from a Halloween aesthetic website board, but he did. Not only are the decorations perfect, but snacks are *everywhere*. Rome has taken a few trips to the snack table more than once. He's like a kid in a candy store.

I don't know Rome very well, other than he's a prodigy football player. He's funny—a bit of an airhead, but I can relate to that. Anytime he looks at me, Ash shoots daggers at him, something else I can appreciate. When Ash is across the room, I feel his smoldering eyes on me. It's not the kind of stare I'm used to though. This one is longing, like he wants to create a world for just the two of us. Like he never wants to let me go, and I don't want him to. I'd give anything to have our own little world, to have his eyes on me and only me.

The Ash in my mind was cool, slick, a mixture of various characters from books and TV shows. But the Ash in front of me is infinitely better than the one I conjured in my fantasies.

This Ash is down to earth, naturally generous, and a damn sweetheart. He makes my stomach flutter and twist in the best possible ways. The only common trait my two Ashes share? They're both suffocatingly sexy. I mean, who can make a cardigan look hot? It should be a crime. And the glasses? *Fuck me.*

I take a sip from the cup Chrissy handed me and shiver.

"Fuck, Chrissy, what is this?" I sputter on the alcohol that burns my throat.

"Vodka." She plops down next to me on the couch and grins ear to ear.

"And?"

"Just vodka." She wiggles her eyebrows at me, and I'm pretty sure my face is frozen in a *what the fuck?* expression.

"I'm going to go get some soda, crazy lady," I mumble.

"Wimp!" she shouts after me.

Stepping into the kitchen, I'm surprised to find Zack and Ash joking with one another. I'm glad they're getting along. They were friends before Roselyn weaseled her way into Zack's life. She tried her best to isolate him, and she almost succeeded.

I pour myself a cup of soda and lock my eyes on Ash, regretting it instantly because now I'm turned on.

I groan into my cup, and, of course, Ash notices because he winks at me. That son of a bitch knows how to burrow into my skin in the most intoxicating way possible. Backing away, I maintain eye contact.

Thankfully, the only light illuminating the room is from the faint decor bulbs, so no one notices when I climb the stairs and sneak into Ash's room. I'm curious to see if he gets the hint or if I have to text him a blatant message.

I shouldn't have doubted his intelligence because not a

Chapter Fifty

minute later, he opens and shuts the door, followed by clicking the lock.

"What are you doing up here, princess?" He steps forward as I step back. "Are you being sneaky again?"

I shrug in response. "Just wanted to see if you had any good books in here."

The backs of my legs hit his bed, giving him the opportunity to close the space between us.

"Find anything good?" His tone drops, lust and desire lacing his words.

"Depends. Can I check you out?" I grin while tugging on his sweater.

Ash's chuckle vibrates against my lips. "For you? I think we can make that happen."

Our lips meet in a frenzy. He balls his hands in my hair and places his knee between my thighs. A groan rumbles in his chest when I part his lips with my tongue. I've never needed anyone so desperately in my life.

I reach for the tiara on my head and toss it on the floor. He pushes me back onto the bed with his knee, and my legs part. I reach down to unbutton his jeans, but his hands stop me.

"I'm not done playing with you," he whispers, hot against my ear.

My leggings end up on the floor in one swift motion, and he trails his lips over my neck and growls when he rests his fingers over my panties.

"How are you so wet already?" he asks while kissing the underside of my jaw.

"It's the damn glasses," I blurt out without thinking.

He hovers over me, melting me under his hot chocolate eyes. Ash pulls my underwear to the side, his mere touch enough to send me over the edge.

"Is that it, sneaky girl?" he teases, and I shake my head.

Every word I want to say gets stuck in my throat as he rubs circles on my clit, the spot that he knows drives me crazy.

"Talk to me, Gwen."

I gasp for air and moan. "It's the sweater," I confess before he pulls on my lower lip with his teeth.

"What else?"

He moves his finger down, dancing around my folds and torturing me with the thought of him being inside me.

"Your—"

"Ash, are you in there?" Ash's free hand covers my mouth as Zack knocks on the door.

He doesn't stop moving his finger, and I have to fight the cry building in my chest.

"Can you be quiet for me?" he whispers.

The thought of him removing his hand is devastating. I would be left cold, lonely, and aching in his absence, so I nod.

"That's my good girl."

My back arches when he inches his finger inside me.

"Yeah, what's up?" Ash calls over his shoulder.

"Have you seen Gwen?"

His eyes land back on me, and he bites his lower lip.

"Yeah." He removes his hand from my mouth and kisses me desperately. "And she's fucking gorgeous," he growls against my lips. "She's in the bathroom," Ash calls back while pumping his finger inside me, expertly hitting the spot that sends goose bumps over my skin.

"Is she okay?"

With his free hand, he tugs my shirt down and kisses my chest. "She's fucking perfect," Ash grunts as my toes curl. "She's fine. Said something about her period." He raises his voice so Zack can hear him.

"Ash," I whimper.

Chapter Fifty

He covers my mouth again as my eyes roll to the back of my head.

"Are you going to come?" he asks in a sexy, hushed tone. I nod but end up whimpering when he removes his finger. "Sorry, sneaky girl, I need you to come on something else." Ash steps out of his jeans and boxers. "We'll be down in a few minutes, Zack." Ash trails his eyes over my body hungrily.

He moves to unbutton his sweater, but I sit up and stop him.

"Leave that on," I plead, and Ash smirks at my request.

"Remind me to buy more sweaters in the future," he says before Zack speaks from the other side of the door.

"Okay, let me know if she needs anything."

Ash climbs on top of me, resting his hand on the underside of my thigh and bending my knee in the perfect position.

"I got her, don't worry." He presses himself inside me, and the groan that escapes me is louder than I anticipated. Ash clashes into my lips with a chuckle. "You're gonna get me killed," he moans as he fills me to completion, giving me everything he has. "*Fuck*, you feel so good."

His rhythm is slow and passionate, but I'm so wound up. I need more.

"Ash, harder," I beg against his lips.

He takes my hands and pins them over my head.

"Is that what you want?" He grabs my other leg and hooks it over his arm. "Think you can be quiet, princess?"

He gives me a taste by retreating and slamming back into me.

I inhale sharply and bite my lower lip while nodding.

"That's my girl."

He thrusts in and out of me, hitting me deeply, each pump sending hot chills through my body. Ash groans before his eyes flutter closed.

"Fuck, Ash."

I ball the blankets in my fist, struggling to hold back the noises that beg to roll off my tongue. I choke out a curse, but it's silenced by Ash's mouth.

"Who's fucking you senseless right now?" He pumps in and out of me furiously, his bare skin smacking against mine.

"You," I whimper.

"Who?" He bites my ear lobe, making my back arch and muscles tense in anticipation.

"Ash."

"Again," he growls.

"Ash." My mind goes blank, and my eyes fill with blinding white stars.

"*Fuck*. Again," he groans in stark desire.

"Ash!" He covers my lips with his and takes my cry in his mouth.

I shudder and unravel around him, just like he wanted. With one final thrust, he matches my response, groaning and gasping for air.

"Fuck me. Holy shit," he mumbles as he fills me.

With a small kiss on my leg, he places it back on the bed and collapses next to me. We struggle to catch our breath and regain our senses.

I turn my head, scooting closer, and settle against his arm.

"Gwen?" My name barely leaves his lips as his chest heaves up and down, his lungs straining for oxygen.

"Hmm?"

He turns his head and meets my gaze. I trail my thumb over his cheekbone and brush my nose over his.

"I think Halloween's my new favorite holiday."

I caress his cheek and fix his glasses.

"Welcome to the spooky bitch club, darling."

Chapter Fifty-One

Ash

Gwen will be the death of me, in the best way possible. I'm not sure who will get to me first: Zack, my melted bones, or my fucked senseless brain. Either way, it would be a happy ending. Dying between Gwen's thighs would be one hell of a way to go.

I can't take my eyes off her. She makes even the most mundane tasks interesting. Like right now, she's trying to make her hair look like it wasn't just curled around my fingers. I think she gives up, though, because she leaves her hair down and secures the crown on her head.

"Better than nothing." She skips over to me and starts messing with my hair next.

Taking a step back, she observes her handy work.

"How do I look?" I ask.

"Like you just had sex." Her nose does that cute crinkle thing. "How do *I* look?"

I drag my eyes over her body more than once, never getting enough of this woman's curves.

"Like you just had mind-blowing sex."

Gwen snorts and reaches for my hand. We leave my room and descend the stairs.

Zack's suspicious gaze falls on us immediately. Gwen notices and tugs on my hand, leading us to Chrissy, Miles, and Rome. Rome sprawled himself on the loveseat, a bowl of chips resting on his stomach, mindlessly shoving handfuls in his mouth while watching some eighties horror flick someone put on.

Zack still doesn't know about Miles and Chrissy, so they placed themselves on opposite ends of the couch. It isn't difficult catching their tiny glances though. I'm not sure how Zack doesn't notice something is up.

Gwen places herself next to Chrissy, which leaves me sitting between her and Miles.

"We should play a game," Rome suggests with a mouthful of chips.

Gwen reaches for a cupcake, and I smile at her as she removes the paper lining.

"Like what?" Miles asks without looking up from his phone.

"Never have I ever?" Rome's voice fades into the background as Gwen licks the icing from her fingers.

She catches me watching her. "*What?*" she mouths.

"Nothing." I shake my head and chuckle.

She's so damn cute, it hurts.

"I'll play." Zack sits on the floor next to Chrissy. "You in, sis?"

"Fine, but Gwen has to play," Chrissy says just as Gwen's cupcake is halfway in her mouth.

"Play what?" she asks with a mouthful.

Chapter Fifty-One

"We'll play." I pull Gwen closer and rest my knee on hers.

"I'll get the drinks." Chrissy jumps up and dances her way into the kitchen.

Rome slumps off the couch to sit on the floor across from me, and Miles settles on the floor, stretching his legs. Chrissy pops back in and hands drinks out like a bubbly waitress. She sits back in her spot, and her lips curl into a smirk. I glance down at my drink, wondering if she spiked it with something other than alcohol.

"I'll go first," Chrissy says. "Never have I ever gotten drunk at a party, returned home only to throw up all over my mom." Chrissy giggles, knowing damn well who she's calling out.

"Fuck me, here we go." Zack takes a sip from his drink and cringes. "Chrissy, what the hell is this?"

"Straight vodka." My eyebrows raise, slightly impressed. "Don't worry, Gwen." I glance over and catch Chrissy wrapping her arm around Gwen. "I put a splash of orange soda in yours."

Gwen looks down into her cup and sighs. "Gee, thanks."

"Never have I ever fallen flat on my face wearing heels." Zack grins at Gwen and Chrissy.

"Son of a bitch," Gwen mutters before taking a sip.

Chrissy joins, but she takes a longer gulp than necessary.

"Never have I ever had sex under the bleachers during halftime at a high school football game," Chrissy hoots before she and Rome point at one another and down their drinks.

Zack eyes them, and I swear the vein in his forehead pops.

"I didn't have sex with your sister, I swear!" Rome blurts out.

"Or did he?" Chrissy teases just to get under Zack's skin.

"Isn't the point of this game not to drink, Chrissy?" Gwen snorts.

"Where's the fun in that?" Chrissy pouts.

"Never have I ever drunk texted naughty pictures to someone." Miles watches Chrissy, Zack, and myself take a sip.

"Does it count if you accidentally texted them to your best friend?"

I choke on my drink when Gwen asks the question.

"Absolutely." Miles nods his head, and Gwen takes a sip.

"Which best friend?" I raise my eyebrows.

If Zack saw Gwen in her underwear—or worse, naked—I'll rip his eyes out.

"It was me!" Chrissy wraps her arm around Gwen and smiles ear to ear. *Thank god.* "And let me say." Chrissy's words slur. "You're one lucky man, Ash Waylen," she says and follows it with a sloppy wink.

Gwen's hand meets her forehead in utter embarrassment.

"I'll go! Never have I ever snuck upstairs during a party, claimed I got my period, but was instead getting railed by a rather hot-looking librarian," Chrissy teases with a wide grin.

All eyes land on Gwen and me. I dare flick my eyes over to Zack, and as Gwen takes a sip, I swear, I'm a dead man. Chrissy, Rome, and Miles whoop and holler.

All I can do is mouth *"Sorry, man"* to Zack.

"Never have I ever had a summer fling," Gwen snaps back and stares Chrissy down.

Chrissy goes snow white as she takes a sip at the same time as Miles. I sit back and hope Zack doesn't catch the hint for Chrissy's sake. Lucky for her, he might be denser than I originally thought.

"Never have I ever streaked across a football field," Chrissy says.

She and Rome down their cups and slam them on the table.

"That's what I'm talking about!" Rome cheers before high-fiving Chrissy.

"Chrissy . . ." Zack groans. "What the hell?"

Chapter Fifty-One

"It was a dare," she offers innocently.

"That doesn't make it better." Zack runs his hands over his face before releasing a sigh.

"Never have I ever dated a siren," Chrissy teases, but the room falls silent.

Gwen's eyes fly over to Zack, and I meet his sunken eyes. His normally pink cheeks drain of color, and his grin fades.

"Zack," Gwen whispers as he stands.

"I'm sorry, Zack. I didn't mean it like that." Chrissy attempts to apologize, but Zack is standing and walking out the door before she can finish her sentence. "Fuck."

"I'll go talk to him," Gwen mumbles.

I place my hand on Gwen's knee to stop her from going after him. "I'll go," I offer without a second thought.

"Thank you," Gwen says as I kiss her on the cheek.

When I pass Chrissy, I ruffle her hair.

"I'm sorry," she offers solemnly.

Gwen pats at her blonde curls as I head outside.

A crisp autumn breeze welcomes me when I step through the front door. Luckily, Zack isn't hard to find.

"Hey, man." I lean against the car next to him.

"Hey."

"Are you okay?"

His dark hair shimmers against the moon's reflection. "I will be."

"Do you want to talk about it?"

Zack tilts his head in response.

"I can relate to what you're going through," I say

"I feel like I was a pawn in some sick, twisted master plan. I remembered how she treated my sister and Gwen, but I thought she changed. She was sweet, loving even."

Absentmindedly, I nod. Looking back, that's exactly how it

Forever Crushed

started for me too. It's as though girls like Alex and Roselyn secrete some kind of brainwashing perfume.

"It took a turn for the worse not even a full week into dating. I noticed a strange text on her phone from some guy I can't remember the name of. Before I could register it, she snatched her phone from the table and dismissed my curiosity." Zack's tone softens.

"And then it got worse," I added.

I don't need to ask him because I *know* it got worse. His timeline matches mine perfectly.

"I thought I was going crazy," he mumbles.

"You saw her kiss someone, didn't you? And when you asked her about it, she said you're *crazy* and *out of your mind*?"

He nods.

"You know you're not crazy, right?"

"I do now, thanks to Chrissy and Gwen. I don't know what would have happened to me if they didn't intervene. I would be a crazy asshole." He looks at me, realizing what he just said.

I stop him before he can say anything else. "No need to apologize because you're right. I'm glad you got away before she could hurt you. You're so unbelievably lucky you have Gwen and Chrissy. If I had friends like them, I don't think they would have let me stay with someone like Alex."

A genuine smile spreads across his lips. "I am lucky, but you are too. You have Gwen, Chrissy, and me behind you now. No one will ever hurt you again. That's what friends do, protect one another."

This is the Zack I know. This Zack would go down fighting to protect everyone he loves and walk through fire to save anyone he cared for. Roselyn poisoned him for a while, but he's back, and that's all that matters.

"So, when are you going to tell her?" Zack asks.

"What are you—"

Chapter Fifty-One

"When are you going to tell Gwen you love her?" Zack smirks at my dumbfounded expression.

My gaze falls to the concrete, and a silly smirk paints across my lips. "Do you think she knows?"

Zack snorts in response. "Gwen's a smart girl, but she's never been in love. She might have an inkling, but I don't think she knows the full extent of it."

"I don't want to scare her."

I thought I loved Alex, but the words never left my mouth. What if I tell Gwen I love her and she runs? What if, after I drop those words, she never talks to me again? The thought makes me sick.

"Ash, you've had her heart for years. I don't think anything you could say will ever scare her. Besides, I'm ninety-nine point nine percent sure she loves you too. And I'm not talking about the Ash she conjured in her head; she loves the Ash right in front of her. I'm glad she met you, you're a good guy. I wish Chrissy could find someone like you. Maybe then my heart will stop aggravating me all the time."

A deep chuckle rises from my chest. "I'll tell her soon. Thanks, Zack. I'm glad you're back, buddy." I pat his back.

"But if you ever fuck her while I'm on the other side of the door again, I'll put all those true crime docs I was forced to watch for the past five years to the test." Zack smiles at me, and while I don't think he meant to sound menacing, he definitely did.

"Understood," I blurt out.

Zack wraps his arm around my shoulder and leads us back inside.

"There they are!" Chrissy shouts before shoving two shot glasses into our hands. "Cheers, motherfuckers!"

"All right, missy, no more shots for you." Zack plants Chrissy back on the couch.

"You're no fun," she whines as Gwen stands.

"Are you—"

Zack pulls Gwen into his chest and hugs the life out of her. Normally, jealousy would rise and run through my veins, but I don't feel it this time. Gwen is mine, as I'm hers.

"Oh, Chrissy." I pull Chrissy's attention from the empty shot glass. "Do you still have those pictures of Gwen?"

Zack and Gwen watch us intently.

"You bet your ass I do."

We both giggle for a few seconds.

I stop laughing and drop my grin. "Delete them."

"What? No fair, she's seen me naked," Chrissy whines.

"More often than I'd like to admit," Gwen mumbles.

"I can't help it. Your home is so freeing. I don't get to walk around naked in my dorm room."

Rome stands in the kitchen doorway, his mouth hitting the floor the second the word "naked" was dropped. "Hey, Gwen, can I come over to your place sometime?"

Zack and I shoot Rome a glare that makes him backtrack.

"I take that back. Forget I'm even here." He holds his arms up in surrender and disappears back into the kitchen, where Miles is eating more cupcakes.

"You guys are no fun." Chrissy crosses her arms over her chest and pouts.

"Chrissy, want to do one last round of shots with me?" Gwen steps forward and offers her hand.

"I just said—" Zack sighs before he finishes his sentence.

Chrissy jumps up, ignoring Zack. "Come on, guys. Shots, shots, shots, shots!"

She and Gwen bounce up and down all the way into the kitchen. Zack follows behind them and smirks.

"One more, and then that girl needs some carbs ASAP," Zack calls after them.

Chapter Fifty-One

Miles and Rome join us as we down one last round of shots. I don't think I've ever been surrounded by a group of friends such as this. I can't quite describe the feeling fluttering behind my ribs. When I look at Gwen, the fluttering hastens and makes me feel like my heart might fly out of my chest.

I have to tell her soon. If I don't, I fear the words will fly out at the wrong time and blindside her.

I love Gwen Roman. There's no doubt about it.

Chapter Fifty-Two

Gwen

The rest of the evening went by without a hitch. Zack lightened up after a few drinks, and it wasn't long before he was laughing along with Rome, Miles, and Chrissy. I don't think he and Roselyn had an in-depth connection, but that didn't lessen his heartache.

I forgot just how much Zack can make me laugh. The whole night, everyone was doubling over in pain from laughing so hard. No one left until one in the morning, and not long after that, Ash and I collapsed in his bed and passed out.

When I wake up, Ash is still asleep, and I don't have the heart to wake him. I slip out of bed, grab a pair of his sweatpants and a baggy T-shirt, and jump in the shower. The hot water stings my skin, and my head throbs because Chrissy kept shoving straight vodka in my face all evening. It's not the worst hangover I've ever had, but it definitely sucks. I think the mountain load of cupcakes I devoured was my saving grace.

Chapter Fifty-Two

Once I step out of the shower, I get dressed, tying the sweatpants as tight as possible so they don't spill around my ankles. I love wearing Ash's clothes, being surrounded by his scent, and knowing the fabric along my skin touched his at one point. I keep reminding myself that this isn't a dream. It just feels so unreal. Who would have thought shy little Gwen would be in her crush's room? The same man that plagued my mind for years is outside this door, resting peacefully. Maybe some dreams are worth hanging on to.

"Gwen?" Ash hums sleepily and flails his arms in the air when I open the door. "Where'd you go?"

Thankful he has carpet in his Arctic-like bedroom, I stroll over to him and kneel. He blindly touches my face and squishes it.

"What are you—" His finger lands in my mouth and hooks my cheek. "Ash."

He squints one eye open and grins. "Oh, there you are."

I kiss the palm of his hand before resting on it.

"Come back to bed," he says before his eyes flutter closed again.

"I will—Ash?"

His breathing slows, and a cute, restful grin pulls on the corners of his mouth.

"Did you really just fall back asleep within five milliseconds?" I whisper in awe. Placing his hand back on the bed, I kiss his cheek. "I'll be right back."

The first thing Ash is going to need when he wakes up is Tylenol and water. I could use some myself as well. Maybe another cupcake or two . . .

I don't know where to find the Tylenol, but I do know where to find the water. Careful not to trip, I take the stairs one at a time. Stepping under the archway to the kitchen, I freeze.

The sound of pans clanging together and humming takes over my ears. Before I can back away, the man spins around, and holy shit, does he look just like an older Ash.

"Hi, Gwen."

He even has the same dimples. It's like looking in a mirror that foretells the future.

"Hi, Max."

It doesn't take a rocket scientist to make the connection. I mean, who else would be in the kitchen cooking at ten in the morning? I guess I was expecting him to be at work, but maybe he's skipping his responsibilities today like Ash and I are.

"Did you guys have fun last night?" His voice is deep, a tad more monotone than Ash's.

"We did. Don't worry, I plan on making Ash help me clean up the mess." I giggle awkwardly.

He smiles, and I'm starting to wonder why Ash calls him an asshole. There's no way, not with a grin like that.

"Ash did say I would like you. Speaking of Ash, is he still sleeping?" He gestures to the stool across the kitchen island.

I nod while taking a seat.

"Yeah, wish I knew what his trick was. He woke up, talked for a minute, then passed back out within five seconds."

Max nods his head in amusement. "Sounds like Ash. When we were kids, we used to try to stay up to catch Santa. That sucker was always fast asleep by nine. One time we were playing hide-and-seek, and that asshole fell asleep while he was it. I hid in a pantry for an hour and a half."

My hand flies over my mouth as I snort. Max slides me a bottle of Tylenol and a glass of water like he just pulled it out of his hat. Funny thing is, he's not wearing a hat.

"Thank you," I manage to say midchuckle.

I take two painkillers and gulp down as much water as possible.

Chapter Fifty-Two

"So, Gwen, tell me about yourself." Max sets the pan on the stove.

"Oh boy, where do I start? I go to Castle Brook with Ash, work part-time at a cat café, and I'm majoring in Biochemical Engineering."

He whips around with wide eyes. "My brother is dating a woman in STEM? My best friend owes me ten bucks. We bet he would end up with someone in marketing or something equally as boring."

I chuckle again. This guy's funny. "Would you believe me if I said I knew Ash in high school?"

He spins around, turns the stove off, then spins around again. "You have my attention." He props his elbows on the island, and his grin makes me smile wider.

"We never talked or anything. I wish we did. Any room he walked in would light up. It was easy to smile just knowing he was near. I guess some people just have that kind of natural energy."

"You had a crush on him, didn't you?"

My cheeks flush before I get the chance to protest. "Everyone did." I fiddle with my hands, embarrassed to make eye contact with him again.

"Can I tell you a secret?" He earns my attention again. "He didn't have many girlfriends growing up. But I can tell you this, I've never heard Ash giggle before. Never seen him so happy or relaxed either. It was only when you walked into his life that his heart started to settle and mend. I think you're going to be the one to show him the kind of person he's meant to be."

I can't fight the tears that coat my eyes. If it wasn't for the hangover and my lack of sleep, I think I would be able to fight them, but they betray me within seconds.

"I'm sorry, I didn't mean to overstep."

I shake my head. "No, it's just—I don't think he knows

what he's done for me. I hear all the time how I fixed his broken heart and mended his trust, but he's helped me too. Before Ash, I didn't know what it was like to be cared for. Like you two, my parents aren't the greatest. They were too self-absorbed to bother with me until I was eighteen. I have two best friends, and I became part of their family, but I never had something that was *mine* and *mine* alone. For the first time, I feel a part of something bigger than myself. Like I belong to something grander and stable. I lo—" I stumble over the word.

A faint knowing smile paints Max's lips as he shifts his attention over my shoulder. "Morning, Ash."

My damn cheeks flush again. I'm starting to wonder if I'm still tipsy from last night.

Turning around, I grin at Ash. "Hey, Ash, I met your brother. Oh, you look terrible."

He rubs his eyes, still fatigued and hungover. "I guess we don't need to have that dinner after all," Ash grumbles.

What the hell is he talking about?

"Nope," Max says with a wide grin. "I asked Ash to invite you to dinner so we could meet, but this works just as well."

"I was bound to run into you sooner or later." I smile while standing from the chair to offer Ash two painkillers and a glass of water.

"Want to go back to bed?" I ask as Ash throws his head back to swallow the Tylenol.

"Please." He pouts and extends his arms out to me.

I wrap my arm around his waist and lean against his chest. "Let's go. It was nice to finally meet you, Max." I peer over my shoulder and meet his smirk.

"You too, Gwen. And Ash?"

Ash loses his balance, leaning on me for support as he looks over his shoulder.

Chapter Fifty-Two

"You were right."

Ash kisses the top of my head in response.

Before we reach the stairs, he places his lips against my ear and whispers, "You're one hundred percent mine, Gwen Roman. As I am yours."

Chapter Fifty-Three

Ash

When did Max and Gwen become best friends? Was it when I was sleeping? When I walked in on them talking in the kitchen? Or was it just now, as we're cleaning up the mess from last night? It seems Gwen has some magical ability to bring out the best in people. Not saying my brother isn't a good guy. I just haven't seen this side of him in a very long time. Gwen put on some music and started dance cleaning. When Max caught me slacking off, he opted to join her. *Since when did this guy clean?*

"Can you guys please turn the music down?" I groan, hoping they'll pity me. That last round of shots really did me over.

"What?" Max and Gwen ask in sync.

"Wannabe" by Spice Girls comes on, and I know I'm screwed. Their faces light up, and I welcome the headache from hell. I would be lying if I said it's not amusing though. I knew Gwen awakened a part of me I forgot existed. Seeing

Chapter Fifty-Three

Max's grin, seeing his eyes light up, makes my heart sing. She's already working her magic on him, too.

"Ash, join us." Gwen tugs on my hand.

"Come on, Ash, stop being such a hungover baby." Max tugs on my other hand.

Yeah, Gwen's magic is in full effect.

"All right." I give in.

Gwen wraps her arms around my waist, swaying to the music, and Max wears a strand of lights like a scarf, shaking his ass like it's got somewhere to go.

"You guys are ridiculous." I chuckle.

Gwen leaps into my arms and kisses the exact spot where my head is pounding.

"You said Max is an asshole, I don't see it," she whispers.

"Let me have a turn." Max picks Gwen up and spins her around like a giddy schoolboy.

"Don't steal my girlfriend, Max," I tease.

Max whirls Gwen around. They're both a grinning, laughing mess.

"I would never." He drops Gwen and places his hand over his heart. "He's always hurting my feelings, Gwen."

"Says the guy who literally threatens to kill his coworker daily."

Max points at me. "That's different. He's not my brother." He feigns a pout and suckers Gwen right into it. "Speaking of my brother, Ash has something to ask you."

I sigh in annoyance and defeat. "You son of a bitch."

Max winks and walks backward into the kitchen, waving his arms like he's doing the wave. I run my hand over my forehead.

"What's wrong, Ash?" Gwen embraces me again.

I take her hand and lead her over to the couch. "Max wanted me to ask you something," I say while we sit. "And it's completely up to you. I'll understand if you say no." Her eyes glint in curiosity. "What are you doing for Thanksgiving?"

"Oh, um. I'm not sure actually. My parents are going to Hawaii—"

"Without you?" I didn't mean to cut her off. I just can't believe her parents take grand vacations without her.

"It's fine." She smiles down at her hands. "I'm used to it. Anyway . . ." It's official, I hate her parents. "I normally go to Chrissy and Zack's parents' back in Pennsylvania, but I haven't asked them their plans yet."

"They can come here!" Max slides into view with a leftover cupcake in his hand.

"Really? I don't want to impose." Her gloomy tone flips to excitement.

"There's one more thing." I sigh, hating that I have to ruin what would possibly be a decent idea. "My parents are coming, and they want to meet you."

"I'm fine with that."

I have to blink a few times because surely this has to be a dream.

"You are?" Max and I ask at the same time.

"Yeah, I don't mind. I mean, you don't know what you're getting yourselves into. You think Chrissy is bad, wait until you meet her mom."

I pull her in and wrap my arms around her. I can't remember the last time I had an actual Thanksgiving with more than just Max and me. I don't care if Mom and Dad are coming. I can tolerate their fighting, secret hoarding, cheating asses for one day. Gwen will be here, and I know I can survive them for one day—as long as she's by my side.

"Great. Now, does anyone know how to cook?" Max asks before shoving the cupcake in his mouth.

Chapter Fifty-Three

Gwen snickers, and I swear it's enough to talk me into just about anything.

"Want to cook with me?" I ask Gwen.

Her baby-blue eyes sparkle in response. I think I just said the five words she's been waiting to hear her entire life.

"I would love to."

Under the blasting music, Max's phone rings. He strolls to the arm of the couch and answers it.

"What do you want, Rodney? I'm busy. What do you mean you lost the contract?!" Gwen's eyes bug out. "Well, you better find it before I get to the office tomorrow. If you don't, I'll drown you in a river and ask my brother's new girlfriend to help me hide the body, and they'll never find you. Do you want to know why, Rodney? Because she watches true crime docs, asshole." Max drops his phone back on the couch and dances to the music like he didn't just threaten to murder his intern.

I can't help but laugh at Gwen's baffled expression.

"Oh, I get it now," she mumbles, and I giggle.

Chapter Fifty-Four

Gwen

I never thought my cooking skills were superior. Growing up, I learned to cook at a young age. Since my parents were always out and about most nights, I was left to fend for myself. I can cook the basics, and whatever I don't know, I look up on the internet, like every other millennial out there. Never would I have expected Ash and his brother to be so hopeless in the kitchen. I thought I was clumsy. These two make me look like the most coordinated human on the planet.

"Max, please don't cut toward your fingers."

He stops chopping in a panic.

"We don't need you losing one, yeah?" I don't care if it takes him ages to cut one carrot, as long as he does it carefully. "Wait, Ash! Don't eat that. There are raw eggs in the batter."

Ash backs away with his hands in the air.

Boys . . .

When I signed up to help Ash cook Thanksgiving dinner, I didn't think it would be stressful. It's not just Max and Ash I'm

Chapter Fifty-Four

stressed over. I'm petrified I'm going to cut myself or burn something. My skills aren't great, even if they surpass Ash's and Max's kitchen knowledge. *Which isn't saying a lot.*

I open the oven and check the turkey's temperature. It should be ready in another two hours. The Willowses will be here any minute now, and Ash's mom texted Max to tell him they'll be here in an hour.

I wouldn't say I'm nervous to meet Ash's parents. He told me time and time again he doesn't care about their opinion or blessing. He only cared about Max's approval, which was easy to get. It's funny how alike those two are. They have the same eyes, the same dimples that appear when they smile, and the same shade of chestnut hair. The only differences I have noted are their personalities and their haircuts.

Max is goofy, but he has this pretentious side that pops up when work appears. Ash is goofy too, but he's more laid back and sweet. I can't wait for Faye, Chrissy and Zack's mom, to meet him. I know their dad, Ethan, will love him, too.

I'm excited to see them. The last time I saw them was last Christmas. They really are like my parents. Blood never mattered to them. If it weren't for the Willows family, I would have been a lost cause. My parents should take a lesson or two out of the Willows parenting book.

"Are you okay?" Ash asks while he places his hand over mine.

"I'm fine. Keeping an eye on you two is more exhausting than I thought," I admit as Max curses and sucks on his finger. "Are you okay?" I call after him.

"Just a scratch, don't worry about me." He scurries into the bathroom.

Ash chuckles, pulling my attention back to him.

"I'm sorry, sneaky girl." He pulls my hands up to his lips, placing a gentle kiss on them. "You're not thinking of running away, are you? Max and I will end up burning the house down without you."

I giggle and meet his beautiful gaze. "You're lucky you're pretty," I tease.

His eyebrows raise in amusement. "Pretty?"

With a nod, I step back. "You're so pretty, Ash. It's a crime."

Ash scoffs, and his lips curl into a beaming grin, releasing those bone-melting dimples.

"If I'm pretty, what word would I use to describe you?"

My phone buzzes in my back pocket just as Ash winks. I peer down at the screen as my cheeks burn, smoldering red.

> We're here!

"They're here." I spin around and jump up and down excitedly. "Are you ready to meet Chrissy and Zack 1.0?"

Ash takes my face in his hands and plants a knee-buckling kiss on my lips. "With you, I'm ready for anything."

I fling the front door open and race down the driveway. The second I see Faye, I crash into her open arms, completely bypassing Zack's bear hug.

"I see how it is, Roman," Zack whines as Faye and I squeal in delight.

"Oh, how I missed you." She tightens her arms around me, reminding me of Zack's hugs.

"There she is!" Ethan swoops us both in his arms.

"Don't forget about me!" Chrissy jumps in, making us look like a big loving family.

When we peel apart, I gasp for much-needed air. Faye hasn't aged a day since I was eight years old. She and Chrissy share the same shade of blonde curly locks, her lips are painted blush pink, and her eyes are hazel with specks of green.

Chapter Fifty-Four

"Is that him?" Faye asks in her natural, sweet tone.

I glance over my shoulder to find Ash approaching us. I breathe out my nerves and swallow past the lump in my throat.

"Ash, my man! Gwen didn't hug me, so you have to fill in." Zack barrels into Ash.

They pat each other on the back like the tension and hostility they held for the past two months never happened.

Ash locks eyes with me, and my stomach jostles with more than just butterflies. The way he admires me is different than it was before. It's like I'm a dream, and he's begging the universe to never wake him up. I can't help but smile when he looks at me like that. It cements something within me that I didn't dare wish into reality solely because I was scared.

"You must be, Ash." Faye strolls up the driveway to her son and Ash.

Ash extends his hand, but Faye ignores him and pulls him into a bear hug.

Ethan places his hand on my shoulder. His royal-blue eyes glimmer, and his hair, slightly grayer than it was last year, is neatly slicked back.

"Don't be nervous. If you like him, we'll like him too."

My shoulders relax at the sound of his father-like voice.

Faye is squeezing Ash's cheeks when we approach them.

"You are so cute," Faye coos.

Ethan rushes in to save Ash from permanently pink cheeks.

"Did you even introduce yourself before you started with the cheek thing, Faye?" Ethan shakes Ash's hand. "Nice to meet you, Ash. I'm Ethan, and you had the pleasure of meeting my wife, Faye."

"I couldn't help it. I'm sorry."

I can't tell if Ash is blushing or if the sudden color painting his cheeks is from Faye's fingers.

"She has a cheek problem. Sorry, Ash." Chrissy skips by, holding some kind of book.

"What's that, Chrissy?" I wrinkle my forehead.

She stops at the front door and smiles wickedly. "Our yearbook from twelfth grade. More specially, *your* copy that you left in my room." She raises and drops her eyebrows.

"You didn't."

She opens the book and flips through the pages. "You're right. I didn't. Mom did."

I whirl around only to meet a shrugging Faye. "She said she needed it for a project."

Poor Faye, she didn't know the trick Chrissy had up her sleeve.

"Now, let's see. Oh, here it is."

"Chrissy," I chastise.

"Ash, wanna see your senior year portrait?"

I charge after her before she can turn the book around. Chrissy runs into the house right past a very confused Max.

"Hey, Max, the Willowses are outside!" I shout over my shoulder as I turn into the kitchen.

Chrissy plants herself on the opposite side of the island. "Come on, Gwen, it's cute." Chrissy holds the book against her chest and dances with it.

"It's not cute, it's embarrassing."

Every year since the tenth grade, I circled Ash's picture with a big red heart. If I was in the mood, I traced it thousands of times until the page threatened to rip.

"What's not cute?" Ash strolls in without warning and unexpectedly snatches the book from Chrissy's hands.

I glare at her as she smiles as innocently as possible.

"Aw, Gwen, you really did like me." He flashes me the page.

I groan and shield myself behind my hands. "Kill me now."

Chapter Fifty-Four

"Not before I get my hug!" Zack lifts me by my waist and spins me around the room until I can't stop myself from laughing and grinning.

Family sucks sometimes, but mine isn't too bad.

I guess.

Chapter Fifty-Five

Ash

Faye and Ethan Willows are everything I hoped they would be. I didn't expect Faye to grab my cheeks and pinch them red. I did expect her to be kind and loving, especially to her two girls. Ethan is nothing like his other family members. He seems shier and more laid back. Yet, he's talking my brother up about some crazy legal case. I tried listening in, but all the jargon and big words rattled my brain.

Gwen rests her head on Faye's shoulder, and Faye plays with Gwen's hair while chatting with Chrissy. I'm glad Gwen found a mother figure in Faye. Heaven knows the one that birthed her never took on the task. Her parents didn't even text her today. Those assholes are living it up in Hawaii without her. The selfish part of me is glad because it means I get to have Gwen all to myself. The selfless part is sad for her. That girl does nothing but work and study. She deserves a nice vacation on the beach, holding a drink in her hand, a book in her face.

Chapter Fifty-Five

She deserves the world. And if they refuse to give it to her, I will.

It'll take some time to get my career off the ground, and she'll be busy launching her mastermind into the world of science. But I know I can give her a good life, one that she deserves and more.

"Ash, are you okay?" Gwen asks me with her kind smile.

"Yeah, was just thinking." I shake my head and focus back on her.

"When will your parents be here?"

I pull my phone out of my pocket. No texts. Normally that would be a good thing. Today though? I'm a bit concerned.

"I'll ask Max if he heard from them. Do you guys need anything from the kitchen?"

Faye jumps up and links her arm through mine. "I'll go with you. We have a lot to talk about." She pats my shoulder.

It's eerie just how much she and Chrissy look alike.

The entire kitchen smells like Thanksgiving, an aroma I can't say I remembered until today. Gwen found a citrus herb butter recipe she wanted to try, so orange, lemon, thyme, and other roasting herbs circulate the kitchen. Combine that with mashed potatoes, stuffing, and green bean casserole. My stomach growls angrily, knowing I won't get to eat for another hour.

"Have you heard from Mom or Dad, Max?"

Max shakes his head. "No, but if they're not here on time, we're eating without them," he announces as Ethan smiles at me.

"Your brother was just telling me you're majoring in computer analytics. I did a little bit of coding back in my university days."

I rest my elbows on the counter across from him. "Really, did you like it?"

We go back and forth discussing various coding software mechanisms. I share my love of science and how I ran into Gwen and Chrissy because of it. I tell him about the corn maze and how bad at trivia those two are. Faye found that particular part hilarious.

"I'm so glad those two stuck together. Sometimes childhood friendships don't last, but they're more than friends. Gwen is a part of this family, but they were sisters way before that," Faye says as she smiles at Ethan.

I would kill to discover what they know about Gwen, all the memories and adventures. I hope I get to hear it all one day.

When the doorbell chimes, Max and I lock eyes and sigh in sync.

"I'll get it." My shoulders slump forward as I walk out of the kitchen.

Gwen is standing by the couch, fiddling with her thumbs. I offer her a reassuring smile and wink. As I place my hand on the doorknob, I take one last breath of parent-free air.

Mom hasn't aged a day. Her waist-length, straight black hair is tied back with a scrunchie, and her dark chocolate eyes reflect in mine. I wish I could say her smile meant something to me, but I don't think it ever did.

"Hey, Mom."

She wraps her arms around me, her fur coat tickling my nose, threatening a sneeze.

"Where's Dad?" I look around her only to find an empty street.

"He had other plans," she tells me, and I roll my eyes.

That means he has other plans involving a hotel room and his secretary. Always placing strange women before his family. At least he's predictable.

"You must be Gwen."

The second Mom brushes past me, I want to take it all

Chapter Fifty-Five

back. I don't want Gwen to meet my mother. She doesn't deserve the toxicity that woman holds. But it's too late. I can only watch as Mom wraps her arms around Gwen to hug her. I close the door, keeping my eyes rooted on Gwen. She doesn't look terrified, anxious maybe, but not scared shitless.

"Ash, you didn't tell me she was so pretty." Mom steps back to look me over.

"How can I tell you if you never call or text me?" Sure, it's a two-way street. The last I talked to my parents was last summer, the same day I put up my boundaries.

Mom shrugs off her jacket and tosses it to me.

Zack appears with his mouth full of bread, and only I know he's screwed.

"And who are you?" Mom's tone drops into one I remember all too well.

"Run," I whisper urgently, not caring if my mom hears me.

With wide eyes, Zack glances around the room. Poor guy doesn't know what he just walked into. He takes careful steps backward and points back to the kitchen.

"I think my mom is calling me." Zack retreats back to where he came from.

He's safe—for now.

"Mom, please don't flirt with my friends." I sigh in disappointment.

"Hi there." Chrissy dances in Mom's view. "I'm Chrissy, Gwen and Ash's best friend."

And there's the look, the one I despise so much. She tips her lips downward, exposing wrinkles even though she gets Botox once a month.

"Chrissy, why don't you go check on your brother," I suggest.

She looks my way and nods in understanding.

I place Mom's jacket on the railing and move to stand next to Gwen.

"So." Mom clasps her hands together. "How's Alex doing?"

And here we go.

"No idea. We broke up. Remember?" I weave my fingers through Gwen's for support.

"I remember, I just don't understand why."

I swear I hear Gwen's heart plummet through the hardwood floor.

"Dinner's ready!"

I've never been more grateful for Max and his shouting.

Mom strolls to the kitchen to make her grand entrance, and I pull Gwen against my chest and nuzzle against the top of her head.

"It'll be okay," she whispers. "She won't scare me away, I promise." She stands on her tippy-toes and kisses me. "You and me, right?"

She offers me her pinkie, and I take it instantly.

"Right."

"I'll kidnap you if it gets too bad, deal?" Gwen's grin grounds me, reminding me I can do anything as long as she's by my side.

"Deal."

Chapter Fifty-Six

Gwen

I wasn't sure what to expect from Ash's mom. I know about his parents' pasts, how they not so secretly have affairs, yet never tried to split or get a divorce. I wonder if they have some kind of strange arrangement. I would ask Ash, but I doubt he would know or care to know the answer.

Everyone piled their plates high and sat around the kitchen table. Ash pulled my chair close to him so our knees would touch. I think it's cute that he wants some part of us touching at all times. It makes me wonder if he gets a sense of strength from it. The universe knows he needs all the courage he can get to survive this dinner.

The only noise that dares to cut the boiling tension in the room is silverware clattering and clanging against glass plates. Leighann, Ash and Max's mom, placed herself at the head of the table. Off the bat, I didn't think she was as bad as Ash painted her to be. But the moment she brought up Alex, I retracted my original thought. From what Ash told me, his mom liked Alex. She and his father didn't find anything wrong with Alex's indiscretion. In fact, they berated Ash for breaking ties with her because, at the end of the day, she's a *decent* girl. No wonder Ash cemented walls around his heart.

"How's work going, Mom?" Max dares to break the silence.

"Fine. I got a new intern," she says.

Max rolls his eyes in response.

"Since when does a marketing manager need an intern?" Ash asks.

I choke on my water. That bet Max said he had with his best friend makes sense now.

"They need one if they're as busy as I am, Ash."

My lips curl in response to her tone. It reminds me of Roselyn's. Smooth yet full of attitude. She thinks she's better than everyone in this room. My plan is to keep shoving food in my mouth, hoping to finish eating in record time so I can leave the table and bring Ash with me.

"Gwen, how's Pickles?" I meet Faye's refreshing gaze.

After unlocking my phone, I hand it to her while finishing the food in my mouth.

"Look how big he's gotten."

The picture I show her is of Pickles in his signature spot lounging in the café's front window. He's doubled in size since we first took him in three months ago, and thankfully, he doesn't chew on me like he used to.

"Who's Pickles?" My eyes flicker Leighann's way.

Faye stands and passes her my phone. The second she sees Pickles, her eyes crinkle.

"He's a cat I take care of at a cat café." I reach for my phone, making sure not to brush my fingers along hers.

"You work at a cat café?"

Ash's hand lands on my knee.

Chapter Fifty-Six

"I do, part-time." I plaster a fake, broad smile on my lips, hoping to appease her.

"How cute."

I drop the smile the second she focuses back on Zack.

Oh no, you don't.

"Zack, how are your hemorrhoids?" I blurt out in an attempt to save him.

Chrissy snorts water out of her nose, and Zack's mouth hangs open, the food on his fork inches from his face. Slowly, he drops his fork and peers over at me.

"They're *grand*, thanks for asking," he deadpans.

I don't think he knows what I'm up to.

"Are you sure? The last I heard, one of them popped, right, Chrissy?" I look at Chrissy and catch a glimpse of Leighann, her attention now on her phone. *Phew.*

"Right, almost had to rush him to the ER. There was *so* much blood."

Okay, maybe that was too far.

"Girls, we're trying to eat," Ethan manages to say while holding back a laugh.

"Sorry," we mumble at the same time.

Ash leans into my ear and kisses the side of my head. "Nice save," he whispers with a hint of laughter.

"Ash, you never answered my question. How's Alex?"

I've never seen Ash roll his eyes so much.

"Fuck me," he whispers while pulling back to look at his mom.

"I don't know, Mom, we broke up. Remember?" He drops his fork and groans.

"I still don't understand why. She was such a nice girl," she says.

"Because he caught Alex bouncing on his best friend's dick," Max spews at Leighann. His cheeks burn red, his tone now resembling the one he used when he was talking to his intern.

"I don't see—" Leighann starts but stops when Max stands from his chair.

"Just because you and Dad get a kick out of sleeping with your interns and secretaries doesn't mean other people share the same kink. Ash's trust was betrayed by the two people he relied on the most. Naturally, he cut ties and moved on. I don't appreciate you asking about his ex when his current girlfriend is sitting right here."

Faye's and Ethan's eyes land on me, and Ash squeezes my thigh.

"I just don't—" She starts again but is cut off.

"That's enough, Mom." Ash's eyes dart over to her. "There's a reason we don't talk anymore, why I don't text or call you. Have you ever considered why? Or are you too busy fucking other men to care about your two sons?"

Leighann is taken aback, her cheeks draining of color. "Ash, you can't talk to me like that." Her tone rises to match Max's.

"He most certainly can because he's in my house, not yours. There's a reason we moved the second we graduated. You're just too blind to see it."

She opens her mouth, but Ash cuts her off this time. "Be careful what you say next, Mom. You're talking about my girlfriend. And whether you want to believe it or not, I like Gwen, and I'm sure her family won't tolerate any more of your nonsense."

He's right. Faye's pursing her lips, trying to hold back, Chrissy is twitching in her seat, and Zack and Ethan both wear the same *fuck with her and you fuck with me* expression. Don't even get me started on Ash. The poor guy looks like his head is about to combust. His fingers are digging into my thigh, and his lips turn down in aggression.

Chapter Fifty-Six

I place my hand over his, securing him by my side.

"I'll be in town until tomorrow evening. You boys can come and apologize to me when you've come to your senses," she says before stomping away.

She grabs her coat, flings the door open, and slams it shut, causing the whole room to both shudder and sigh in relief upon her exit.

"I'm sorry about her. I thought she had good intentions this year, should have known better." Max looks over at Ash, wearing a sympathetic smile. "I should have listened to you. Like always, you were right."

"Don't be sorry. If anything, I now know cutting ties with them was a good decision. I'm just sorry we ruined everyone's Thanksgiving." Ash apologizes, but Ethan shakes his head in response.

"No need to be sorry. It isn't an official Willows holiday until someone gets yelled at or embarrassed. We just happened to hit both of those this year. If I knew my son had hemorrhoids, I would have brought some cream for him."

Zack sputters out his water all over Faye. Her mouth hangs open in shock.

"Sorry, Mom." He flashes her his famous broad smile.

Chrissy and I look at each other and start cracking up. We both end up leaning on Ash for support as Faye wipes her face clean.

"How many times do we have to go over this, Zack?" she groans. "Dad started it!" Zack stands and points at Ethan.

"Hey, I wasn't the one who spit on your mother." Ethan holds his hands up and leans back in his chair.

"Payback's a bitch." Faye takes a gulp of water and swooshes it around in her mouth.

She stands and rushes over to Zack, and he stumbles over his chair. The whole room erupts in laughter as Zack runs into the kitchen screaming, and Faye chases after him. Seconds later, she returns with a pleased smirk on her face.

"Why are you like this?!" Zack appears in the doorway, dripping wet.

"So, when's dessert?" Faye clasps her hands together triumphantly.

Chrissy falls out of her chair and wraps her arms around her waist, crying from laughter. Ash's smile matches my own, like the whole mom incident never happened. I rest my head on his shoulder and watch the world around us. Ethan is right. It's not officially Thanksgiving unless one argument occurs or someone gets embarrassed, and while this day may have started tense, it won't end that way. Ash kisses the top of my head and wraps his hand around mine.

"Thank you," he whispers around the noise.

I tilt my head and kiss the underside of his jaw. "You and me, always."

Chapter Fifty-Seven

Ash

Seeing Gwen in my bed, wearing my T-shirt and a pair of flannel pajama pants, is one of my favorite sights in the world. She's lying on her back with her hands cradling her stomach. That girl has a weakness for apple crumb pie with a mountain load of whip cream.

I put on a pair of sweatpants and a plain white tee before collapsing next to her.

"Are you okay?" I can't help but snicker knowing how bloated she is right now.

"I'm so full, yet I want more pie," she groans. I wrap my arm around her waist to pull her closer, but she grumbles, "Don't touch me. I might explode."

Her phone starts to vibrate on the bedside table next to her.

"Want me to get that?" I don't think Gwen will be moving anytime soon.

"Please."

Very carefully, I reach over her and see the text from her parents.

"Let me guess. It's a picture from my mom saying they're having a great time."

I open the message and frown.

"Was I right? Your facial expression is telling me I'm right."

I place her phone down behind me.

"Doesn't it bother you?" I ask.

She shrugs. "It used to, but not anymore. I have the Willowses, and now I have you and Max." She tilts her head to look at me. "We have something else in common, you know. We both picked our families, regardless of blood. I picked the Willowses, and you picked your brother. Now, we're picking each other." Her thumb brushes over my cheekbone. "Family doesn't define us, Ash. The ones we pick to surround ourselves with do. And I think we have a good circle of people."

I place my chest on top of hers and shove my face in the crook of her neck. Her hand lands on my back, tracing random shapes along my shoulder blade.

"Do you ever wish I was more like the Ash you had in your head?"

She shakes her head. "No, he's unrealistic. Besides, the Ash I had in my head doesn't live up to you. I couldn't have imagined someone like you because I never knew anyone like you existed." I reach under her shirt and rest my hand on her skin. "You're so much more than I originally took you for, and I know you overheard me talking to Max the other day, so you heard how much you mean to me, but you don't know how much you changed me. I'll never be outgoing or flashy like the other girls you've dated, but you're popping the bubble I secured around myself. I don't let others walk over me anymore. I don't let anyone talk down to me either. I think it started when you first said hi to me in biochem, which is weird to say out loud. How

Chapter Fifty-Seven

can one interaction change someone? I wish I had the answer, but I know it's true. Because of you, I'm finally figuring out the kind of person I'm meant to be, and she's not bad." Her nose wrinkles when I weave my hand into her wavy locks. "You changed me, Ash Waylen. I just hope you stick around to see the final product."

I press my lips against hers, desperate for her to know just how much I love her.

"I'm not going anywhere," I whisper as our lips part. "I would be crazy to leave you. If I do, you should assume someone has brainwashed me." Her giggle fans my lips. "I'm nothing without you. When I saw you that first day of fall semester, I felt a pull that urged me to be near you. Something inside yelled at me to get to know you, that you were someone special. I tried to hold back because I was scared. I didn't want to get hurt again. But those feelings overpowered me, and I'm so glad they did. You're it for me, Gwen Roman. There can never be anyone else. The thought of losing you is maddening." I stare into her eyes, the words I want to say on the tip of my tongue. "Gwen, I—"

She closes the gap between us and kisses me with such devotion and desire I know she won't run. Gwen Roman would never run away from me. Her grip around me is proof.

"I love you," I say as our lips part. Fuck that feels good to say. "I love you, Gwen."

Her eyes flutter open, and the anxiety I had washes away. My muscles finally relax and release built-up tension I didn't know I had.

"I love you, Ash."

"Really?"

She nods enthusiastically. "I do."

I kiss her over and over again, her giggle the only other sound other than our lips against each other.

"I love you so much. Fuck, I've wanted to say that for so long." I move from her lips and kiss her cheek, her jawline, her neck. I need to kiss every inch of her.

"How long were you holding that in?" she snickers as I move down her body. "Ash, Ash, please, not my stomach!" she cries in laughter and rolls on her side to protect her pie-filled belly.

"I wanted to tell you last month, but I was scared you would run. I now know you won't. I love you." I cup her face in my palms and kiss her long and hard. "And now that you know, you can never leave me."

"I would be crazy to leave, but if you don't stop kissing me like that, I'll have to spend the night in Max's room."

I roll Gwen onto her back and secure myself over her.

"You wouldn't dare, you'd miss me too much." I rest my head on her breasts and listen to her breathing.

"You're right." She plays with my hair and laughs.

"You wouldn't last five minutes knowing you left me in here all by myself." I tug on the waistband of her pants.

"You're right," she repeats, out of breath.

I take her pants off and throw them across the room. The sight of her bare legs, her simple violet panties with lace trim, makes my heart stutter.

"Especially knowing you left me all alone and this hard." I hover over her so we're face to face.

"You're right." She unties the drawstring on my pants and glides them down my legs.

"Is that all you can say?" I ask while kicking my pants to the floor.

She reaches into my boxers to release my cock. The touch of her hand against me is almost enough to make me come.

"What do you want me to say?" she whispers while stroking me.

Chapter Fifty-Seven

"Fuck me," I moan.

"Fuck me," she repeats in the same hypnotized tone.

"Since when did you become a smart-ass?"

She increases her pressure and strokes faster. "Not sure. What are you going to do about it?"

I flip onto my back and arch my eyebrows at her. "Wrap that smart-ass mouth around my cock."

Gwen places herself over my right leg and licks her lips. She hovers over me, taking her sweet ass time.

"Gwen," I urge.

She wraps her mouth around me, and my back arches at the contact. I ball her hair in my fist so I can see how her lips look around my erection, and damn, I've never seen anything more beautiful.

"Fuck me." My whimper of pleasure ignites something within her.

Gwen starts grinding her clit on my thigh, groaning from the pressure.

"Does that feel good, baby?"

She nods while peering up at me. Somehow, she manages to take all of me in her mouth.

"Fuck, you're such a good girl, taking every inch of my cock."

Her eyes glisten as I whimper. I don't have to take control or guide her with my hands because this woman knows my body and how to please it. The muscles in my thighs tighten, and Gwen moans louder as her grinding quickens.

She takes my length in her hand and removes her mouth. "Are you going to come for me?"

All I can do is nod and mumble an incoherent response.

She unwraps her hand and slips her underwear off over her right thigh. "Sorry, I need you to come in something else."

"You fucking smart-ass—*yes*."

She takes all of me without a moment's notice. My mouth hangs open, savoring how her muscles contract around me. When my hands land on her hips, I realize I can watch Gwen ride me like this all day. She leans over to press her chest against mine before she sucks my bottom lip and pulls on it tenderly.

"What were you saying?" she whispers.

I rest my hands on her sides and lift my hips to thrust into her. "I fucking love you."

It takes all I have not to come. I was close before, but now? I'm barely holding on.

"I love you," she mumbles into my mouth as I drive into her. "Ash."

Her back tightens under my palm as she groans loudly in my mouth, and I take all of it. She rides me fast, gyrating her hips and bouncing up and down my shaft, her pussy massaging my cock.

I squeeze her hips, and she screams, "Fuck, Ash!" Then she falls against my chest.

I drive into her, and she screams once more in finality.

"Gwen, oh baby, fuck." Releasing everything I have inside her, my groans of pleasure fill the air.

I'm still fighting for air when she rolls off me and snuggles against my right arm. The sound of her own struggle satisfies me. I like hearing her tiny gasps for air after we make love.

"Ash?"

I turn my head and smile down at her. "Yeah?"

"Can you get me some more pie?" She flutters those damn eyelashes at me, and I'm completely under her control.

"Anything for you, my love."

Chapter Fifty-Eight

Gwen

Ash loves me.

Ash Waylen loves me.

When I told Chrissy, all she said was "I knew it." Chrissy has a knack for little things like this. What I didn't expect was for Zack to have the same reaction. How did he know before I did? Wish I could say. I had a suspicion that Ash loved me, I just didn't want to voice the idea out loud. Because what if he didn't, and I got my hopes up about nothing?

One week later, I can't stop myself from skipping all the way to work. I didn't know I could feel this good, feel this loved. I can't wrap my head around it. One thing is for sure, now that December is here, I need to start planning for Christmas and a surprise or two beforehand. I want to show Ash I remember his favorite holiday, just as he did mine.

And maybe show him up a little . . .

"There she is!" Blake sings as I step through the door.

Pickles races over to me, the grin already on my face growing wider. "Love looks good on you, girl."

"Are you gonna say that every time you see me?" I ask.

Blake goes back to sweeping and nods. "Yes, I am!"

He's lucky he has a good singing voice.

"How are you today, handsome?" I soak up all the snuggles Pickles has to offer and clock in.

I'm not used to this kind of attention from Pickles. Normally he would be tangled in my hair by now. I'm going to take full advantage of this kind, loving boy.

"There you are." Ryan strolls in from the back with a weird, forlorn expression.

"Why do I feel like I'm about to get the worst news of my life?"

Blake's whistling dies down. Yep, I'm about to get in trouble for something.

"Gwen." Ryan looks down at Pickles and sighs. "I have some goodish bad news."

"Tell me the good news first."

"It's one piece of news, unfortunately."

Pickles leaps out of my hands to harass Blake and his sweeping.

"Pickles got adopted," Ryan tells me, and I laugh in disbelief.

"No, he didn't. Who would want to adopt that maniac?"

Right on cue, Pickles jumps Blake, and Blake's screaming fills the room.

"I can't say."

I squint my eyes. "Since when are adoptions confidential?"

"Since the person adopting Pickles doesn't want their name disclosed." Ryan places his hands on his hips, another sigh escaping his chest.

"Then I challenge their application," I say.

Chapter Fifty-Eight

"You can't challenge someone's approved application."

"Says who?" I copy his posture to assert dominance.

"Says me."

I poke my bottom lip out to try to pull on his heartstrings.

"You really want to adopt that crazy thing?" He points over to Pickles, who's chasing Blake around a line of tables.

He's right. What would I do with a cat like Pickles? My tiny apartment could never house that crazy boy. Just because I want him doesn't mean it's meant to be.

"He's going to a good home, I promise." Ryan flashes me that *it'll all be okay* smile.

"How long until he leaves?" I ask with a trembling tone.

"Christmas Eve, about three weeks. And don't even think about catnapping him." He points at me as I purse my lips.

"Me? I would never."

I so would . . .

But I wouldn't do that to Pickles. He deserves a good home. I have three weeks left with him, so I'll have to make the best of it.

Chapter Fifty-Nine

Ash

I love December, not just because of Christmas. I love it because of the chill in the air and how snow threatens the sky each day. While everyone huddles inside, I'm walking the ice-covered paths. I feel awakened when winter comes around. Perhaps I was a polar bear in a past life.

A thin layer of ice crunches under my feet as I walk to the computer lab. With the fall semester almost over, I need to make sure my final coding project runs with no errors. As I walk along the sidewalk, I slow my pace when I spot Alex. I haven't heard from her in weeks, and now I know why. Her attention is on her next victim, and as much as I don't want memories to trickle into my brain, they do.

So, in an attempt to ignore these recollections, I pull my phone from my jacket pocket to check the time, but I see a text from Gwen, and my whole day brightens.

Chapter Fifty-Nine

> Look who decided to pay Pickles and me a visit!

Attached is a picture of Gwen holding Pickles with Chrissy throwing bunny ears behind the chaotic cat, and surprisingly, he's not biting her. That kitten will always remain a mystery to me. Somehow, though, I kind of love him.

The center is crowded, so I plop down in a free computer station and type in my credentials without looking at the keyboard. I can't pull my eyes away from the photo of Gwen. This woman's hold on me just doesn't let up, not that I'm complaining.

Reluctantly, I close the text and open the coding software. If I keep my head straight, I can finish this today and prepare for my other finals a bit earlier than I originally planned. That's easier said than done though, isn't it?

Memes will always be my downfall. Twenty minutes in, and I'm already scrolling through my phone, smirking to myself, desperate for a change of scenery. One can only focus on codes on a computer screen for so long . . .

> Are you finishing that project, or are you looking at memes again?

I hold back the chuckle that rises in my throat. We've only been together a few months now, but she knows me like the back of her hand. Instead of texting back, I send her a meme that had me cracking up.

> You dork! Get back to work xD

> Okay, okay. See you in a few hours.

I send her one last meme before shoving my phone back in

Forever Crushed

my bag. As always, she's right. I need to finish this damn thing before I go cross-eyed.

Normally, I would notice the first snowfall of the year. But I was holed up inside that musty computer lab for hours. The second I step outside, the snowflakes pelt my face, melting on contact.

I opt out of driving back to Tea and Kittens. I'm sure Gwen won't mind walking back and spending the night at her apartment. I need to clear my head of codes and relish the first snowfall.

When I told Gwen why I love Christmas, it was the truth. It's the only time of year my parents got along and didn't bring random strangers into the house. I was actually the center of their attention, and I didn't have to worry about them fighting.

Following the pavement, I round the upcoming bend. Tea and Kittens comes into view, and my pace quickens. I can't wait to walk back to Gwen's place and watch the rest of the snow while we cuddle in her bed.

Just as I reach the storefront, I stop.

In the window's reflection, I witness the moment my jaw tightens. Gwen steps back from embracing some guy as Chrissy wraps her scarf around her neck. The smile Gwen is offering him makes time slow. I look over the man wearing a baseball cap, trying to figure out if I know him or not. *Why does he look so familiar?*

"*Who is that?*" The question I used to ask Alex rings in my head.

I would always find her embracing someone, and she would always deny my feelings.

"*My best friend!?*" Tears sting my eyes as the memory collides into the forefront of my mind.

Is this strange guy someone Gwen knows? Why is she hugging him? Who the fuck is he?

Chapter Fifty-Nine

The bell above the door sends sharp signals right to my eardrums. Gwen pulls her beanie over her head and grins at me as she steps outside.

"Hey, you," she says.

I don't meet her smile like I usually do. My eyes stay plastered on the guy talking to Chrissy.

"Who's that?" I nod toward the man standing next to Chrissy inside the café, not caring to identify any distinguishable features.

"David, Chrissy's lab partner. He stopped by to swap some notes to prepare for the final."

I peer at him, trying my best to remember whether or not I've seen him in class before.

"You remember, don't you? You paid Chrissy five bucks to sit with him so you could sit next to me."

"Oh, yeah." My tone is emotionless.

That doesn't answer the pounding question in my head. *Why were you hugging him?*

"Are you okay?" Gwen tilts her head as concern floods her expression.

My eyes flicker over him as they step outside. I don't mean to ignore Chrissy when she waves at me, but I don't bother saying hi to *David*.

"Ash? What crawled up your butt?" Chrissy grins, not knowing the state of my mind from the jealousy racking my nerves.

"Nothing, my coding project kicked my ass, is all."

With a subtle nod, Chrissy squeezes my shoulder. "Go take a nap or something. You look awful. See you guys tomorrow!" Chrissy beams again.

David nods his head at me, but I don't respond. None of my motor functions seem to be working right now.

"Ash, talk to me." Gwen grabs my hands, her fingerless gloves soft against my frigid limbs.

"How well do you know him?" I glance over my shoulder even though they're out of sight now.

"Not well. He seems nice though."

"Then why were you hugging him?" I can't stop the question from rolling off my tongue.

"I was saying bye and thanking him for letting me copy some of his notes." She shrugs like it's nothing, but it's not *nothing*, not to me. "Ash, what's going on?"

"I just wasn't expecting it . . ."

"Ash Waylen, are you jealous?" She clicks her tongue with a smirk.

But I'm not in the mood for jokes. "It's not funny, Gwen. I didn't expect to see that." I gesture to the window, painting the picture as it's replaying in my mind.

"It was just a hug," she states.

I drop her hands and run my fingers through my hair.

"Are you seriously upset over this?"

I let out a huff, trying my best to simmer down the envy thickening my blood.

"I just didn't like it." My tone drops, and the image of Gwen doing more than just hugging David creeps into my mind.

"Do you honestly think I could ever hurt you like that? Especially right after we said 'I love you' to one another?"

Tears coat my eyes as my blood-boiling thoughts start to run wild.

"I don't know, Gwen." I shrug in frustration.

Shaking my head, I try to free myself of these unnecessary thoughts, but it's not long before the image of David's lips on hers stabs me in the heart.

Chapter Fifty-Nine

Next thing I know, I'm saying the unthinkable. "I didn't think Alex would cheat on me, and she did."

My stomach drops the second the words fly from my mouth, but I don't take them back. Regret pools in my veins, but I'm standing up for myself. Because what if Gwen is cheating on me, and I was blinded once again?

Gwen's eyes widen, and a puff of hot air blows past her lips. "Did you just compare me to Alex?"

"It's true though. The last thing I expected was for Alex to cheat on me. Who's to say I won't walk in on you bouncing on some random guy's dick." *Fuck, wrong choice of words, asshole.*

"Did you really just say that to me?" An irritated scoff leaves her lips. "Answer me, dammit!"

The wind picks up, and even though she tries not to shiver, she does. The fury that rages in my blood keeps me warm. If we were in different circumstances, I would pull her close and share all the body heat I could muster for her. Pretty sure she would punch me if I did that now, and I wouldn't blame her.

"Gwen, I—" I stumble over my words, trying to string together whatever cohesive thought I can from my brain.

But I can't. The images of Alex riding Brandon manage to free themselves, releasing a new wave of anger.

"I'm not perfect, okay? I'm not the Ash in your fantasies. I'm real, and I have feelings. I didn't like what I saw, and I won't apologize for it."

"I never thought I'd say this." Her normal tone is long gone, replaced with disappointment and fury. "You're a fucking asshole. I'm not cheating on you. The fact that I have to say that hurts. Since the first day of the fall semester, I've only tried to comfort you. I knew you were broken, and any normal person would've run away. But you know what I did? I *stayed*, and I tried my damn best to help you. I thought I did. But I was wrong. What you're doing right now, even though I did nothing, only proves it."

All I can do is breathe as the silence surrounding us becomes deafening.

"Are you going to say anything?"

I meet her once caring eyes, and the shiver that sets deep in my bones misses the kind spark she once carried.

"I don't have anything else to say . . ." The wind hits my back, but the cold doesn't sting. If anything, it's the same temperature as my heart.

"I'm going to walk away now. Don't follow me. Text me once you've calmed down." She doesn't wait for a response.

The second she leaves, the air around me becomes bitter.

Chapter Sixty

Gwen

> Ash is a fucking asshole.

My thumbs pound into the phone screen. I wonder if there's a word to describe this level of anger settling into my bones.

> Why? What happened?

My fingers slam the screen as I type out my response to Chrissy. I let my rage blind all logical parts of my senses. I should be watching the ground, especially now that it's snowing and brisk. I shouldn't be focusing on sending a maddening text or how my head throbs. I shouldn't let Ash's words get to me.

But I do.

There's a reason I say I'm aging like a sixty-year-old man. I can't tell you how many times I've slipped both up and down stairs. There's a reason I watch my feet. So how come I'm not doing what I should be doing? Because Ash pissed me off.

I don't get the chance to react or brace myself. Everything happens in slow motion. My feet slip out from under my body. My phone flies out of my hands and straight into the air. My hands try to soften the blow I'm about to make, but that was the wrong move. The cry that escapes my chest doesn't deafen the crack I both hear and feel from my wrist.

I roll on my side as blinding hot tears well in my eyes. How can my wrist feel both numb and like it's on fire at the same time? Sweat beads across my forehead, and I yank my hat off with my free hand, stifling the cry that builds in my core.

"Fuck." My tears melt the ice that surrounds me. "You fucking idiot." I try to right my vision, but the pain is so brutal that I can't focus.

With ragged gasps of air, I scramble for my phone, making sure to keep my left wrist stable. Flipping it over, I'm not surprised to find the screen cracked. I'm just shocked it still works.

"Call Chrissy."

The phone begins to ring. *Thank you!*

"Hello?"

"Chrissy, where are you?" I can't hide the panic in my voice.

"I'm almost back at my dorm. Why? What's wrong?"

I muffle another groan as I attempt to stand straight. *Nope, not happening.*

"What did Ash do?" Her tone rises, almost matching my level of panic.

"Besides piss me off? Nothing. I fucking slipped and fell on my wrist. My entire arm is numb." I'm trying not to hyperventilate, but my lungs are desperate for air.

Chapter Sixty

"Where are you?" I hear her shuffle on the other end of the line.

I glance around to try to make out my surroundings.

"One block from my apartment."

"Okay, I'm coming. I'll call Zack, and we'll take you to the ER. Gwen, you need to call Ash."

"Why?" I hold back another cry through clenched teeth.

"He's probably close by, and I need someone to check your head. Knowing your luck, you hit it on the way down."

If I could gauge whether or not she's right, I would, but my vision is still fuzzy.

"Fine, just please hurry."

"Twenty minutes tops." She hangs up.

I stare at my phone, willing myself to not be stubborn and call Ash for help. But I don't want to. The fury that's settled in my veins is too strong.

Chapter Sixty-One

Ash

I don't know if I should answer Chrissy's call. Not sure I can handle another ear lashing. I have a strong inkling that Gwen told Chrissy what happened, and because Chrissy is a good friend, she's calling to give me the shit I deserve.

I don't want to feel the way I do. Frustration got the better of me, only solidifying that I'm the biggest fucking idiot on the planet. I swipe right to answer the call, ready to receive what's coming to me.

"Before you yell at me—" I start, but Chrissy's urgent tone cuts me off.

"Shut the fuck up and listen. I need you to walk to Gwen's. She slipped, and I'm afraid she hit her head. I told her to call you, but knowing her, she won't because she's furious at whatever dumb stunt you pulled."

I don't waste a second. "Okay, I'm on my way." I start down the block immediately.

Chapter Sixty-One

"Zack and I will be there in fifteen minutes." She hangs up, and I haul ass.

The snow doesn't lighten up, and a light dusting coats the sidewalk. It doesn't take long for me to find Gwen; she made it a block from her apartment before slipping.

"Hey, Gwen, whoa . . ." Okay, that's where she slipped, no doubt about it.

My knees hit the pavement beside her. Gwen rolls onto her back, her face wrinkling in utter discomfort.

"What are you doing here?" she snaps at me.

"Chrissy called."

Gwen lets out a brief, annoyed chuckle. "Of course she did," Gwen groans, cradling her wrist against her chest.

"What happened?" I ask, noticing her wrinkled brow.

"My clumsy ass slipped." Her whimper snaps my heart into a thousand glass-like shards.

"I need to check your head, okay?"

Gwen nods reluctantly. Reaching around her, I weave my fingers in her hair to feel her scalp. Doesn't seem sticky or damp, and I can't locate any kind of bump.

"Can you see straight?"

"I can now, but I couldn't before," she says through chattering teeth.

I unzip my coat and drape it over her legs, my eyes moving to her wrist again.

"Did you land on your wrist?" I try to hide the concern in my voice, knowing she doesn't want my sympathy right now.

"Unfortunately," she cries.

"That's okay, I'm sure it's fine." I try to comfort her.

"I heard it crack."

Fuck. Even I know that's not good.

"You're not making me feel any better." Her feisty chuckle is visible in the chilly air.

Thankfully, the snow is nothing more than a flurry at the moment.

"Chrissy and Zack will be here soon," I say, hoping to reassure her.

She shifts uncomfortably. "The snow is melting under my ass, and I'm freezing."

I place my hands on her back to provide support. Against her will, she falls against me.

"You're a fucking asshole, but you're warm." She lets out a short chuckle.

How this girl manages to laugh right now is beyond me, but if she's laughing, she'll be okay. She *has* to be okay.

Ten minutes pass before a car pulls up beside us, parking along the curb. Chrissy flings the door open and falls to her knees in front of Gwen.

"Hey, girly," she greets her with a mother-like tone.

Zack rushes in next, his cheeks both pale and red from the brisk air.

"Is she okay?" Zack squats down next to me as Chrissy checks Gwen over.

"I don't think she hit her head, but she said she heard her wrist crack."

"We need to get her to the car, she's beyond cold." Chrissy secures her scarf around Gwen's neck.

"I can stand by myself."

"No way," Zack and I say at the same time.

I don't trust Gwen not to fall again, and the last thing she needs is to injure her other wrist in the process of being stubborn.

"Fine, help me to the car," she says with an eye roll.

"I got her." I'm about to lift her, but she stops me.

"No, Zack will help me." Her words shoot a flaming arrow right into my heart.

Chapter Sixty-One

Zack side-eyes me. He must not know about the fight Gwen and I just had. Standing to the side, Zack offers her his strength. She lets him wrap his arm around her for support. Chrissy scurries to open the door, and Gwen secures her left arm to her chest as she settles into the backseat. As Chrissy closes the door, Zack climbs in the driver seat to blast the heat.

Offering me a frustrated sigh, Chrissy stands in front of me.

"Keep me updated, please?" I beg, trying to fight the tears that threaten me.

"Oh, don't worry, I'll be calling you later."

Zack turns the steering wheel to get back on the road. As he presses on the accelerator, I catch Gwen's expression. Only two words can describe it, pain and utter disappointment.

Chapter Sixty-Two

Gwen

"Ready to go?" Zack asks, sounding like he's ready to break a world record to get me to the hospital.

"Let's go, man. Gwen's about to hurl from the amount of pain she's in." Chrissy pounds the dashboard.

As Zack presses on the gas, I catch the look on Ash's face. He's a potent mixture of envy, anger, and hurt. But that doesn't even begin to explain how I'm feeling right now.

"I am not." A wave of nausea hits me, and I double over as we speed down the road. "No, wait, oh shit, I take it back," I groan.

Chrissy reaches over the front seat and rests her hand on my head. She keeps it there until we pull into the parking lot, and I'm thankful her touch grounded me.

I'm used to hospitals. The dull white tile, the smell of sterile medical equipment, how the gowns are always floral patterned and stiff no matter where you go. I'm a klutz, so this isn't my first trip to the ER. When I was a kid, I fell down the

Chapter Sixty-Two

stairs and twisted my ankle. Pretty sure all of my fingers have been jammed at one point or another. I know my wrist is broken because this is the same wrist I broke when I was twelve. Never, I repeat, never put a clumsy child in roller skates.

Zack though? He's never had to take a trip to the ER, and it shows.

"Zack, will you please sit down?" Chrissy not-so-kindly demands.

It's been a little over two hours of not-so-patiently waiting. If I wasn't in pain, I would be pacing too, so I don't intrude on Zack's coping mechanism.

"I'm pretty sure that guy"—he points to a middle-aged man across the way from us—"is only here because he gets a kick out of seeing people in pain." Zack's normally slicked-back hair now sticks to his forehead with sweat.

"Don't be crazy," Chrissy hisses before their bickering fills the room.

My wrist is numb, and when I try to move it, the sensation I feel is a strange tingle, like it's asleep. I'm surprised my phone isn't going off. I expected Ash to check in on me, but maybe Chrissy said something before we drove away.

Don't get me wrong, even if he did text me, I wouldn't respond. I know Ash is broken, but I think we hit the end of the honeymoon phase. Now, his flaws are creeping to the surface. He's still hurting from the past, and I'm starting to wonder if I alone can fix that part of him, and if I do, will I lose myself and him in the process?

"Why does it look like you're going to war with yourself?" Chrissy leans over to ask me.

"Because I am."

The way Ash snapped earlier frightened me. *Did a hug cause that severe of a reaction?* No, absolutely not. I was a fool to think he was healed from his traumatic relationship. I was a fool to think I alone could fix him.

"Gwen Roman."

"Finally." Zack offers me his hand, and I take it.

Chrissy rests her hand on my back as we follow the nurse into the back.

"What happened between you and Ash?" Zack whispers as we pass a group of residents discussing a case study.

"Something stupid. Men always end up doing something stupid," I mutter mainly to myself.

I tell Zack and Chrissy exactly what happened while we wait for my x-ray results. My legs dangle off the hospital bed, swinging carelessly. Pretty sure the pain medicine they gave me is kicking in, *thank goodness*. I don't think I'm very coherent because the words that leave Zack's mouth confuse the living shit out of me.

"Did you place yourself in his shoes?" he asks while resting his elbows on his knees.

"Why the fuck would she do that?" Chrissy snaps, ready to fight any man that crosses her path.

"Think of it like this. You grew up in a household where your parents had a different partner every day. Not only did you know about it, but you saw it. You knew it wasn't normal, and no matter how much you begged for it to stop, no one listened. As you got older, you start to date, but a part of you is afraid to get too close because you don't know how to love another human properly. So, you go to college and meet someone you think is genuine. Only to find out she's not, in a rather earth-shattering way. Your parents don't acknowledge your pain, so you cut them off. Now, you're without your girlfriend and parents all within a month's time. Walls start to tower around your heart, some even reinforcing ones that were already built. To protect yourself, you vow to never love again,

Chapter Sixty-Two

except it doesn't last because you see someone, and you know that person is meant to cross your path. Ash's reaction was uncalled for. I'm not defending him. But if you grew up like that, how would you feel if you saw your partner hugging a stranger?" Zack holds up his hand to cut off both Chrissy and me. "What if you saw your partner giving someone else a friendly hug, and in that precise moment, your mind betrays you, and worse images flood in? For example, Gwen bouncing on some random guy's dick."

My lips purse in response, and Chrissy huffs out a defensive sigh.

"It's no excuse . . ." Chrissy mutters.

"No, it's not. Ash's dark side came out, but he shouldn't have reacted the way he did. He shouldn't have talked to you the way he did. But Gwen, I have to ask. You do know Ash isn't perfect, right?"

"I'm not stupid, Zack." Annoyance coats my words.

"I'm not saying you're stupid. I'm saying you had this image of Ash for years without knowing him, and that Ash was perfect. But the real-life Ash? He's flawed just like everyone else, and his trust in women doesn't stretch far. He has his mom, dad, and Alex to thank for that. I know Ash loves you, anyone can see that. His face softens, the color in his cheeks rises, he gets this goofy grin the guys and I tease him for. He doesn't want to lose you. He can't lose you. Because in his mind, if he does, he's utterly broken and lost."

"What am I supposed to do?" I sigh out all the emotions that cloud my vision.

"You can't fix him yourself; he needs professional help. Help him see that. When you're ready, of course."

I meet Chrissy's gaze as she scrunches her nose. "I hate when he's right . . ."

There's no doubt I love Ash, and I know he loves me. I'm

not going to give up on our relationship, not after everything we've worked through. I do owe it to myself to take a step back. I can't fix him the way he needs fixing. Only a medical professional can offer him that.

"Since when did you start making sense?" I scowl at the newly intelligent Zack.

"That's the pain medicine, darling. It dumbed you down to my level," Zack says with a lopsided smirk. "No one is perfect. You guys fought. That's what couples do."

"Ugh, why are you so annoying and smart?" Chrissy pulls at her hair. "It's so fucking irritating."

I smirk at Chrissy just as the doctor walks in.

"Ms. Roman, how are you feeling?"

"Like my fat ass broke my wrist," I admit.

The doctor lets out an airy chuckle before smirking at me. "Well, you've got one part of that right. Your wrist is broken. But it's a clean break, so it should heal nicely. You need to see an orthopedist for a cast as soon as possible. I sent a prescription to your pharmacy for some stronger Tylenol. A nurse will wrap you up and give you your discharge papers. Sound like a plan?"

"Sounds good, thank you." I smile at her in gratitude, thankful for a stronger dose of Tylenol because two hundred milligrams won't cut the pain I'll be in tomorrow morning. But nothing will ease the ache that now settles in my chest.

I know it's all the emotions catching up with me, and I'm beyond exhausted. In my weak state, I start to miss Ash, and I wish our conversation hadn't taken the turn that it did. I know for sure I'm not willing to give up on him. He does, however, need help. If he doesn't come to that conclusion on his own, I'll be sure to send him down that path. Because I love him, and I know Ash Waylen is and will always be it for me.

Chapter Sixty-Three

Ash

I'm not an emotional driver like some other guys might be. If I was, I'd be driving down the interstate at ninety miles an hour, not giving a shit about anyone's life. I'm not, though, because I'm not completely stupid. I do, however, take the stairs two at a time and slam my bedroom door.

I'm not mad at Gwen. I'm furious at my own dumbass. I let my envy creep back in, and because of that, the images returned, and I took it out on the wrong person. It was ridiculous of me to think Gwen would ever do anything to hurt me. She hasn't done anything to lose my trust. I can't make the fucking connection, and I feel like it's clear as day. No sane person should get jealous over a friendly hug. I thought Gwen healed me, but I now know I'm far from sane. I'm a raging lunatic.

If Max was home, he would be knocking on my door right now, but he's not. So I pace around my room, unsure how to let these emotions free.

Forever Crushed

Gwen slipped because of me.
She broke her wrist because of me.
I sent her down the icy path in a frenzy.
It's all my fault.

I drop my phone on my bed, almost missing all the text messages that highlight the screen. They're all from Miles and Rome.

> What happened, man?

> Chrissy texted me. What's going on?

Part of me doesn't want to text them back because what if I do and they leave me like everyone else? Who wants to be friends with a jealous asswipe?

> I fucked up.

> Well, duh, but how?

> I'm an envious cock sucker.

> That's not what I was gonna say, but that works too.

> I'm coming over.

> Rome, please don't.

> Too late, I'm already in my car.

> I'm coming too.

> Guys, what the fuck? I said no.

No one responds to me after that.

Chapter Sixty-Three

Next thing I know, fists are pounding at the front door like some religious solicitors. This is Miles and Rome, though, and they won't give up. They'd break a window if they had to, and the last thing I need is a furious Max on my hands.

I pull my hood over my head and jog downstairs. The second I open the door, Rome shoves a bag of sour cream and onion chips in my hands and heads straight into the kitchen.

"We need more snacks!" he calls over his shoulder as Miles removes the hood from my head.

"Crawl out of that bag of pity and face the consequences, which is us right now." He squeezes my shoulder in reassurance.

"Look what I found!" Rome skips back into the living room, chugging orange soda right out of the bottle. He takes the bag of chips from my hands and grins ear to ear. "Thanks, bro. Now . . ." He plops down on the loveseat and points to the couch across from him. "Sit."

I follow Miles and take a seat. Running my hands through my hair, I rub my palms against my eyes.

"Start from the beginning."

I side-eye Miles and give in. I start from the very beginning, and by that, I mean from the age of eight to present day. My parents were the start of my lack of trust. I didn't realize how much of an impact it had on me until it was too late. Alex only added to the equation, and I released it on Gwen, the one person who didn't deserve it.

I tell Miles and Rome what happened when I saw David's arms around her. I share the images that rushed to the forefront of my mind. Saying it out loud makes me cringe. One, because I have to witness them again, and two, because I know it's a fucked-up thought.

Rome snaps a chip in his mouth, his eyes glued to the ceiling. "So, let me get this straight. You saw Gwen hugging some dweeb, and *you* got jealous? The same guy who used to exude crazy Mr. Sunshine energy?" Rome swings his legs off the couch and sits up, snagging my full attention. "I didn't know about your parents, and obviously, that had an immense impact on you. I saw you date in high school though. Did you feel that way then? This level of jealousy?"

I think back to the few girlfriends I had back then, but I don't think the thick emotion of envy started until Alex, and I think I know why.

"It didn't start until Alex," I blurt out. "When we first started going out, I had her complete attention. It changed, though, the day I caught her kissing some guy's cheek."

Rome's face remains still.

"And it didn't stop after that, did it?"

I shake my head at Miles's question. "It was sporadic at first. I would walk in on her and a guy in her dorm *studying*. Hugging some stranger longingly in the cafeteria, flirting even though I was right next to her." Fuck, did I block these memories out? Why am I remembering them now?

"And you're afraid Gwen is going to follow the same path, aren't you?"

Tears sting my eyes. Miles always knows my thoughts before I can even speak them into existence.

"You know she won't though." Rome lowers his tone. "She's crazy about you."

"I know . . . it doesn't stop the images and voices in my head."

Silence floats around us. A car pulls into the driveway, and the engine stops humming.

"You know what you need to do, right?"

I meet Miles's kind caramel eyes and nod. "I need to ask for help."

Miles and Rome leave as soon as Max strolls through the

Chapter Sixty-Three

door. He looks around the room, instant worry creasing his forehead.

"Can we talk?" I ask him.

He drops his briefcase at the door and slips his shoes and jacket off. "Is it about Gwen?"

Damn, Chrissy's fast.

"That and something else."

Max plops down next to me, loosening his pristine black tie.

"Let's talk. I'm all ears."

I have a feeling Chrissy told him what happened, but I recount the story. I want him to know why I reacted the way I did. I need him to know I'm more fucked up than I thought I was.

"Mom and Dad really traumatized us, didn't they?" Max's eyes shimmer as I meet his gaze. "You had it extra tough with Alex. I'm glad you know your reaction wasn't called for, and I understand why you got upset," he reassures me.

"I sent her down that path, Max. She got hurt because of me."

He shakes his head. "Did you push her?"

"No."

"Did you trip her?"

"No."

"Then how is it your fault?"

"Is this the asshole lawyer coming into play?"

He chuckles at my question. "No, but I'm starting to wonder if Gwen's smart-ass remarks are rubbing off on you."

A soft grin spreads across my face. That girl knows how to throw back sass without realizing it.

"I get why you think it's your fault, but I'm telling you it's not. Gwen slipped on a sheet of ice. Unless you have some new magical powers that I don't know about . . ."

I smirk again, and he grabs my shoulder and squeezes it.

"I need help, Max." I catch him nodding from the corner of my eye. "Not just from the internet."

"I know. I have someone I can call in the morning."

I turn my head so I can meet his gaze.

"I'm proud of you for coming to this conclusion." He holds out his arms for a hug, and my upper lip twitches. "Get in here, dammit." He pulls me against him, and I let him comfort me. "You and Gwen will be okay. One step at a time."

I nod into the crook on his neck.

One step at a time . . .

Chapter Sixty-Four

Gwen

Pain is the first thing that registers when my eyes peel open. I whimper, patting the right side of the bed, searching for Ash. But my palms don't meet his chest or shoulder. Instead, I'm met with crinkled sheets. Then I remember I'm not in his bed, and he's not next to me. I lie on my back, helpless. The burning, tingling sensation that overtakes my entire left arm is debilitating.

"There's my injured best friend. How are you feeling?" Chrissy asks as she bounces out of the bathroom.

"Miserable," I huff in irritation.

"Well, you look fantastic."

I throw her a look, knowing damn well my hair is sticking up in more places than one. I reach for her with my right arm, and Chrissy pulls me up. Sitting up, I sway for a moment before getting my bearings.

"Where's Zack?" I ask as I scan the room.

Both he and Chrissy opted to spend the night at my place

last night. I told them I didn't need them to, but I'm glad they did.

"He had class today. You know what that means, right?" Chrissy wiggles her eyebrows.

"True crime and snacks?" I grin as she throws her hands in the air. I forget the pain from yesterday for a moment. "I need to shower first." I sigh before swinging my legs off the bed.

"Ugh, fine. I'll get everything set up."

"I'm going to need your help," I say as I open my dresser drawer.

"Pretty sure Ash doesn't want me to see you naked anymore." She pouts, knowing damn well the mention of his name will get a rise out of me.

"Shut the fuck up and help me, woman."

"Geez, so feisty."

I ignore her attempt at being funny. After I grab an oversized movie tee and a pair of baggy flannel pajama pants, Chrissy follows me into the bathroom. I'm able to get my pants off, but the shirt is a bit worrisome. Beyond carefully, Chrissy unwraps my arm, wincing as my skin hits the air for the first time.

"Is it bad?" I ask, afraid to look at it myself.

"It's not *great*." She offers me a sympathetic smile. "We'll call the ortho doctor person today. Get you in a cast in no time."

I scoff at her comment. "You mean an orthopedist?"

"Yeah, whatever. Let's get this shirt off."

She helps me out of the shirt on the right side first. Once it's over my head, she shimmies it over my injured wrist. Relief washes over me when the shirt lands on the floor. Of course, I wore a sports bra, so this part is going to be tricky.

Chrissy amps herself up by jumping in place. "Okay, let's do this."

We start at the band, lifting it over my breasts. I free my

Chapter Sixty-Four

right arm and head just like I did with the tee. This time, I wince in pain as the bra snaps against my armpit. Ignoring the sharp pain, I shrug it off and take in a shaky breath through my nose.

"Thank you," I say as Chrissy starts the shower for me.

"One blazing hot waterfall coming right up."

I hop in the shower, thankful that I hurt my left wrist instead of my right. At least I can perform one-handed tasks by myself. I wash my hair and soak in the steam. Flashbacks from yesterday flood in my mind, and it fucking hurts just as much as it did when I first heard it.

"Who's to say I won't walk in on you bouncing on some random guy's dick."

I glance down at my wrist. I'm already pale, but my complexion is ghostly. The bruise that creeps up my wrist and into my palm is angry purple with splotches of blue and it's swollen, like two times the size of my other wrist. I fucked myself up . . . Combine this pain, Ash's words, and the ache in my heart, and I'm a piping hot mess.

With a sigh, I step out of the shower. Chrissy strolls back in with a bagel in her mouth. She helps me slip on the baggy shirt I grabbed and even ties my pants for me. Remind me why I deserve such a great friend again.

I'm brushing my hair when a knock sounds at the door. Glancing over at Chrissy, I wonder if she's expecting anyone.

I walk toward the door, and just as I turn the doorknob and pull, Chrissy shouts, "Oh fuck, I forgot—"

But it's too late because now I'm face to face with a rather frazzled-looking Max.

"Gwen, I have the best news."

My eyes widen at the sight of him. His hair is messy, somehow crazier than mine was a few minutes ago. His dark chestnut hair is normally slicked back, no frizz to be found.

Now? It's standing up, longer pieces drape across his forehead, and his eyes are wild from caffeine.

"We're gonna sue the city." He looks like the alien meme guy, hand gestures and all.

"Dammit, Max, I specifically said leave the bag and don't knock." Ash's voice sounds from downstairs, echoing up the stairwell and right into my ears.

"I had to tell her my plan!" Max calls down.

A smirk plays on my lips because this Max is damn hilarious.

The sound of Ash's feet on the stairs sends my stomach into an anxious frenzy. When I see him, it fucking hurts in more ways than one.

"Sorry, Gwen, I told him to deliver the bag and leave, I promise." He has a black hoodie on, with the hood pulled over his head, and heavy bags shadow under his eyes. "He gets in these kinds of moods when he hasn't slept." Ash offers me a weary smile, like he's unsure where we stand right now.

"It's okay." I meet Max's bug eyes and grin sweetly. "Max, we can't sue the city. Last I checked, the city can't control ice."

He holds a finger up to stop me from talking. "I'll find a way. Don't doubt me."

I respond the way a mother might to a child. "Uh-huh, sure, whatever you say." I reach for the bag Max is holding. "What's this?"

"Your medicine and some other things. The plan was to leave it and go. I'm sorry we bothered you." I meet Ash's solemn grin, and a rush of emotions runs through me.

"That's okay, it's no bother." I offer him a soft smile because he didn't have to get my medicine for me. But he did, so he must not be angry anymore, not that I warranted his rage to begin with . . .

"Okay, Max, let's go. I have somewhere to be, remember?"

Chapter Sixty-Four

Max's eyes light up as he remembers. "Oh yeah, let's go. We can't be late!"

Max scurries down the stairs, and worry sits in my gut.

"Where are you going?" I ask, trying to prolong the conversation.

"Max got me in with a therapist. It's about time I get some professional help," he says before his cheeks redden.

I nod, trying to appear indifferent. "Okay, just do yourself a favor, and don't give him any more caffeine," I whisper while indicating down to Max, who is currently doing jumping jacks in the middle of the foyer.

"I'm trying. He keeps whipping shots out from secret pockets."

I choke back a laugh as Ash smirks. "Listen, I know we have to talk. I just need to make sure I don't say the wrong thing again."

I nod in understanding. I also need to take some time to work out my thoughts.

"Okay," I respond in a hushed tone.

Ash glances down at my wrist. The regret that registers on his face is blinding. "I'm sorry . . ." His eyes flicker to mine, but he doesn't stay.

He descends the stairs and walks out the door with Max. I watch as they get in their car and leave, and I fucking wish he didn't take my heart with him. I should be angry. I should yell at him until my throat is sore. Deep down, I know he knows he fucked up. Anyone can see it. I pull my phone out before turning back to Chrissy, sending one important message.

> I'm proud of you, Waylen.

Chapter Sixty-Five

Ash

It's been one week since I saw Gwen. Leaving her in front of her apartment door, pulling myself away from her was harder than anything I've ever done. I couldn't tear my eyes away from her shattered wrist. I couldn't stop lingering over the disappointment and hurt written on her face. I did that to her. No amount of therapy can tell me otherwise.

I've been attending classes here and there. I talked to Professor Stilts and asked him if I could study at home and only show up for quizzes and whatnot. He approved, only because I'm a straight A student in his class. Once I told him it was for my mental health, he didn't hesitate.

I've been seeing Dr. Lukin every day for a week. The second he saw me, he knew I needed help, and he cleared his schedule for me. The sessions are draining. Who knew expressing your feelings was so damn exhausting? After every appointment, I go home and collapse in bed, passing out until dinner, just to wake up, eat, and then go back to sleep.

Chapter Sixty-Five

Dr. Lukin suggested I give Gwen some space. I insulted and hurt her. She needs to recover, just as I need to heal from my shit. That doesn't mean I haven't checked in on her. Every day I ask her how she's doing. If she needs her medicine refilled, I fetch it for her, adding in an order of fries from her favorite takeout restaurant. I overheard her, Zack, and Chrissy on the other side of the door as I dropped off her last care package. Part of me wanted to knock, but the other part knew it wasn't the right time. So I left the bag and texted her.

Miles and Rome have been the best friends any guy can ask for. If they're not at my place, they check in on me. They're the only ones besides Gwen who knows the shit I went through when I was a child, and they've been a great support system. I text Rome if I need a laugh and Miles if I need someone to listen to me recap a therapy session. Each time they follow through, I'm beyond grateful I have them in my life again. Christmas is a couple of weeks away, which only means one thing—

Finals.

I walk along the cobblestone path toward the computer technology center, ready to turn in my coding project and take whatever test is thrown at me. I secure my hood over my head, not wanting to socialize or catch anyone's eye. Just as my hand meets the revolving door, a voice stops me in my tracks.

"Waylen!"

I turn around as Chrissy's boots clack against the cement.

"Where the hell have you been?"

"Here and there," I respond.

Chrissy squints at me, knowing damn well I haven't been *here and there*. I've been to two places these past few weeks: my bed and Dr. Lukin's office.

"You look tired." Her blonde hair shines bright gold in the sunlight, and her soft smile offers genuine concern.

"It's been rough." I drop my gaze, staring at my sneakers instead of her sympathy.

"I can tell . . ."

"How's Gwen?" I can't help but ask.

Chrissy knows how Gwen really is. I just hope she tells me the truth.

"She's okay. Her arm is in a cast, and she keeps hitting her head with it . . ."

I smirk at the thought. That girl is so clumsy . . .

"She's not angry anymore."

I meet Chrissy's gaze again, and the smallest weight lifts off my shoulders at her words.

"She should be. I said some fucked-up shit to her."

She tilts her head as she scans my expression. "Oh, don't get me wrong. She was *pissed*. I watched that girl go through so many mood swings I thought she was in a constant state of insanity. And you did say some fucked-up shit, but I'm willing to bet that you're beating yourself up more than anyone else could right now."

Boy, does she know it . . . that was one thing Dr. Lukin said. He could sense the hurt radiating from my body. I was inflicting pain upon myself.

One day at a time. I repeat his words a lot. They help ground me.

"I won't hold you up. Go take your final. I'll see you in biochem, whether you like it or not." She winks at me before reaching under my hood to mess with my hair. "Keep that head up, you hear me? Don't let Alex corrupt what's left of you." She slaps my cheek gently before skipping away.

I'm trying. It's just hard, especially today. Dr. Lukin and I are going to talk about what my parents and Alex put me through. I'm already emotionally tired—the thought of it is draining beyond belief.

Chapter Sixty-Six

Gwen

"Zack, I swear to god. Back. The. Fuck. Up." I'm getting sick of this man.

"I'm just trying to help you!"

I'm tired of Nurse Zack and his constant attention. I can get out of the car on my own. Hell, I could walk to campus like I normally do, but no. He has to pick me up. How did my injury turn into a Zack care-fest?

"I will hit you with this thing, I swear." I threaten him with my cast, and he steps aside.

With his hands in the air, I start down the path toward my first final.

"Wait!" he calls after me, but I haul ass, hoping to lose him in the upcoming crowd.

I have one test today, and it'll be a piece of cake. Who really needs to study for an English final, anyway? Read the book, answer the questions, done.

My phone goes off in my pocket, and I pull it out, hoping to see a message from the one person I haven't seen in weeks. But disappointment rushes over me instead. I love Max, but I need the other Waylen to text me more than once a day.

I miss you! When can we hang out again? :)

I wish I knew how to respond. If I go over, I'll see Ash and his pained expression. I don't think he would appreciate me showing up out of the blue. I know he's in therapy, and I know firsthand how exhausting it can be. Ash needs patience and love right now. A week ago, I wasn't ready to provide either. Now I'm dying to see him. I would be lying if I said I didn't scan the campus grounds when walking to class like I used to do in high school. I know his schedule, and I tried *accidentally* bumping into him, but I always just miss him. He hasn't been in biochem either. I now sit next to an empty seat, one that used to be filled with flirtatious winks and longing gazes.

Fuck. Woman up, Gwen. I blink back the tears and walk straight into the arts center. Let's get this over with.

I can't believe you ditched me!

I read Zack's text just as I leave English class.

Chapter Sixty-Six

> Zack, I love you. But you're smothering me! I'm walking home, okay? Go bother someone else for a bit ;)

> After all I've done for you. :'(

> You'll survi—

My phone smacks against the ground as I bump into someone's chest, but I don't rush to see the damage. The screen is already bits and pieces. I need to get a replacement like yesterday.

"I'm so sorry, I wasn't paying attention." I reach down to pick up the already shattered phone.

His hand hovers over mine, and I pause.

The familiar scent of apples, pine, and home dances in my nose. The muscles in my neck move before my brain fires off the signals, and I meet his eyes for the first time in days.

"Hey." I'm breathless. How am I already out of air?

"Hi." His dark irises are clouded, and he has heavy bags under his eyes.

I grab my phone, and we stand simultaneously.

"Where have you been? I was about to send the dogs to find you." I grin while shoving my phone in my fleece pocket.

"I've been around." His eyes flick down to my purple-casted arm.

"Do you like it? It's a great self-defense weapon," I say, trying my best to get him to crack a smile.

"Chrissy said you've hit yourself more than anything else."

I scrunch my nose in response, knowing damn well she's right. "You weren't supposed to know that bit."

The anger I felt a few weeks ago has vanished. The only thing that remains is the need for closure. I just want to move forward. I don't want us avoiding one another.

"Listen, um." I fumble over my words as the wind pushes against my back.

I lose my footing and stumble forward, but Ash catches me, his arms holding me tight. Our gazes lock, and time slows just for us. He leans his forehead against mine, and his eyes flutter closed.

"I miss you." I can't stop the words as they leave my lips.

I used to go months without seeing him, but I barely survived this last week without him by my side. Sleeping has been a nightmare. Not even my comfort show provides relief anymore.

"I miss you too." His words cement me, setting free a breath that rested deep in my lungs.

"I'm here whenever you're ready to talk."

He nods his head against mine, opening his eyes, and I'm happy to see a spark of life within them. With a sharp intake of air, he steps away, and time resumes. People around us pass by, the clouds roll in, the wind picks up again, everything goes back to normal. Everything besides the ache in my chest.

"I have an appointment, but, um, would you want to talk later?"

I can't fight the grin that lifts my cheeks. "I'd really like that."

"Can I pick you up at seven?"

I nod eagerly, and I finally get a reaction.

"See you then, sneaky girl," he says before throwing a quick smile at me.

I don't care that it was brief, it was a smile, and I'm going to lock it away forever.

Chapter Sixty-Seven

Ash

Dr. Lukin's office is always immaculate. When I first came here, I noticed his *Star Wars: A New Hope* poster. That was a favorite movie of mine growing up. It was then that I knew I was in the right place. Plopping down on the couch across from him, I remove my hood.

Dr. Lukin is around Max's age. His black hair is neatly trimmed, he wears these big, thick-rimmed glasses that slip down his nose every once in a while, and he's always wearing a cardigan. I think men are catching on to the whole *women's gaze* thing...

"How was your day, Ash?" He clicks his pen and prepares to take notes.

"Not too bad. I turned in my final project and took the last test for my coding class. Bumped into Chrissy."

He shoots his eyes toward me. He knows who Chrissy is. He also knows I've been trying to avoid her because I wasn't ready for the ear lashing I couldn't handle.

"How did that go?"

"She checked in on me, said to not let Alex corrupt me."

Dr. Lukin nods. "How did that make you feel?"

It's a cliché question, but it works. Each session I get better at processing it.

I think back to when she said those words.

"It made me feel like Alex *is* still corrupting me."

Because she is. She tainted a part of my mind I can't regain control of. I lashed out at the one person I love most in life because of my past relationship. Any normal person wouldn't imagine their partner fucking some guy just because they hugged someone. I'm far from normal, and anyone can see it.

"Great segue, my friend." Dr. Lukin beams at me. "Let's talk about Alex. When was the first time you walked in on her and another guy?"

"A month after we started dating, she was embracing someone I had never seen before."

Dr. Lukin nods like he's connecting the dots. "After that?" he asks, keeping eye contact with me.

"She kissed another guy on the cheek."

Cue another nod . . . "And it didn't stop after that?"

"No, it got worse."

Dr. Lukin flips through his notebook until he finds what he's searching for.

"Another embrace, some flirtatious comments, more cheek kissing, but this time while you were in the room, and then the explosion. Let me ask you this, Ash, do you regret how you handled that night?"

I take a second to roll the thought around in my head.

"I wish I didn't let my anger control me . . ." My tone drops. "I beat the shit out of my best friend, and I didn't stop until someone pulled me away."

"Why do you think you reacted that way?"

Chapter Sixty-Seven

My gaze drops to the gray carpet beneath our feet. "I have anger problems—"

"I screened you for anger management issues. You passed."

Surprisingly.

"Want to hear my theory?"

I hold my hands together and prepare myself for a major aha moment.

"When you were growing up, did you ever talk to your parents about their infidelity?"

I nod.

"And how did they react?"

"They brushed me off."

"How did you react when they brushed you off?" he asks while arching his right eyebrow.

"I was angry. I hated them. I wanted to scream until I couldn't anymore."

"But they didn't let you, and I'm willing to bet you wanted a fight because you wanted a reaction from the two people who were in the wrong. You wanted them to own up to their mistakes, to voice them out loud, so you didn't feel crazy."

And there's the lightbulb.

"You got a reaction from Alex and Brandon that night. They didn't continue or act like you weren't there. What was the first thing Alex did when you walked in on them?" He clicks his pen again, jotting down notes like it's his job.

"She screamed at me . . ."

"And what did Brandon do?"

I think back to the moment Brandon approached me before I beat him shitless. He was drunk, but his words didn't slur.

"He said, 'She's just so hot, I couldn't stop myself.'"

"You got a reaction, and that's what you wanted. You craved it from the moment you knew what your parents were doing. They brushed you off and didn't consider your feelings.

You got a reaction from Alex and Brandon, and looking back, I know you regret how you handled it. But, at the moment, those repressed emotions blinded you, and they won."

Tears sting my eyes, and I wipe them away before they become overwhelming.

"Fuck, I hate therapy."

Dr. Lukin chuckles at my admission. "Our goal here is to ensure the past doesn't happen again, Ash. You did the right thing in asking for help. You noticed the way you reacted to Gwen hugging that guy wasn't right, and while you yelled and said things you regret, it had to happen, because look where you are now." He gestures to me, crying on his sofa, sniffling past my tears and snotty nose. "What's our next step?"

"I can tell you what I *want* my next step to be, but I don't know if you'll agree." I run my fingers through my hair, trying to regain my composure.

"You handle things in your time, no one else's. Tell me what *you* want to do."

"I want to talk to Gwen. I need to tell her what happened, what played through my mind. I need to apologize for how I reacted and for what I said. I need her to know it wasn't her fault and that I shouldn't have lashed out the way I did. I need her to know I still love her."

"And what if she isn't ready to hear any of it?" He wrinkles his forehead curiously.

"I accept it and take things one day at a time."

"Sounds like a good plan to me."

Chapter Sixty-Eight

Gwen

I made the mistake of telling Max I would see him later in the evening. Not only did I get a spam warning on my phone from all the text messages, but now he's right outside my door.

"Oh gee, I wonder who this is." I open the door only to have flowers shoved in my face. I sputter out a few petals.

"I got you a flower for each day we were apart."

You'd think I was dating Max with the way he's professing his feelings and whatnot.

"Did the Waylen brothers swap brains or something?"

He pops around the pastel-colored roses and beams at me. "You missed me, and you know it."

I wiggle my nose, trying not to sneeze. "I did. Thank you, Max." I accept the flowers and walk over to the sink. *What the hell am I supposed to put these in?*

"I have the best day set up for us."

I scan my cupboards for a vase or large glass as Max talks.

"I set up a snack table, loaded the couches with blankets and pillows, found a shit ton of menus so we can order out..." He rambles on as I reach for an oversized coffee mug.

I fill the cup with water and place the roses in it, making sure the cup doesn't topple over.

"Geez, Max, is this a date or something?" I purse my lips, cutting him off midsentence.

"I missed you, and because I missed you, you're getting me tenfold. Now let's go, missy." He links my arm through his and pulls me out of my apartment.

He barely lets me lock the door. He's in such a rush to start this little hang-out session he planned out for us.

Max wasn't kidding when he said he had everything set up. The coffee table is lined with various chips, chocolates, and gummy snacks. Max curls up on the couch next to me and starts the show. He picked a good one, too. Hopefully, Chrissy doesn't find out because this one has been on our watch list for years. I can't stop myself from snickering when Max gasps or makes little comments only a lawyer would know to make. We're two episodes in, and he's pretty sure he's got the case figured out.

"It was the husband, one hundred percent," Max says before tossing a piece of milk-chocolate-caramel-drizzled popcorn in his mouth.

"Really? What about the brother though? He seems shady," I say before taking a sip of cola.

"Not as suspicious as the husband. I mean, that guy had two secret girlfriends and multiple online dating accounts."

"Start the next episode, Mr. Lawyer Man." I chuckle before glancing at the clock. "Oh shit, I forgot to text Ash."

I reach for my phone, but Max stops me.

"I told him, don't worry."

Chapter Sixty-Eight

Butterflies rampage in my chest. "How has he been?" Curiosity fills my tone.

"He's going through it, I'm not gonna lie. I'm hoping since he asked you to come over, it means he's moving in the right direction. I'll let him tell you everything." Max smiles before looking down at my cast. "How many times have you hit yourself in the head with that thing?" He smirks, pretending like Chrissy hasn't told him the exact number already.

"Shut up, Waylen." Normally, I say that to the other Waylen.

Ash and Max are more alike than I originally accounted for.

Halfway through the third episode, the front door opens, and my nerves return. Max pauses the episode and sighs.

"I need her back before bedtime. We *need* to finish this episode." Max approaches Ash in front of the staircase and drops his voice. He tells him something, but I can't make it out.

With a quick shoulder squeeze, Max slips into the kitchen, leaving Ash and me alone.

"How was your session?" I break the silence.

His eyes are red and puffy, hinting he may have been crying.

"Eye-opening and exhausting." He unzips his navy-blue fleece and shoves his hands in his hoodie pocket. "Is now a good time?" he asks.

I nod with a sharp intake of air. I don't know what to expect from this conversation. I just hope neither of our hearts ends up shattered like glass on the floor.

I follow Ash up the stairs and step into his room, my nerves ravaging my stomach. The familiar scent of faint apples and musk relaxes my shoulders. The sudden urge to crawl in his bed, snuggle in his arms, and sleep for years is overwhelming.

There are more pressing matters though. This is a talk that needs to happen.

"Do you want to sit?" He gestures for me to take a seat at the foot of his bed.

When I settle in, he places himself next to me, giving me plenty of space.

His eyes meet the floor while mine take in his features, trying to gauge what's going through his head.

"Do you want me to start, or do you want to?" he asks as he releases a puff of air.

I prop my leg on the bed and adjust myself to face him.

"You can start." I need to hear what he has to say. Why he reacted the way he did. I'm tired of speculating.

"I wasn't ready to date after Alex. I told myself I was because I was being selfish. I wanted to be with you, so I fooled myself into thinking I was ready, even though I wasn't. I regret nothing, Gwen." He meets my eyes, and a knife pierces my heart. "Not one second." His eyes gloss over just as my vision blurs. "I was selfish to give you the role to heal me, and while I think you mended part of my soul, deep cracks still remain, and I can't rely on you to fix them because it's not fair to you. You saw what happened. You saw how broken I still am. When I saw you hug David, pictures of his lips on yours invaded my mind. After that, I saw Alex and Brandon, and it clouded my senses. I took it out on you, the one person who didn't deserve it."

I take a deep breath through my nose, trying to stifle the sobs that threaten me.

"I'm sorry. It's my fault you stormed off. It's my fault you broke your wrist. I shouldn't have let you leave. My fury blinded me, and I lost control. I should know by now I can trust you. I don't know how you can look at me without punching me

Chapter Sixty-Eight

in the face." A tear slips down his cheek. "That fight was my fault. I take full responsibility."

"You scared me, Ash. Your personality did a complete one-eighty, and it fucking terrified me. You understand that, right?"

He nods, more tears falling down his face. "I know, and I regret every second of it." He sniffles, breaking down right in front of me. "I fucked everything up. That's why . . . that's why I'm letting you go. You deserve someone who isn't broken beyond repair. You deserve someone who won't care if you hug another guy. You deserve someone who will make you happy. You can go home and never worry about seeing me again. I won't bother you, I promise."

I shake my head, my tears burning my eyes as they free themselves. "Don't you fucking dare." I grab his hands and hold on to him for dear life.

"I need you to be happy, Gwen. You can't be happy with someone like me."

New anger rises in my throat. "Shut the fuck up, Waylen." I grip his hands, not willing to let go. "Listen to me." Urgency fills my tone. "You made me a promise, remember? Back in the library?"

"Gwen—"

"Shut up and listen. I'm not willing to accept this solution you came up with. Want to know why? It's giving up, and I refuse to give up on us. You didn't break my wrist. You didn't push me and leave me in the cold. You ran when you found out what happened, and even though I fought against you, you helped me. You're taking steps to better yourself. Hell, I was going to tell you to go to therapy, but you made that decision on your own. You're recognizing your own red flags and fixing them. We're all broken in our own way, Ash. Some more than others, but we're all human, and humans are a mess. So don't you fucking give up on us."

"I don't want to," he whispers through his sobs.

"Then don't." I bring his hand to my lips to kiss his knuckles. "I'm not giving up. We're stronger than one stupid fight. We're stronger than that voice inside your head."

"It's so loud, Gwen."

I rest my forehead against his. "And what are you doing to silence it?" I thumb numerous tears off his cheek.

"What I should have done months ago. Working on myself."

I rest my hand on his cheek. "Which is more than a lot of other people can say. It's hard to accept when we need help, and you did it that same day. I don't think you want us to break up. I think you're being selfless." His eyes shimmer in his now-darkened room. "Do you really want me to leave?"

He shakes his head and falls against me.

"Good, even if you said yes, I wouldn't have left. You're stuck with me, Waylen." I chuckle through my own clogged nose. "You and me, that was the deal, remember?"

"I love you." He tangles his hand into my hair and takes a deep breath.

"And I love you."

Chapter Sixty-Nine

Ash

Everything snaps back into place, like a puzzle begging to be finished. Gwen and I were a blubbering mess last night. We fell asleep in each other's arms and didn't wake until noon. I'll say one thing; I thought a normal headache was bad, but no, crying-induced headaches are the worst.

Crying is one of the things I didn't do growing up. I was told to suck it up and move on. Crying is like a damn drug. Once you start, you can't stop. When you get a good cry in, you feel like gold afterward.

The next morning, I felt renewed. It was like I released all my pent-up sadness from my childhood to present day, and with the weight gone, I felt like me again.

Gwen strolls out of the bathroom wearing a pair of my basketball shorts and another tee of mine, one of the many sights I've missed.

"How'd you sleep?" I ask her as she plops down on the bed.

"Like I haven't slept in months."

I smile down at her. "Same."

She grins at me in response. "Aw, did you miss my snoring?"

I can't help but giggle—something else I haven't done without her. I twirl a loose strand of her wet hair around my finger.

"I am sorry." I can't say it enough. I put Gwen through hell, and she deserves more than just my apology, but right now, it's all I can offer.

"I know." She kisses my forehead before closing her eyes. "It's going to be okay," she soothes.

"Gwen!"

Her eyes snap open as we both sit up.

"Is that—"

Before Gwen can finish her question, Chrissy storms through my bedroom door.

"You watched that true crime doc without me?!"

"Uh," is all Gwen can register.

"Sup, Ash." Chrissy greets me with a head nod. "You're looking better."

"Thanks—" I don't get to finish my sentence.

Max's door closes, and Chrissy whirls around.

"You, legal man! You owe me!" she shouts at him.

"For what?" Max peers over Chrissy and smirks at Gwen and me.

"You and Gwen watched the one true crime doc I've been dying to see. You. Owe. Me." She stabs his chest with each word.

"Fine, we'll start over so you can catch up," he suggests with a simple shrug.

"And you'll order lunch," she adds like she's negotiating the deal of the lifetime.

"Deal."

Chapter Sixty-Nine

They firmly shake hands and head down the stairs.

"You guys coming?" Max calls.

"What the hell just happened . . ." Gwen mumbles.

"I wish I knew."

I have to blink more than once to fully register what's transpiring in the living room. Chrissy, Max, and Rome are in the middle of shoving popcorn in their mouths. The TV is on full volume, blasting the true crime documentary Gwen was watching with Max yesterday. Gwen itches her head, clearly just as perplexed as I am.

When the hell did Rome get here?

"You couldn't wait ten minutes?" Aggravated shushes follow Gwen's question, and she shuts her mouth.

I peek over at her and drop my shoulders. Best not to ask questions, I guess.

It takes thirty minutes and the end of the episode before the room reawakens. I still can't figure out why Rome is here.

"Not that I'm not glad to see you, Rome, but why are you here?" I ask.

"I heard Gwen was here, and I wanted to check in on her."

My eyes twitch, and I squint.

"Aw, how sweet," Chrissy coos as Gwen sits on the couch next to her.

"You're hungry, aren't you?" I ask, unamused.

Rome grins ear to ear. "Well, since you mentioned it."

I fucking knew it. This guy's stomach is a bottomless pit, and now that he knows where I live, my refrigerator is his.

"You know, I was really touched for a minute," Gwen mumbles as Rome jogs into the kitchen.

"Is that the kid Mom and Dad were always bitching about?" Max points behind his back.

"Unfortunately," I grumble.

"He better not touch my Norwegian Greek yogurt!" Max leaps over the love seat, charging into the kitchen.

"I'm going to referee. Be right back." I kiss the side of Gwen's head, hesitating for a moment.

We didn't talk about boundaries or anything, and I'm afraid I just crossed one.

"Have fun." Gwen ruffles my hair and smiles.

Stepping back, I try my best not to get lost in her eyes. Before I walk away, I tease Chrissy. I have weeks of torture to make up for, so I mess with Chrissy's curls before strolling into the kitchen.

"I'll get you for that, Waylen!" is the last thing I hear before I walk in on Rome raiding the fridge.

Chapter Seventy

Gwen

Rome is the main character in any room he walks in. From my spot on the couch, I can see straight into part of the kitchen. Rome got his hands on Max's fancy yogurt, so while Max chases him around the pristine marble island, Ash stands in the corner with his palm against his forehead. Rome made himself right at home.

It's nice seeing Ash smile again. When I woke up this morning, I caught him staring at the ceiling, deep in thought. When he saw me stroll out of the bathroom, he looked relieved.

Chrissy's thumbs hammer away at her phone screen. That little indent in the crease of her brow wrinkles, which can only mean one thing.

"Boy trouble?"

Chrissy loves to love, but she has commitment issues. That's why she ended things with Miles this past August. I can't say for sure why she runs though. She grew up in a stable, loving home. Sometimes it's embedded in your DNA to be afraid of commitment, and that's okay.

"Why do you know me so well?" She releases a huff and leans back. Her eyes get a faraway look. "Why can't I have what you and Ash have?"

"Rome, I swear to god, please drop that yogurt." Ash jogs after Max and Rome, joining the fray.

"We're a fucking mess. You don't want what we have," I chuckle. We just made up yesterday. Things are going to take time to get back to normal. "I thought you and Miles were doing okay. Did something change?"

Chrissy shakes her head solemnly. "Not exactly. I thought things would pick back up, especially after what we shared a few months ago. Instead, I was trying to force emotions that used to come naturally."

I feather my fingers along her open palm, something she does for me when I'm feeling down.

"What changed?" I ask.

With a forlorn smile, she gives me her full attention. "I know what love looks like. I saw it every day growing up. Mom and Dad are the perfect example of what love is. You and Ash, you're the true example of strength. You two love one another, and you're willing to work past each other's flaws. What you guys went through took guts. It's beyond impressive, almost contemporary romance-worthy. I think what really got me though—and you're going to laugh at me for this—is when we went to Horror Fest, and Miles didn't wear a jacket, even though I told him one of my favorite gestures is when a guy offers you a jacket when it's cold. Ash didn't hesitate to give me his hoodie. I guess I want someone like that. How bad does that make me sound?" Her eyes gloss over with tears.

This girl held this in since October, and I didn't see it.

Chapter Seventy

Holding feelings in like that must weigh a person down. I don't know how she did it. Being honest with yourself takes a lot of guts, and this girl just let it all out.

"Oh, Chrissy, that doesn't make you a bad person. It makes you strong. You know how long it takes some people to realize what they want out of love and life? It's okay to feel that way. I'm sorry I didn't notice the internal battle you were going through." I pull her in with my free arm, and she rests her head on my shoulder and sighs. "I just want you to be happy, and if Miles isn't making you happy, I know you'll do the right thing."

"Thank you." She sniffles before pulling back, wiping away the few tears that stain her pink cheeks.

"You can't catch me, suckers!" Rome's feet pound against the carpet, but the second he sees Chrissy's swollen face, he stops dead in his tracks. "Are you okay, Bubbles?"

Bubbles? What the fuck?

"I'm okay. Thanks, Rome." Her lips form the faintest smile, one that makes my forehead crinkle in pure confusion.

"Rome, I will personally end your football career before it even starts!" Max flies into the room.

"Shit, gotta go. See y'all later!" Rome bursts out the front door just as Ash crosses the threshold to the living room. "Nice to meet you, Max!"

Chrissy and I snort at Rome's distant voice.

"That son of a bitch," Max curses even though his lips twitch, fighting a grin.

"What did I just miss?" Zack looks over his shoulder as he strolls in.

"Rome just stole all my food. Not gonna lie though, I kinda like him," Max admits.

Ash runs his fingers through his hair, letting out an airy chuckle. "Good because he'll be back."

"You've got some explaining to do, Bubbles." I drop my tone so only Chrissy can hear me.

The second I drop her new nickname, her cheeks flush pink and her eyes dart to the carpet.

Yeah, there's definitely something going on there.

Chapter Seventy-One

Gwen

One of the many downsides of my recent injury is that I can't get comfortable. I've also done nothing but sit around and watch TV all day. Once Ryan found out I broke my wrist, he put me on leave for a few weeks. I protested immediately. I need to work, not just for the money, but because Pickles will be leaving the café soon and I wanted to spend as much time as I could with him. Ryan wouldn't hear it though. He kept saying I needed rest and whatnot. He told me I could come in and visit Pickles before Christmas Eve. It won't be enough though. Guess I should be grateful I get to see him one more time.

Not only is Ash's room pitch black, but it's cold, like teeth-chattering freezing. He wasn't lying when he told me he's a hot sleeper back when I first walked into his room.

Right now, Ash is sleeping on his back, and I can barely make out his features against the dim light from my phone. It's crazy how comfortable we've gotten around one another again.

Forever Crushed

Within a couple of days, we fell into our normal routine, except his now includes a buttload of therapy sessions.

I'm so proud of him for coming to that conclusion on his own. He has no idea the big step he took in bettering himself. He's about twelve sessions in, and his improvement is already showing. He doesn't look at me like I'm a broken puppy anymore. His eyes scan my cast now and then, but certainly not as often as he did before. Dr. Lukin is working wonders on Ash, and I'm forever grateful for him.

The clock in the corner of my phone reads 1:07. I snuggle closer to Ash, letting my knee rest against his leg. His thigh twitches in response, and a breath of air escapes his nose.

I play the next episode in the series I'm watching. Who doesn't love a good forbidden fantasy romance show in the middle of a snowy night?

Like many people, I rely on fantasy for an escape. I didn't read much when I was younger, just the one book I have on my bookshelf. The one with the princess and the necklace. I more so fell into the world of video games and movies. Something about physically seeing a different world draws me in. Not that I don't like visualizing them myself, but sometimes it can be a bit too heavy. My head lands on Ash's arm. I can't get over how comfortable this man is.

Ash always ran through my mind. Now? He rushes through me. I crave his touch when he's not nearby. I think about him every moment of every day, wondering if he ate or studied for an upcoming test. Addiction is no joke, and while there are worse things to become addicted to, I'm pretty sure love should be near the top of the list.

I don't know how I survived without him. I lived years without his comfort and endearing gaze. How did I not feel empty or incomplete? How did my blood course through my body without him? It's like my body needs him to function

Chapter Seventy-One

now. Biologically, I know it's not true. Something tells me love plays some part though. Even back in high school, I felt a rush whenever he was close by. I could pass it off as my silly crush then, but do I dare wonder if it was something else entirely? What if, even back then, my body knew it needed Ash? The universe just wasn't ready for us yet.

My icy accident was two weeks ago. I still haven't told my parents, and they haven't texted to check in. The Willowses found out before I got the chance to tell them. Thank you, Zack and Chrissy. They called me right away, wanting to hear me say I was okay. I'm pretty sure that's how parents are supposed to react. If I reach out to Mom and Dad, they won't express that kind of reaction. Hell, there's a ninety percent chance I wouldn't hear from them at all.

"Oh shit." My phone lands right on my face, vibrating with a call.

"What's going on?" Ash groans before rolling on his side to face me.

I flip my phone around and curse. "I just summoned the devil."

"What?" Ash chuckles before squinting at my phone.

"Oh, *that* devil."

The word *Mom* appears on my shattered phone screen.

"Want me to answer it?"

I chuckle at the thought. "That would be fucking hilarious."

Before I can react, Ash snatches my phone from my hand and swipes right.

"Hello?" he answers, sounding as casual as possible. "Gwen? Gwen Roman?" He taps his pointer finger against his chin, feigning deep thought.

I can't wipe the broad, mischievous grin from my face, knowing the thought path my mom is going down.

"Oh, yeah, I know Gwen. She's right next to me, actually." Ash pulls the phone away from his ear when she shouts *What?!* "Hey, you're the one who called at one in the morning. Want me to wake her up?"

My eyes widen as I shake my head. He sticks his tongue out at me.

"Oh wait, she just ran into the bathroom. Something about bad tacos."

I punch his arm, and he mouths "*ow*" at me.

"Well, it was nice chatting with you. Sorry we had to meet this way."

Meet this way?! is the last thing I hear from my mother's shrill voice before Ash hangs up and offers me back my phone.

"That was fun."

I send her a quick text to make sure everything's okay and quickly discover she is when she sends me a picture of a range of snowy mountains.

Typical.

"You're trouble, Ash Waylen," I giggle as he plops back down on the bed.

"You love it." He winks at me, and my stomach flips upside down.

Move over old Ash, here comes a new and improved Ash.

Chapter Seventy-Two

Ash

The biochem final is in two days, which means Christmas is officially one week away. Gwen wants to visit Pickles before it's too late. She's worried time will pass her by, and she'll never see that maniac again.

It's crazy to think I first met Pickles over three months ago. When Gwen approached me with him that night, I knew she was special. Even Pickles showed me compassion when I got a rare cuddle session before he bit me.

Gwen is brushing her hair when I step into the hallway. Max's door is open, so I pop my head in to check on him. His room is a chaotic mess, literally. He doesn't like folding laundry, so he has a chair for clean clothes and a chair for dirty clothes. The only part of his room that is tidy is his closet, where he keeps his dry-cleaned suits, iron-pressed ties, and polished leather shoes. Max puts on a pristine front, but I know the mess he truly is.

"Ready, Max?" I walk into his room just as he finishes slipping on his sneakers.

"If this cat sends me to the ER, remind me to get Gwen's punch card," Max teases.

"Hilarious..." I sigh at his lame joke.

"It's nice to see you smiling again." Max drops his jokester persona. "I'm glad you didn't push her away."

"I tried to," I admit.

"She didn't let you, did she?"

I shake my head.

"Smart girl. You did say I would like her." He winks at me before grabbing his windbreaker.

"I get the feeling you don't just *like* her." I chuckle at him.

Max has gone out of his way to spoil Gwen. They have nightly true crime sessions, he orders out whatever she wants, and they snack and binge their hearts out.

"Oh, I fucking love her. She's the sister I never had." He wipes a fake tear from his eye. "All the fucking around Mom and Dad did, and we never got another sibling."

On that note, I leave the room. "You're the worst," I say, trying to hold back a laugh.

"Dad always said to wrap your—oh, hey, Gwen." Max comes to a halt.

Gwen's eyes widen as she steps out of my room, a smile tugging on her lips. "No, go ahead, Max, finish that sentence."

My gut has a tickling kind of sensation. No matter how many times I see her, I can't fight the sappy smile that creeps along my lips. The pom-pom on her beanie bounces as she zips her fleece jacket.

"I was just saying that safe sex is important." He deepens his tone to try to make himself seem serious.

"Uh-huh, sure. Are you guys ready?" she asks.

Chapter Seventy-Two

I close the brief distance between us and press my palms against her face.

"Did I mention how much I love you?" I drop my tone so only she can hear me.

She rolls her eyes around like she's counting. "No, I don't think you did."

"I love you so, so much." I press my forehead against hers, wanting to kiss her but too nervous to make the move.

We haven't kissed since the day before the accident, and it feels like I'd be breaking an unspoken rule.

"Shut up and kiss me, Waylen."

"When did you become a mind reader?"

Gwen closes the gap between us, and the second her lips make contact with mine, my body ignites in fireworks. Not just any fireworks. I'm talking extravagant theme park displays with fire and music. My lips tingle, and my body sings. This is a feeling no human should experience. It's not of this world.

She pulls away, leaving us both breathless and aching for more.

"I love you," she says with a sweet grin.

"I love you, too." I lean in again, but our moment is interrupted as quickly as it started.

"Aw, I love you guys." Max collides with us, wrapping his arms around us both.

Gwen giggles, and I can't help but emit the same sound.

Max was right. Apparently, I giggle now.

Chapter Seventy-Three

Gwen

"There's my boy!"

Pickles rushes me the second I walk through the door to Tea and Kittens. He leaps into my arms, not caring about my cast. I snuggle his face, and he freaking nuzzles back.

"Aw, I thought you were talking about me." Blake pouts and feigns tears.

"Sorry, Blake, this was the man I missed the most."

"Whatever, I didn't miss you anyway."

Pickles purrs and collapses against my shoulder.

"Is she always this cruel?" Blake directs the question to the two men behind me.

"When it comes to Pickles, yes." Ash's husky chuckle fills the room.

Ryan strolls in from the back room and grins. "Well, well, well, who do we have here? Check her pockets before she leaves. She might try to catnap Pickles."

Blake and Ryan step forward and meet Max. They go back

Chapter Seventy-Three

and forth discussing, well, I can't say for sure because I'm not paying attention.

"I missed you," I whisper in Pickles's ear. "What am I going to do without you?"

And here come the waterworks.

We took Pickles in when he was a kitten. I personally fed and played with him from day one. He scared Ryan and Blake immediately. He was always chewy and flighty. I mean, what cat chases you around the room for hours on end? What kind of cat chews the little plastic off your shoelaces while you're wearing them? Pickles does, and while he's an asshole, he's my asshole.

"All right, let me meet the little monster." Max steps in front of me and reaches out to pat his head. "Hey, dude." He lowers his tone and strokes the underside of his chin. "Am I missing something here?" Max asks, knowing all the warning signs but not seeing any on display.

Ash steps forward and chuckles. "Let Max hold him."

I scrunch my nose and groan.

"Gwen." Ash prolongs my name and grins. "Two minutes. Let Max meet Pickles properly."

"Fine." I peel Pickles off my jacket and offer him to Max.

He holds Pickles a few inches from his face, and Pickles observes him, tilting his head curiously.

"Let him smell you, Max."

Max side-eyes me before pulling him in closer. Pickles sniffs Max's nose, and it's not long before he's dragging his sandpaper tongue against him.

"I thought you said this cat was—ow, fucker!"

There it is. Pickles nibbles on the tip of Max's nose and pats his paw against his forehead. The room erupts in laughter as Max struggles with a now hyper and chaotic Pickles. He leaps from Max's arms and runs laps around the empty café.

"He's a character, isn't he?" Max asks.

"You have no idea," Blake sighs.

Pickles stops in his tracks. His pupils dilate as he crouches low in front of Blake.

"Don't you even." Blake points at Pickles and backs away. "Pickles, no. Dammit!"

Blake stumbles and books it away from Pickles. Their chase scenes are my favorite, and they always will be.

"Gwen, tell me again why you love him." Max points at Pickles and grins. "Oh, I get it now."

"Do you?" Ash raises his eyebrows. "Pickles is the one aspect of Gwen's life I don't understand."

"She loves him because he's like Chrissy."

The aha moment hits me as Pickles bumps into my legs and collapses.

"That makes perfect sense. Gwen loves chaotic people and animals."

I grin at Ash's words.

Blake doubles over with laughter and fights for air. "Damn, I think Castle Brook's football team needs that cat during training sessions."

I reach down and cradle Pickles in my arms again. Ryan captures my eyes and smiles, but we don't exchange words. Ryan knows no matter how many times he offers sympathy, it won't be enough. I can't take Pickles. It doesn't matter how much I want to. I know if I could, Ryan would terminate the current adoption and give him to me. I can't provide the space or time Pickles needs in his life. My love isn't enough.

"Hey, little fucker." Ash reaches out and scratches Pickles's chin. "Remember when you first introduced us?" he asks while returning his gaze to me.

"How could I forget?" I smile at the memory.

September seems like a lifetime ago. When Ash and Alex

Chapter Seventy-Three

strolled through those doors, I didn't know what to expect. I certainly didn't expect to walk up to his booth, hand him Pickles, then hold his hand. I think that was the day I started fitting into the shoes of the person I am today. It's funny how I didn't notice how fearless I was in the moment. Looking back now, I can safely say that day defined me, but not because of Ash. I saw someone in need that day. I sucked up my anxiety and summoned the nerve to comfort him. I did it because I felt the urge to ease his pain, not because of my silly crush. I was beginning to evolve into the person I'm meant to be.

"What's going through your head, sneaky girl?" Ash weaves his hands underneath my beanie and curls them into my hair.

"Just reminiscing."

He flashes me his dimples and grins. "Good thoughts?"

"Good thoughts." I lean into his palm for support.

I don't want to say goodbye. I'm not good at goodbyes. So instead, I kiss Pickles on his nose. I let the tears trickle from my eyes and slide down my cheeks.

"I'll see you later, okay?" Ash presses his forehead against my shoulder, offering me as much strength as he can. "I love you, crazy boy." I snuggle against his furry cheek. "You're going to have the best life, you hear me? You're going to forget all about me and love your new family. I will be a blip in your timeline, nothing more." The tears flood down my cheeks. I sniff past my stuffy nose and choke. "I love you, baby boy. Always will."

I place him down on the floor.

My eyes meet Ryan's against my will.

"It'll be okay."

I nod at his words, then look at Blake.

"Your shoes will thank you," he teases, and I chuckle.

Blake always tries to lighten any gloomy situation.

"See you guys later?" Ash intertwines his fingers with mine.

"We'll be here. Have a lovely Christmas, Gwen." Ryan smiles sympathetically as Ash tugs on my hand gently.

"You guys wait in the car. I have a question for Ryan." Max steps in front of Ash and me. "Five minutes, then we'll go find something to eat."

I drop my gaze, meeting Pickles and his sea-green eyes.

"Have a great holiday, guys. See you later," Ash says and pulls on my hand.

I mouth, "*I love you*" to Pickles.

He slowly blinks and tilts his head.

"He'll be okay. Let's go," Ash whispers before tugging on my hand again.

I let myself fall under his command. My feet step back, ignoring the burning defiance in my mind. I force my thoughts away and spin around. I let Ash wrap his arm around my shoulders. He pulls me against his chest, and I close my eyes. Pickles will be okay.

Sometimes, the best way to love someone—or something—is to let them go.

Chapter Seventy-Four

Gwen

I basically live at Ash's now. He and Max won't let me leave. *Wait, does that make me their captive?* If Ash wasn't so damn good-looking, I think I'd be more concerned.

I miss Pickles, and he's not even gone yet. Lucky for me, school has been keeping me busy. The rest of my finals are today, so I poured myself into my studies and books preparing for them.

Ash has been a great study partner. We all know he's brilliant in biochem, but biology? That man is a flat-out genius. No surprise there.

I have two finals today. The first of the day is biology, followed by biochem. Ash and I walk hand in hand along the freshly shoveled path on campus. Ash is usually a fast walker, and I have a hard time keeping up with him on a normal snowless day. Today, though, he's keeping his pace slow and methodical. His eyes never leave the path, scanning for black ice like some kind of slip-protection robot. It's the small things that fill my heart.

I gasp for air when we enter the science center.

"Are you okay?" Ash asks while trying his best to hide his laugh.

"I fucking hate winter." I'm still out of breath from clenching my muscles. It's not *totally* true.

I don't mind the snow as long as I get to stay inside. Otherwise, winter can suck mother nature's ass.

Ash walks me to biology since he doesn't have any other finals today besides biochem. He opted to hang outside until I'm done.

"Go kick its ass, sneaky girl."

I give him a thumbs-up before strolling to my seat.

And, of course, I did kick its ass. There's a reason I love biology. It just comes naturally to me. By the time I step outside, Chrissy and Ash are waiting for me.

"Sup, Bubbles," I smirk at Chrissy, knowing full well she has yet to disclose the origin of her new nickname.

"Bubbles?" Ash raises his eyebrow.

"Oh, she didn't tell you? Rom—"

Chrissy rushes over and slaps her hand over my mouth. "Zack started calling me Bubbles. Isn't it cute?"

I squint at her suspiciously. This lady has a big secret she's hiding from me.

"I'm starting to see why Zack runs when he sees the two of you," Ash says.

"He does what?" Chrissy and I ask at the same time, but my voice is muffled by her hand.

"You guys didn't hear me say that." Ash throws his hands in the air. "Let's go before anyone else reveals a secret they shouldn't tell."

Chrissy removes her hand from my mouth.

Chapter Seventy-Four

I wipe my lips dry and grin. "You owe me, Bubbles. Ow!"

Her fist makes contact with my arm, and I swear this woman packs more of a punch than a muscle head.

"You two are going to be the death of me." Ash sighs and covers his forehead with his hand.

"I'll tell you later. I just don't want Zack to find out," Chrissy whispers.

Oh yeah, this is gonna be good.

The three of us stroll into biochem, each of us wearing a different expression. Ash is confident, as always. He and I studied night and day for this final. For someone who majors in computer analytics, he's perfect with memorizing different equations and balancing them. Chrissy bops all the way to her desk, but I know once we sit down, she's going to dive back into her notes and textbook, aiming to take mental pictures of everything we already went over fifty times. I'm pretty sure my face is going to get stuck in a permanently wrinkled kind of situation. It doesn't matter how many times I study or for how long. The tension in my shoulders won't relax until the final is over and done with. At this point, I don't care if I get an A. If I can get a B, I'll be a happy duck. I have a high enough grade in this class that a B will maintain my grade point average.

"Ready, ladies?" Ash pulls out his glasses and winks at me.

Strange to think that only four months ago I captured his attention. When he sat next to me, I thought I was going to faint. Hell, I almost booked it straight out of the room altogether. Then a day later, he was passing me notes.

If I had known back when I signed up for this class that it would change my life, I would have prepared myself better. Nothing could prepare me for Ash though. Everyone says I changed his life, but I never hear how he changed mine.

A mere four months ago, I was stuck in my perfect bubble of solitude. When I saw him, his sharp pin locked on me. When he sat next to me and said, "Hi, Gwen." I couldn't register the fact that he knew my name. That moment, the pin took aim. Then in the evening, when he strolled into the café with Alex, not only did I work up the nerve to approach him, I reached out and offered comfort, and my bubble popped. From day one, Ash realigned my DNA, shaping me into someone I only dared dream to be.

"I think I'm going to hurl."

I chuckle as Chrissy groans to my left in response to Ash's question.

His lopsided grin makes all the color rush to my cheeks. Those glasses will forever be the end of me.

"As I'll ever be, Mr. Biochem." I throw his signature wink back at him just as Professor Stilts walks in.

Chapter Seventy-Five

Ash

This woman, I swear to god. Not only did she just wink at me, she giggled afterward. Professor Stilts is going over the rules: no talking, no phones, blah blah blah. I'm chewing on the cap of my pen as he hands the tests out, staring at Gwen like she's a mystical creature from another world.

And that's because she is.

Who else can love a man with a shattered heart and almost nonexistent trust? One person in the whole world, and her name is Gwen Roman. Don't get me wrong, I know I'm still fucked up, but I'm different than I was four months ago. When Alex cheated on me, the speck of trust that floated in my veins dissolved. My heart snapped into a million pieces. The moment I saw Gwen, my body erupted in butterflies. As cliché as that is, there's no other way to describe it. I couldn't keep my eyes off her. The only reason I did was because of the walls I had cemented around my heart and mind.

Then I saw her in class. The smallest shards of my heart

glued to one another, slowly rebuilding who I was before Alex Finnley. I couldn't help but tease her; the way her cheeks flushed when I said her name was intoxicating. Not only did I need to see more of it, I wanted to witness the glimmer in her ocean-blue eyes. Gwen created this feeling deep in my gut that no one had ever summoned before. How did I live so long without it? Don't ask me because I'm still trying to figure it out.

While I miss part of the person I was before Alex, I'm not him anymore. Gwen molded me into a new and stronger version of myself I didn't think could ever exist. Her love redefined my life. Because of Gwen, I know I'm deserving and cared for. I know I can defeat any challenges that stand in my way as long as she's beside me. I'm not perfect. I would be stupid to think I am. With Gwen, she makes me feel like I can go toe to toe with the universe and win. She's all I want. She's all I need.

"You're gonna pay for that, sneaky girl." I drop my tone so only she can hear me.

Grabbing the stack of extra tests, I hand them off to the person behind me. Gwen sticks her tongue out at me, and I swear the snicker that escapes my lips should be embarrassing, but it's not. Nothing about this girl could ever embarrass me.

Damn, not only did that test kick my ass, it handed it right back to me. I'm pretty sure everyone else feels the same way.

Chapter Seventy-Five

Gwen's nose is doing that deep in thought wrinkle. Chrissy's face is scrunched and ghostly pale. No one has turned the test in yet, which either means I'm the first to finish or no one has the guts to be the first to stand. There are only ten minutes left, and while I should go over my exam to double-check my answers, my track record for doing that never ends well.

Releasing a puff of air through my lips, I stand. I sling my bag over my arm and grin as I hand the test back to Professor Stilts.

"Willing to bet it's perfect as always, Mr. Waylen. Have a lovely holiday break."

"Thanks, Professor. See you around." I peek over my shoulder and smirk at a hyperfocused Gwen.

She's got this. That girl is smarter than she gives herself credit for.

Ten minutes later, Gwen and Chrissy stroll out, looking like their souls were drained from their bodies. Gwen presses her face into my chest and slumps her shoulders.

"I'm so glad that's over." Her voice is muffled by my shirt.

Chrissy sighs and rests her head on my shoulder.

"Can we go home and take a nap?" Chrissy whines.

"I second that." Gwen holds her finger up in favor of the nap proposition.

"I was going to treat you guys to lunch, but if you want to take naps instead . . ."

"Lunch, then nap." Gwen and Chrissy say at the same time.

"You owe me." Gwen points at Chrissy with what I can only assume is a knowing smirk on her lips.

"No, you owe me," Chrissy fires back.

"No, I'm pretty sure—"

The laugh that bubbles up my chest is genuine. I don't think I'll ever get sick of their bickering; it's too entertaining.

"Shut up, Bubbles. You totally owe me a soda."

"You wanna play that game, snore queen?"

"I don't snore!"

Oh boy...

From the corner of my eye, I see Zack peer around the hall. The split second he sees Gwen and Chrissy going back and forth, he backtracks. Sorry, buddy, you can't get away that easily.

"Chrissy, I just saw Zack across the hallway. Want to ask him if he wants to join us?"

"Good idea!" Chrissy books it down the corridor.

The squeal she emits and the groan Zack releases is the only indication we get that Chrissy found her prey.

"Ready for your session with Dr. Lukin today?"

"Yes and no."

It's been two weeks since I started my sessions. I'm happy to say we dialed back to having only three sessions a week rather than five. I was more fucked up than I originally thought...

"Want me to go with you?"

I love how supportive she is. Gwen knows how important mental health is, and she's a great advocate and cheerleader.

"Soon." I smile at her.

Dr. Lukin would love to meet Gwen, and I know it will only strengthen our relationship. I can't wait for her to work her magic on him. I'd pay good money to see him crack a real laugh.

"Got him!" Chrissy calls from down the hall.

Zack purses his lips, but the second he sees Gwen, he's all smiles.

"There she is!" He trots down the hallway, scooping Gwen in his arms without a care in the world. "I need to sign that cast of yours, missy."

Chapter Seventy-Five

"Yeah, yeah. Let's go eat first." Gwen takes my hand and leads the way back down to Chrissy.

"I'm starting to see why you're losing your hair at the ripe age of twenty-one," I tease Zack as we watch Chrissy pump her arms in the air.

"Welcome to my club. Isn't it fabulous?" he whispers while combing his fingers through his hair.

Gwen releases my hand and joins Chrissy. They link arms and skip down the hallway, not caring about the glances of others.

The smile that spreads on my lips whenever Gwen is around is noticeable. But when I see her with her best friend, when she forgets about that introverted part of her soul and lets herself be free, the smile on my face marks my soul.

They're crazy, don't get me wrong. And I might lose my hair at an early age from dealing with their antics. But the thought of them not being in my life has an iron fist gripping my heart. The thought of Gwen having no one to skip down the halls with is devastating. If I go bald by the age of thirty, it'll all be worth it.

As long as Gwen's smile never leaves her face.

Chapter Seventy-Six

Gwen

How is it Christmas Eve already? The entire month soared right by. I didn't get to plan any fun surprises for Ash. I mean, I understand why I lost track of time. Just look at my arm. No way I could go ice skating, sledding, skiing, or snowboarding with this thing. Not sure I could even if I wasn't injured. The one thing I did do is grab a few gifts that I think he'll love. And with Chrissy's help, I was able to set something up last minute.

"Think he'll like it?" I ask Chrissy while stepping back to observe our handy work.

"If he doesn't, I call dibs."

I smirk as she admires our hard work. "Think they're back yet?"

Ash and Zack went out to finish shopping. Leave it up to them to go outside during Christmas Eve mayhem.

"Knowing those two, they might be gone for a few more hours."

Chapter Seventy-Six

"That's fine. There's a certain someone who hasn't told me their secret yet."

Chrissy purses her lips as I grin knowingly.

"Spill it."

She plops down on the edge of Ash's bed and runs her fingers through her golden curls. "There's nothing to tell."

I land beside her as she sighs.

"Then why are you blushing and trying to hide something from me?"

Since the second grade, Chrissy and I have told each other everything. She told me about her awkward first kiss. I got all the unwanted details of her dates and spicy rendezvous. She knows all about my cringy "first time." Every little secret I have, she knows, just as I know hers.

"If you really don't want to tell me . . ."

She pops up, her cheeks kissed crimson. "Rome and I share the same English class. I was minding my own business, and you know I have a resting bitch face. He saw me and said, 'Are you okay, Bubbles?' And I couldn't help but perk up. I have this feeling though . . ." She clutches her midsection, and a soft grin forms on her lips. "It's weird, I can't explain it. When he called me Bubbles and ruffled my hair, I got all flustered, which only made him smile like a damn fool. His smirk . . . it's nothing like I've ever seen. Since that day, he's made it his mission to check on me. It's nice."

Rome? The same Rome who eats all the snacks? The same one who I could've sworn lost his brain in a football accident?

"Do you *like* a football player?" Her forehead wrinkles in deep thought as I ask her.

"I think I do." She lets out a breathless giggle.

"Zack is going to kill you," I mumble even though he's not here.

"I know, but nothing is going on between Rome and me," she states, but I smile like the smart-ass I am.

"Not yet."

One thing about Chrissy is even when she tries to hold back, the universe deals her the hand she's meant to have. If Chrissy and Rome are meant to be, it'll happen.

"Do you think he likes you?" I wiggle my eyebrows.

"I don't know."

I shimmy my shoulders and giggle at her response. "He would be crazy not to. I mean, have you seen you?"

Chrissy knows she's pretty, but I don't think she knows the beauty she holds in her heart. This woman is a goddess walking the plains of the earth, and she doesn't even know it.

"Promise me something, Gwen."

I meet her gaze and nod.

"Don't tell anyone, not even Ash. I don't want to work anyone up if there's nothing to get worked up about."

I give her a thumbs-up. "My lips are sealed."

"What's going on in here?"

When the door creaks open, I leap toward it in hopes of reaching it before Ash waltzes in. But that man is way too fast.

"Dammit, Ash."

The second his eyes land in the corner of the room, they light up, and he chuckles in disbelief.

Well, there goes my attempt at a grand surprise.

Chapter Seventy-Seven

Ash

"Surprise!" Chrissy cheers from my bed. Zack and I were gone for two hours, and somehow, these two built a magical makeshift fort right in front of the TV in my room. Multicolored Christmas string lights are stung delicately in and out of the navy-blue sheet tent. For a pair of girls with only a total of three working arms, I'm impressed.

"You were supposed to text me before you got back." Gwen pouts.

"I'm sorry, love. It slipped my mind." I can't wipe away the smile that tugs on my lips. "What is this?"

"My attempt at a surprise to make up for the entire month of December. Do you like it?" Gwen smiles while peering up at me.

Chrissy bounces on my bed with her knees, nodding in excitement.

"I love it." I tear my eyes off the magical fort and meet Gwen's grin.

"All right, I'm outta here. Don't fuck in the tent because I'm hanging out in it tomorrow. Peace, bitches!" Chrissy walks out the door while throwing us the peace sign.

"She's not kidding," Gwen states seriously.

I tilt my head and nod. Seems about right.

"Ready to get comfy and watch movies?" Gwen asks.

"Absolutely."

Gwen and I get changed into our pajamas and grab a ton of snacks before turning the lights off and huddling under the fort. I tell her my favorite Christmas movie is "The Grinch" from 2000, so she puts it on and rests her head on my shoulder.

I wasn't expecting Gwen to do anything for me, not because I didn't want her to. I didn't even think about it. I planned all those surprises in October because I knew it would make her happy, and in turn, it would make me happy. Whenever her face lights up and her cheeks turn that cute shade of pink, I feel like I did something right in my life. Like I'm not a total failure.

"I originally wanted to take you ice skating."

I can't fight the chuckle that flies out of my mouth.

"What?" she asks with a wide grin.

"You ice skating? Didn't you break your wrist rollerblading?"

She scrunches up her face. "Shut up, Waylen." Carefully she rolls onto her back.

I lie on my back and smile at her in admiration. "Being here with you is all I need. This"—I gesture to the light-clustered tent—"is more than I could've ever dreamed. You're more than I could've ever dreamed."

"Really?"

I prop myself up and lean over to close the distance between us. "Really," I say while feathering my nose over hers.

Chapter Seventy-Seven

Her lips meet mine, pulling me against her. It starts off slow, but with Gwen, it never remains that way. Her legs part, and I waste no time in settling between them. I wrap my hands into her hair and groan because, damn, I'll never get tired of kissing this woman. I glide my tongue over her bottom lip and gently bite it.

"You drive me crazy," I moan into her mouth.

"Prove it." That damn laugh will be the end of me.

"Are you sure?" My question comes out shaky and nervous.

We haven't made love in weeks, and the last thing I want to do is make her uncomfortable or force her into something she doesn't want to do.

"I'm ready, but only if you are."

Cautiously, I tug her pants off with one hand.

"I'm ready," I whisper before kissing her again.

"Prove it," she repeats, and before she can even register what she said, my finger lands on the spot that I know she melts over.

"Wanna say that one more time?" I tease her.

She cries incoherently, the sound making my cock twitch under my boxers. Brushing my finger right above her clit, I glide my other hand under her shirt.

"Say it again, I dare you." As tenderly as I can, I brush her nipple and clit in time with one another. "Say it, Gwen."

The look in her eyes sends emotions crashing over me like a wave, but I don't worry about drowning; such a death would be satisfying.

"Prove it," she rasps.

"What do you want?" I whisper against her lips.

She whimpers against me, and I glide my finger downward.

"You."

"You have me."

"I swear if I didn't have this cast, I would have you in the palm of my hand," she groans in annoyance.

I collide our lips together, kissing her in hungry desire. I kick my pants off and pull myself out of my boxers.

"Is this what you want?" I pull her panties aside and rub the tip of my cock along her pussy.

"Please."

"Are you begging me?"

"Ash," she chastises.

I pull on her thighs to bring her closer. Given her tone, I'm afraid that if I don't give her what she wants, she might take matters into her own hands. *Not that the sight wouldn't be pleasing.*

I press into her, and the moan of pure desire that echoes through my chest is out of this world. Gwen feels like undiluted magic, something no one should ever experience or ruin. She takes every inch of me, and I swear, she pulsates when I'm fully inside her.

"How's that?" I ask her completely out of breath.

"Fantastic."

I withdraw and press back into her, her chest heaving each time I do. Her nipples harden underneath her shirt, something else I could watch every day and never grow tired of.

"Fuck, Gwen. You're so hot." I can't help but move faster. The noises she makes are enough to make me come.

"Don't stop." Her free hand rests on my cheek, holding me against her lips. "Please, don't stop." Her cry floats into my mouth, vibrating everything within me.

I force myself to keep the rhythm she wants, even though everything within me is begging me to go harder and faster.

"Ash."

"Gwen," I growl.

Chapter Seventy-Seven

I ram into her, making sure to hold still for a second before resuming my thrusts. She tugs on my lower lip with hers. The second her body tenses, I kiss her hard, selfishly taking every sound she releases. She pulls on my hair when she tightens her thighs around me. She's almost there.

"Fuck, Ash, don't stop."

And I obey. With every inch she takes, I feel her stretch around me. She's so fucking tight it drives me crazy, and knowing I'm the only person to make her orgasm kills me. Lifting her shirt, I take her nipple in my mouth.

"Yes, don't stop!"

I flick my tongue over her nipple before gently sucking on it. I try to go in time with my rhythm, but I can't keep up. With every blissful sound that leaves her mouth, my movements turn sloppy. I can't control myself anymore.

"Fuck, I need you to come for me," I growl against her breast before sucking on her hardened nipple. "I'm about to fill your pussy." I dig my fingers into the back of her thigh, each millisecond blazing by.

"Oh my god—"

I take her mouth against mine to cut her off.

"I'm doing this to you, Gwen, no one else. Say *my* name."

Her mouth drops open, and a moan dances along her tongue.

"Ash! Ash!" she cries as she comes undone.

Her muscles grip and squeeze around my cock. Her thighs relax around me as she whimpers in contentment.

"Yes, fuck yes."

I finally let go, pressing my forehead against hers.

Fuck, making love with Gwen is beyond me. How does she manage to always feel addicting and wonderful?

We're both fighting for air, staring at the artificial stars. I glance at her in awe as "The Grinch" continues in the background.

"Ash, I think Christmas is my new favorite holiday," she giggles as she struggles to even out her breathing.

I roll over and take her cheeks in my hands. "Welcome to the basic bitch club, my love."

Chapter Seventy-Eight

Gwen

What the? Why does it sound like thunder is rolling up the staircase? I roll over on my back and sit up. No, wait, that's not thunder.

"It's Christmas!" Max pushes the door open while banging two unused wrapping paper tubes together.

"Five more minutes," Ash groans and pulls the blanket over his head.

Max smacks the tubes together, making me wish I had a set of noise-canceling earplugs.

"What time is it?" I shout over the most annoying sound in the world.

"Six AM, baby!"

I swear, how do I always find the early birds?

"Four more hours." Ash flops onto his stomach and shields his face with his pillow.

"Gwen." Max puckers his lower lip at me, quivering it more and more as the seconds pass.

"Five minutes?" I ask while rubbing Ash's back.

Max pumps his arms in the air in victory. His feet thump down the stairs like a five-year-old would on Christmas morning.

"Ash?"

His sleepy mumble makes me smile. Why does he have to be so cute? I scooch down and join him under the blankets.

"Merry Christmas, sleepy head." I kiss his forearm until he peels his eyes open. "Did you have good dreams?" I trail my thumb over his cheekbone.

"Last night's dream involved you pressed against my co— ow, woman!"

I sucker punch him in the arm. It's way too early for this man's dirty mouth.

"Watch it, mister."

He scrunches his nose as I wiggle my pointer finger at him.

"Gwen!" Max whines from the living room.

Ash scoffs and rolls his eyes.

"Let's go. Our child is waiting," I say while Ash secures a hoodie over his body.

"Just wait until we have children."

My cheeks flush, and, of course, he notices it because he fucking winks at me.

"You stay away from me." I raise my casted arm. "I'll whack you with this thing."

Ash raises his hands and chuckles. "You won't be saying that later tonight."

Ash books it into the hallway as my feet thud against the carpeted floor.

"You're a fucking pervert, Waylen!"

Ash leaps down the stairs, wearing the biggest grin I've ever seen.

Chapter Seventy-Eight

Stepping off the final stair, I understand why Max was so damn excited for us to get out of bed.

"Surprise!"

"No fucking way," I mutter.

Ash nearly squeals when he sees my reaction. Max is standing right next to the Christmas tree, holding none other than Pickles himself.

"What did you do?" I whisper in disbelief.

Pickles jumps out of his arms, crashing right into me and my casted arm.

"Guys." Tears threaten my eyes. "How did you get the bow on him?" is the only question I can ask.

Both Ash and Max chuckle in response.

"How was I supposed to let him go off to some other family after seeing how much you love him?" Max grins proudly.

Ash wipes the tears that escape my eyes as Pickles nuzzles against my jawline, his purrs vibrating against my ribcage.

"I don't know what to say." I lean against Ash's palm, feeling happy and confused at the same time. "Thank you."

Pickles leaps out of my arms and tears straight into the kitchen.

"You know you just released a furry monster into your home, right?" Ash warns the very second a crash sounds from the other room.

"It's fine." Max shrugs. "He'll calm down."

A sharp shatter echoes from the kitchen. *There goes a glass cup...*

"You guys start opening presents. I'm going to try to tame the wild beast. Merry Christmas!"

I thumb the remaining tears from my eyes as Max scurries off.

"Did you have any say in that?"

Ash traces my jawline with his thumb and presses his nose to mine.

"Who do you think talked him into going to the cat café in the first place?"

Aw man, here come the waterworks. Ash pulls me against his chest, not caring that I'm soaking his hoodie straight through to his chest. Is this what family does for one another? Putting someone else's wants and needs before their own? I've seen the Willowses do it a thousand times, so why does it only feel real at this moment?

"Not sure if you've noticed, but Max really likes you."

I snicker against his warm, soothing chest.

"You might be stuck with us forever."

I peer up at him. The feeling that soars through my veins, right to my heart, is something I didn't understand three months ago. Now, I can define it without a second thought.

"I love you."

He presses his lips against mine, welcoming me straight into our own little world. "And I love you."

Chapter Seventy-Nine

Ash

Gwen is the definition of magic. As soon as her gaze landed on Pickles, the room became brighter. The feeling in my chest lightened and tingled beyond belief. Just when I thought I had this girl down, she surprises me all over again. We both plop down in front of the lit ten-foot Christmas tree. Max went out as soon as he knew we were spending Christmas here. He bought the biggest tree he could find, all the color LED lights, and as many ornaments he could get his hands on. The tree itself is chaos. Not one thing looks alike, and it fits in perfectly. I hand Gwen a crudely wrapped present.

"I don't think this will top Pickles, but I think you'll like it."

The way she tears into it makes me wonder how many presents she's gotten over the years. If it wasn't many, she doesn't have to worry about that anymore.

Her eyes light up when she pulls out the Halloween hoodie I had made just for her. "Now we'll match next Halloween."

She grips the sweater and clutches it against her chest.

"Do you get a kick out of making me cry?" She chokes on built-up tears in the middle of her sentence.

"You didn't even get the big one yet." I reach behind the tree and hand her a tiny box.

"This isn't what I think it is, is it?" She flips the box over, examining it.

It does look very similar to a ring box now that I'm thinking about it.

"Just open it."

She unwraps this one slowly. When she removes the lid, her shoulders relax at the sight of the golden key.

"You kind of live here already, so I thought it was time you had a key."

"Ash." Gwen sniffles before wiping her eyes dry. "Thank you."

She wraps her free arm around my neck, and I take her in my arms, sighing from pure happiness.

"Okay, your turn." Gwen bounces on her knees as I take the present she offers me. Her smile grows as I unwrap it.

"You little—" I giggle at the zombie video game resting in my hands.

"Thought you could use some practice."

This is the very game Gwen whooped my ass in when we went to the arcade. That day seems so distant now when, in reality, it was only a few months ago. To think I was still afraid of my feelings back then, but I'm glad I got my head on straight.

"One more." She beams while handing me one more gift.

I rip the paper, and this time, I'm the one threatened by tears.

"Do you like it?"

Is that even a question? Gwen framed the first photo I took of her, the one with her and Pickles. The one I thought I was

Chapter Seventy-Nine

creepy for taking. I reach out for her, and when she snuggles against my shoulder, I take a deep breath.

"I love it, thank you."

She kisses my cheek over and over again.

I fucking love her. There's no other way to explain the way my body reacts to her. There's no other way to explain the fireworks that light off in my head when she's around. Hell, just hearing her name brings a smile to my face.

I love this woman.

I'll do anything to protect her, to keep that smile on her face. Without Gwen, life isn't worth living. Without Gwen, I simply can't exist. Gwen is my person. I didn't know that in high school, but I know it now.

And that's all that matters.

Chapter Eighty

Gwen

Chrissy and Zack show up around noon, and we gather around the tree to exchange gifts. It doesn't take long for Pickles to find Zack, and when Zack notices who now roams this house, I think he's scarred for life. Max ordered a shit ton of Chinese food for lunch, so we all huddle around the coffee table in the living room and eat. The laughter that fills the room is music to my ears.

I didn't hear from Mom or Dad. Normally I might care or let it ruin my day, but today? I'm realizing I don't want to hear from them. I don't *need* to hear from them. Glancing around the room, I realize that the family I need is right here. Ash created this world for me without knowing it. Because of him, I know what love means, what it truly means to be cared for. His knee rests on mine, and I catch him midlaugh.

Years ago, I dreamed of Ash night and day. He consumed my mind effortlessly. How I got so lucky to have him in my life,

Chapter Eighty

I'll never know. And that's fine. Some answers can remain a mystery.

I might take a page out of Ash's book and return to therapy myself; the universe knows I need it. My parents are different from Ash's, but the one thing they have in common is the everlasting trauma they left in their wake.

"I'm telling you, cold showers in the morning are the way to go," Zack says with a mouthful of sesame chicken.

"You're fucking crazy. No way am I taking a cold shower in twenty degree weather," Max replies, ready for a debate.

As a laugh leaves my lips, Ash glances over at me. "You okay, sneaky girl?"

I'll never get used to the way he looks at me. I wonder if he knows that and just how much he means to me.

Just how much he changed me.

We've been through some shit, no doubt about that. But the good outweighs the bad, and I'm willing to fight whatever monster comes along the way to keep us together. Love takes work, and what I have with Ash is going to take patience, but I'm going to give him my all. The way he makes me feel is undeniably loved and cared for. Ash isn't perfect; he has his flaws, but he's working on them, and I'm going to be there every step of the way.

"I'm great, Mr. Biochem."

Then Ash Waylen fucking winks at me.

And just like that, I'm forever crushed.

Epilogue Part One

Three Months Later

Ash

"How are you today, Ash?"

I settle on the couch across from Dr. Lukin.

"Pretty good," I say while taking my jacket off.

"How's the new semester treating you?" Dr. Lukin asks while pushing his glasses farther up his nose.

"Busy, but I'm managing. My new coding design class is kicking my ass." I chuckle—mainly to myself. I end up spending most of my free time in the computer lab now, something I'm not too upset about.

"And we're working on our stress-handling techniques, right?"

"One task at a time, one day at a time."

He smiles brightly in response. "Very good, and how's Gwen?"

Epilogue Part One

I smile wider at the mention of her name. "She's great. She started seeing a therapist as well."

Gwen and I don't share any classes this semester, but I still see her every day. It was an easy decision for Gwen to move in with Max and me. Hell, Max pushed for it harder than I did. Gwen took a big leap and decided to take a break from her parents. Gwen did end up calling her mom the day after Christmas. Once her mom started talking about herself and the upcoming vacation to Italy, Gwen took the jump. She wanted to cut all ties, and that started with ending her lease for her studio apartment. I think she was upset about losing the space, but she didn't spend much time there anyway.

Since she moved in, the entire atmosphere at home has changed. Max doesn't work crazy hours anymore. We don't eat frozen junk every night. It's refreshing to walk into the kitchen to see Max cooking with Gwen's supervision. Even he's bettering himself now that she's with us twenty-four seven.

"Excellent. Do you still blame yourself for her injury?" Dr. Lukin gets ready to jot down notes on his notepad.

"I do, and I don't. I know I didn't physically hurt her, but I sent her emotions through the roof. I feel like if she wasn't pissed off at me, she would have taken her time and avoided the ice." My eyes gloss over as the memory of her sprawled across the sidewalk returns.

"And what are we going to do to move forward?" he asks in his doctor-like tone.

"Accept what happened, and remember that I'm working on myself. I didn't hurt her, and she doesn't blame me, so neither should I."

Dr. Lukin gives me a thumbs-up. "One day at a time, right?"

I nod at his calming voice.

"Great, now. Let's return to our favorite topic..."

Epilogue Part One

I groan.

"The only way to heal from our past—"

I finish his sentence for him. "Is to talk about it, I know. All right, let's talk about my parents."

Max and I decided to take a break from Mom and Dad. After last Thanksgiving, we're both rightfully pissed. Hell, I still am. The thought of reaching out to Mom makes me sick. I can imagine the look on her face. She would gloat about how she was right and we were wrong. Like always, she would paint herself to be the victim, even though that's not the case. She needs to know she fucked up and there are consequences to her actions. I regret nothing I said that day. If anything, I wish I said more.

Talking about your feelings is not an easy task, and anyone who says it is, is lying through their teeth. When I leave Dr. Lukin's office, I take in as much air as I can. Normally, I would go home and take a nap after my sessions, but today I promised Gwen and Chrissy I would treat them to lunch. So I hop in my car and drive back to Castle Brook. Beyond ready to see my girl.

"Chrissy, how many times do I have to tell you? I'm not drinking that!" I hear Gwen say from down the path.

I smile at Gwen's attempt at being defiant.

"Come on. It's good for you!" Chrissy shoves the green juice in Gwen's face.

Epilogue Part One

I watch as she reluctantly tries it, and I know she hates it because she jumps up and down in disgust.

"That's terrible!"

Chrissy bursts into laughter before twirling the straw around her tongue.

"What are you two up to?"

Gwen spins around, and the whole world stops. Her dirty-blonde waves bounce as she closes the distance between us. She leaps into my arms, no longer needing to be careful about hitting me in the head with her cast.

"Hey, sneaky girl," I manage to say before her lips press into mine.

I'll never fully be able to express how much I love this woman. She deserves the world and so much more. One day, I'll give her everything she deserves. Right now, I give her all the love I can, and I know it's enough. Loving Gwen is all I want and need, and I know she feels the same way.

Epilogue Part Two

Gwen

"Hey, sneaky girl."

Damn, I love him. I love the way his lips form a natural lopsided grin when my cheeks flush. I love how his shimmering brown eyes dance along my features like he's trying to memorize every inch of me.

I love how much I love him.

"Hey, you," I whisper as our lips part. "How was therapy?" I ask as he sets me back on the ground.

"Heavy." He releases a deep sigh before fixing his glasses. "I'm going to need a nap after we eat."

I ruffle his hair and grin. "Count me in." I link my free arm around his and grin at Chrissy, who is currently smiling down at her phone.

"Ready, blondie?" I ask.

Chrissy snaps her attention back up and shoves her phone into her back pocket.

Epilogue Part Two

"Yes, I'm starving!" She skips over to Ash's side and links her arm through his.

"All right, ladies, what did we have in mind?" Ash asks as we start down the path.

"Pizza."

"Ice cream."

I peer over at Chrissy as she glances over at me.

"We had pizza a few days ago," she starts.

"So? I want fries. Why do you want ice cream for lunch?"

"Because I just had that gross smoothie, and I deserve a treat."

"Ha! So, you admit it was gross!" I fire back.

Straight ahead, I spot Zack, and my smile falters. Grabbing Chrissy's arm, I shush her. Zack is talking to the one person he knows he shouldn't be talking to. What on earth is this man thinking?

"Oh, hell no." Chrissy starts forward, but Ash grabs her by her shoulders and holds her back.

"Just wait a moment."

My right foot is planted on the cement, ready to pounce and defend Zack against Roselyn's toxicity, and Chrissy grunts in response to Ash. I'm about to follow my instincts and take action, but then I see Zack's jaw tense, his cheeks flush hot red, and his Adam's apple bobs.

"He and I talked about this the other day. He said he needed closure. He needed her to know what she did to him and that it wasn't okay. He understands it now, thanks to you two," Ash informs us.

Chrissy's posture relaxes, and my stance eases. Roselyn stomps away in the other direction with a visible huff. Not a moment later, Zack turns his head and spots us. When he sees Chrissy and I, his posture relaxes in relief.

We all start toward one another, and I don't waste a second when he's close enough.

"Zack, pizza or ice cream for lunch?" My question brings a grin to his face.

The last thing he needs right now is to rehash the conversation. He'll talk to us when he's ready.

"Why not both?" He flashes his famous smile, hoping his answer will please his sisters.

"Deal," Chrissy and I say at the same time.

We start down the path to Ash's car. With Ash and Chrissy on my right side, I wrap my left arm around Zack's and squeeze him.

While Ash drives us to get ice cream, I call in the order at a local pizza restaurant. We manage to get back to his place just as the delivery guy pulls into the driveway. I carry the ice cream inside while the boys take the mountain of food we ordered from the driver's hands.

"Here, let me get that for you." Chrissy bounces in front of me.

Just as she opens the door, I panic.

"Wait, be careful! Pickles has been—"

The second the door opens, Pickles bursts onto the lawn.

"Escaping," I mumble in defeat.

"Hey, lawyer man, come get your cat," Chrissy calls before taking the various ice cream orders from my hands.

Max almost bumps into Chrissy, but he misses her by a mere centimeter.

"I got him!" he shouts over his shoulder.

"Did he get out again?" Ash asks as he and Zack make it to the front door.

"Man, I wasn't ready for another chase today . . ." I groan while stretching my legs.

"Wait, we're chasing Pickles? I'm so in. It's time that squirt got a taste of his own medicine." Zack places the food on the front step before jogging after Max.

"Ready, sneaky girl?" Ash kisses my cheek before smirking.

"You're lucky I love you."

He beams at my confession and takes my cheeks in his hands, pulling me in for a kiss.

"And I love you. I always will."

"Promise?" I offer him my pinkie, and he wastes no time accepting it.

"Promise."

Chrissy

"Coming, blondie?" Ash asks before he and Gwen chase after my brother and his archnemesis.

"All right, you're lucky I wore my sneakers today."

Gwen and Ash are so stinkin' cute it hurts. I can't help but smile when I'm around them. I wonder what it feels like to be in love like that. Knowing you have someone in this world who loves you more than life itself. What is it like having someone look out for you twenty-four seven? And by someone, I mean someone other than your best friend and brother.

My thigh vibrates just as Ash starts down the block. When I glance down at my phone, my lips reach my cheeks involuntarily.

> How's my ray of sunshine today?

I blush as I stare at his words. I knew Rome in high school, but only because he was an insane football star. I didn't feel this way about him before. So, why do my insides flip and twist in on themselves whenever I hear his name? Why do butterflies roam through my veins in a frenzy?

> I'm good :) About to eat with Gwen, Ash, and Zack. Want to join us?

The little bubbles at the bottom of the screen pop up to indicate he's typing. Before I can see what he has to say, I get another notification.

> Who's making you smile like that, Bubbles?

I glance up from my phone screen only to meet an intrigued Gwen, smiling knowingly. I don't even have to say it. Gwen knows me better than I know myself. I get the feeling this summer is going to be a very eventful and interesting adventure.

Afterword

Forever Crushed was my first real spicy novel. The idea started from the pool/bedroom scene (which I obsessed over for months.) I decided to try and write a story around it, and this story was born.

I remember when I started it. I was sitting in my office at work, it was right after I finished writing Symbol of Hope. The daydream was playing in my head nonstop. So, I started to write.

I would have never guessed I would be able to create a world from one daydream, but here we are. Gwen, Ash, Chrissy, Zack, Max, and Pickles are and will always be my favorite, found family.

Maybe you can add them to yours too.

Acknowledgments

To my husband, I'm really sorry about all my cackling when I write spicy scenes. But hey, at least you always know what I'm up to.

To my sisters, if you read this book, please don't tell Dad what I write. And maybe I can offer you a censored version?

To my first and forever writing companion, Eerie. I miss you more than words can ever express. While you and Pickles are vastly different, I pulled your experiences and made them his. You'll always be on page and in my heart.

To my lovely supporters and readers, thank you! Thank you for tagging along on this journey with me and for dealing with my crazy antics. I wouldn't be where I am today without you. And get ready because there is so much more yet to come.

About the Author

Amber Paige is an indie author who is focusing on fluffy, HEA's, and spicy novels. She's a big mood reader and writer, but once something captures her attention, she hyperfocuses on it. She mainly writes fiction, romance, and fantasy but isn't afraid to dive into another genre if it calls to her. She writes from her laptop, either in bed or on the couch with a cat by her side.

When she's not overanalyzing commas or letting her imposter syndrome get the best of her, you can find her playing video games, watching too much TV, reading, writing, or hanging out with her husband and three cats.

The Forever Series

The story isn't over!

Stay tuned for the following installment (coming summer 2024) and the next book in the series (winter 2025). I plan to release the final book in spring of 2026. There will also be either a full book or a novella that will showcase the crew's future. I can't wait to write their stories and share them with everyone!

Also by Amber Paige

Symbol of Hope

The Academy Games (Coming 2024)

Made in the USA
Middletown, DE
10 April 2025

73969489R00266